INCREDIBLE ADVENTURES

Algernon Blackwood

Incredible Adventures

Algernon Blackwood

With an Introduction by S. T. Joshi

Hippocampus Press

New York

Published by Hippocampus Press
P.O. Box 641, New York, NY 10156.
http://www.hippocampuspress.com

Cover art by W. Graham Robertson (1866–1948) from *The Centaur*
by Algernon Blackwood (Macmillan & Co., 1916).

Frontispiece from "Algernon Blackwood: Pan's Gardener" by Neil Austin
in *Famous Fantastic Mysteries* (April 1948).

Cover design and Lovecraft's Library series logo by Barbara Briggs Silbert.
Hippocampus Press logo designed by Anastasia Damianakos.

First Edition
1 3 5 7 9 8 6 4 2

ISBN 0-9748789-0-1

To

M. S.-K.

Contents

Introduction

A weird story, to be a serious aesthetic effort, must form primarily a *picture of a mood*—and such a picture certainly does not call for any clever jack-in-the-box fillip. There *are* weird stories which more or less conform to this description . . . especially in Blackwood's *Incredible Adventures*."[1] So wrote H. P. Lovecraft in 1935, echoing a comment he had made nearly a decade earlier in "Supernatural Horror in Literature," where he observed:

> In the volume titled *Incredible Adventures* occur some of the finest tales which the author has yet produced, leading the fancy to wild rites on nocturnal hills, to secret and terrible aspects lurking behind stolid scenes, and to unimaginable vaults of mystery below the sands and pyramids of Egypt; all with a serious finesse and delicacy that convince where a cruder or lighter treatment would merely amuse. Some of these accounts are hardly stories at all, but rather studies in elusive impressions and half-remembered snatches of dream. Plot is everywhere negligible, and atmosphere reigns untrammeled.[2]

That final comment, reflecting as it does Lovecraft's chosen gauge of excellence in weird fiction ("Atmosphere is the all-important thing, for the final criterion of authenticity is not the dovetailing of a plot but the creation of a given sensation"[3]), makes us realise why he valued this distinctive Blackwood collection so highly: in many ways it represented the goal to which he himself aspired in his own weird writing—a goal that, toward the end of his life, he felt he was farther and farther from achieving.

The curious thing about all this is that Lovecraft's first exposure to Blackwood was exactly by way of *Incredible Adventures*—but his reaction was far different, and far less favourable. Writing to the Gallomo around April 1920, Lovecraft delivered a somewhat cocksure verdict upon the volume:

> At the recommendation of James F. Morton, Jr., I am perusing the works of a modern imaginative author named Algernon Blackwood . . . I can't say that I am very much enraptured, for somehow Blackwood lacks the power to create a really haunting atmosphere. He is too diffuse, for one thing; and for another thing, his horrors and weirdness are too obviously symbolical—

---

1. H. P. Lovecraft, letter to R. H. Barlow, [11 May 1935]; *Selected Letters 1934–1937*, ed. August Derleth and James Turner (Sauk City, WI: Arkham House, 1976), p. 160.

2. *The Annotated Supernatural Horror in Literature*, ed. S. T. Joshi (New York: Hippocampus Press, 2000), pp. 66–67.

3. Ibid., p. 23.

symbolical rather than convincingly outré. And his symbolism is not of that luxuriant kind which makes Dunsany so phenomenal a fabulist. Just to see what he's like, youse fellers might read "Incredible Adventures", a collection of five very long "short" stories. It ain't half bad, and if the first one tires you out, you are not compelled to swallow the remainder.[4]

It is difficult to credit how so diametrically opposite a judgment could have been delivered, one that would be reversed in only five or six years. If we find the passage in "Supernatural Horror in Literature" insufficient evidence for such a reversal, we need only turn to a letter written a few months after the publication of that essay in the *Recluse* (1927), when Lovecraft remarked: "I am dogmatic enough to call 'The Willows' the finest weird story that I have ever read, & I find in the *Incredible Adventures* & *John Silence* material a serious & sympathetic understanding of the human illusion-weaving process which makes Blackwood rate far higher as a creative artist than many another crafts-man of mountainously superior word-mastery & general technical ability."[5] It is not to our purpose to discuss how this revision in Lovecraft's critical judg-ment occurred; suffice it to say that his maturer view of *Incredible Adventures* seems a far more judicious evaluation of this remarkable volume than his ear-lier, cruder opinion.

The very manner in which Blackwood wrote this book is a testament to an-other central component of Lovecraft's aesthetic stance. Convinced that the greatest literature emerges from a purely non-commercial focus on "self-expression" without thought of markets or audience, Lovecraft himself strove in his work to repudiate prevailing standards in both pulp fiction and in the scarcely less trite and hackneyed material that appeared in the popular "slick" magazines of the day. It is no accident that he held up Lord Dunsany, that titled nobleman who conjoined the aristocracy of blood with the aristocracy of art, as a literary model of disinterested aesthetic achievement. He would have been similarly heartened by the remarkable fertility of Blackwood's decade or so of writing following the spectacular success of *John Silence—Physician Extraordinary* (1908), an unexpected best-seller that allowed its author to settle in Switzerland for the period 1908–14 and write some of his most celebrated and brilliant works. While it is true that such well-known stories as "The Willows" and "The Wendigo" had been written a few years earlier, Blackwood used his freedom from monetary concerns to generate such works as the powerful mystical fan-tasy *The Human Chord* (1910), the substantial collection *Pan's Garden* (1912), and,

4. Lovecraft, letter to the Gallomo [c. April 1920]; *Letters to Alfred Galpin,* ed. S. T. Joshi and David E. Schultz (New York: Hippocampus Press, 2003), p. 73.

5. Lovecraft, letter to Vincent Starrett (6 December 1927); *Selected Letters: 1925–1929,* ed. August Derleth and Donald Wandrei (Sauk City, WI: Arkham House, 1968), p. 211.

most significant of all, *The Centaur* (1911), the novel that defines Blackwood's entire work and can be regarded as his spiritual autobiography. *Incredible Adventures*, published in 1914, came toward the end of this vital period of writing. Although his career extended for another three and a half decades, Blackwood never produced any body of work to match the volumes of 1908–14 in concentrated excellence, complexity, and depth.

Lovecraft's frequent comments regarding the relative absence of conventional plot in the tales in *Incredible Adventures* are part and parcel of his oft-expressed scorn of the pulp-magazine standard that insisted on "action" plots to sustain the interest of lazy readers. Blackwood himself reflects this stance when, in one of the two times he cites the title phrase in the volume, he notes poignantly: "The incredible adventure was literally true, but, being spiritual, may not be told in the terms of a detective story." This notion of the "spiritual" was highly important to Blackwood, and it really structures his entire work. A mystic who had early absorbed the teachings of Hinduism and Buddhism as an antidote to the stifling and rigid Christian orthodoxy of his parents, Blackwood was perennially searching for an expansion of consciousness that would allow for the perception of what he believed to be the essential unity of all entity. It is this expansion that Lord Ernie, in "The Regeneration of Lord Ernie," experiences as he participates in a ritual in the fastnesses of the Swiss Alps; it is this that the protagonists of "A Descent into Egypt" experience as they wait for the dawn in hoary, aeon-weighted Egypt.

It could well be said that religion—although scarcely of a conventional sort—is at the heart of all the stories in *Incredible Adventures*. "The Damned" is, in this sense, the most obvious and straightforward tale in the volume. In the figure of the rigidly doctrinaire Samuel Franklyn, who even in death exercises a baleful influence over both his own widow and his rambling house in Sussex, we can detect a hint of what Blackwood felt about his own father, who expressed alarm that his son's soul was in peril when he caught him studying Eastern religious texts. Blackwood's biographer, Mike Ashley, also sees a reflection of another real-life figure in the portrayal of Franklyn. *Incredible Adventures* is dedicated to "M. S.-K."—Maya Stuart-King, a woman whom Blackwood met around 1911. At that time she was married to Johann, Baron Knoop, a Russian nobleman. The lifelong bachelor Blackwood appears to have had a complex but platonic relationship with Maya: far from being merely an object of affection, carnal or otherwise, she seems to have been a kind of Muse for Blackwood, who dedicated many books to her. Ashley believes that there is something of Baron Knoop in Samuel Franklyn; certainly, the house that serves as the setting of "The Damned" is manifestly modelled upon a home, South Park, near the village of Wadhurst on the border between Sussex and Kent. Blackwood was staying in this houue in the summer of 1913 when he was working on three of the stories in *Incredible Adventures*, "The Damned," "The Regeneration of Lord Ernie," and "A Descent into Egypt."[6]

That last story is only the greatest of many tales by Blackwood set in Egypt, which he visited for the first time in early 1912. Perhaps only "Sand" (in *Pan's Garden*) can compare to this tale in its cumulative intensity and its remarkable fusion of horror, awe, and pathos; certainly, the diffuse reincarnation novel *The Wave* (1916), although Blackwood's most exhaustive treatment of Egypt, can by no means be regarded as among his successes. The reincarnation theme enters into "Wayfarers," a tale that renounces horror altogether for wistful delicacy. "The Sacrifice" is an almost unclassifiable story that takes as its theme the notion that "all of life is a Ceremony on a giant scale, and that by performing the movements accurately, with sincere fidelity, there may come—Knowledge." What is remarkable in this tale is how, with every act being a ceremony, every sentence becomes a metaphor. It may have been this "symbolical" quality in the tale that evoked Lovecraft's disapproval in 1920.

What, then, did *Incredible Adventures* mean to Lovecraft? Can we detect any demonstrable literary influence upon any of his own works of fiction? Such an influence is, precisely because of the extreme subtlety and lack of obvious plot-elements in the tales, difficult to specify. Whereas we can tell that "The Wendigo," with its use of footprints to signal the advent of an invisible monster, unmistakably influenced "The Dunwich Horror"; that "Ancient Sorceries" (a tale in *John Silence*), depicting an entire town turning into cats at night, must have played a role in the conception of "The Shadow over Innsmouth"; and, a bit more nebulously, that "The Willows," with its imperishable depiction of a locale haunted by the most intangible of entities, had some impact on "The Colour out of Space" (1927), we struggle to find any direct correlation of the tales in *Incredible Adventures* with those of Lovecraft's later period. It is unlikely that the subtle but inexpressibly powerful evocation of Egypt in "A Descent into Egypt" had any role in Lovecraft's much cruder depiction in "Under the Pyramids" (1924). But perhaps a more remote influence of that story upon two of Lovecraft's narratives can be detected. George Isley, after participating in the ritual that is at the heart of that tale, returns to his normal, present-day life a mere shell of a man—just as Thomas Olney, in "The Strange High House in the Mist," appears to have left his spirit in that inaccessible house perched on the cliff outside of Kingsport. And the narrator of "A Descent into Egypt," torn between pursuing the inexplicable mysteries of

---

6. See Mike Ashley, *Algernon Blackwood: An Extraordinary Life* (New York: Carroll & Graf, 2001), pp. 189–90.

Egypt with his friend or holding back in order to maintain his sanity and identity, bears some faint resemblance to Albert N. Wilmarth in "The Whisperer in Darkness" (1930), who cannot decide whether to follow his correspondent Henry Akeley into the exploration of the wonders being revealed by the fungi from Yuggoth or to remain in the safety of the known and familiar.

Perhaps, in the end, the most significant influence of *Incredible Adventures* upon Lovecraft was that it set so high a standard of excellence. These tales, by incorporating the weird within the framework of a coherent philosophical system; by focusing not upon the "dovetailing of a plot" but, almost in the manner of Henry James, upon the shifting perceptions of a human consciousness encountering the bizarre; by utilising prose in a virtually poetic manner to convey the most delicate shades of meaning and the subtlest turns of thought and feeling, transmute the crude emotions of fear and horror into the broader, deeper emotions of awe and wonder. There is, then, some truth in Lovecraft's rueful comment, made at the very end of his life: "To compare any of my stuff with Machen's *Hill of Dreams* or Blackwood's *Incredible Adventures* or Dunsany's 'Bethmoora' or M. R. James's 'Count Magnus' or Poe's 'Ligeia' would be simply to subvert the soundest principles of criticism."[7] Lovecraft was, as was his custom, being a bit hard on himself; but it may well be the case that in only the very best of his narratives did he attain the depth and substance that make *Incredible Adventures* an authentic contribution to the literature of its time.

—S. T. JOSHI

---

7. Lovecraft, letter to Willis Conover (10 January 1937); *Selected Letters: 1934–1937*, p. 384.

The Regeneration of Lord Ernie

I

John Hendricks was bear-leading at the time. He had originally studied for Holy Orders, but had abandoned the Church later for private reasons connected with his faith, and had taken to teaching and tutoring instead. He was an honest, upstanding fellow of five-and-thirty, incorruptible, intelligent in a simple, straightforward way. He played games with his head, more than most Englishmen do, but he went through life without much calculation. He had qualities that made boys like and respect him; he won their confidence. Poor, proud, ambitious, he realised that fate offered him a chance when the Secretary of State for Scotland asked him if he would give up his other pupils for a year and take his son, Lord Ernie, round the world upon an educational trip that might make a man of him. For Lord Ernie was the only son, and the Marquess's influence was naturally great. To have deposited a regenerated Lord Ernie at the castle gates might have guaranteed Hendricks' future. After leaving Eton prematurely the lad had come under Hendricks' charge for a time, and with such excellent results—"I'd simply swear by that chap, you know," the boy used to say—that his father, considerably impressed, and rather as a last resort, had made this proposition. And Hendricks, without much calculation, had accepted it. He liked "Bindy" for himself. It was in his heart to "make a man of him," if possible. They had now been round the world together and had come up from Brindisi to the Italian Lakes, and so into Switzerland. It was middle October. With a week or two to spare they were making leisurely for the ancestral halls in Aberdeenshire.

The nine months' travel, Hendricks realised with keen disappointment, had accomplished, however, very little. The job had been exhausting, and he had conscientiously done his best. Lord Ernie liked him thoroughly, admiring his vigour with a smile of tolerant good-nature through his ceaseless cigarette smoke. They were almost like two boys together. "You *are* a chap and a half, Mr. Hendricks. You really ought to be in the Cabinet with my father." Hendricks would deliver up his useless parcel at the castle gates, pocket the thanks and the hard-earned fee, and go back to his arduous life of teaching and writing in dingy lodgings. It was a pity, even on the lowest grounds. The tutor, truth to tell, felt undeniably depressed. Hopeful by nature, optimistic, too, as men of action usually are, he cast about him, even at the last hour, for something that might stir the boy to life, wake him up, put zest and energy into him. But there was only Paris now between them and the end; and Paris certainly could not be relied upon for help. Bindy's desire for Paris even was not strong enough to count. No desire in him was ever strong. There lay the crux of the problem in a word—Lord Ernie was without desire which is life.

Tall, well-built, handsome, he was yet such a feeble creature, without the energy to be either wild or vicious. Languid, yet certainly not decadent, life ran slowly, flabbily in him. He took to nothing. The first impression he made was fine—then nothing. His only tastes, if tastes they could be called, were out-of-door tastes: he was vaguely interested in flying, yet not enough to master the mechanism of it; he liked motoring at high speed, being driven, not driving himself; and he loved to wander about in woods, making fires like a Red Indian, provided they lit easily, yet even this, not for the poetry of the thing nor for any love of adventure, but just "because." "I like fire, you know; like to watch it burn." Heat seemed to give him curious satisfaction, perhaps because the heat of life, he realised, was deficient in his six-foot body. It was significant, this love of fire in him, though no one could discover why. As a child he had a dangerous delight in fireworks—anything to do with fire. He would watch a candle flame as though he were a fire-worshipper, but had never been known to make a single remark of interest about it. In a wood, as mentioned, the first thing he did was to gather sticks—though the resulting fire was never part of any purpose. He had no purpose. There was no wind or fire of life in the lad at all. The fine body was inert.

Hendricks did wrong, of course, in going where he did—to this little desolate village in the Jura Mountains—though it was the first time all these trying months he had allowed himself a personal desire. But from Domo Dossola the Simplon Express would pass Lausanne, and from Lausanne to the Jura was but a step—all on the way home, moreover. And what prompted him was merely a sentimental desire to revisit the place where ten years before he had fallen violently in love with the pretty daughter of the Pasteur, M. Leysin, in whose house he lodged. He had gone there to learn French. The very slight detour seemed pardonable.

His spiritless charge was easily persuaded.

"We might go home by Pontarlier instead of Bâle, and get a glimpse of the Jura," he suggested. "The line slides along its frontiers a bit, and then goes bang across it. We might even stop off a night on the way—if you cared about it. I know a curious old village—Villaret—where I went at your age to pick up French."

"Top-hole," replied Lord Ernie listlessly. "All on the way to Paris, ain't it?"

"Of course. You see there's a fortnight before we need get home."

"So there is, yes. Let's go." He felt it was almost his own idea and that he decided it.

"If you'd *really* like it."

"Oh, yes! Why not? I'm sick of cities." He flicked some dust off his coat sleeve with an immaculate silk handkerchief, then lit a cigarette. "Just as you like," he added, with a drawl and a smile. "I'm ready for anything." There was no keenness, no personal desire, no choice in reality at all; flabby good-nature merely.

A suggestion was invariably enough, as though the boy had no will of his own, his opposition rarely more than negative sulking that soon flattened out because it was forgotten. Indeed, no sign of positive life lay in him anywhere—no vitality, aggression, coherence of desire and will; vacuous rather than imbecile; unable to go forward upon any definite line of his own, as though all wheels had slipped their cogs; a pasty soul that took good enough impressions, yet never mastered them for permanent use. Nothing stuck. He would never make a politician, much less a statesman. The family title would be borne by a nincompoop. Yet all the machinery was there, one felt—if only it could be driven, made to go. It was sad. Lord Ernie was heir to great estates, with a name and position that might influence thousands.

And Hendricks had been a good selection, with his virility and gentle, understanding firmness. He understood the problem. "You'll do what no one else could," the anxious father told him, "for he worships you, and you can sting without hurting him. You'll put life and interest into him if anybody in this world can. I have great hopes of this tour. I shall always be in your debt, Mr. Hendricks." And Hendricks had accepted the onerous duty in his big, high-minded way. He was conscientious to the backbone. This little side-trip was his sole deflection, if such it can be called even. "Life, light and cheerful influences," had been his instructions; "nothing dull or melancholy; an occasional fling, if he wants it—I'd welcome a fling as a good sign—and as much intercourse with decent people, and stimulating sight-seeing as you can manage—or can stand," the Earl added with a smile. "Only you won't over-tax the lad, will you? Above all, let him think *he* chooses and decides, when possible."

Villaret, however, hardly complied with these conditions; there was melancholy in it; Hendricks' mind—whose reflexes the spongy nature of the empty lad absorbed too easily—would be in a minor key. Yet a night could work no harm. Whence came, he wondered, the fleeting notion that it might do good? Was it, perhaps, that Leysin, the vigorous old Pasteur, might contribute something? Leysin had been a considerable force in his own development, he remembered; they had corresponded a little since; Leysin was out of the common, certainly, restless energy in him as of the sea. Hendricks found difficulty in sorting out his thoughts and motives but Leysin was in them somewhere—this idea that his energetic personality might help. His vitalising effect, at least, would counteract the melancholy.

For Villaret lay huddled upon unstimulating slopes, the robe of gloomy pine-woods sweeping down towards its poverty from bleak heights and desolate gorges. The peasants were morose, ill-living folk. It was a dark untaught corner in a range of otherwise fairy mountains, a backwater the sun had neglected to clean out. Superstitions, Hendricks remembered, of incredible kind still lingered there; a touch of the sinister hovered about the composite mind of its inhabitants. The Pasteur fought strenuously this blackness in their lives and thoughts; in the village itself with more or less success—though even there the drinking and habits of living were utterly unsweetened—but on the heights, among the somewhat arid pastures, the mountain men remained untamed, turbulent, even menacing. Hendricks knew this of old, though he had never understood too well. But he remembered how the English boys at *la cure* were forbidden to climb in certain directions, because the life in these scattered châlets was somehow loose and violent. There was danger there, the danger, however, never definitely stated. Those lonely ridges lay cursed beneath dark skies. He remembered too, the savage dogs, the difficulty of approach, the aggressive attitude towards the plucky Pasteur's visits to these remote upland *pâturages*. They did not lie in his parish: Leysin made his occasional visits as man and missionary; for extraordinary rumours, Hendricks recalled, were rife, of some queer worship of their own these lawless peasants kept alive in their distant, windy territory, planted there first, the story had it, by some renegade priest whose name was now forgotten.

Hendricks himself had no personal experiences. He had been too deeply in love to trouble about outside things, however strange. But Marston's case had never quite left his memory—Marston, who climbed up by unlawful ways, stayed away two whole days and nights and came back suddenly with his air of being broken, shattered, appallingly used up, his face so lined and strained it seemed aged by twenty years, and yet with a singular new life in him, so vehement, loud, and reckless, it was like a kind of sober intoxication. He was packed off to England before he could relate anything. But he had suffered shocks. His white, passionate face, his boisterous new vigour, the way M. Leysin screened his view of the heights as he put him personally into the Paris train—almost as though he feared the boy would see the hills and make another dash for them!—made up an unforgettable picture in the mind.

Moreover, between the sodden village and that string of evil châlets that lay in their dark line upon the heights there had been links. Exactly of what nature he never knew, for love made all else uninteresting; only, he remembered swarthy, dark-faced messengers descending into the sleepy hamlet from time to time, big, mountain-limbed fellows with wind in their hair and fire in their eyes; that their visits produced commotion and excitement of difficult kinds; that wild orgies invariably followed in their wake; and that, when the messengers went back, they did not go alone. There was life up there, whereas the village was moribund. And none who went ever cared to return. Cudrefin, the young giant *vigneron*, taken in this way, from the very side of his sweetheart too, came back two years later as a messenger himself. He did not even ask for the girl, who had meanwhile married another. "There's life up there with us," he told the drunken loafers in the "Guillaume Tell," "wind and fire to make you spin to the devil—or to heaven!" He was enthusiasm personified. In the village he had been merely drinking himself stupidly to death. Vaguely, too, Hendricks remembered visits of police from the neighbouring towns, some of them on horseback, all armed, and that once even soldiers accompanied them, and on another occasion a bishop, or whatever the church dignitary was called, had arrived suddenly and promised radical assistance of a spiritual kind that had never materialised—oh, and many other details that now trooped back with suggestions time had certainly not made smaller. For the love had passed along its way and gone, and he was free now to the invasion of other memories, dwarfed at the time by that dominating, sweet passion.

Yet all the tutor wanted now, this chance week in late October, was to see again the corner of the mossy forest where he had known that marvellous thing, first love; renew his link with Leysin who had taught him much; and see if, perchance, this man's stalwart, virile energy might possibly overflow with benefit into his listless charge. The expenses he meant to pay out of his own pocket. Those wild pagans on the heights—even if they still existed—there was no need to mention. Lord Ernie knew little French, and certainly no word of patois. For one night, or even two, the risk was negligible.

Was there, indeed, risk at all of any sort? Was not this vague uneasiness he felt merely conscience faintly pricking? He could not feel that he was doing wrong. At worst, the youth might feel depression for a few hours—speedily curable by taking the train.

Something, nevertheless, did gnaw at him in subconscious fashion, producing a sense of apprehension; and he came to the conclusion that this memory of the mountain tribe was the cause of it—a revival of forgotten boyhood's awe. He glanced across at the figure of Bindy lounging upon the hotel lawn in an easy-chair, full in the sunshine, a newspaper at his feet. Reclining there, he looked so big and strong and handsome, yet in reality was but a painted lath without resistance, much less attack, in all his many inches. And suddenly the tutor recalled another thing, the link, however, undiscoverable, and it was this:

that the boy's mother, a Canadian, had suffered once severely from a winter in Quebec, where the marquess had first made her acquaintance. Frost had robbed her, if he remembered rightly, of a foot—with the result, at any rate, that she had a wholesome terror of the cold. She sought heat and sun instinctively—fire. Also, that asthma had been her sore affliction—sheer inability to take a full, deep breath. This deficiency of heat and air, therefore, were in her mind. And he knew that Bindy's birth had been an anxious time, the anxiety justified, moreover, since she had yielded up her life for him.

And so the singular thought flashed through him suddenly as he watched the reclining, languid boy, Cudrefin's descriptive phrase oddly singing in his head—

"Heat and fire, fire and wind—why, it's the very thing he lacks! And he's always after them. I wonder—!"

II

The lumbering yellow *diligence* brought them up from the Lake shore, a long two hours, deposited them at the opening of the village street, and went its grinding, toiling way towards the frontier. They arrived in a blur of rain. It was evening. Lowering clouds drew night before her time upon the world, obscuring the distant summits of the Oberland, but lights twinkled here and there in the nearer landscape, mapping the gloom with signals. The village was very still. Above and below it, however, two big winds were at work, with curious results. For a lower wind from the east in gusty draughts drove the body of the lake into quick white horses which shone like wings against the deep *basses Alpes,* while a westerly current swept the heights immediately above the village. There was this odd division of two weathers, presaging a change. A narrow line of clear bright sky showed up the Jura outline finely towards the north, stars peeping sharply through the pale moist spaces. Hurrying vapours, driven by the upper westerly wind, concealed them thinly. They flashed and vanished. The entire ridge, five thousand feet in the air, had an appearance of moving through the sky. Between these opposing winds at different levels the village itself lay motionless, while the world slid past, as it were, in two directions.

"The earth seems turning round," remarked Lord Ernie. He had been reading a novel all day in train and steamer, and smoking endless cigarettes in the *diligence,* his companion and himself its only occupants. He seemed suddenly to have waked up. "What is it?" he asked with interest.

Hendricks explained the queer effect of the two contrary winds. Columns of peat smoke rose in thin straight lines from the blur of houses, untouched by the careering currents above and below. The winds whirled round them.

Lord Ernie listened attentively to the explanation.

"I feel as if I were spinning with it—like a top," he observed, putting his hand to his head a moment. "And what are those lights up there?"

He pointed to the distant ridge, where fires were blazing as though stars had fallen and set fire to the trees. Several were visible, at regular intervals. The sharp summits of the limestone mountains cut hard into the clear spaces of northern sky thousands of feet above.

"Oh, the peasants burning wood and stuff, I suppose," the tutor told him.

The youth turned an instant, standing still to examine them with a shading hand.

"People live up there?" he asked. There was surprise in his voice, and his body stiffened oddly as he spoke.

"In mountain châlets, yes," replied the other a trifle impatiently, noticing his attitude. "Come along now," he added, "let's get to our rooms in the carpenter's house before the rain comes down. You can see the windows twinkling over there," and he pointed to a building near the church. "The storm will catch us." They moved quickly down the deserted street together in the deepening gloom, passing little gardens, doors of open barns, straggling manure heaps, and courtyards of cobbled stones where the occasional figure of a man was seen. But Lord Ernie lingered behind, half loitering. Once or twice, to the other's increasing annoyance, he paused, standing still to watch the heights through openings between the tumble-down old houses. Half a dozen big drops of rain splashed heavily on the road.

"Hurry up!" cried Hendricks, looking back, "or we shall be caught. It's the mountain wind—the *coup de joran*. You can hear it coming!" For the lad was peering across a low wall in an attitude of fixed attention. He made a gesture with one hand, as though he signalled towards the ridges where the fires blazed. Hendricks called pretty sharply to him then. It was possible, of course, that he misinterpreted the movement; it may merely have been that he passed his fingers through his hair, across his eyes, or used the palm to focus sight, for his hat was off and the light was quite uncertain. Only Hendricks did not like the lingering or the gesture. He put authority into his tone at once. "Come along, will you; come along, Bindy!" he called.

The answer filled him with amazement.

"All right, all right. I'll follow in a moment. I like this."

The tutor went back a few steps towards him. The tone startled him.

"Like what?" he asked.

And Lord Ernie turned towards him with another face. There was fighting in it. There was resolution.

"This, of course," the boy answered steadily, but with excitement shut down behind, as he waved one arm towards the mountains. "I've dreamed this sort of thing; I've known it somewhere. We've seen nothing like it all our stupid trip." The flash in his brown eyes passed then, as he added more quietly, but with firmness: "Don't wait for me; I'll follow."

Hendricks stood still in his tracks. There was a decision in the voice and manner that arrested him. The confidence, the positive statement, the eager desire, the hint of energy—all this was new. He had never encouraged the boy's habit of vivid dreaming, deeming the narration unwise. It flashed across him suddenly now that the "deficiency" might be only on the surface. Energy and life hid, perhaps, subconsciously in him. Did the dreams betray an activity he knew not how to carry through and correlate with his everyday, external world? And were these dreams evidence of deep, hidden desire—a clue, possibly, to the energy he sought and needed, the exact kind of energy that might set the inert machinery in motion and drive it?

He hesitated an instant, waiting in the road. He was on the verge of understanding something that yet just evaded him. Bindy's childish, instinctive love of fire, his passion for air, for rushing wind, for oceans of limitless—

There came at that moment a deep roaring in the mountains. Far away, but rapidly approaching, the ominous booming of it filled the air. The westerly wind descended by the deep gorges, shaking the forests, shouting as it came. Clouds of white dust spiralled into the sky off the upper roads, spread into sheets like snow, and swept downwards with incredible velocity. The air turned suddenly cooler. More big drops of rain splashed and thudded on the roofs and road. There was a feeling of something violent and instantaneous about to happen, a sense almost of attack. The *joran* tore headlong down into the valley.

"Come on, man," he cried at the top of his voice. "That's the *joran!* I know it of old! It's terrific. Run!" And he caught the lad, still lingering, by the arm.

But Lord Ernie shook himself free with an excitement almost violent.

"I've been up there with those great fires," he shouted. "I know the whole blessed thing. But where was it? Where?" His face was white, eyes shining, manner strangely agitated. "Big, naked fellows who dance like wind, and rushing women of fire, and—"

Two things happened then, interrupting the boy's wild language. The *joran* reached the village and struck it; the houses shook, the trees bent double, and the cloud of limestone dust, painting the darkness white, swept on between Hendricks and the boy with extraordinary force, even separating them. There was a clatter of falling tiles, of banging doors and windows, and then a burst of icy rain that fell like iron shot on everything, raising actual spray. The air was in an instant thick. Everything drove past, roared, trembled. And, secondly—just in that brief instant when man and boy were separated—there shot between them with shadowy swiftness the figure of a man, hatless, with flying hair, who vanished with running strides into the darkness of the village street beyond—all so rapidly that sight could focus neither the manner of his coming nor of his going. Hendricks caught a glimpse of a swarthy, elemental type of face, the swing of great shoulders, the leap of big loose limbs— something rushing and elastic in the whole appearance—but nothing he could claim for definite detail. The figure swept through the dust and wind like an animal—and was gone. It was, indeed, only the contrast of Lord Ernie's whitened skin, of his graceful, half-elegant outline, that enabled him to recall the details that he did. The weather-beaten visage seemed to storm away. Bindy's delicate aristocratic face shone so pale and eager. But that a real man had passed was indubitable, for the boy made a flurried movement as though to follow. Hendricks caught his arm with a determined grip and pulled him back.

"Who was that? Who was it?" Lord Ernie cried breathlessly, resisting with all his strength, but vainly.

"Some mountain fellow, of course. Nothing to do with us." And he dragged the boy after him down the road. For a second both seemed to have lost their heads. Hendricks certainly felt a gust of something strike him into momentary consternation that was half alarm.

"From up there, where the fires are?" asked the boy, shouting above the wind and rain.

"Yes, yes, I suppose so. Come along. We shall be soused. Are you mad?" For Bindy still held back with all his weight, trying to turn round and see. Hendricks used more force. There was almost a scuffle in the road.

"All right, I'm coming. I only wanted to look a second. You needn't drag my arm out." He ceased resistance, and they lurched forward together. "But what a chap he was! He went like the wind. Did you see the light streaming out of him—like fire?"

"Like what?" shouted Hendricks, as they dashed now through the driving tempest.

"Fire!" bawled the boy. "It lit me up as he passed—fire that lights but does not burn, and wind that blows the world along—"

"Button your coat and run!" interrupted the other, hurrying his pace, and pulling the lad forcibly after him.

"Don't twist! You're hurting! I can run as well as you!" came back, with an energy Bindy had never shown before in his life. He was breathless, panting, charged with excitement still. "It touched me as he passed—fire that lights but doesn't burn, and wind that blows the heart to flame—let me go, will you? Let go my hand."

He dashed free and away. The torrential rain came down in sheets now from a windless sky, for the *joran* was already miles beyond them, tearing across the angry lake. They reached the carpenter's house, where their lodging was, soaked to the skin. They dried themselves, and ate the light supper of soup and omelette prepared for them—ate it in their dressing-gowns. Lord Ernie went to bed with a hot-water bottle of rough stone. He declared with decision that he felt no chill. His excitement had somewhat passed.

"But I say, Mr. Hendricks," he remarked, as he settled down with his novel and a cigarette, calmed and normal again, "this *is* a place and a half, isn't it? It stirs me all up. I suppose it's the storm. What do *you* think?"

"Electrical state of the air, yes," replied the tutor briefly.

Soon afterwards he closed the shutters on the weather side, said good-night, and went into his own room to unpack. The singular phrase Bindy had used kept singing through his head: "Fire that lights but doesn't burn, and wind that blows the heart to flame"—the first time he had said "blows the world along." Where on earth had the boy got hold of such queer words? He still saw the figure of that wild mountain fellow who had passed between them with the dust and wind and rain. There was confusion in the picture, or rather in his memory of it, perhaps. But it seemed to him, looking back now, that the man in passing had paused a second—the briefest second merely—and had spoken, or, at any rate, had stared closely a moment into Bindy's face, and that some communication had been between them in that moment of elemental violence.

III

Pasteur Leysin Hendricks remembered very well. Even now in his old age he was a vigorous personality, but in his youth he had been almost revolutionary; wild enough, too, it was rumoured, until he had turned to God of his own accord as offering a larger field for his strenuous vitality. The little man was possessed of tireless life, a born leader of forlorn hopes, attack his métier, and heavy odds the conditions that he loved. Before settling down in this isolated spot—*pasteur de l'église indépendente* in a protestant Canton—he had been a missionary in remote pagan lands. His horizon was a big one, he had seen strange things. An uncouth being, with a large head upon a thin and wiry body supported by steely bowed legs, he had that courage which makes itself known in advance of any proof. Hendricks slipped over to *la cure* about nine o'clock and found him in his study. Lord Ernie was asleep; at least his light was out, no sound or movement audible from his room. The *joran* had swept the heavens of clouds. Stars shone brilliantly. The fires still blazed faintly upon the heights.

The visit was not unexpected, for Hendricks had already sent a message to announce himself, and the moment he sat down, met the Pasteur's eye, heard his voice, and observed his slight imperious gestures, he passed under the influence of a personality stronger than his own. Something in Leysin's atmosphere stretched him, lifting his horizon. He had come chiefly—he now realised it—to borrow help and explanation with regard to Lord Ernie; the events of two hours before had impressed him more than he quite cared to own, and he wished to talk about it. But, somehow, he found it difficult to state his case; no opening presented itself; or, rather, the Pasteur's mind, intent upon something of his own, was too preoccupied. In reply to a question presently, the tutor gave a brief outline of his present duties, but omitted the scene of excitement in the village street, for as he watched the furrowed face in the light of the study lamp, he realised both anxiety and spiritual high pressure at work below the surface there. He hesitated to intrude his own affairs at first. They discussed, nevertheless, the psychology of the boy, and the unfavourable chances of regeneration, while the old man's face lit up and flashed from time to time, until at length the truth came out, and Hendricks understood his friend's preoccupation.

"What you're attempting with an individual," Leysin exclaimed with ardour, "is precisely what I'm attempting with a crowd. And it's difficult. For poor sinners make poor saints, and the lukewarm I will spue out of my mouth." He made an abrupt, resentful gesture to signify his disgust and weariness, perhaps his contempt as well. "Cut it down! Why cumbereth it the ground?"

"A hard, uncharitable doctrine," began the tutor, realising that he must discuss the Parish before he could introduce Bindy's case effectively. "You mean, of course, that there's no material to work on?"

"No energy to direct," was the emphatic reply. "My sheep here are—real sheep; mere negative, drink-sodden loafers without desire. Hospital cases! I could work with tigers and wild beasts, but who ever trained a slug?"

"Your proper place is on the heights," suggested Hendricks, interrupting at a venture. "There's scope enough up there, or used to be. Have they died out, those wild men of the mountains?" And hit by chance the target in the bull's-eye.

The old man's face turned younger as he answered quickly.

"Men like that," he exclaimed, "do not die off. They breed and multiply." He leaned forward across the table, his manner eager, fervent, almost impetuous with suppressed desire for action. "There's evil thinking up there," he said suggestively, "but, by heaven, it's alive; it's positive, ambitious, constructive. With violent feeling and strong desire to work on, there's hope of some result. Upon vehement impulses like that, pagan or anything else, a man can work with a will. Those are the tigers; down here I have the slugs!"

He shrugged his shoulders and leaned back into his chair. Hendricks watched him, thinking of the stories told about his missionary days among savage and barbarian tribes.

"Born of the vital landscape, I suppose?" he asked. "Wind and frost and blazing sun. Their wild energy, I mean, is due to—"

A gesture from the old man stopped him. "You know who started them upon their wild performances," he said gravely in a lower voice; "you know how that ambitious renegade priest from the Valais chose them for his nucleus, then died before he could lead them out, trained and competent, upon his strange campaign? You heard the story when you were with me as a boy—?"

"I remember Marston," put in the other, uncommonly interested, "Marston—the boy who—" He stopped because he hardly knew how to continue. There was a minute's silence. But it was not an empty silence, though no word broke it. Leysin's face was a study.

"Ah, Marston, yes," he said slowly, without looking up; "you remember him. But that is at my door, too, I suppose. His father was ignorant and obstinate; I might have saved him otherwise." He seemed talking to himself rather than to his listener. Pain showed in the lines about the rugged mouth. "There was no one, you see, who knew how to direct the great life that woke in the lad. He took it back with him, and turned it loose into all manner of useless enterprises, and the doctors mistook his abrupt and fierce ambitions for—for the hysteria which they called the vestibule of lunacy. . . . Yet small characters may have big ideas. . . . They didn't understand, of course. . . . It was sad, sad, sad." He hid his face in his hands a moment.

"Marston went wrong, then, in the end?" for the other's manner suggested disaster of some kind. Hendricks asked it in a whisper. Leysin uncovered his face, looped his neck with one finger, and pointed to the ceiling.

"Hanged himself!" murmured Hendricks, shocked.

The Pasteur nodded, but there was impatience, half anger in his tone.

"They checked it, kept it in. Of course, it tore him!"

The two men looked into each other's eyes for a moment, and something in the younger of them shrank. This was all beyond his ken a little. An odd hint of bleak and cruel reality was in the air, making him shiver along nerves that were normally inactive. The uneasiness he felt about Lord Ernie became alarm. His conscience pricked him.

"More than he could assimilate," continued Leysin. "It broke him. Yet, had outlets been provided, had he been taught how to use it, this elemental energy drawn direct from Nature—" He broke off abruptly, struck perhaps by the expression in his listener's eyes. "It seems incredible, doesn't it, in the twentieth century? I know."

"Evil?" asked Hendricks, stammering rather.

"Why evil?" was the impatient reply. "How can any force be evil? That's merely a question of direction."

"And the priest who discovered these forces and taught their use, then—?"

"Was genuinely spiritual and followed the truth in his own way. He was not necessarily evil." The little Pasteur spoke with vehemence. "You talk like the religion-primers in the kindergarten," he went on. "Listen. This man, sick and weary of his lukewarm flock, sought vital, stalwart systems who might be clean enough to use the elemental powers he had discovered how to attract. Only the bias of the users could make it 'evil' by wrong use. His idea was big and even holy—to train a corps that might regenerate the world. And he chose unreasoning, unintellectual types with a purpose—primitive, giant men who could assimilate the force without risk of being shattered. Under his direction he intended they should prove as effective as the twelve disciples of old who were fisher-folk. And, had he gone on—"

"He, too, failed then?" asked the other, whose tangled thoughts struggled with incredulity and belief as he heard this strange new thing. "He died, you mean?"

"Maison de santé," was the laconic reply, "straight waistcoats, padded cells, and the rest; but still alive, I'm told. It was more than he could manage."

It was a startling story, even in this brief outline, deep suggestion in it. The tutor's sense of being out of his depth increased. After nine months with a lifeless, devitalised human being, this was—well, he seemed to have fallen in his sleep from a comfortable bed into a raging mountain torrent. Strong currents rushed through and over him. The lonely, peaceful village outside, sleeping beneath the stars, heightened the contrast.

"Suppressed or misdirected energy again, I suppose," he said in a low tone, respecting his companion's emotion. "And these mountain men," he asked abruptly, "do they still keep up their—practices?"

"Their ceremonies, yes," corrected the other, master of himself again. "Turbulent moments of nature, storms and the like, stir them to clumsy rehearsals of once vital rituals—not entirely ineffective, even in their incompleteness, but dangerous for that very reason. This *joran*, for instance, invariably communicates something of its atmospherical energy to themselves. They light their fires as of old. They blunder through what they remember of *his* ceremonies. With the glasses you may see them in their dozens, men and women, leaping and dancing. It's an amazing sight, great beauty in it, impossible to witness even from a distance without feeling the desire to take part in it. Even my people feel it—the only time they ever get alive,"—he jerked his big head contemptuously towards the street—"or feel desire to act. And some one from the heights—a messenger perhaps—will be down later, this very evening probably, on the hunt—"

"On the hunt?" Hendricks asked it half below his breath. He felt a touch of awe as he heard this experienced, genuinely religious man speak with conviction of such curious things. "On the hunt?" he repeated more eagerly.

"Messengers do come down," was the reply. "A living belief always seeks to increase, to grow, to add to itself. Where there's conviction there's always propaganda."

"Ah, converts—?"

Leysin shrugged his big black shoulders. "Desire to add to their num-ber—desire to *save*," he said. "The energy they absorb overflows, that's all."

The Englishman debated several questions vaguely in his mind; only his mind, being disturbed, could not hold the balance exactly true. Leysin's influ-ence, as of old, was upon him. A possibility, remote, seductive, dangerous, be-gan to beckon to him, but from somewhere just outside his reasoning mind.

"And they always know when one of their kind is near," the voice slipped in between his tumbling thoughts, "as though they get it instinctively from these universal elements they worship. They select their recruits with marvel-lous judgment and precision. No messenger ever goes back alone; nor has a recruit ever been known to return to the lazy squalor of the conditions whence he escaped."

The younger man sat upright in his chair, suddenly alert, and the gesture that he made unconsciously might have been read by a keen psychiatrist as evidence of mental self-defence. He felt the forbidden impulse in him gather-ing force, and tried to call a halt. At any rate, he called upon the other man to be explicit. He enquired point-blank what this religion of the heights might be. What were these elements these people worshipped? In what did their wild ceremonies consist?

And Leysin, breaking bounds, let his speech burst forth in a stream of explanation, learned of actual knowledge, as he claimed, and uttered with a vehement conviction that produced an undeniable effect upon his astonished listener. Told by no dreamer, but by a righteous man who lived, not merely preached his certain faith, Hendricks, before the half was heard, forgot what age and land he dwelt in. Whole blocks of conventional belief crumbled and fell away. Brick walls erected by routine to mark narrow paths of proper con-duct—safe, moral, advisable conduct—thawed and vanished. Through the ruins, scrambling at him from huge horizons never recognised before, came all manner of marvellous possibilities. The little confinement of modern thought appalled him suddenly. Leysin spoke slowly, said little, was not even speculative. It was no mere magic of words that made the dim-lit study swim these deep waters beyond the ripple of pert creeds, but rather the overwhelm-ing sense of sure conviction driving behind the statements. The little man had witnessed curious things, yes, in his missionary days, and that he had found truth in them in place of ignorant nonsense was remarkable enough. That silly superstitions prevalent among older nations could be signs really of their former greatness, linked mightily close to natural forces, was a startling notion, but it paved the way in Hendricks' receptive mind just then for the belief that certain so-called elements might be worshipped—known intimately, that is—to the uplifting advantage of the worshippers. And what elements more suitable for adoring imitation than wind and fire? For in a human body the first signs of what men term life are heat which is combustion, and breath which is a measure of wind. Life means fire, drawn first from the sun, and breathing, borrowed from the omnipresent air; there might credibly be ways of assaulting these elements and taking heaven by storm; of seizing from their inexhaustible stores an abnormal measure, of straining this huge raw supply into effective energy for human use—vitality. Living with fire and wind in their most active moments; closely imitating their movements, following in their footsteps, understanding their "laws of being," going *identically* with them—there lay a hint of the method. It was once, when men were primitively close to Nature, instinctual knowledge. The ceremony was the teaching. The Powers of fire, the Principalities of air, existed; and humanity *could* know their qualities by the ritual of imitation, could actually absorb the fierce enthusiasm of flame and the tireless energy of wind. Such transference was conceivable.

Leysin, at any rate, somehow made it so. His description of what he had personally witnessed, both in wilder lands and here in this little mountain range of middle Europe, had a reality in it that was upsetting to the last degree. "There is nothing more difficult to believe," he said, "yet more certainly true, than the effect of these singular elemental rites." He laughed a short dry laugh. "The mediæval superstition that a witch could raise a storm is but a remnant of a once completely efficacious system," he concluded, "though how that strange being, the Valais priest, re-discovered the process and introduced it here, I have never been able to ascertain. That he did so results have proved. At any rate, it lets in life, life moreover in astonishing abundance; though, whether for destruction or regeneration, depends, obviously, upon the use the recipient puts it to. That's where direction comes in."

The beckoning impulse in the tutor's bewildered thoughts drew closer. The moment for communicating it had come at last. Without more ado he took the opening. He told his companion the incident in the village street, the boy's abrupt excitement, his new-found energy, the curious words he used, the independence and vitality of his attitude. He told also of his parentage, of his mother's disabilities, his craving for rushing air in abundance, his love of fire for its own sake, of his magnificent physical machinery, yet of his uselessness.

And Leysin, as he listened, seemed built on wires. Searching questions shot forth like blows into the other's mind. The Pasteur's sudden increase of enthusiasm was infectious. He leaped intuitively to the thing in Hendricks' thought. He understood the beckoning.

The tutor answered the questions as best he could, aware of the end in view with trepidation and a kind of mental breathlessness. Yes, unquestionably, Bindy *had* exchanged communication of some sort with the man, though his excitement had been evident even sooner.

"And you saw this man yourself?" Leysin pressed him.

"Indubitably—a tall and hurrying figure in the dusk."

"He brought energy with him? The boy felt it and responded?"

Hendricks nodded. "Became quite unmanageable for some minutes," he replied.

"He assimilated it though? There was no distress exactly?" Leysin asked sharply.

"None—that I could see. Pleasurable excitement, something aggressive, a rather wild enthusiasm. His will began to act. He used that curious phrase about wind and fire. He turned alive. He wanted to follow the man—"

"And the face—how would you describe it? Did it bring terror, I mean, or confidence?"

"Dark and splendid," answered the other as truthfully as he could. "In a certain sense, rushing, tempestuous, yet stern rather."

"A face like the heights," suggested Leysin impatiently, "a windy, fiery aspect in it, eh?"

"The man swept past like the spirit of a storm in imaginative poetry—" began the tutor, hunting through his thoughts for adequate description, then stopped as he saw that his companion had risen from his chair and begun to pace the floor.

The Pasteur paused a moment beside him, hands thrust deep into his pockets, head bent down, and shoulders forward. For twenty seconds he stared into his visitor's face intently, as though he would force into him the thought in his own mind. His features seemed working visibly, yet behind a mask of strong control.

"Don't you see what it is? Don't you see?" he said in a lower, deeper tone. "*They knew.* Even from a distance they were aware of his coming. He is one of themselves." And he straightened up again. "He belongs to them."

"One of them? One of the wind-and-fire lot?" the tutor stammered.

The restless little man returned to his chair opposite, full of suppressed and vigorous movement, as though he were strung on springs.

"He's *of* them," he continued, "but in a peculiar and particular sense. More than merely a possible recruit, his empty organism would provide the very link they need, the perfect conduit." He watched his companion's face with careful keenness. "In the country where I first experienced this marvellous thing," he added significantly, "he would have been set apart as the offering, the sacrifice, as they call it there. The tribe would have chosen him with honour. He would have been the special bait to attract."

"Death?" whispered the other.

But Leysin shook his head. "In the end, perhaps," he replied darkly, "for the vessel might be torn and shattered. But at first charged to the brim and crammed with energy—with transformed vitality they could draw into themselves through him. A monster, if you will, but to them a deity; and superhuman, in our little sense, most certainly."

Then Hendricks faltered inwardly and turned away. No words came to him at the moment. In silence the minds of the two men, one a religious, the other a secular teacher, and each with a burden of responsibility to the race, kept pace together without speech. The religious, however, outstripped the pedagogue. What he next said seemed a little disconnected with what had preceded it, although Hendricks caught the drift easily enough—and shuddered.

"An organism needing heat," observed Leysin calmly, "can absorb without danger what would destroy a normal person. Alcohol, again, neither injures nor intoxicates—up to a given point—the system that really requires it."

The tutor, perplexed and sorely tempted, felt that he drifted with a tide he found it difficult to stem.

"Up to a point," he repeated. "That's true, of course."

"Up to a given point," echoed the other, with significance that made his voice sound solemn. "Then rescue—in the nick of time."

He waited two full minutes and more for an answer; then, as none was audible, he said another thing. His eyes were so intent upon the tutor's that this latter raised his own unwillingly, and understood thus all that lay behind the pregnant little sentence.

"With a number it would not be possible, but with an individual it could be done. Brim the empty vessel first. Then rescue—in the nick of time! Regeneration!"

IV

In the Englishman's mind there came a crash, as though something fell. There was dust, confusion, noise. Moral platitudes shouted at conventional admonitions. Warnings laughed and copy-book maxims shrivelled up. Above the lot, rising with a touch of grandeur, stood the pulpit figure of the little Pasteur, his big face shining clear through all the turmoil, strength and vision in the flaming eyes—a commanding outline with spiritual audacity in his heart. And Hendricks saw then that the man himself was standing erect in the centre of the room, one finger raised to command attention—listening. Some considerable interval must have passed while he struggled with his inner confusion.

Leysin stood, intently listening, his big head throwing a grotesque shadow on wall and ceiling.

"Hark!" he exclaimed, half whispering. "Do you hear that? Listen."

A deep sound, confused and roaring, passed across the night, far away, and slightly booming. It entered the little room so that the air seemed to tremble a moment. To Hendricks it held something ominous.

"The wind," he whispered, as the noise died off into the distance; "yet a moment ago the night was still enough. The stars were shining." There was tense excitement in the room just then. It showed in Leysin's face, which had gone white as a cloth. Hendricks himself felt extraordinarily stirred.

"Not wind, but human voices," the older man said quickly. "It's shouting. Listen!" and his eyes ran round the room, coming to rest finally in a corner where his hat and cloak hung from a nail. A gesture accompanied the look. He wanted to be out. The tutor half rose to take his leave. "You have duties to-night elsewhere," he stammered. "I'm forgetting." His own instinct was to get away himself with Bindy by the first early *diligence*. He was afraid of yielding.

"Hush!" whispered Leysin peremptorily. "Listen!"

He opened the window at the top, and through the crack, where the stars peeped brightly, there came, louder than before, the uproar of human voices floating through the night from far away. The air of the great pine forests came in with it. Hendricks listened intently a moment. He positively jumped to feel a hand upon his arm. Leysin's big head was thrust close up into his face.

"That's the commotion in the village," he whispered. "A messenger has come and gone; someone has gone back with him. To-night I shall be needed—down here, but to-morrow night when the great ritual takes place—up there—!"

Hendricks tried to push him away so as not to hear the words; but the little man seemed immovable as a rock. The impulse remained probably in the mind without making the muscles work. For the tutor, sorely tempted, longed to dare, yet faltered in his will.

"—if you felt like taking the risk," the words continued seductively, "we might place the empty vessel near enough to let it fill, then rescue it, charged with energy, in the nick of time." And the Pasteur's eyes were aglow with enthusiasm, his voice even trembling at the thought of high adventure to save another's soul.

"Watch merely?" Hendricks heard his own voice whisper, hardly aware that he was saying it, "without taking part?" He said it thickly, stupidly, a man wavering and unsure of himself. "It would be an experience," he stammered.

"I've never—"

"Merely watch, yes; look on; let him see," interrupted the other with eagerness. "We must be very careful. It's worth trying—a last resort."

They still stood close together. Hendricks felt the little man's breath on his face as he peered up at him.

"I admit the chance," he began weakly.

"There is no chance," was the vigorous reply, "there is only Providence. You have been guided."

"But as to risk and failure, what of them? What's involved?" he asked, recklessness increasing in him.

"New wine in old bottles," was the answer. "But here, you tell me, the vessel is not damaged, but merely empty. The machinery is all right. If he merely watches, as from a little distance—"

"Yes, yes, the machinery *is* there, I agree. The boy has breeding, health, and all the physical qualities—good blood and nerves and muscles. It's only that life refuses to stay and drive them." His heart beat with violence even as he said it; he felt the energy and zeal from the older man pour into him. He was realising in himself on a smaller scale what might take place with the boy in large. But still he shrank. Leysin for the moment said no more. His spiritual discernment was equal to his boldness. Having planted the seed, he left it to grow or die. The decision was not for him.

In the light of the single lamp the two men sat facing each other, listening, waiting, while Leysin talked occasionally, but in the main kept silence. Some time passed, though how long the tutor could not say. In his mind was wild confusion. How could he justify such a mad proposal? Yet how could he refuse the opening, preposterous though it seemed? The enticement was very great; temptation rushed upon him. Striving to recall his normal world, he found it difficult. The face of the old marquess seemed a mere lifeless picture on a wall—it watched but could not interfere. Here was an opportunity to take or leave. He fought the battle in terms of naked souls, while the ordinary four-cornered morality hid its face awhile. He heard himself explaining, delaying, hedging, half-toying with the problem. But the redemption of a soul was at stake, and he tried to forget the environment and conditions of modern thought and belief. Sentences flashed at him out of the battle: "I must take him back worse than when I started, or—what? A violent being like Marston, or a redeemed, converted system with new energy? It's a chance, and my last." Moreover, odd, half-comic detail—there was the support of the Church, of a protestant clergyman whose fundamental beliefs were similar to the evangelical persuasions of the boy's family. Conversion, as demoniacal possession,

were both traditions of the blood. After all, the old Marquess might understand and approve. "You took the opening God set in your way in his wisdom. You showed faith and courage. Far be it from me to condemn you."
The picture on the wall looked down at him and spoke the words.

The wild hypothesis of the intrepid little missionary-pasteur swept him
with an effect like hypnotism. Then, suddenly, something in him seemed to
decide finally for itself. He flung himself, morality and all, upon this vigorous
other personality. He leaned across the table, his face close to the lamp. His
voice shook as he spoke.

"Would *you?*" he asked—then knew the question foolish, and that such a
man would shrink from nothing where the redemption of a soul was at stake;
knew also that the question was proof that his own decision was already
made.

There was something grotesque almost in the torrent of colloquial French
Leysin proceeded to pour forth, while the other sat listening in amazement,
half ashamed and half exhilarated. He looked at the stalwart figure, the wiry
bowed legs as he paced the floor, the shortness of the coat-sleeves and the
absence of shirt-cuffs round the powerful lean wrists. It was a great fighting
man he watched, a man afraid of nothing in heaven or earth, prepared to lead
a forlorn hope into a hostile unknown land. And the sight, combined with
what he heard, set the seal upon his half-hearted decision. He would take the
risk and go.

"Pfui!" exclaimed the little Pasteur as though it might have been an oath,
his loud whisper breaking through into a guttural sound, "pfui! Bah! Would
that *my* people had machinery like that so that I could use it! I've no material
to work on, no force to direct, nothing but heavy, sodden clay. Jelly!" he
cried, "negative, useless, lukewarm stuff at best." He lowered his voice suddenly, so as to listen at the same time. "I might as well be a baker kneading
dough," he continued. "They drink and yield and drink again; they never attack and drive; they're not worth labouring to save." He struck the wooden
table with his fist, making the lamp rattle, while his listener started and drew
back. "What good can weak souls, though spotless, be to God? The best have
long ago gone up to them," and he jerked his leonine old head towards the
mountains. "Where there's *life* there's hope," he stamped his foot as he said it,
"but the lukewarm—pfui!—I will spue them out of my mouth!"

He paused by the window a moment, listened attentively, then resumed
his pacing to and fro. Clearly, he longed for action. Indifference, half-
heartedness had no place in his composition. And Hendricks felt his own
slower blood take fire as he listened.

"Ah!" cried Leysin louder, "what a battle I could fight up there for God, could I but live among them, stem the flow of their dark strong vitality, then twist it round and up, up, up!" And he jerked his finger skywards. "It's the great sinners we want, not the meek-faced saints. There's energy enough among those devils to bring a whole Canton to the great Footstool, could I but direct it." He paused a moment, standing over his astonished visitor. "Bring the boy up with you, and let him drink his fill. And pray, pray, I say, that he become a violent sinner first in order that later there shall be something worth offering to God. Over one *sinner* that repenteth—"

A rapid, nervous knocking interrupted the flow of words, and the figure of a woman stood upon the threshold. With the opening of the door came also again the roaring from the night outside. Hendricks saw the tall, somewhat di-shevelled outline of the wife—he remembered her vaguely, though she could hardly see him now in his darker corner—and recalled the fact that she had been sent out to Leysin in his missionary days, a worthy, illiterate, but adoring woman. She wore a shawl, her hair was untidy, her eyes fixed and staring. Her husband's sturdy little figure, as he rose, stood level with her chin.

"You hear it, Jules?" she whispered thickly. "The *joran* has brought them down. You'll be needed in the village." She said it anxiously, though Hendricks understood the patois with difficulty. They talked excitedly to-gether a moment in the doorway, their outlines blocked against the corridor where a single oil lamp flickered. She warned, urging something; he expostu-lated. Fragments reached Hendricks in his corner. Clearly the woman wor-shipped her husband like a king, yet feared for his safety. He, for his part, comforted her, scolded a little, argued, told her to "believe in God and go back to bed."

"They'll take you too, and you'll never return. It's not your parish anyhow . . ." a touch of anguish in her tone.

But Leysin was impatient to be off. He led her down the passage. "My par-ish is wherever I can help. I belong to God. Nothing can harm me but to leave undone the work He gives me." The steps went farther away as he guided her to the stairs. Outside the roar of voices rose and fell. Wind brought the drifting sound, wind carried it away. It was like the thunder of the sea.

And the Englishman, using the little scene as a flashlight upon his own attitude, saw it for an instant as God might have seen it. Leysin's point of view was high, scanning a very wide horizon. His eye being single, the whole body was full of light. The risk, it suddenly seemed, was—nothing; to shirk it, indeed, the merest cowardice.

He went up and seized the Pasteur's hand.

"To-morrow," he said, a trifle shakily perhaps, yet looking straight into his eyes. "If we stay over—I'll bring the lad with me—provided he comes willingly."

"You will stay over," interrupted the other with decision. "Come to supper at seven. Come in mountain boots. Use persuasion, but not force. He shall see it from a distance—without taking part."

"From a distance—yes," the tutor repeated, "but without taking part."

"I know the signs," the Pasteur broke in significantly. "We can rescue him in the nick of time—charged with energy and life, yet before the danger gets—"

A sudden clangour of bells drowned the whispering voice, cutting the sentence in the middle. It was like an alarm of fire. Leysin sprang sharply round.

"The signal!" he cried; "the signal from the church. Some one's been taken. I must go at once—I shall be needed." He had his hat and cloak on in a moment, was through the passage and into the street, Hendricks following at his heels. The whole place seemed alive. Yet the roadway was deserted, and no lights showed at the windows of the houses. Only from the farther end of the village, where stood the cabaret, came a roar of voices, shouting, crying, singing. The impression was that the population was centred there. Far in the starry sky a line of fires blazed upon the heights, throwing a lurid reflection above the deep black valley. Excitement filled the night.

"But how extraordinary!" exclaimed Hendricks, hurrying to overtake his alert companion; "what life there is about! Everything's on the rush." They went faster, almost running. "I feel the waves of it beating even here." He followed breathlessly.

"A messenger has come—and gone," replied Leysin in a sharp, decided voice. "What you feel here is but the overflow. This is the aftermath. I must work down here with my people—"

"I'll work with you," began the other. But Leysin stopped him.

"Keep yourself for to-morrow night—up there," he said with grave authority, pointing to the fiery line upon the heights, and at the same time quickening his pace along the street. "At the moment," he cried, looking back, "your place is yonder." He jerked his head towards the carpenter's house among the vineyards. The next minute he was gone.

V

And Hendricks, accredited tutor to a sprig of nobility in the twentieth century, asked himself suddenly how such things could possibly be. The adventure took on abruptly a touch of nightmare. Only the light in the sky above the cabaret windows, and the roar of voices where men drank and sang, brought home the reality of it all. With a shudder of apprehension he glanced at the lurid glare upon the mountains. He was committed now; not because he had merely promised, but because he had definitely made up his mind.

Lighting a match, he saw by his watch that the visit had lasted over two hours. It was after eleven. He hurried, letting himself in with the big house-key, and going on tiptoe up the granite stairs. In his mind rose a picture of the boy as he had known him all these weary, sight-seeing months—the mild brown eyes, the facile indolence, the pliant, watery emotions of the listless creature, but behind him now, like storm clouds, the hopes, desires, fears the Pasteur's talk had conjured up. The yearning to save stirred strongly in his heart, and more and more of the little man's reckless spiritual audacity came with it. His own affection for the lad was genuine, but impatience and adventure pushed eagerly through the tenderness. If only, oh, if only he could put life into that great six-foot, big-boned frame! Some energy as of fire and wind into that inert machinery of mind and body! The idea was utterly incredible, but surely no harm could come of trying the experiment. There *were* the huge and elemental forces, of course, in Nature, and if . . . A sound in the bed-room, as he crept softly past the door, caught his attention, and he paused a moment to listen. Lord Ernie was not asleep, then, after all. He wondered why the sound got somehow at his heart. There was shuffling behind the door; there was a voice, too—or was it voices? He knocked.

"Who is it?" came at once, in a tone he hardly recognised. And, as he answered, "It's I, Mr. Hendricks; let me in," there followed a renewal of the shuffling, but without the sound of voices, and the door flew open—it was not even locked. Lord Ernie stood before him, dressed to go out. In the faint starlight the tall ungainly figure filled the doorway, erect and huge, the shoulders squared, the trunk no longer drooping. The listlessness was gone. He stood upright, limbs straight and alert; the sagging limp had vanished from the knees. He looked, in this semi-darkness, like another person, almost monstrous. And the tutor drew back instinctively, catching an instant at his breath.

"But, my dear boy! why aren't you asleep?" he stammered. He glanced half nervously about him. "I heard you talking, surely?" He fumbled for a match; but, before he found it, the other had turned on the electric switch. The light flared out. There was no one else in the room. "Is anything wrong with you? What's the matter?"

But the boy answered quietly, though in a deeper voice than Hendricks had ever known in him before: "I'm all right; only I couldn't sleep. I've been watching those fires on the mountains. I—I wanted to go out and see."

He still held the field-glasses in his hand, swinging them vigorously by the strap. The room was littered with clothes, just unpacked, the heavy shooting boots in the middle of the floor; and Hendricks, noticing these signs, felt a wave of excitement sweep through him, caught somehow from the presence of the boy. There was a sense of vitality in the room—as though a rush of active movement had just passed through it. Both windows stood wide open, and the roar of voices was clearly audible. Lord Ernie turned his head to listen.

"That's only the village people drinking and shouting," said Hendricks, closely watching each movement that he made. "It's perfectly natural, Bindy, that you feel too excited to sleep. We're in the mountains. The air stimulates tremendously—it makes the heart beat faster." He decided not to press the lad with questions.

"But I never felt like this in the Rockies or the Himalayas," came the swift rejoinder, as he moved to the window and looked out. "There was nothing in India or Japan like *that!*" He swept his hand towards the wooded heights that towered above the village so close. He talked volubly. "All those things we saw out there were sham—done on purpose for tourists. Up there it's real. I've been watching through the glasses till—I felt I simply must go out and join it. You can see men dancing round the fires, and big, rushing women. Oh, Mr. Hendricks, isn't it all glorious—all too glorious and ripping for words!" And his brown eyes shone like lamps.

"You mean that it's spontaneous, natural?" the other guided him, welcoming the new enthusiasm, yet still bewildered by the startling change. It was not mere nerves he saw. There was nothing morbid in it.

"They're doing it, I mean, because they have to," came the decided answer, "and because they feel it. They're not just copying the world." He put his hand upon the other's arm. There was dry heat in it that Hendricks felt even through his clothes. "And that's what *I* want," the boy went on, raising his voice, "what I've always wanted without knowing it—real things that can make me alive. I've often had it in my dreams, you know, but now I've found it."

"But I didn't know. You never told me of those dreams."

The boy's cheeks flushed, so that the colour and the fire in his eyes made him positively splendid. He answered slowly, as out of some part he had hitherto kept deliberately concealed.

"Because I never could get hold of it in words. It sounded so silly even to myself, and I thought Father would train it all away and laugh at it. It's awfully far down in me, but it's so real I knew it must come out one day, and that I should find it. Oh, I say, Mr. Hendricks," and he lowered his voice, leaning out across the window-sill suddenly, "*that* fills me up and feeds me"—he pointed to the heights—"and gives me life. The life I've seen till now was only a kind of show. It starved me. I want to go up there and feel it pouring through my blood." He filled his lungs with the strong mountain air, and paused while he exhaled it slowly, as though tasting it with delight and under-standing. Then he burst out again, "I vote we go. Will you come with me? What d'you say. Eh?"

They stared at each other hard a moment. Something as primitive and ir-resistible as love passed through the air between them. With a great effort the older man kept the balance true.

"Not to-night, not now," he said firmly. "It's too late. To-morrow, if you like—with pleasure."

"But to-morrow *night*," cried the boy with a rush, "when the fires are blazing and the wind is loose. Not in the stupid daylight."

"All right. To-morrow night. And my old friend, Monsieur Leysin, shall be our guide. He knows the way, and he knows the people too."

Lord Ernie seized his hands with enthusiasm. His vigour was so discon-certing that it seemed to affect his physical appearance. The body grew almost visibly; his very clothes hung on him differently; he was no longer a nonentity yawning beneath an ancient pedigree and title; he was an aggressive personal-ity. The boy in him rushed into manhood, as it were, while still retaining boy-ish speech and gesture. It was uncanny. "We'll go more than once, I vote; go again and again. This *is* a place and a half. It's *my* place with a vengeance—!"

"Not exactly the kind of place your father would wish you to linger in," his tutor interrupted. "But we might stay a day or two—especially as you like it so."

"It's far better than the towns and the rotten embassies; better than fifty Simlas and Bombays and filthy Cairos," cried the other eagerly. "It's just the thing I need, and when I get home I'll show 'em something. I'll prove it. Why, they simply won't know me!" He laughed, and his face shone with a kind of vivid radiance in the glare of the electric light. The transformation was more than curious. Waiting a moment to see if more would follow, Hendricks moved slowly then towards the door, with the remark that it was advisable now to go to bed since they would be up late the following night—when he noticed for the first time that the pillow and sheets were crumpled and that the bed had already been lain in. The first suspicion flashed back upon him with new certainty.

Lord Ernie was already taking off his heavy coat, preparatory to undress-ing. He looked up quickly at the altered tone of voice.

"Bindy," the tutor said with a touch of gravity, "you *were* alone just now—weren't you—of course?"

The other sat up from stooping over his boots. With his hands resting on the bed behind him, he looked straight into his companion's eyes. Lying was not among his faults. He answered slowly after a decided interval.

"I—I was asleep," he whispered, evidently trying to be accurate, yet hesitating how to describe the thing he had to say, "and had a dream—one of my real, vivid dreams when something happens. Only, this time, it was more real than ever before. It was"—he paused, searching for words, then added—"sweet and awful."

And Hendricks repeated the surprising sentence. "Sweet and awful, Bindy! What in the world do you mean, boy?"

Lord Ernie seemed puzzled himself by the choice of words he used.

"I don't know exactly," he went on honestly, "only I mean that it was awfully real and splendid, a bit of my own life somewhere—somewhere else—where it lies hidden away behind a lot of days and months that choke it up. I can never get at it except in woods and places, quite alone, hearing the wind or making fires, or—in sleep." He hid his face in his hands a moment, then looked up with a hint of censure in his eyes. "Why didn't you tell me that such things *were* done? You never told me," he repeated.

"I didn't know it myself until this evening. Leysin—"

"I thought you knew everything," Lord Ernie broke in in that same half-chiding tone.

"Monsieur Leysin told me to-night for the first time," said Hendricks firmly, "that such people and such practices existed. Till now I had never dreamed that such superstitions survived anywhere in the world at all." He resented the reproach. But he was also aware that the boy resented his authority. For the first time his ascendency seemed in question; his voice, his eye, his manner did not quell as formerly. "So you mean, when you say 'sweet and awful,' that it was very real to you?" he asked. He insisted now with purpose. "Is that it, Bindy?"

The other replied eagerly enough. "Yes, that's it, I think—partly. This time it was more than dreaming. It was real. I got there. I remembered. That's what I meant. And after I woke up the thing still went on. The man seemed still in the room beside the bed, calling me to get up and go with him—"

"Man! What man?" The tutor leant upon the back of a chair to steady himself. The wind just then went past the open windows with a singing rush.

"The dark man who passed us in the village, and who pointed to the fires on the heights. He came with the wind, you remember. He pulled my coat."

The boy stood up as he said it. He came across the naked boarding, his step right and dancing. "Fire that heats but does not burn, and wind that blows the heart alight, or something—I forget now exactly. *You* heard it too." He whispered the words with excitement, raising his arms and knees as in the opening movements of a dance.

Hendricks kept his own excitement down, but with a distinctly conscious effort.

"I heard nothing of the kind," he said calmly. "I was only thinking of getting home dry. You say," he asked with decision, "that you *heard* those words?"

Lord Ernie stood back a little. It was not that he wished to conceal, but that he felt uncertain how to express himself. "In the street," he said, "I heard nothing; the words rose up in my own head, as it were. But in the dream, and afterwards too, when I was wide awake, I heard them out loud, clearly: Fire that heats but does not burn, and wind that blows the heart to flame—that's how it was."

"In French, Bindy? You heard it in French?"

"Oh, it was no language at all. The eyes said it—both times." He spoke as naturally as though it was the Durbah he described again. Only this new aggressive certainty was in his voice and manner. "Mr. Hendricks," he went on eagerly, "*you* understand what I mean, don't you? When certain people look at one, words start up in the mind as though one heard them spoken. I heard the words in my head, I suppose; only they seemed so familiar, as though I'd known them before—always—"

"Of course, Bindy, I understand. But this man—tell me—did he stay on after you woke up? And how did he go?" He looked round at the barely furnished room for hiding-places. "It was really the dream you carried on after waking, wasn't it?"

Then Bindy laughed, but inwardly, as to himself. There was the faintest possible hint of derision in his voice. "No doubt," he said; "only it was one of my big, real dreams. And how he went I can't explain at all, for I didn't see. You knocked at the door; I turned, and found myself standing in the room, dressed to go out. There was a rush of wind outside the window—and when I looked he was no longer there. The same minute you came in. It was all as quick as that. I suppose I dressed—in my sleep."

They stood for several minutes, staring at each other without speaking. The tutor hesitated between several courses of action, unable, for the life of him, to decide upon any particular one. His instinct on the whole was to stop nothing, but to encourage all possible expression, while keeping rigorous watch and guard. Repression, it seemed to him just then, was the least desirable line to take. Somewhere there was truth in the affair. He felt out of his depth, his authority impaired, and under these temporary disadvantages he might so easily make a grave mistake, injuring instead of helping. While Lord Ernie finished his undressing he leaned out of the window, taking great draughts of the keen night air, watching the blazing fires and listening to the roar of voices, now dying down into the distance.

And the voice of his thinking whispered to him, "Let it all come out. Repress nothing. Let him have the entire adventure. If it's nonsense it can't injure, and if it's true it's inevitable." He drew his head in and moved towards the door. "Then it's settled," he said quietly, as though nothing unusual had happened; "we'll go up there to-morrow night—with Monsieur Leysin to show us the way. And you'll go to sleep now, won't you? For to-morrow we may be up very late. Promise me, Bindy."

"I'm dead tired," came the answer from the sheets. "I certainly shan't dream any more, if that's what you mean. I promise."

Hendricks turned the light out and went softly from the room. He could always trust the boy.

"Good-night, Bindy," he said.

"Good-night," came the drowsy reply.

Upstairs he lingered a long time over his own undressing, listening, waiting, watching for the least sound below. But nothing happened. Once, for his own peace of mind, he stole stealthily downstairs to the boy's door; then, reassured by the heavy breathing that was distinctly audible, he went up finally and got into bed himself. The night was very still now. It was cool, and the stars were brilliant over lake and forest and mountain. No voices broke the silence. He only heard the tinkle of the little streams beyond the vineyards. And by midnight he was sound asleep.

VI

And next day broke as soft and brilliant as though October had stolen it from June; the Alps gleamed through an almost summery haze across the lake; the air held no hint of coming winter; and the Jura mountains wore the true blue of memory in Hendricks' mind. Patches of red and yellow splashed the great pine-woods here and there where beech and ash put autumn in the vast dark carpet.

The tutor woke clear-headed and refreshed. All that had happened the night before seemed out of proportion and unreasonable. There had been exaggerated emotion in it: in himself, because he returned to a place still charged with potent memories of youth; and in Lord Ernie, because the lad was overwrought by the electrical disturbance of the atmosphere. The nearness of the ancestral halls, which they both disliked, had emphasised it; the ominous, wild weather had favoured it; and the coincidence of these pagan rites of superstitious peasants had focussed it all into a melodramatic form with an added touch of the supernatural that was highly picturesque and—dangerously suggestive. Hendricks recovered his common sense; judgment asserted itself again.

Yet, for all that, certain things remained authentic. The effect upon the boy was not illusion, nor his words about fire and wind mere meaningless invention. There hid some undivined and significant correspondence between the gaps in his deficient nature and these two turbulent elements. The talk of Leysin, as the conduct of his wife, remained authentic; those facts were too steady to be dismissed, the Pasteur too genuinely in earnest to be catalogued in dream. Neither daylight nor common sense could dissipate their actuality. Truth lay somewhere in it all.

Thus the day, for the tutor, was a battle that shifted with varying fortune between doubt and certainty. In the morning his mind was decided: the wild experiment was unjustifiable; in the afternoon, as the sunshine grew faint and melancholy, it became "interesting, for what harm could come of it?" but towards evening, when shadows lengthened across the purple forests and the trees stood motionless in the calm and windless air, the adventure seemed, as it had seemed the night before, not only justifiable, but right and necessary. It only became inevitable, however, when, after tea together on the balcony, Lord Ernie, mentioning the subject for the first time that day, asked pointedly what time the Pasteur expected them to supper; then, noticing the flush of hesitancy in his companion's eyes, added in his strange deep voice, "You promised we should go." Withdrawal after that was out of the question. To retract would have meant, for one thing, final loss of the boy's confidence—a possibility not to be contemplated for a moment.

Until this moment no word of the preceding night had passed the lips of either. Lord Ernie had been quiet and preoccupied, silent rather, but never listless. He was peaceful, perhaps subdued a little, yet with a suppressed energy in his bearing that Hendricks watched with secret satisfaction. The tutor, closely observant, detected nothing out of gear; life stirred strongly in him; there was purpose, interest, will; there was desire; but there was nothing to cause alarm.

Availing himself then of the lad's absorption in his own affairs, he wandered forth alone upon his sentimental tour of inspection. No ghost of emotion rose to stalk beside him. That early tragedy, he now saw clearly, had been no more than youthful explosion of mere physical passion, wholesome and natural, but due chiefly to propinquity. His thoughts ran idly on; and he was even congratulating himself upon escape and freedom when, abruptly, he remembered a phrase Bindy had used the night before, and stumbled suddenly upon a clue when least expecting it.

He came to a sudden halt. The significance of it crashed through his mind and startled him. "There are big rushing women . . ." It was the first reference to the other sex, as evidence of their attraction for him, Hendricks had ever known to pass his lips. Hitherto, though twenty years of age, the lad had never spoken of women as though he was aware of their terrible magic. He had not discovered them as females, necessary to every healthy male. It was not purity, of course, but ignorance: he had felt nothing. Something had now awakened sex in him, so that he knew himself a man, and naked. And it had revolutionised the world for him. This new life came from the roots, transforming listless indifference into positive desire; the will woke out of sleep, and all the currents of his system took aggressive form. For all energy, intellectual, emotional, or spiritual, is fundamentally one: it is primarily sexual.

Hendricks paused in his sentimental walk, marvelling that he had not realised sooner this simple truth. It brought a certain logical meaning even into the pagan rites upon the mountains, these ancient rites which symbolised the marriage of the two tremendous elements of wind and fire, heat and air. And the lad's quiet, busy mood that morning confirmed his simple discovery. It involved restraint and purpose. Lord Ernie was alive. Hendricks would take home with him to those ancestral halls a vessel bursting with energy—creative energy. It was admirable that he should witness—from a safe distance—this primitive ceremony of crude pagan origin. It was the very thing. And the tutor hurried back to the house among the vineyards, aware that his responsibility had increased, but persuaded more than ever that his course was justified.

The sky held calm and cloudless through the day, the forests brooding beneath the hazy autumn sunshine. Indications that the second hurricane lay brewing among the heights were not wanting, however, to experienced eyes. Almost a preternatural silence reigned; there was a warm heaviness in the placid atmosphere; the surface of the lake was patched and streaky; the extreme clarity of the air an ominous omen. Distant objects were too close. Towards sunset, moreover, the streaks and patches vanished as though sucked below, while thin strips of tenuous cloud appeared from nowhere above the northern cliffs. They moved with great rapidity at an enormous height, touched with a lurid brilliance as the sun sank out of sight; and when Hendricks strolled over with Lord Ernie to *la cure* for supper there came a sudden rush of heated wind that set the branches sharply rattling, then died away as abruptly as it rose.

They seemed reflected, too, these disturbances, in the human atmospheres about the supper table—there was suppression of various emotions, emotions presaging violence. Lord Ernie was exhilarated, Hendricks uneasy and preoccupied, the Pasteur grave and thoughtful. In Hendricks was another feeling as well—that he had lightly summoned a storm which might carry him off his feet. The boy's excitement increased it, as wind-puffs fan a starting fire. His own judgment had somewhere played him false, betraying him into this incredible adventure. And yet he could not stop it. The Pasteur's influence was over him perhaps. He was ashamed to turn back. He was committed. The unusual circumstances found the weakness in his character.

For somewhere in the preposterous superstition there lay a big forgotten truth. He could not believe it, and yet he did believe it. The world had forgotten how to live truly close to Nature.

A desultory conversation was carried on, chiefly between the two men, while the boy ate hungrily, and Mme. Leysin watched her husband with anxiety as she served the simple meal.

"So you are coming with us, and you like to come?" the Pasteur observed quietly, Hendricks translating.

Lord Ernie replied with a gesture of unmistakable enthusiasm.

"A wild lot of men and women," Leysin went on, keeping his eye hard upon him, "with an interesting worship of their own copied from very ancient times. They live on the heights, and mix little with us valley folk. You shall see their ceremonies to-night."

"They get the wind and fire into themselves, don't they?" asked the boy keenly, and somewhat to the distress of the translator who rendered it, "They get into wind and fire."

"They worship wind and fire," Leysin replied, "and they do it by means of a wonderful dance that somehow imitates the leap of flame and the headlong rush of wind. If you copy the movements and gestures of a person you discover the emotion that causes them. You share it. Their idea is, apparently, that by imitating the movements they invite or attract the force—draw these elemental powers into their systems, so that in the end—"

He stopped suddenly, catching the tutor's eye. Lord Ernie seemed to understand without translation; he had laid down his knife and fork and was leaning forward across the table, listening with deep absorption. His expression was alert with a new intelligence that was almost cunning. An acute sensibility seemed to have awakened in him.

"As with laughing, I suppose?" he said in an undertone to Hendricks quickly. "If you imitate a laughter, you laugh yourself in the end and feel all the jolly excitement of laughter. Is that what he means?"

The tutor nodded with assumed indifference. "Imitation is always infectious," he said lightly; "but, of course, you will not imitate these wild people yourself, Bindy. We'll just look on from a distance."

"From a distance!" repeated the boy, obviously disappointed. "What's the good of that?' A look of obstinacy passed across his altered face.

Hendricks met his eyes squarely. "At a circus," he said firmly, "you just watch. You don't imitate the clown, do you?"

"If you look on long enough, you do," was the rather dogged reply.

"Well, take the Russian dancers we saw in Moscow," the other insisted patiently, "you felt the power and beauty without jumping up and whirling in your stall?"

Bindy half glared at him. There was almost contempt in his quiet answer: "But your mind whirled with them. And later your body would too; otherwise it's given you nothing." He paused a second. "I can only get the fun of riding by being on a horse's back and doing his movements exactly with him—not by watching him."

Hendricks smiled and shrugged his shoulders. He did not wish to discourage the enthusiasm lying behind this analysis. The uneasiness in him grew apace. He said something rapidly in French, using an undertone and laughter to confuse the actual words.

"Of course we must not interfere with their ceremonies," put in the Pasteur with decision. "It's sacred to them. We can hide among the trees and watch. You would not leave your seat in church to imitate the priest, would you?" He glanced smilingly at the eager youth before him.

"If he did something real, I would." It was said with a bright flash in the eyes. "Anything real I'd copy like a shot. Only, I never find it."

The reply was disconcerting rather: and Hendricks, as he hurriedly translated, made a clatter with his knife and fork, for something in him rose to meet the truth behind the curious words. From that moment, as though catching a little of the boy's exhilaration, he passed under a kind of spell perhaps. It was, in spite of the exaggeration, oddly stimulating. This dull little meal at the village *cure* masked an accumulating vehemence, eager to break loose. He heard the old father's voice: "Well done, Hendricks! You have accomplished wonders!" He would take back the boy—alive. . . .

Yet all the time there were streaks and patches on his soul as upon the surface of the lake that afternoon. There were signs of terror. He felt himself letting go, an increasing recklessness, a yielding up more and more of his own authority to that of this triumphant boy. Bindy understood the meaning of it all and felt secure; Hendricks faltered, hesitated, stood on the defensive. Yet, ever less and less. Already he accepted the other's guidance. Already Lord Ernie's leadership was in the ascendant. Conviction invariably holds dominion over doubt.

They ate little. It was near the end of the meal when the wind, falling from a clear and starlit sky, struck its first violent blow, dropping with the force of an explosion that shook the wooden house, and passing with a roar towards the distant lake. The oil lamp, suspended from the ceiling, trembled; the Pasteur looked apprehensively at the shuttered windows; and Lord Ernie, with startling abruptness, stood up. His eyes were shining. His voice was brisk, alert, and deep.

"The wind, the wind!" he cried. "Think what it'll be up there! We shall feel it on our bodies!" His enthusiasm was like a rush of air across the table. "And the fire!" he went on. "The flames will lick all over, and tear about the sky. I feel wild and full of them already! How splendid!" And the flame of the little lamp leaped higher in the chimney as he said it.

"The violence of the *coup de joran* is extraordinary," explained Leysin as he got up to turn down the wick, "and the second outburst—" The rest of his sentence was drowned by the noise of Hendricks' voice telling the boy to sit down and finish his supper. And at the same moment the Pasteur's wife came in as though a stroke of wind drove behind her down the passage. The door slammed in the draught. There was a momentary confusion in the room above which her voice rose shrill and frightened.

"The fires are alight, Jules," she whispered in her half intelligible patois, "the forest is burning all along the upper ridge." Her face was pale and her speech came stumbling. She lowered her lips to her husband's ear. "They'll be looking out for recruits to-night. Is it necessary, is it right for you to go?" She glanced uneasily at the English visitors. "You know the danger—"

He stopped her with a gesture. "Those who look on at life accomplish nothing," he answered impatiently. "One must act, always act. Chances are sent to be taken, not stared at." He rose, pushing past her into the passage, and as he did so she gave him one swift comprehensive look of tenderness and admiration, then hurried after him to find his hat and cloak. Willingly she would have kept him at home that night, yet gladly, in another sense, she saw him go. She fumbled in her movements, ready to laugh or cry or pray. Hendricks saw her pain and understood. It was singular how the woman's attitude intensified his own misgivings; her behaviour, the mere expression of her face alone, made the adventure so absolutely real.

Three minutes later they were in the village street. Hendricks and Lord Ernie, the latter impatient in the road beyond, saw her tall figure stoop to embrace him. "I shall pray all night: I shall watch from my window for your return. God, who speaks from the whirlwind, and whose pathway is the fire, will go with you. Remember the younger men; it is ever the younger men that they seek to take . . .!" Her words were half hysterical. The kiss was given and taken; the open doorway framed her outline a moment; then the buttress of the church blotted her out, and they were off.

VII

And at once the curious confusion of strong wind was upon them. Gusts howled about the corners of the shuttered houses and tore noisily across the open yards. Dust whirled with the rapidity as of some spectral white machinery. A tile came clattering down about their feet, while overhead the roofs had an air of shifting, toppling, bending. The entire village seemed scooped up and shaken, then dropped upon the earth again in tottering fashion.

"This way," gasped the little Pasteur, blown sideways like a sail, "follow me closely." Almost arm-in-arm at first they hurried down the deserted street, past lampless windows and tight-fastened doors, and soon were beyond the cabaret in that open stretch between the village and the forest where the wind had unobstructed way. Far above them ran the fiery mountain ridge. They saw the glare reflected in the sky as the tempest first swept them all three together, then separated them in the same moment. They seemed to spin or whirl. "It's far worse than I expected," shouted their guide; "here! Give me your hand!" then found, once disentangled from his flapping cloak, that no one stood beside him. For each of them it was a single fight to reach the shelter of the woods, where the actual ascent began. An instant the Pasteur seemed to hesitate. He glanced back at the lighted window of *la cure* across the fields, at the line of fire in the sky, at the figure disappearing in the blackness immediately ahead. "Where's the boy?" he shouted. "Don't let him get too far in front. Keep close. Wait till I come!" They staggered back against each other. "Look how easily he's slipped ahead already!"

"This howling wind—" Hendricks shouted, as they advanced side by side, pushing their shoulders against the storm.

The rest of the sentence vanished into space. Leysin shoved him forward, pointing to where, some twenty yards in front, the figure of Lord Ernie, head down, was battling eagerly with the hurricane. Already he stood near to the shelter of the trees waving his arms with energy towards the summits where the fire blazed. He was calling something at the top of his voice, urging them to hurry. His voice rushed down upon them with a pelt of wind.

"Don't let him get away from us," bawled Leysin, holding his hands cupwise to his mouth. "Keep him in reach. He may see, but must not take part . . ." A blow full in the face that smote him like the flat of a great sword clapped the sentence short. "That's *your* part. He won't obey me!" Hendricks heard it as they plunged across the wind-swept reach, panting, struggling, forcing their bodies sideways like two-legged crabs against the terrific force of the descending *joran*. They reached the protection of the forest wall without further attempt at speech. Here there was sudden peace and silence, for the tall, dense trees received the tempest's impact like a cushion, stopping it. They paused a moment to recover breath.

But although the first exhaustion speedily passed, that original confusion of strong wind remained—in Hendricks' mind at least,—for wind violent enough to be battled with has a scattering effect on thought and blows the very blood about. Something in him snapped its cables and blew out to sea. His breath drew in an impetuous quality from the tempest each time he filled his lungs. There was agitation in him that caused an odd exaggeration of the emotions. The boy, as they came up, leaped down from a boulder he had climbed. He opened his arms, making of his cloak a kind of sail that filled and flapped.

"At last!" he cried, impatient, almost vexed. "I thought you were never coming. The wind blew me along. We shall be late—"

The tutor caught his arm with vigour. "You keep by us, Ernest; d'you hear now? No rushing ahead like that. Leysin's the guide, not you." He even shook him. But as he did so he was aware that he himself resisted something that he did not really want to resist, something that urged him forcibly; a little more and he would yield to it with pleasure, with abandon, finally with reck-lessness. A reaction of panic fear ran over him.

"It was the wind, I tell you," cried the boy, flinging himself free with a hint of insolence in his voice, "for it's alive. I mean to see everything. The wind's our leader and the fire's our guide." He made a movement to start on again.

"You'll obey me," thundered Hendricks, "or else you'll go home. D'you understand?"

With exasperation, yet with uneasy delight, he noted the words Bindy made use of. It was in him that he might almost have uttered them himself. He stepped already into an entirely new world. Exhilaration caught him even now. Putting the brake on was mere pretence. He seized the lad by both shoulders and pushed him to the rear, then placed himself next, so that Leysin moved in front and led the way. The procession started, diving into the com-parative shelter of the forest. "Don't let him pass you," he heard in rapid French; "guide him, that's all. The power's already in his blood. Keep yourself in hand as well, and follow me closely." The roar of the storm above them carried the words clean off the world.

Here in the forest they moved, it seemed, along the floor of an ocean whose surface raged with dreadful violence; any moment one or other of them might be caught up to that surface and whirled off to destruction. For the procession was not one with itself. The darkness, the difficulty of hearing what each said, the feeling, too, that each climbed for himself, made every-thing seem at sixes and sevens. And the tutor, this secret exultation growing in his heart, denied the anxiety that kept it pace, and battled with his turbulent emotions, a divided personality. His power over the boy, he realised, had gravely weakened. A little time ago they had seemed somehow equal. Now, however, a complete reversal of their relative positions had taken place. The boy was sure of himself. While Leysin led at a steady mountaineer's pace on his wiry, short, bowed legs, Hendricks, a yard or two behind him, stumbled a good deal in the darkness, Lord Ernie for ever on his heels, eager to push past. But Bindy never stumbled. There was no flagging in his muscles. He moved so lightly and with so sure a tread that he almost seemed to dance, and often he stopped aside to leap a boulder or to run along a fallen trunk. Path there was none. Occasional gusts of wind rushed gustily down into these depths of forest where they moved, and now, from time to time, as they rose nearer to the line of fire on the ridge, an increasing glare lit up the knuckled roots or glimmered on the bramble thickets and heavy beds of moss. It was astonishing how the little Pasteur never missed his way. Periods of thick silence alternated with moments when the storm swept down through gullies among the trees, reverberating like thunder in the hollows.

Slowly they advanced, buffeted, driven, pushed, the wildness of some Walpürgis night growing upon all three. In the tutor's mind was this strange lift of increasing recklessness, the old proportion gone, the spiritual aspect of it troubling him to the point of sheer distress. He followed Leysin as blindly with his body as he followed this new Bindy eagerly with his mind. For this languid boy, now dancing to the tune of flooding life at his very heels, seemed magical in the true sense: energy created as by a wizard out of nothing. From lips that ordinarily sighed in listless boredom poured now a ceaseless stream of questions and ejaculations, ringing with enthusiasm. How long would it take to reach the fiery ridge? Why did they go so slowly? Would they arrive too late? Would their intrusion be welcomed or understood? Already one great change was effected—accepted by Hendricks, too—that the rôle of mere spectator was impossible. The answers Hendricks gave, indeed, grew more and more encouraging and sympathetic. He, too, was impatient with their leader's crawling pace. Some elemental spell of wind and fire urged him towards the open ridge. The pull became irresistible. He despised the Pasteur's caution, denied his wisdom, wholly rejected now the spirit of compromise and prudence. And once, as the hurricane brought down a flying burst of voices, he caught himself leaping upon a big grey boulder in their path. He leaped at the very moment that the boy behind him leaped, yet hardly realised that he did so; his feet danced without a conscious order from his brain. They met together on the rounded top, stumbled, clutched one another frantically, then slid with waving arms and flying cloaks down the slippery surface of damp moss—laughing wildly.

"Fool!" cried Hendricks, saving himself. "What in the world—?"

"*You* called," laughed Bindy, picking himself up and dropping back to his place in the rear again. "It's the wind, not me; it's in our feet. Half the time you're shouting and jumping yourself!"

And it was a few minutes after this that Lord Ernie suddenly forged ahead. He slipped in front as silently as a shadow before a moving candle in a room. Passing the tutor at a moment when his feet were entangled among roots and stones, he easily overtook the Pasteur and found himself in the lead. He never stumbled; there seemed steel springs in his legs.

From Leysin, too breathless to interfere, came a cry of warning. "Stop him! Take his hand!" his tired voice instantly smothered by the roaring skies. He turned to catch Hendricks by the cloak. "You see *that!*" he shouted in alarm. "For the love of God, don't lose sight of him! He must see, but not take part—remember—!"

And Hendricks yelled after the vanishing figure, "Bindy, go slow, go slow! Keep in touch with us." But he quickened his pace instantly, as though to overtake the boy. He passed his companion the same minute, and was out of sight. "I'll wait for you," came back the boy's shrill answer through the thinning trees. And a flare of light fell with it from the sky, for the final climb of a steep five hundred feet had now begun, and overhead the naked ridge ran east and west with its line of blazing fires. Boulders and rocky ground replaced the pines and spruces.

"But you'll never find the way," shouted Leysin, while a deep trumpeting roar of the storm beyond muffled the remainder of the sentence.

Hendricks heard the next words close beside him from a clump of shadows. He was in touching distance of the excited boy.

"The fires and the singing guide me. Only a fool could miss the way."

"But you *are* a—"

He swallowed the unuttered word. A new, extraordinary respect was suddenly in him. That tall, virile figure, instinct with life, springing so cleverly through the choking darkness, guiding with decision and intelligence, almost infallible—it was no fool that led them thus. He hurried after till his very sinews ached. His eyes, troubled and confused, strained through the trees to find him. But these same trees now fled past him in a torrent.

"Bindy, Bindy!" he cried, at the top of his voice, yet not with the imperious tone the situation called for. The sentence dropped into a lull of wind. Instead of command there was entreaty, almost supplication, in it. "Wait for me, I'm coming. We'll see the glorious thing together!"

And then suddenly the forest lay behind him, with a belt of open pastureland in front below the actual ridge. He felt the first great draught of heat, as a line of furnaces burst their doors with a mighty roar and turned the sky into a blaze of golden daylight. There was a crackling as of musketry. The flare shot up and burned the air about him, and the voices of a multitude, as yet invisible, drove through it like projectiles on the wind. This was the first impression, wholesale and terrific, that met him as he paused an instant on the edge of the sheltering forest and looked forward. Leysin and Lord Ernie seemed to leave his mind, forgotten in this first attack of splendour, but forgotten, as it were, the first with contempt, the latter with an overwhelming regret. For the Pasteur's mistake in that instant seemed obvious. In half measures lay the fatal error, and in compromise the danger. Bindy all along had known the better way and followed it. The lukewarm was the worthless.

"Bindy, boy, where are you? I'm coming . . ." and stepping on to the grassy strip of ground, soft to his feet, he met a wind that fell upon his body with a shower of blows from all directions at once and beat him to his knees. He dropped, it seemed, into the cover of a sheltering rock, for there followed then a moment of sudden and delicious stillness in which the weary muscles recovered themselves and thought grew slightly steadier. Crouched thus close to the earth he no longer offered a target to the hurricane's attack. He peered upwards, making a screen of his hands.

The ridge, some fifty feet above him, he saw, ran in a generous platform along the mountain crest; it was wide and flat; between the enormous fires of piled-up wood that stretched for half a mile coiled a medley of dense smoke and tearing sparks. No human beings were visible, and yet he was aware of crowding life quite near. On hands and knees, crawling painfully, he then slowly retreated again into the shelter of the forest he had sought to leave. He stood up. The awful blaze was veiled by the roof of branches once more. But, as he rose, seizing a sapling to steady himself by, two hands caught him with violence from behind, and a familiar voice came shouting against his ear. Leysin panting, dishevelled and half broken with the speed, stood beside him.

"The boy! Where is he? We're just in time!" He roared the words to make them carry above the din. "Hurry, hurry! I'll follow. . . . My older legs . . . See, for the love of God, that he is not taken. . . . I warned you!"

And for a second, as he heard, Hendricks caught at the vanished sense of responsibility again. He saw the face of the old Marquess watching him among the tree trunks. He heard his voice, amazed, reproachful, furious: "It was criminal of you, criminal—!"

"Where is the boy—*your* boy?" again broke in the shout of the Pasteur with a slap of hurricane, as he staggered against the tutor, half collapsing, and trying to point the direction. "Watch him, find him for the love of heaven before it is too late—before they see him . . .!"

The tutor's normal and responsible self dived out of sight again as he heard the cry of weakness and alarm. It seemed the wind got under him, lifting him bodily from his feet. He did not pause to think. Like a man midway in a whirling prize-fight, he felt dazed but confident, only conscious of one thing—that he must hold out to the end, take part in all the splendid fighting—*win*. The lust of the arena, the pride of youth and battle, the impetuous recklessness of the charge in primitive war caught at his heart, brimming it with headlong courage. To play the game for all it might be worth seemed shouted everywhere about him, as the abandon of wind and fire rushed through him like a storm. He felt lifted above all possibility of little failure. The Marquess with his conventional traditions, the Pasteur with his considerations of half-way safety, both vanished utterly; safety, indeed, both for himself and for the boy in his charge lay in unconditional surrender. This was no time for little thought-out actions. It was all or nothing!

"God bless the whirlwind and the fire!" he shouted, opening wide his arms.

But his voice was inaudible amid the uproar, and the forward movement of his body remained at first only in the brain. He turned to push the old man aside, even to strike him down if necessary. "Lukewarm yourself and a coward!" rose in his throat, yet found no utterance, for in that moment a tall, slim figure, swift as a shadow, steady as a hawk, shot hard across the open space between the forest and the ridge. In the direction of the blazing platform it disappeared against a curtain of thick smoke, emerged for one second in a storm of light, then vanished finally behind a ruin of loose rocks. And Hendricks, his eyes wounded by heat and wind, his muscles paralysed, understood that the boy deliberately invited capture. The multitude that hid behind the smoke and fire, feeding the blazing heaps with eager hands, had become aware of him, and presently would appear to claim him. They would take him to themselves. Already answering flares ran east and west along the desolate ridge.

"I'll join you! I'm coming! Wait for me!" he tried to cry. The uproar smothered it.

VIII

And this uproar, he now perceived, was composed entirely of wind and fire. Here, on the roof of the hills beneath a starry sky, these two great elements expressed their nature with unhampered freedom, for there was neither rain to modify the one, nor solid obstacle to check the other. Their voices merged in a single sound—the hollow boom of wind and the deep, resounding clap of flame. The splitting crackle of burning branches imitated the high, shrill whistle of the tearing gusts that, javelin-like, flew to and fro in darts of swifter sound. But one shout rose from the summit, no human cry distinguishable in it, nor amid the thousand lines of skeleton wood that pierced the golden background was any human outline visible. Fire and wind encouraged one another to madness, manifesting in prodigious splendour by themselves.

Then, suddenly, before a gigantic canter of the wind, the driving smoke rolled upwards like a curtain, and the flames, ceasing their wild flapping, soared steadily in gothic windows of living gold towards the stars. In towering rows between columns of black night they transformed the empty space between them into a colossal temple aisle. They tapered aloft symmetrically into vanishing crests. And Hendricks stood upright. Rising so that his shoulders topped the edge of the boulder, and utterly contemptuous of Leysin's hand that sought with violence to drag him into shelter, he gazed as one who sees a vision. For at first he could only stand and stare, aware of sensation but not of thought. An enormous, overpowering conviction blew his whole being to white heat. Here was a supply of elemental power that human beings—empty, needy, starved, deficient human beings—could use. His love for the boy leaped headlong at the skirts of this terrific salvation. A majestic possibility stormed through him.

Yet it was no nightmare wonder that met his staring and half-shielded eyes, although some touch of awful dream seemed in it, set, moreover, to a scale that scantier minds might deem distortion. The heat from some thirty fires, placed at regular intervals, made midnight quiver with immense vibrations. Of varying, yet calculated size, these towering heaps emitted notes of measured and alternating depth, until the roar along the entire line produced a definite scale almost of melody, the near ones shrilly singing, those more distant booming with mountainous pedal notes. The consonance was monstrous, yet conformed to some magnificent diapason. This chord of fire-music paced the starlit sky, directed, but never overmastered, by the wind that measured it somehow into meaning. Repeated in quick succession, the notes now crashing in a mass, now singing alone in solitary beauty, the effect suggested an idea of ordered sequence, of gigantic rhythm. It seemed, indeed, as though some controlling agency, mastering excess, coerced both raging elements to express through this stupendous dance some definite idea. Here, as it were, was the alphabet of some natural, undifferentiated language, a language of sight and sound, predating speech, symbolical in the ultimate, deific sense. Some Lord of Fire and some Lord of Air were in command. Harnessed and regulated, these formless cohorts of energy that men call stupidly mere flame and wind, obeyed a higher power that had invoked them, yet a power that, by understanding their laws of being, held him most admirably in control.

This, at least, seems a hint of the explanation that flashed into Hendricks as he stared in amazed bewilderment from the shelter of the nearest boulder. He read a sentence in some natural, forgotten script. He watched a primitive ritual that once invoked the gods. He was aware of rhythm, and he was aware of system, though as yet he did not see the hand that wrote this marvellous sentence on the night. For still the human element remained invisible. He only realised—in dim, blundering fashion—that he witnessed a revelation of those two powers which, in large, lie at the foundations of the Universe, and, in little, are the basic essentials of human existence—the powers behind heat and air. Fragments of that talk with Leysin stammered back across his mind, like letters in some stupendous word he dared not reconstruct entire. He shuddered and grew wise. Realms of forgotten being opened their doors before his dazzled sight. Vision fluttered into far, piercing vistas of ancient wonder, haunting and half-remembered, then lost its way in blindness that was pain. For a moment, it seemed, he was aware of majestic Presences behind the turmoil, shadowy but mighty, charged with a vague potentiality as of immense algebraical formulæ, symbolical and beyond full comprehension, yet willing and able to be used for practical results. He *felt* the elements as nerves of a living Universe. . . . Yet thinking was not really in him anywhere; feeling was all he knew. The world he moved in, as the script he read, belonged to conditions too utterly remote for reason to recover a single clue to their intelligible reconstruction. Glory, clean and strong as of primitive star-worship, passed between what he saw and all that he had ever known before. The curtain of conventional belief was rent in twain. The terrific thing was true. . . .

For an unmeasured interval the tutor, oblivious of time and actual place, stood on the brink of this majestic pageant, staring with breathless awe, while the swaying of the entire scenery increased like the sway of an ocean lifted to the sky by many winds. Then, suddenly, in one of those temporary lulls that passed between the beat of the great notes, his searching eyes discovered a new thing. The focus of his sight was altered, and he realised at last the source of the directing and the controlling power. Behind the fires and beyond the smoke he recognised the disc-like, shining ovals that upon this little earth stand in the image of the one, eternal Likeness. He saw the human faces, symbols of spiritual dominion over all lesser orders, each one possessed of belief, intelligence and will. Singly so feeble, together so invincible, this assemblage, unscorched by the fire and by the wind unmoved, seemed to him impressive beyond all possible words. And a further inkling of the truth flashed on him as he stared: that a group of humans, a crowd, combining upon a given object with concentrated purpose, possessed of that terrific power, certain faith, may know in themselves the energy to move great mountains, and therefore that lesser energy to guide the fluid forces of the elements. And a sense of cosmic exultation leaped into his being. For a moment he knew a touch of almost frenzy. Proud joy rose in him like a splendour of omnipotence. Humanity, it seemed to him, here came into a grand but long neglected corner of its kingdom as originally planned by Heaven. Into the hands of a weakling and deficient boy the guidance had been given.

Motionless beneath the stars, lit by the glare till they shone like idols of yellow stone, and magnified by the sheets of flying, intolerable light the wind chased to and fro, these rows of faces appeared at first as a single line of undifferentiated fire against the background of the night. The eyes were all cast down in prayer, each mind focussed steadily upon one clear idea—the control and assimilation of two elemental powers. The crowd was one; feeling was one; desire, command and certain faith were one. The controlling power that resulted was irresistible.

Then came a remarkable, concerted movement. With one accord the eyes all opened, blazing with reflected fire. A hundred human countenances rose in a single shining line. The men stood upright. Swarthy faces, tanned by sun and wind, heads uncovered, hair and beards tossing in the air, turned all one way. Mouths opened too. There came a roar that even the hurricane could not drown—a word of command, it seemed, that sprang into the pulses of the dancing elements and reduced their turmoil to a wave of steadier movement. And at the same moment a hundred bodies, naked above the waist, arms outstretched and hands with the palms held upwards, swayed forwards through the smoke and fire. They came towards the spot, where, half concealed from view, the tutor crouched and watched.

And Hendricks, thinking himself discovered, first quailed, then rose to meet them. No power to resist was in him. It was, rather, willing response that he experienced. He stepped out from the shelter of the boulder and entered the brilliant glare. Hatless himself, shoulders squared, cloak flying in the wind, he took three strides towards the advancing battalion—then, undecided, paused. For the line, he saw, disregarded him as though he were not there at all. It was not him the worshippers sought. The entire troop swept past to a point some fifty feet below where the end of the ridge broke out of the thinning trees. Beautiful as a curving wave of flame, the figures streamed across the narrow, open space with a drilled precision as of some battle line, and Hendricks, with a sense of wild, secret triumph saw them pause at the brink of the platformed. ridge, form up their serried ranks yet closer, then open two hundred arms to welcome some one whom the darkness should immediately deliver. Simultaneously, from the covering trees, the tall, slim shadow of Lord Ernie darted out into the light.

"Magnificent!" cried Hendricks, but his voice was smothered instantly in a mightier sound, and his movement forward seemed ineffective stumbling. The hundred voices thundered out a single note. Like a deer the boy leaped; like a tongue of flame he flew to join his own; and instantly was surrounded, borne shoulder high upon those upturned palms, swept back in triumph towards the procession of enormous fires. Wrapped by smoke and sparks, lifted by wind, he became part of the monstrous rhythm that turned that mountain ridge alive. He stood upright upon the platform of interlacing arms; he swayed with their movements as a thing of wind and fire that flew. The shining faces vanished then, turned all towards the blazing piles so that the boy had the appearance of standing on a wall of living black. His outline was visible a moment against the sky, firelight between his wide-stretched legs, streaming from his hair and horizontal arms, issuing almost, as it seemed, from his very body. The next second he leaped to the ground, ran forward— appallingly close—between two heaped-up fires, flung both hands heavenwards, and—knelt.

And Hendricks, sympathetically following the boy's performance as though his own mind and body took part in it, experienced then a singular result: it seemed the heart in him began to roar. This was no rustle of excited blood that the little cavern of his skull increased, but a deeper sound that proclaimed the kinship of his entire being with the ritual. His own nature had begun to answer. From that moment he perceived the spectacle, not with the senses of sight and hearing, separately, but with his entire body—synthetically. He became a part of this assembly that was itself one single instrument: a cosmic sounding-board for the rhythmical expression of impersonal Nature Powers. Leysin, he dimly realised, fixed in his churchy tenets, remained outside, apart, and compromising; Hendricks accepted and went with. All little customary feelings dipped utterly away, lost, false, denied, even as a unit in a crowd loses its normal characteristics in the greater mood that sways the whole. The fire no longer burned him, for he was the fire; nor did he stagger against the furious wind, because the wind was in his heart. He moved all over, alive in every point and corner. With his skin he breathed, his bones and tissue ran with glorious heat. He cried aloud. He praised. "I am the whirlwind and I am the fire! Fire that lights but does not burn, and wind that blows the hearts to flame!" His body sang it, or rather the elements sang it through his body; for the sound of his voice was not audible, and it was wind and fire that thundered forth his feeling in their crashing rhythm.

IX

And so it was that he no longer saw this thing pictorially, nor in the little detached reports the individual senses brought, but knew it in himself complete, as a man knows love and passion. Memory afterwards translated these vast central feelings into pictures, but the pictures touched reality without containing it. Like a vision it happened all at once, as a room or landscape happens, and what happens all at once, coming through a synthesis of the senses, is not properly describable later. To instantaneous knowledge mere sequence is a falsehood. The sequence first comes in with the telling afterwards. That kneeling form, he understood, was the empty vessel to which conventional life had hitherto denied the heat and air it craved. The breath of life now poured at full tide into it, the fire of deity lit its heart of touchwood, wind blew into desire; and later flame would burst forth in action, consuming opposition. He must let it fill to the brim. It was not salvation, but creation. Then thought went out, extinguished by a puff of something greater. . . .

For beyond the smoke and sparks, beyond the space the men had occupied, a new and gentler movement, lyrical with bird-like beauty, ran suddenly along the ridge. What Hendricks had taken for branches heaped in rows for the burning, stirred marvellously throughout their whole collective mass, stirred sweetly, too, and with an exquisite loveliness. The entire line rose gracefully into the air with a whirr as of sweeping birds. There was a soft and undulating motion as though a draught of flowing wind turned faintly visible, yet with an increasing brilliance, like shining lilies of flame that now flocked forward in a troop, bending deliciously all one way. And in the same second these tall lilies of fire revealed themselves as figures, naked above the waist, hair streaming on the wind, eyes alight and bare arms waving. Above the men's deep pedal bass their voices rose with clear, shrill sweetness on the storm. The band swept forwards swift as wind towards the kneeling boy. The long line curved about him foldingly. The women took him as the south wind takes a bird.

There may have been—indeed, there was—an interval, for Hendricks caught, again and again repeated, the boy's great cry of passionate delight above the tumult. Ringing and virile it rose to heaven, clear as a fine-wrought bell. And instantaneously the knitted figures of flame disentangled themselves again, the mass unfolded like an opening flower, and, as by a military word of command, dissolved itself once more into a long thin line of running fire. The women advanced, and the waiting men flowed forward in a stream to meet them. This interweaving of the figures was as easily accomplished as the mingling of light and heavy threads upon some living loom. Hands joining hands, all singing, these naked worshippers of fire and wind passed in and out among the blazing piles with a headlong precision that was torrential and yet orderly. The speed increased; the faces flashed and vanished, then flashed and passed again; each woman between two men, each man between two women, and Lord Ernie, radiantly alive, between two girls of rich, o'erflowing beauty. Their movements were undulating, like the undulations of fire, yet with sudden, unexpected upward leaps as when fire is partnered abruptly by a cantering wind. For the women were fire, and the men were wind. The imitative dance was in full swing. The marvellous wind and fire ritual unrolled its old-world magic.

It was awe-inspiring certainly, but for Hendricks, as he watched, the terror of big conflagrations was wholly absent: rather, he felt the sense of deep security that rhythmic movement causes. Bathed in a sea of elemental power, he burned to share the pagan splendour and the rush of primitive delight. It seemed he had a cosmic body in which new centres stirred to life, linking him on to this source of natural forces. Through these centres he drew the chaotic energy into nerves and blood and muscle, into the very substance of his thought, indeed, transmuting them into the magic of the will. Abundant and inexhaustible vigour filled the air, pouring freely into whatever empty receptacle lay at hand. Sheets of flame, whole separate fragments of it, torn at the edges, raced, loudly, hungrily flapping on vehement gusts of wind; curved as they flew; leaped, twisted, flashed and vanished. And the figures closely copied them. The women tossed their bodies aloft, then dipped suddenly to the earth, invisible, till the rushing men urged them into view again with wild impetuous swing, so that the entire line stretched and contracted like an immense elastic band of life, now knotted, now dissolved.

Yet, while of raging and terrific beauty, there was never that mad abandon which is disorder; but rather a kind of sacred natural revel that prohibited mere licence. There was even a singular austerity in it that betrayed a definite ritual and not mere reckless pageantry. No walls could possibly have contained it. In cathedral, temple, or measured space, however grand, it could only have seemed exaggerated and apostate; here, beneath the open sky, it was beautiful and true. For overhead the stars burned clear and steady, the constellations watching it from their immovable towers—a representation of their own leisured and hierarchic dance in swifter miniature. And indeed this relationship it bore to a universal rhythm was the key, it seemed, to its deep significance; for the close imitation of natural movements seduced the colossal powers of fire and wind to swell human emotions till they became mould and vessel for this elemental manifestation in men and women. Golden yellow in the blaze, the limbs of the women flashed and passed; their hair flew dark a moment across gleaming breasts; and their waving arms tossed in evershifting patterns through the driving smoke. The fires boiled and roared, scattering torrents of showering sparks like stars; and amid it all the slim, white shoulders of the boy, his clothes torn from him, his eyes ablaze, and his lips opened to the singing as though he had known it always, drove to and fro on the crest of the ritual like some flying figure of wind and fire incarnate.

All of which, instantaneously yet in sequence, Hendricks witnessed, painted upon the wild night sky. A volcanic energy poured through him too. He knew a golden enthusiasm of immeasurable strength, of unconquerable hope, of irresistible delight. Wind set his feet to dancing, and fire swept across his face without a trace of burning.

Nature was part of him. He had stepped inside. No obstacle existed that could withstand for a single second the torrential energy that fired his heart and blood. There was lightning in his veins. He could sweep aside life's difficult barriers with the ease of a tornado, and shake the rubbish of doubt and care from the years with earthquake shocks. Empires he could mould, and play with nations, drive men and women before him like a flock of sheep, shatter convention, and dislocate the machinery time has foisted upon natural energies. He knew in himself the omnipotence of the lesser elemental deities. Yet, as sympathetic observer, he can but have felt a tithe of what Lord Ernie felt.

"We are the whirlwind and we are the fire!" he cried aloud with the rushing worshippers. "We are unconquerable and immense! We destroy the lukewarm and absorb the weak! For we can make evil into good by bending it all one way! . . ."

The roar swept thunderingly past him, catching at his voice and body. He felt himself snatched forward by the wind. The fire licked sweetly at him. It was the final abandonment. He plunged recklessly towards the surge of dancers. . . .

X

What stopped him he did not know. Some hard and steely thing pricked sharply into him. An opposing power, fierce as a sword, stabbed at his heart—and he heard a little sound quite close beside him, a sound that pierced the babel, reaching his consciousness as from far away.

"Keep still! Cling tight to this old rock! Hold yourself in, or else they'll have you too!"

It was as if some insect scratched within his ear. His arm, that same instant, was violently seized. He came down with a crash. He had been half in the air. He had been dancing.

"Turn your eyes away, away! Take hold of this big tree!" The voice cried furiously, but with a petty human passion in it that marred the world. There was an intolerable revulsion in him as he heard it. He felt himself dragged forcibly backwards. He lost his balance, stumbling among loose stones.

"Loose me! Let me go!" he shouted, struggling like a wild animal, yet vainly, against the inflexible grip that held him. "I am one with the fire that lights but does not burn. I am the wind that blows the worlds along. Damnation take you. . . . Let me free! . . ."

Confusion caught him, smothering speech and blinding sight. He fell backwards, away from the heat and wind. He was furious, but furious with he knew not whom or what. The interference had destroyed the rhythm, broken it into fragments. Violent impulses clashed through him without the will to choose or guide them. For power had deserted him and flowed elsewhere. He stood no longer in the stream of energy. He was emptied. And at first he could not tell whether his instinct was to return himself, to rescue his precious boy, or—to crush the interfering object out of existence with what was left to him of raging anger. He turned, stood up, and flung the Pasteur aside with violence. He raised his feet to stamp and kill . . . when a phrase with meaning darted suddenly across his wild confusion and recalled him to some fragment of truer responsibility and life.

". . . There'll be only violence in him—reckless violence instead of strength—destructive. Save him before it is too late!"

"It *is* too late," he roared in answer. "What devil hinders me?"

But his roar was feeble, and his ironed boots refused the stamping. Power slipped wholly out of him. The rhythm poured past, instead of through him. Interference had destroyed the circuit. More glimmerings of responsibility came back. He stooped like a drunken man and helped the other to his feet. The rapidity of the change was curious, proving that the spell had been put upon him from without. It was not, as with the boy, mere development of pre-existing tendencies.

"Help me," he implored suddenly instead, "help me! There has been madness in me. For God's sake, help me to get him out!" It seemed the face of the old Marquess, stern and terrible, broke an instant through the smoky air, black with reproach and anger. And, with a violent effort of the will, Hendricks turned round to face the elemental orgy, bent on rescue. But this time the heat was intolerable and drove him back. The hair, hitherto untouched, now singed upon his head. Fire licked his very breath away. He bent double, covering his face with arms and cloak.

"Pray!" shouted Leysin, dropping to his knees. "It is the only way. My God is higher than this. Pray, pray!"

And, automatically, Hendricks fell upon his knees beside him, though to pray he knew not how. For no real faith was in him as in the other, and his eye was far from single. The fast fading grandeur of what he had experienced still left its pagan tumult in his blood. The pretence of prayer could only have been blasphemy. He watched instead, letting the other invoke his mighty Deity alone, that Deity he had served, unflinchingly all his life with faith and fasting, and with belief beyond assault.

It was an impressive picture, fraught with passionate drama. On his knees behind a sheltering boulder, a blackened pine-tree tossing scorched branches above his head, this righteous man prayed to his God, sure of his triumphant answer. Hendricks watched with an admiration that made him realise his own insignificance. The eyes were closed, the leonine big head set firm upon the diminutive body, the face now lit by flame, now veiled by smoke, the strong hands clasped together and upraised. He envied him. He recognised, too, that the elements themselves, with all their chaos of might and terror, were after all but servants of the Vastness which dips the butterflies in colour and puts down upon the breasts of little robins. And, because the Pasteur's life had been always prayer in action, his little human will invoked the Will of Greatness, merged with it, used it, and directed it steadily against the commotion of these unleashed elements. Certain of himself and of his God, the Pasteur never doubted. His prayer set instantly in action those forces which balance suns and keep the stars afloat.

Thus, trembling with terror that made him wholly ineffective, Hendricks watched, and, as he watched, became aware of the amazing change. For it seemed as if a stream of power, steady and in opposition to the tumult, now poured audaciously against the elemental rhythm, altering its direction, modifying gradually its stupendous impetus. There were pauses in the huge vibrations: they wavered, broke, and fled. They knew confusion, as when the prow of a steel-nosed vessel drives against the tide. The tide is vaster, but the steel is—different. The whole sky shivered, as this new entering force, so small, so soft, yet of such incalculable energy, began at once its overmastering effect. Signs of violence or rout, or of anything disordered, had no part in it; excess before it slipped into willing harness; there was light that sponged away all glare, as when morning sunshine cleans a forest of its shadows. Some little whispering power sang marvellously as of old across the desolate big mountains, "Peace! Be still!" turning the monstrous turbulence into obedient sweetness. And upon his face and hands Hendricks felt faint, delicate touches of some refreshing softness that he could not understand.

Yet not instantly was this harmony restored; at first there was the stress of vehement opposition. The night of wind and fire drove roaring through the sky. There were bursts of triumphant tumult, but convulsion in them and no true steadiness as before. The human figures hitherto had danced with that fluid appearance which belongs to fire, and with that instantaneous rush which is of wind, the men increasing the women, and the women answering with joy; limbs and faces had melted into each other till the circular ritual looked like a glowing wheel of flame rotating audibly. But slowly now the speed of the wheel decreased; the single utterance was marred by the crying of many voices, all at different pitch, discordant, inharmonious, dismayed. The fires somehow dwindled; there came pauses in the wind; and Hendricks became aware of a curious hissing noise, as more and more of these odd soft touches found his face and hands. Here and there, he saw, a figure stumbled, fell, then gathered itself clumsily together again with a frightened shout, breaking violently out of the circle. More and more these figures blundered and dropped out; and although they returned again, so that the dance apparently increased, these were but moments in the final violence of the dispersing hurricane. The rejected ones dashed back wildly into the wrong places; men and women no longer stood alternate, but in groups together, falsely related. The entire movement was dislocated; the ceremony grew rapidly incoherent; meaning forsook it. The composite instrument that had transmuted the elemental forces into human, emotional storage was imperfect, broken, out of tune. The disarray turned rout.

And then it was, while Leysin continued without ceasing his burning and successful prayer, that his companion, conscious of returning harmony, rose to his feet, aware suddenly that he could also help. A portion of the powers he had absorbed still worked in him, but in a new direction. He felt confident and unafraid. He did not stumble. With unerring tread he advanced towards the lessening fires, feeling as he did so the cold soft touches multiply with a rush upon his skin. From all sides they came by hundreds, like messengers of help.

"Ernest!" he cried aloud, and his voice, though little raised, carried resonantly above the dying turmoil; "Ernest! Come back to us. Your father calls you!"

And from threescore faces hurrying in confusion through the smoke, one paused and turned. It stood apart, hovering as though in air, while the mob of disordered figures rushed in a body along the ridge. Plunging like frightened cattle below the farther edge, then vanishing into thick darkness, they left behind them this one solitary face. A final dying flame licked out at it; a rush of smoke drove past to hide it; there was a high, wild scream—and the figure shot forward with a headlong leap and fell with a crash at Hendricks' feet. Lord Ernie, blackened by smoke and scorched by fire, lay safe outside the danger zone.

And Hendricks knelt beside him. Remorse and shame made him powerless to do more as he pulled the torn clothing over the neck and chest and heard his own heart begging for forgiveness. He realised his own weakness and faithlessness. A great temptation had found him wanting. . . .

It was owing to Leysin that the rescue was complete. The Pasteur was instantly by his side.

"Saved as by water," he cried, as he folded his cloak about the prostrate body, and then raised the head and shoulders; "saved by His ministers of rain. For His miracles are love, and work through natural laws."

He made a sign to Hendricks. Carrying the boy between them, they scrambled down the slope into the shelter of the trees below. The cold, soft touches were then explained. The *joran* had dropped as suddenly as it rose, and the torrential rain that invariably follows now poured in rivers from the sky. Water, drenching the fires and padding the savage wind, had stopped the dancers midway in their frenzied ritual. It was the element they dreaded, for it was hostile. Rain soused the mountain ridge, extinguishing the last embers of the numerous fires. It rushed in rivulets between their feet. The heated earth gave out a hissing steam, and the only sound in the spaces where wind and fire had boomed and thundered a little while before was now the splash of water and the drip of quenching drops.

In the cover of the sheltering trees the body stirred, lifted its head, and sat up slowly. The eyes opened.

"I'm cold. I'm frightened," whispered a shivering voice. "Where am I?"

Only the pelt and thud of the rain sounded behind the quavering words.

"Where are the others? Have I been away? Hendricks—Mr. Hendricks— is that you—?"

He stared about him, his face now a mere luminous disc in the thick darkness. No breath of wind was loose. They spoke to him till he answered with assurance, groping to find their hands with his own, his words confused and strange with hidden meaning for a time. "I'm all right now," he kept repeating. "I know exactly. It was one of my big dreams. . . . I suppose I fell asleep . . . and the rain woke me. Great heavens! What a night to be out." And then he clambered vigorously to his feet with a sudden movement of great energy again, saying that hunger was in him and he must eat. There was no complaint of heat or cold, of burning or of bruises. The boy recovered marvellously. In ten minutes, breaking away from all support, he led, as they descended through the dripping forest in the gloom and chill of very early morning. It was the others who called to him for guidance in the tangled woods. Lord Ernie was in the lead. Throughout the difficult woods he was ever in front, and singing:

"Fire that lights but does not burn! And wind that blows the heart to flame! They both are in me now for ever and ever! Oh, praise the Lord of Fire and the Lord of Wind . . .!"

And this voice, now near, now distant, sounding through the dripping forest on their homeward journey, was an experience weird and unforgettable for those other two. Leysin, it seemed, had one sentence only which he kept repeating to himself—"Heaven grant he may direct it all for good. For they have filled him to the brim, and he is become an instrument of power."

But Hendricks, though he understood the risk, felt only confidence. Lord Ernie's regeneration had begun.

Soaked and bedraggled, all three, they reached the village about two o'clock. The boy, utterly unmanageable, said an emphatic No to spirits, soup, or medical appliances. His skin, indeed, showed no signs of burning, nor was there the smallest symptom of cold or fever in him. "I'm a perfect furnace," he laughed; "I feel health and strength personified." And the brightness of his eyes, his radiant colour, the vigour of his voice and manner—both in some way astonishing—made all pretence of assistance unnecessary and absurd. "It's like a new birth," he cried to Hendricks, as he almost cantered beside him down the road to their house, "and, by Jove, I'll wake 'em up at home and make the world go round. I know a hundred schemes. I tell you, sir, I'm simply bursting! For the first time I'm alive!"

And an hour later, when the tutor peeped in upon him, the boy was calmly sleeping. The candle light, shaded carefully with one hand, fell upon the face. There were new lines and a new expression in it. Will and purpose showed in the stern set of the lips and jaw. It was the face of a man, and of a man one would not lightly trifle with. Purpose, will, and power were established on their thrones. To such a man the entire world might one day bow the head.

"If only it will last," thought Hendricks, as, shaken, bewildered, and more than a little awed, he tiptoed out of the room again and went to bed. But through his dreams, sheeted in flame and veiled in angry smoke, the face of the old Marquess glowered upon him from a heavy sky above ancestral towers.

XI

From the obituary notices of the 9th Marquess of Oakham the following selections have their interest: He succeeded to his father, then in the Cabinet as Minister for Foreign Affairs, at the age of twenty-one. His career was brief but singular, the early magnificence of the younger Pitt offering a standard of comparison, though by no means a parallel, to his short record of astonishing achievement. His effect upon the world, first as Chief of the Government Labour Department and subsequently as Home Secretary, and Minister of War, is described as shattering, even cataclysmic. His public life lasted five years. He died at the age of twenty-nine. His personality was revolutionary and overwhelming.

For, judging by these extracts, he was a "Napoleonic figure whose personal influence combined the impetus of Mirabeau and the dominance of Alexander. His authority held an incalculable element, precisely described as uncanny. His spirit was puissant, elemental, his activity irresistible." Yet, according to another journal, "he was, properly speaking, neither intellectual, astute, nor diplomatic, and possessed as little subtlety as might be expected of a miner whose psychology was called upon to explain the Trinity. In no sense was he Statesman, and even less strategist, yet his name swept Europe, changed the map of the Nearer East, its mere whisper among the Chancelleries convulsing men's counsels with an influence almost menacing."

His enthusiasm appears to have been amazing. "Some stupendous and untiring energy drove through him, paralysing attack, and rendering the bitterest and most skilful opposition nugatory. His hand was imperious, upsetting with a touch the chessboards set by the most able statecraft, and his voice was heard with a kind of reverence in every capital."

The brevity of his astonishing career called for universal comment, as did the hypnotising effect of his singular ascendancy. "In five short years of power he achieved his sway. He rushed upon the world, he shook it, he retired," as one journal picturesquely phrased it. "The manner of his ending, moreover—a stroke of lightning,—seemed in keeping with his life. There was neither lingering, delay, nor warning. Of distinguished stock, noble, yet ordinary enough in all but name, his power is unexplained by heredity; his family furnished no approach to greatness, as history supplied no parallel to his dynamic intensity. Nor, we are informed, among his near of kin, does any inherit his volcanic energy."

The world, however, was apparently well relieved of his tumultuous presence, for his influence was generally surveyed as "destructive rather than constructive." He was unmarried, and the title went to a nephew.

The cheaper journals abounded, of course, in details of his personal and private life that were freely copied into the foreign press, and supply curious material for the student of human nature and the psychologist. The amazing revelations no doubt were picturesquely exaggerated, yet the substratum of truth in them all was generally admitted. No contradictions, at any rate, appeared. They read like the story of some primitive, wild giant let loose upon the world— primitive, because his specific brain power was admittedly of no high order; wild, because he was in favour of fierce, spontaneous action, and his mere presence, on occasions, could stir a nation, not alone a crowd, to vehement, terrific methods. His energy seemed inexhaustible, his fire inextinguishable.

Legends were rife, even before he died, among the peasantry of his Scotch estates, that he was in league with the devil. His habit of keeping enormous fires in his private rooms, fires that burned day and night from January to December, and in open hearths widened to thrice their natural size, stimulated the growth of this particular myth among those of his personal environment. All manner of stories raged. But it was his strange custom out-of-doors that provided the diabolical suggestion. For, "behind a specially walled-in space on an open ridge, denuded of pines, in a distant part of the estate, a series of gigantic heaps of wood, all ready to ignite, were—it was said—kept in a state of constant preparedness. And on stormy nights, especially when winds were high, and invariably at the period of the equinoctial tempests, his lordship would himself light these tremendous bonfires, and spend the nocturnal hours in their blazing presence, communing, the stories variously relate, with the witches at their Sabbath, or with hordes of fire-spirits, who emerged from the Bottomless Pit in order to feed his soul with their unquenchable supplies. From these nightly orgies, it seems clear, at any rate, he returned at dawn with a splendour of energy that no one could resist, and with a mien whose grandeur invited worship rather than inspired alarm."

His biography, it was further stated, would be written by Sir John Hendricks, Bt., who began life as Private Secretary to his father, the 8th Marquess, but whose rapid rise to position was due to his intimate association as trusted friend and adviser to the subject of these obituary notices. The biography, however, had not appeared, within five years of Lord Oakham's sudden death, and curiosity is only further stimulated by the suggestive whisper that it never will, and never can appear.

The Sacrifice

I

Limasson was a religious man, though of what depth and quality were un-known, since no trial of ultimate severity had yet tested him. An adherent of no particular creed, he yet had his gods; and his self-discipline was proba-bly more rigorous than his friends conjectured. He was so reserved. Few guessed, perhaps, the desires conquered, the passions regulated, the inner tendencies trained and schooled—not by denying their expression, but by transmuting them alchemically into nobler channels. He had in him the mak-ings of an enthusiastic devotee, and might have become such but for two limitations that prevented. He loved his wealth, labouring to increase it to the neglect of other interests; and, secondly, instead of following up one steady line of search, he scattered himself upon many picturesque theories, like an actor who wants to play all parts rather than concentrate on one. And the more picturesque the part, the more he was attracted. Thus, though he did his duty unshrinkingly and with a touch of love, he accused himself sometimes of merely gratifying a sensuous taste in spiritual sensations. There was this un-balance in him that argued want of depth.

As for his gods—in the end he discovered their reality by first doubting, then denying their existence.

It was this denial and doubt that restored them to their thrones, convert-ing his dilettante skirmishes into genuine, deep belief; and the proof came to him one summer in early June when he was making ready to leave town for his annual month among the mountains.

With Limasson mountains, in some inexplicable sense, were a passion almost, and climbing so deep a pleasure that the ordinary scrambler hardly understood it. Grave as a kind of worship it was to him; the preparations for an ascent, the ascent itself in particular, involved a concentration that seemed symbolical as of a ritual. He not only loved the heights, the massive grandeur, the splendour of vast proportions blocked in space, but loved them with a respect that held a touch of awe. The emotion mountains stirred in him, one might say, was of that profound, incalculable kind that held kinship with his religious feelings, half realised though these were. His gods had their invisible thrones somewhere among the grim, forbidding heights. He prepared himself for this annual mountaineering with the same earnestness that a holy man might approach a solemn festival of his church.

And the impetus of his mind was running with big momentum in this direction, when there fell upon him, almost on the eve of starting, a swift series of disasters that shook his being to its last foundations, and left him stunned among the ruins. To describe these is unnecessary. People said, "One thing after another like that! What appalling luck! Poor wretch!" then wondered, with the curiosity of children, how in the world he would take it. Due to no apparent fault of his own, these disasters were so sudden that life seemed in a moment shattered, and his interest in existence almost ceased. People shook their heads and thought of the emergency exit. But Limasson was too vital a man to dream of annihilation. Upon him it had a different effect—he turned and questioned what he called his gods. They did not answer or explain. For the first time in his life he doubted. A hair's breadth beyond lay definite denial.

The ruin in which he sat, however, was not material; no man of his age, possessed of courage and a working scheme of life, would permit disaster of a material order to overwhelm him. It was collapse of a mental, spiritual kind, an assault upon the roots of character and temperament. Moral duties laid suddenly upon him threatened to crush. His *personal* existence was assailed, and apparently must end. He must spend the remainder of his life caring for others who were nothing to him. No outlet showed, no way of escape, so diabolically complete was the combination of events that rushed his inner trenches. His faith was shaken. A man can but endure so much, and remain human. For him the saturation point seemed reached. He experienced the spiritual equivalent of that physical numbness which supervenes when pain has touched the limit of endurance. He laughed, grew callous, then mocked his silent gods.

It is said that upon this state of blank negation there follows sometimes a condition of lucidity which mirrors with crystal clearness the forces driving behind life at a given moment, a kind of clairvoyance that brings explanation and therefore peace. Limasson looked for this in vain. There was the doubt that questioned, there was the sneer that mocked the silence into which his questions fell; but there was neither answer nor explanation, and certainly not peace. There was no relief. In this tumult of revolt he did none of the things his friends suggested or expected. He merely followed the line of least resistance. He yielded to the impetus that was upon him when the catastrophe came. To their indignant amazement he went out to his mountains.

All marvelled that at such a time he could adopt so trivial a line of action, neglecting duties that seemed paramount; they disapproved. Yet in reality he was taking no definite action at all, but merely drifting with the momentum that had been acquired just before. He was bewildered with so much pain, confused with suffering, stunned with the crash that flung him helpless amid undeserved calamity. He turned to the mountains as a child to its mother, instinctively. Mountains had never failed to bring him consolation, comfort, peace. Their grandeur restored proportion whenever disorder threatened life. No calculation, properly speaking, was in his move at all; but a blind desire for a violent physical reaction such as climbing brings. And the instinct was more wholesome than he knew.

In the high upland valley among lonely peaks whither Limasson then went, he found in some measure the proportion he had lost. He studiously avoided thinking; he lived in his muscles recklessly. The region with its little Inn was familiar to him; peak after peak he attacked, sometimes with, but more often without a guide, until his reputation as a sane climber, a laurelled member of all the foreign Alpine Clubs, was seriously in danger. That he overdid it physically is beyond question, but that the mountains breathed into him some portion of their enormous calm and deep endurance is also true. His gods, meanwhile, he neglected utterly for the first time in his life. If he thought of them at all, it was as tinsel figures imagination had created, figures upon a stage that merely decorated life for those whom pretty pictures pleased. Only—he had left the theatre and their make-believe no longer hypnotised his mind. He realised their impotence and disowned them. This attitude, however, was subconscious; he lent to it no substance, either of thought or speech. He ignored rather than challenged their existence.

And it was somewhat in this frame of mind—thinking little, feeling even less—that he came out into the hotel vestibule after dinner one evening, and took mechanically the bundle of letters the porter handed to him. They had no possible interest for him; in a corner where the big steam-heater mitigated the chilliness of the hall, he idly sorted them. The score or so of other guests, chiefly expert climbing men, were trailing out in twos and threes from the dining-room; but he felt as little interest in them as in his letters: no conversation could alter facts, no written phrases change his circumstances. At random, then, he opened a business letter with a typewritten address—it would probably be impersonal, less of a mockery, therefore, than the others with their tiresome sham condolences. And, in a sense, it was impersonal; sympathy from a solicitor's office is mere formula, a few extra ticks upon the universal keyboard of a Remington. But as he read it, Limasson made a discovery that startled him into acute and bitter sensation. He had imagined the limit of bearable suffering and disaster already reached. Now, in a few dozen words, his error was proved convincingly. The fresh blow was dislocating.

This culminating news of additional catastrophe disclosed within him entirely new reaches of pain, of biting, resentful fury. Limasson experienced a momentary stopping of the heart as he took it in, a dizziness, a violent sensation of revolt whose impotence induced almost physical nausea. He felt like—death.

"Must I suffer all things?" flashed through his arrested intelligence in letters of fire.

There was a sullen rage in him, a dazed bewilderment, but no positive suffering as yet. His emotion was too sickening to include the smaller pains of disappointment; it was primitive, blind anger that he knew. He read the letter calmly, even to the neat paragraph of machine-made sympathy at the last, then placed it in his inner pocket. No outward sign of disturbance was upon him; his breath came slowly; he reached over to the table for a match, holding it at arm's length lest the sulphur fumes should sting his nostrils.

And in that moment he made his second discovery. The fact that further suffering was still possible included also the fact that some touch of resignation had been left in him, and therefore some vestige of belief as well. Now, as he felt the crackling sheet of stiff paper in his pocket, watched the sulphur die, and saw the wood ignite, this remnant faded utterly away. Like the blackened end of the match, it shrivelled and dropped off. It vanished. Savagely, yet with an external calmness that enabled him to light his pipe with untrembling hand, he addressed his futile deities. And once more in fiery letters there flashed across the darkness of his passionate thought:

"Even this you demand of me—this cruel, ultimate sacrifice?"

And he rejected them, bag and baggage; for they were a mockery and a lie. With contempt he repudiated them for ever. The stage of doubt had passed. He denied his gods. Yet, with a smile upon his lips; for what were they after all but the puppets his religious fancy had imagined? They never had existed. Was it, then, merely the picturesque, sensational aspect of his devotional temperament that had created them? That side of his nature, in any case, was dead now, killed by a single devastating blow. The gods went with it.

Surveying what remained of his life, it seemed to him like a city that an earthquake has reduced to ruins. The inhabitants think no worse thing could happen. Then comes the fire.

Two lines of thought, it seems, then developed parallel in him and simultaneously, for while underneath he stormed against this culminating blow, his upper mind dealt calmly with the project of a great expedition he would make at dawn. He had engaged no guide. As an experienced mountaineer, he knew the district well; his name was tolerably familiar, and in half an hour he could have settled all details, and retired to bed with instructions to be called at two.

But, instead, he sat there waiting, unable to stir, a human volcano that any moment might break forth into violence. He smoked his pipe as quietly as though nothing had happened, while through the blazing depths of him ran ever this one self-repeating statement: "Even this you demand of me, this cruel, ultimate sacrifice! . . ." His self-control, dynamically estimated, just then must have been very great and, thus repressed, the store of potential energy accumulated enormously.

With thought concentrated largely upon this final blow, Limasson had not noticed the people who streamed out of the *salle à manger* and scattered themselves in groups about the hall. Some individual, now and again, approached his chair with the idea of conversation, then, seeing his absorption, turned away. Even when a climber whom he slightly knew reached across him with a word of apology for the matches, Limasson made no response, for he did not see him. He noticed nothing. In particular he did not notice two men who, from an opposite corner, had for some time been observing him. He now looked up—by chance?—and was vaguely aware that they were discussing him. He met their eyes across the hall, and started.

For at first he thought he knew them. Possibly he had seen them about in the hotel—they seemed familiar—yet he certainly had never spoken with them. Aware of his mistake, he turned his glance elsewhere, though still vividly conscious of their attention. One was a clergyman or a priest; his face wore an air of gravity touched by sadness, a sternness about the lips counteracted by a kindling beauty in the eyes that betrayed enthusiasm nobly regulated. There was a suggestion of stateliness in the man that made the impression very sharp. His clothing emphasised it. He wore a dark tweed suit that was strict in its simplicity. There was austerity in him somewhere.

His companion, perhaps by contrast, seemed inconsiderable in his conventional evening dress. A good deal younger than his friend, his hair, always a tell-tale detail, was a trifle long; the thin fingers that flourished a cigarette wore rings; the face, though picturesque, was flippant, and his entire attitude conveyed a certain insignificance. Gesture, that faultless language which challenges counterfeit, betrayed unbalance somewhere. The impression he produced, however, was shadowy compared to the sharpness of the other. "Theatrical" was the word in Limasson's mind, as he turned his glance elsewhere. But as he looked away he fidgeted. The interior darkness caused by the dreadful letter rose about him. It engulfed him. Dizziness came with it. . . .

Far away the blackness was fringed with light, and through this light, stepping with speed and carelessness as from gigantic distance, the two men, suddenly grown large, came at him. Limasson, in self-protection, turned to meet them. Conversation he did not desire. Somehow he had expected this attack.

Yet the instant they began to speak—it was the priest who opened fire—
it was all so natural and easy that he almost welcomed the diversion. A phrase
by way of introduction—and he was speaking of the summits. Something in
Limasson's mind turned over. The man was a serious climber, one of his own
species. The sufferer felt a certain relief as he heard the invitation, and realised, though dully, the compliment involved.

"If you felt inclined to join us—if you would honour us with your company," the man was saying quietly, adding something then about "your great
experience" and "invaluable advice and judgment."

Limasson looked up, trying hard to concentrate and understand.

"The Tour du Néant?" he repeated, mentioning the peak proposed.
Rarely attempted, never conquered, and with an ominous record of disaster, it
happened to be the very summit he had meant to attack himself next day.

"You have engaged guides?" He knew the question foolish.

"No guide will try it," the priest answered, smiling, while his companion
added with a flourish, "but we—we need no guide—if *you* will come."

"You are unattached, I believe? You are alone?" the priest enquired,
moving a little in front of his friend, as though to keep him in the background.

"Yes," replied Limasson. "I am quite alone."

He was listening attentively, but with only part of his mind. He realised
the flattery of the invitation. Yet it was like flattery addressed to some one
else. He felt himself so indifferent, so—dead. These men wanted his skilful
body, his experienced mind; and it was his body and mind that talked with
them, and finally agreed to go. Many a time expeditions had been planned in
just this way, but to-night he felt there was a difference. Mind and body
signed the agreement, but his soul, listening elsewhere and looking on, was
silent. With his rejected gods it had left him, though hovering close still. It did
not interfere; it did not warn; it even approved; it sang to him from great distance that this expedition cloaked another. He was bewildered by the clashing
of his higher and his lower mind.

"At one in the morning, then, if that will suit you . . ." the older man concluded.

"I'll see to the provisions," exclaimed the younger enthusiastically, "and I
shall take my telephoto for the summit. The porters can come as far as the
Great Tower. We're over six thousand feet here already, you see, so . . ." and
his voice died away in the distance as his companion led him off.

Limasson saw him go with relief. But for the other man he would have
declined the invitation. At heart he was indifferent enough. What decided him
really was the coincidence that the Tour du Néant was the very peak he had

intended to attack himself *alone,* and the curious feeling that this expedition cloaked another somehow—almost that these men had a hidden motive. But he dismissed the idea—it was not worth thinking about. A moment later he followed them to bed. So careless was he of the affairs of the world, so dead to mundane interests, that he tore up his other letters and tossed them into a corner of the room—unread.

II

Once in his chilly bedroom he realised that his upper mind had permitted him to do a foolish thing; he had drifted like a schoolboy into an unwise situation. He had pledged himself to an expedition with two strangers, an expedition for which normally he would have chosen his companions with the utmost caution. Moreover, he was guide; they looked to him for safety, while yet it was they who had arranged and planned it. But who were these men with whom he proposed to run grave bodily risks? He knew them as little as they knew him. Whence came, he wondered, the curious idea that this climb was really planned by another who was no one of them?

The thought slipped idly across his mind; going out by one door, it came back, however, quickly by another. He did not think about it more than to note its passage through the disorder that passed with him just then for thinking. Indeed, there was nothing in the whole world for which he cared a single brass farthing. As he undressed for bed, he said to himself: "I shall be called at one . . . but why am I going with these two on this wild plan? . . . And who made the plan?" . . .

It seemed to have settled itself. It came about so naturally and easily, so quickly. He probed no deeper. He didn't care. And for the first time he omitted the little ritual, half prayer, half adoration, it had always been his custom to offer to his deities upon retiring to rest. He no longer recognised them.

How utterly broken his life was! How blank and terrible and lonely! He felt cold, and piled his overcoats upon the bed, as though his mental isolation involved a physical effect as well. Switching off the light by the door, he was in the act of crossing the floor in the darkness when a sound beneath the window caught his ear. Outside there were voices talking. The roar of falling water made them indistinct, yet he was sure they were voices, and that one of them he knew. He stopped still to listen. He heard his own name uttered— "John Limasson." They ceased. He stood a moment shivering on the boards, then crawled into bed beneath the heavy clothing. But in the act of settling down, they began again. He raised himself again hurriedly to listen. What little wind there was passed in that moment down the valley, carrying off the roar of falling water; and into the moment's space of silence dropped fragments of definite sentences:

"They are close, you say—close down upon the world?" It was the voice of the priest surely.

"For days they have been passing," was the answer—a rough, deep tone that might have been a peasant's, and a kind of fear in it, "for all my flocks are scattered."

"The signs are sure? You know them?"

"Tumult," was the answer in much lower tones. "There has been tumult in the mountains . . ."

There was a break then as though the voices sank too low to be heard. Two broken fragments came next end of a question—beginning of an answer.

". . . the opportunity of a life-time?"

". . . if he goes of his own free will, success is sure. For acceptance is . . ."

And the wind, returning, bore back the sound of the falling water, so that Limasson heard no more. . . .

An indefinable emotion stirred in him as he turned over to sleep. He stuffed his ears lest he should hear more. He was aware of a sinking of the heart that was inexplicable. What in the world were they talking about, these two? What was the meaning of these disjointed phrases? There lay behind them a grave significance almost solemn. That "tumult in the mountains" was somehow ominous, its suggestion terrible and mighty. He felt disturbed, uncomfortable, the first emotion that had stirred in him for days. The numbness melted before its faint awakening. Conscience was in it—he felt vague prickings—but it was deeper far than conscience. Somewhere out of sight, in a region life had as yet not plumbed, the words sank down and vibrated like pedal notes. They rumbled away into the night of undecipherable things. And, though explanation failed him, he felt they had reference somehow to the morrow's expedition: how, what, wherefore, he knew not; his name had been spoken—then these curious sentences; that was all. Yet to-morrow's expedition, what was it but an expedition of impersonal kind, not even planned by himself? Merely his own plan taken and altered by others—made over? His personal business, his personal life, were not really in it at all.

The thought startled him a moment. He had no personal life . . .!

Struggling with sleep, his brain played the endless game of disentanglement without winning a single point, while the under-mind in him looked on and smiled—because it *knew*. Then, suddenly, a great peace fell over him. Exhaustion brought it perhaps. He fell asleep; and next moment, it seemed, he was aware of a thundering at the door and an unwelcome growling voice, *"'s ist bald ein Uhr, Herr! Aufstehen!"*

Rising at such an hour, unless the heart be in it, is a sordid and depressing business; Limasson dressed without enthusiasm, conscious that thought and feeling were exactly where he had left them on going to sleep. The same confusion and bewilderment were in him; also the same deep solemn emotion stirred by the whispering voices. Only long habit enabled him to attend to detail, and ensured that nothing was forgotten. He felt heavy and oppressed, a kind of anxiety about him; the routine of preparation he followed gravely, utterly untouched by the customary joy; it was mechanical. Yet through it ran the old familiar sense of ritual, due to the practice of so many years, that cleansing of mind and body for a big Ascent—like initiatory rites that once had been as important to him as those of some priest who approached the worship of his deity in the temples of ancient time. He performed the ceremony with the same care as though no ghost of vanished faith still watched him, beckoning from the air as formerly. . . . His knapsack carefully packed, he took his ice-axe from beside the bed, turned out the light, and went down the creaking wooden stairs in stockinged feet, lest his heavy boots should waken the other sleepers. And in his head still rang the phrase he had fallen asleep on—as though just uttered:

"The signs are sure; for days they have been passing—close down upon the world. The flocks are scattered. There has been tumult—tumult in the mountains." The other fragments he had forgotten. But who were "they"? And why did the word bring a chill of awe into his blood?

And as the words rolled through him Limasson felt tumult in his thoughts and feelings too. There had been tumult in his life, and all his joys were scattered—joys that hitherto had fed his days. The signs were sure. Something was close down upon his little world—passing—sweeping. He felt a touch of terror.

Outside in the fresh darkness of very early morning the strangers stood waiting for him. Rather, they seemed to arrive in the same instant as himself, equally punctual. The clock in the church tower sounded one. They exchanged low greetings, remarked that the weather promised to hold good, and started off in single file over soaking meadows towards the first belt of forest. The porter—mere peasant, unfamiliar of face and not connected with the hotel—led the way with a hurricane lantern. The air was marvellously sweet and fragrant. In the sky overhead the stars shone in their thousands. Only the noise of falling water from the heights and the regular thud of their heavy boots broke the stillness. And, black against the sky, towered the enormous pyramid of the Tour du Néant they meant to conquer.

Perhaps the most delightful portion of a big ascent is the beginning in the scented darkness while the thrill of possible conquest lies still far off. The hours stretch themselves queerly; last night's sunset might be days ago; sunrise and the brilliance coming seem in another week, part of dim futurity like children's holidays. It is difficult to realise that this biting cold before the dawn, and the blazing heat to come, both belong to the same to-day.

There were no sounds as they toiled slowly up the zigzag path through the first fifteen hundred feet of pinewoods; no one spoke; the clink of nails and ice-axe points against the stones was all they heard. For the roar of water was felt rather than heard; it beat against the ears and the skin of the whole body at once. The deeper notes were below them now in the sleeping valley; the shriller ones sounded far above, where streams just born out of ponderous snow-beds tinkled sharply. . . .

The change came delicately. The stars turned a shade less brilliant, a softness in them as of human eyes that say farewell. Between the highest branches the sky grew visible. A sighing air smoothed all their crests one way; moss, earth, and open spaces brought keen perfumes; and the little human procession, leaving the forest, stepped out into the vastness of the world above the tree-line. They paused while the porter stooped to put his lantern out. In the eastern sky was colour. The peaks and crags rushed closer.

Was it the Dawn? Limasson turned his eyes from the height of sky where the summits pierced a path for the coming day, to the faces of his companions, pale and wan in the early twilight. How small, how insignificant they seemed amid this hungry emptiness of desolation. The stupendous cliffs fled past them, led by headstrong peaks crowned with eternal snows. Thin lines of cloud, trailing half way up precipice and ridge, seemed like the swish of movement—as though he caught the earth turning as she raced through space. The four of them, timid riders on the gigantic saddle, clung for their lives against her titan ribs, while currents of some majestic life swept up at them from every side. He drew deep draughts of the rarefied air into his lungs. It was very cold. Avoiding the pallid, insignificant faces of his companions, he pretended interest in the porter's operations; he stared fixedly on the ground. It seemed twenty minutes before the flame was extinguished, and the lantern fastened to the pack behind. This Dawn was unlike any he had seen before.

For, in reality, all the while, Limasson was trying to bring order out of the extraordinary thoughts and feelings that had possessed him during the slow forest ascent, and the task was not crowned with much success. The Plan, made by others, had taken charge of him, he felt; and he had thrown the reins of personal will and interest loosely upon its steady gait. He had abandoned himself carelessly to what might come. Knowing that he was leader of the expedition, he yet had suffered the porter to go first, taking his own place as it was appointed to him, behind the younger man, but before the priest. In this order, they had plodded, as only experienced climbers plod, for hours without a rest, until half way up a change had taken place. He had wished it, and instantly it was effected. The priest moved past him, while his companion dropped to the rear—the companion who for ever stumbled in his speed, whereas the older man climbed surely, confidently. And thereafter Limasson walked more easily—as though the relative positions of the three were of importance somehow. The steep ascent of smothering darkness through the woods became less arduous. He was glad to have the younger man behind him.

For the impression had strengthened as they climbed in silence that this ascent pertained to some significant Ceremony, and the idea had grown insistently, almost stealthily, upon him. The movements of himself and his companions, especially the positions each occupied relatively to the other, established some kind of intimacy that resembled speech, suggesting even question and answer. And the entire performance, while occupying hours by his watch, it seemed to him more than once, had been in reality briefer than the flash of a passing thought, so that he saw it within himself—pictorially. He thought of a picture worked in colours upon a strip of elastic. Some one pulled the strip, and the picture stretched. Or some one released it again, and the picture flew back, reduced to a mere stationary speck. All happened in a single speck of time.

And the little change of position, apparently so trivial, gave point to this singular notion working in his under-mind—that this ascent was a ritual and a ceremony as in older days, its significance approaching revelation, however, for the first time—now. Without language, this stole over him; no words could quite describe it. For it came to him that these three formed a unit, himself being in some fashion yet the acknowledged principal, the leader. The labouring porter had no place in it, for this first toiling through the darkness was a preparation, and when the actual climb began, he would disappear, while Limasson himself went first. This idea that they took part together in a Ceremony established itself firmly in him, with the added wonder that, though so often done, he performed it now for the first time with full comprehension, knowledge, truth. Empty of personal desire, indifferent to an ascent that formerly would have thrilled his heart with ambition and delight, he understood that climbing had ever been a ritual for his soul and of his soul, and that power must result from its sincere accomplishment. It was a symbolical ascent.

In words this did not come to him. He felt it, never criticising. That is, he neither rejected nor accepted. It stole most sweetly, grandly, over him. It floated into him while he climbed, yet so convincingly that he had felt his relative position must be changed. The younger man held too prominent a post, or at least a wrong one—in advance. Then, after the change, effected mysteriously as though all recognised it, this line of certainty increased, and there came upon him the big, strange knowledge that all of life is a Ceremony on a giant scale, and that by performing the movements accurately, with sincere fidelity, there may come— knowledge. There was gravity in him from that moment.

This ran in his mind with certainty. Though his thought assumed no form of little phrases, his brain yet furnished detailed statements that clinched the marvellous thing with simile and incident which daily life might apprehend: That knowledge arises from action; that to do the thing invites the teaching and explains it. Action, moreover, is symbolical; a group of men, a family, an entire nation, engaged in those daily movements which are the working out of their destiny, perform a Ceremony which is in direct relation somewhere to the pattern of greater happenings which are the teachings of the Gods. Let the body imitate, reproduce—in a bedroom, in a wood—anywhere—the movements of the stars, and the meaning of those stars shall sink down into the heart. The movements constitute a script, a language. To mimic the gestures of a stranger is to understand his mood, his point of view—to establish a grave and solemn intimacy. Temples are everywhere, for the entire earth is a temple, and the body, House of Royalty, is the biggest temple of them all. To ascertain the pattern its movements trace in daily life, *could* be to determine the relation of that particular ceremony to the Cosmos, and so learn power. The entire system of Pythagoras, he realised, could be taught without a single word—by movements; and in everyday life even the commonest act and vulgarest movement are part of some big Ceremony—a message from the Gods. Ceremony, in a word, is three-dimensional language, and action, therefore, is the language of the Gods. The Gods he had denied were speaking to him . . . passing with tumult close across his broken life. . . . Their passage it was, indeed, that had caused the breaking!

In this cryptic, condensed fashion the great fact came over him—that he and these other two, here and now, took part in some great Ceremony of whose ultimate object as yet he was in ignorance. The impact with which it dropped upon his mind was tremendous. He realised it most fully when he stepped from the darkness of the forest and entered the expanse of glimmering, early light; up till this moment his mind was being prepared only, whereas now he knew. The innate desire to worship which all along had been his, the momentum his religious temperament had acquired during forty years, the yearning to have proof, in a word, that the Gods he once acknowledged were really true, swept back upon him with that violent reaction which denial had aroused.

He wavered where he stood. . . .

Looking about him, then, while the others rearranged burdens the returning porter now discarded, he perceived the astonishing beauty of the time and place, feeling it soak into him as by the very pores of his skin. From all sides this beauty rushed upon him. Some radiant, wingéd sense of wonder sped past him through the silent air. A thrill of ecstasy ran down every nerve. The hair of his head stood up. It was far from unfamiliar to him, this sight of the upper mountain world awakening from its sleep of the summer night, but never before had he stood shuddering thus at its exquisite cold glory, nor felt its significance as now, so mysteriously *within himself*. Some transcendent power that held sublimity was passing across this huge desolate plateau, far more majestic than the mere sunrise among mountains he had so often witnessed. There was Movement. He understood why he had seen his companions insignificant. Again he shivered and looked about him, touched by a solemnity that held deep awe.

Personal life, indeed, was wrecked, destroyed, but something greater was on the way. His fragile alliance with a spiritual world was strengthened. He realised his own past insolence. He became afraid.

III

The treeless plateau, littered with enormous boulders, stretched for miles to right and left, grey in the dusk of very early morning. Behind him dropped thick guardian pinewoods into the sleeping valley that still detained the darkness of the night. Here and there lay patches of deep snow, gleaming faintly through thin rising mist; singing streams of icy water spread everywhere among the stones, soaking the coarse rough grass that was the only sign of vegetation. No life was visible; nothing stirred; nor anywhere was movement, but of the quiet trailing mist and of his own breath that drifted past his face like smoke. Yet through the splendid stillness there *was* movement; that sense of absolute movement which results in stillness—it was owing to the stillness that he became aware of it—so vast, indeed, that only immobility could express it. Thus, on the calmest day in summer, may the headlong rushing of the earth through space seem more real than when the tempest shakes the trees and water on its surface; or great machinery turn with such vertiginous velocity that it appears steady to the deceived function of the eye. For it was not through the eye that this solemn Movement made itself known, but rather through a massive sensation that owned his entire body as its organ. Within the league-long amphitheatre of enormous peaks and precipices that enclosed the plateau, piling themselves upon the horizon, Limasson felt the outline of a Ceremony extended. The pulses of its grandeur poured into him where he stood. Its vast design was knowable because they themselves had traced—were even then tracing—its earthly counterpart in little. And the awe in him increased.

"This light is false. We have an hour yet before the true dawn," he heard the younger man say lightly. "The summits still are ghostly. Let us enjoy the sensation, and see what we can make of it."

And Limasson, looking up startled from his reverie, saw that the far-away heights and towers indeed were heavy with shadow, faint still with the light of stars. It seemed to him they bowed their awful heads and that their stupendous shoulders lowered. They drew together, shutting out the world.

"True," said his companion, "and the upper snows still wear the spectral shine of night. But let us now move faster, for we travel very light. The sensations you propose will but delay and weaken us."

He handed a share of the burdens to his companion and to Limasson. Slowly they all moved forward, and the mountains shut them in.

And two things Limasson noted then, as he shouldered his heavier pack and led the way: first, that he suddenly knew their destination though its purpose still lay hidden; and, secondly, that the porter's leaving before the ascent proper began signified finally that ordinary climbing was not their real objective. Also—the dawn was a lifting of inner veils from off his mind, rather than a brightening of the visible earth due to the nearing sun. Thick darkness, indeed, draped this enormous, lonely amphitheatre where they moved.

"You lead us well," said the priest, a few feet behind him, as he picked his way unfalteringly among the boulders and the streams.

"Strange that I do so," replied Limasson, in a low tone, "for the way is new to me, and the darkness grows instead of lessening." The language seemed hardly of his choosing. He spoke and walked as in a dream.

Far in the rear the voice of the younger man called plaintively after them:

"You go so fast, I can't keep up with you," and again he stumbled and dropped his ice-axe among the rocks. He seemed for ever stooping to drink the icy water, or clambering off the trail to test the patches of snow as to quality and depth. "You're missing all the excitement," he cried repeatedly. "There are a hundred pleasures and sensations by the way."

They paused a moment for him to overtake them; he came up panting and exhausted, making remarks about the fading stars, the wind upon the heights, new routes he longed to try up dangerous couloirs, about everything, it seemed, except the work in hand. There was eagerness in him, the kind of excitement that saps energy and wastes the nervous force, threatening a probable collapse before the arduous object is attained.

"Keep to the thing in hand," replied the priest sternly. "We are not really going fast; it is you who are scattering yourself to no purpose. It wears us all. We must husband our resources," and he pointed significantly to the pyramid of the Tour du Néant that gleamed above them at an incredible altitude.

"We are here to amuse ourselves; life is a pleasure, a sensation, or it is noth-ing," grumbled his companion; but there was a gravity in the tone of the older man that discouraged argument and made resistance difficult. The other ar-ranged his pack for the tenth time, twisting his axe through an ingenious scheme of straps and string, and fell silently into line behind his leaders. Limasson moved on again . . . and the darkness at length began to lift. Far overhead, at first, the snowy summits shone with a hue less spectral; a delicate pink spread softly from the east; there was a freshening of the chilly wind; then suddenly the highest peak that topped the others by a thousand feet of soaring rock, stepped sharply into sight, half golden and half rose. At the same instant, the vast Movement of the entire scene slowed down; there came one or two terrific gusts of wind in quick succession; a roar like an avalanche of falling stones boomed distantly—and Limasson stopped dead and held his breath.

For something blocked the way before him, something he knew he could not pass. Gigantic and unformed, it seemed part of the architecture of the deso-late waste about him, while yet it bulked there, enormous in the trembling dawn, as belonging neither to plain nor mountain. Suddenly it was there, where a mo-ment before had been mere emptiness of air. Its massive outline shifted into visibility as though it had risen from the ground. He stood stock still. A cold that was not of this world turned him rigid in his tracks. A few yards behind him the priest had halted too. Further in the rear they heard the stumbling tread of the younger man, and the faint calling of his voice—a feeble, broken sound as of a man whom sudden fear distressed to helplessness.

"We're off the track, and I've lost my way," the words came on the still air. "My axe is gone . . . let us put on the rope! . . . Hark! Do you hear that roar?" And then a sound as though he came slowly groping on his hands and knees.

"You have exhausted yourself too soon," the priest answered sternly. "Stay where you are and rest, for we go no further. This is the place we sought."

There was in his tone a kind of ultimate solemnity that for a moment turned Limasson's attention from the great obstacle that blocked his further way. The darkness lifted veil by veil, not gradually, but by a series of leaps as when some one inexpertly turns a wick. He perceived then that not a single Grandeur loomed in front, but that others of similar kind, some huger than the first, stood all about him, forming an enclosing circle that hemmed him in.

Then, with a start, he recovered himself. Equilibrium and common sense returned. The trick that sight had played upon him, assisted by the rarefied atmosphere of the heights and by the witchery of dawn, was no uncommon one, after all. The long straining of the eyes to pick the way in an uncertain light so easily deceives perspective. Delusion ever follows abrupt change of focus. These shadowy encircling forms were but the rampart of still distant precipices whose giant walls framed the tremendous amphitheatre to the sky. Their closeness was a mere gesture of the dusk and distance.

The shock of the discovery produced an instant's unsteadiness in him that brought bewilderment. He straightened up, raised his head, and looked about him. The cliffs, it seemed to him, shifted back instantly to their accustomed places; as though after all they *had* been close; there was a reeling among the topmost crags; they balanced fearfully, then stood still against a sky already faintly crimson. The roar he heard, that might well have seemed the tumult of their hurrying speed, was in reality but the wind of dawn that rushed against their ribs, beating the echoes out with angry wings. And the lines of trailing mist, streaking the air like proofs of rapid motion, merely coiled and floated in the empty spaces.

He turned to the priest, who had moved up beside him.

"How strange," he said, "is this beginning of new light! My sight went all astray for a passing moment. I thought the mountains stood right across my path. And when I looked up just now it seemed they all ran back." His voice was small and lost in the great listening air.

The man looked fixedly at him. He had removed his slouch hat, hot with the long ascent, and as he answered, a long thin shadow flitted across his features. A breadth of darkness dropped about them. It was as though a mask were forming. The face that now was covered had been—naked. He was so long in answering that Limasson heard his mind sharpening the sentence like a pencil.

He spoke very slowly: "*They* move perhaps even as Their powers move, and Their minutes are our years. Their passage ever is in tumult. There is disorder then among the affairs of men; there is confusion in their minds. There may be ruin and disaster, but out of the wreckage shall issue strong, fresh growth. For like a sea, They pass."

There was in his mien a grandeur that seemed borrowed marvellously from the mountains. His voice was grave and deep; he made no sign or gesture; and in his manner was a curious steadiness that breathed through the language a kind of sacred prophecy.

Long, thundering gusts of wind passed distantly across the precipices as he spoke. The same moment, expecting apparently no rejoinder to his strange utterance, he stooped and began to unpack his knapsack. The change from the sacerdotal language to this commonplace and practical detail was singularly bewildering.

"It is the time to rest," he added, "and the time to eat. Let us prepare." And he drew out several small packets and laid them in a row upon the ground. Awe deepened over Limasson as he watched, and with it a great wonder too. For the words seemed ominous, as though this man, upon the floor of some vast Temple, said: "Let us prepare a sacrifice . . .!" There flashed into him, out of depths that had hitherto concealed it, a lightning clue that hinted at explanation of the entire strange proceeding—of the abrupt meeting with the strangers, the impulsive acceptance of their project for the great ascent, their grave behaviour as though it were a Ceremonial of immense design, his change of position, the bewildering tricks of sight, and the solemn language, finally, of the older man that corroborated what he himself had deemed at first illusion. In a flying second of time this all swept through him—and with it the sharp desire to turn aside, retreat, to run away.

Noting the movement, or perhaps divining the emotion prompting it, the priest looked up quickly. In his tone was a coldness that seemed as though this scene of wintry desolation uttered words: "You have come too far to think of turning back. It is not possible. You stand now at the gates of birth—and death. All that might hinder, you have so bravely cast aside. Be brave now to the end."

And, as Limasson heard the words, there dropped suddenly into him a new and awful insight into humanity, a power that unerringly discovered the spiritual necessities of others, and therefore of himself. With a shock he realised that the younger man who had accompanied them with increasing difficulty as they climbed higher and higher—was but a shadow of reality. Like the porter, he was but an encumbrance who impeded progress. And he turned his eyes to search the desolate landscape.

"You will not find him," said his companion, "for he is gone. Never, unless you weakly call, shall you see him again, nor desire to hear his voice." And Limasson realised that in his heart he had all the while disapproved of the man, disliked him for his theatrical fondness of sensation and effect, more, that he had even hated and despised him. Starvation might crawl upon him where he had fallen and eat his life away before he would stir a finger to save him. It was with the older man he now had dreadful business in hand.

"I am glad," he answered, "for in the end he must have proved my death—our death!"

And they drew closer round the little circle of food the priest had laid upon the rocky ground, an intimate understanding linking them together in a sympathy that completed Limasson's bewilderment. There was bread, he saw, and there was salt; there was also a little flask of deep red wine. In the centre of the circle was a miniature fire of sticks the priest had collected from the bushes of wild rhododendron. The smoke rose upwards in a thin blue line. It did not even quiver, so profound was the surrounding stillness of the mountain air, but far away among the precipices ran the boom of falling water, and behind it again, the muffled roar as of peaks and snow-fields that swept with a rolling thunder through the heavens.

"They are passing," the priest said in a low voice, "and They know that you are here. You have now the opportunity of a lifetime; for, if you yield acceptance of your own free will, success is sure. You stand before the gates of birth and death. They offer you life."

"Yet . . . I denied Them!" He murmured it below his breath.

"Denial is evocation. You called to them, and They have come. The sacrifice of your little personal life is all They ask. Be brave—and yield it."

He took the bread as he spoke, and, breaking it in three pieces, he placed one before Limasson, one before himself, and the third he laid upon the flame which first blackened and then consumed it.

"Eat it and understand," he said, "for it is the nourishment that shall revive your fading life."

Next, with the salt, he did the same. Then, raising the flask of wine, he put it to his lips, offering it afterwards to his companion. When both had drunk there still remained the greater part of the contents. He lifted the vessel with both hands reverently towards the sky. He stood upright.

"The blood of your personal life I offer to Them in your name. By the renunciation which seems to you as death shall you pass through the gates of birth to the life of freedom beyond. For the ultimate sacrifice that They ask of you is—this."

And bending low before the distant heights, he poured the wine upon the rocky ground.

For a period of time Limasson found no means of measuring, so terrible were the emotions in his heart, the priest remained in this attitude of worship and obeisance. The tumult in the mountains ceased. An absolute hush dropped down upon the world. There seemed a pause in the inner history of the universe itself. All waited—till he rose again. And, when he did so, the mask that had for hours now been spreading across his features, was accomplished. The eyes gazed sternly down into his own. Limasson looked—and recognised. He stood face to face with the man whom he knew best of all others in the world . . . himself.

There had been death. There had also been that recovery of splendour which is birth and resurrection.

And the sun that moment, with the sudden surprise that mountains only know, rushed clear above the heights, bathing the landscape and the standing figure with a stainless glory. Into the vast Temple where he knelt, as into that greater inner Temple which is mankind's true House of Royalty, there poured the completing Presence which is—Light.

"For in this way, and in this way only, shall you pass from death to life," sang a chanting voice he recognised also now for the first time as indubitably his own.

It was marvellous. But the birth of light is ever marvellous. It was anguish; but the pangs of resurrection since time began have been accomplished by the sweetness of fierce pain. For the majority still lie in the pre-natal stage, unborn, unconscious of a definite spiritual existence. In the womb they grope and stifle, depending ever upon another. Denial is ever the call to life, a protest against continued darkness for deliverance. Yet birth is the ruin of all that has hitherto been depended on. There comes then that standing alone which at first seems desolate isolation. The tumult of destruction precedes release.

Limasson rose to his feet, stood with difficulty upright, looked about him from the figure so close now at his side to the snowy summit of that Tour du Néant he would never climb. The roar and thunder of *Their* passage was resumed. It seemed the mountains reeled.

"They are passing," sang the voice that was beside him and within him too, "but They have known you, and your offering is accepted. When They come close upon the world there is ever wreckage and disaster in the affairs of men. They bring disorder and confusion into the mind, a confusion that seems final, a disorder that seems to threaten death. For there is tumult in Their Presence, and apparent chaos that seems the abandonment of order. Out of this vast ruin, then, there issues life in new design. The dislocation is its entrance, the dishevelment its strength. There has been birth. . . ."

The sunlight dazzled his eyes. That distant roar, like a wind, came close and swept his face. An icy air, as from a passing star, breathed over him.

"Are you prepared?" he heard.

He knelt again. Without a sign of hesitation or reluctance, he bared his chest to the sun and wind. The flash came swiftly, instantly, descending into his heart with unerring aim. He saw the gleam in the air, he felt the fiery impact of the blow, he even saw the stream gush forth and sink into the rocky ground, far redder than the wine. . . .

He gasped for breath a moment, staggered, reeled, collapsed . . . and within the moment, so quickly did all happen, he was aware of hands that supported him and helped him to his feet. But he was too weak to stand. They carried him up to bed. The porter, and the man who had reached across him for the matches five minutes before, intending conversation, stood, one at his feet and the other at his head. As he passed through the vestibule of the hotel, he saw the people staring, and in his hand he crumpled up the unopened letters he had received so short a time ago.

"I really think—I can manage alone," he thanked them. "If you will set me down, I can walk. I felt dizzy for a moment."

"The heat in the hall—" the gentleman began, in a quiet, sympathetic voice.

They left him standing on the stairs, watching a moment to see that he had quite recovered. Limasson walked up the two flights to his room without faltering. The momentary dizziness had passed. He felt quite himself again, strong, confident, able to stand alone, able to move forward, able to *climb*.

The Damned

"I'm over forty, Frances, and rather sot in my ways," I said good-naturedly, ready to yield if she insisted that our going together on the visit involved her happiness. "My work is rather heavy just now too, as you know. The question is, *could* I work there—with a lot of unassorted people in the house?"

"Mabel doesn't mention any other people, Bill," was my sister's rejoinder. "I gather she's alone—as well as lonely."

By the way she looked sideways out of the window at nothing, it was obvious she was disappointed, but to my surprise she did not urge the point; and as I glanced at Mrs. Franklyn's invitation lying upon her sloping lap the neat, childish handwriting conjured up a mental picture of the banker's widow, with her timid, insignificant personality, her pale grey eyes and her expression as of a backward child. I thought, too, of the roomy country mansion her late husband had altered to suit his particular needs, and of my visit to it a few years ago when its barren spaciousness suggested a wing of Kensington Museum fitted up temporarily as a place to eat and sleep in. Comparing it mentally with the poky Chelsea flat where I and my sister kept impecunious house, I realised other points as well. Unworthy details flashed across me to entice: the fine library, the organ, the quiet work-room I should have, perfect service, the delicious cup of early tea, and hot baths at any moment of the day—without a geyser!

"It's a longish visit, a month—isn't it?" I hedged, smiling at the details that seduced me, and ashamed of my man's selfishness, yet knowing that Frances expected it of me. "There *are* points about it, I admit. If you're set on my going with you, I could manage it all right."

I spoke at length in this way because my sister made no answer. I saw her tired eyes gazing into the dreariness of Oakley Street and felt a pang strike through me. After a pause, in which again she said no word, I added: "So, when you write the letter, you might hint, perhaps, that I usually work all the morning, and—er—am not a very lively visitor! Then she'll understand, you see." And I half-rose to return to my diminutive study, where I was slaving, just then, at an absorbing article on Comparative Æsthetic Values in the Blind and Deaf.

But Frances did not move. She kept her grey eyes upon Oakley Street where the evening mist from the river drew mournful perspectives into view. It was late October. We heard the omnibuses thundering across the bridge. The monotony of that broad, characterless street seemed more than usually depressing. Even in June sunshine it was dead, but with autumn its melancholy soaked into every house between King's Road and the Embankment. It washed thought into the past, instead of inviting it hopefully towards the future. For me, its easy width was an avenue through which nameless slums across the river sent creeping messages of depression, and I always regarded it as Winter's main entrance into London—fog, slush, gloom trooped down it every November, waving their forbidding banners till March came to rout them. Its one claim upon my love was that the south wind swept sometimes unobstructed up it, soft with suggestions of the sea. These lugubrious thoughts I naturally kept to myself, though I never ceased to regret the little flat whose cheapness had seduced us. Now, as I watched my sister's impassive face, I realised that perhaps she, too, felt as I felt, yet, brave woman, without betraying it.

"And, look here, Fanny," I said, putting a hand upon her shoulder as I crossed the room, "it would be the very thing for you. You're worn out with catering and housekeeping. Mabel is your oldest friend, besides, and you've hardly seen her since *he* died—"

"She's been abroad for a year, Bill, and only just came back," my sister interposed. "She came back rather unexpectedly, though I never thought she would go *there* to live—" She stopped abruptly. Clearly, she was only speaking half her mind. "Probably," she went on, "Mabel wants to pick up old links again."

"Naturally," I put in, "yourself chief among them." The veiled reference to the house I let pass. It involved discussing the dead man for one thing.

"I feel *I* ought to go anyhow," she resumed, "and of course it would be jollier if you came too. You'd get in such a muddle here by yourself, and eat wrong things, and forget to air the rooms, and—oh, everything!" She looked up, laughing. "Only," she added, "there's the British Museum—?"

"But there's a big library there," I answered, "and all the books of reference I could possibly want. It was of you I was thinking. You could take up your painting again; you always sell half of what you paint. It would be a splendid rest, too, and Sussex is a jolly country to walk in. By all means, Fanny, I advise—"

Our eyes met, as I stammered in my attempts to avoid expressing the thought that hid in both our minds. My sister had a weakness for dabbling in the various "new" theories of the day, and Mabel, who before her marriage had belonged to foolish societies for investigating the future life to the neglect of the present one, had fostered this undesirable tendency. Her amiable, impressionable temperament was open to every psychic wind that blew. I deplored, detested the whole business. But even more than this I abhorred the later influence that Mr. Franklyn had steeped his wife in, capturing her body and soul in his sombre doctrines. I had dreaded lest my sister also might be caught.

"Now that she is alone again—"

I stopped short. Our eyes now made pretence impossible, for the truth had slipped out inevitably, stupidly, although unexpressed in definite language. We laughed, turning our faces a moment to look at other things in the room. Frances picked up a book and examined its cover as though she had made an important discovery, while I took my case out and lit a cigarette I did not want to smoke. We left the matter there. I went out of the room before further explanation could cause tension. Disagreements grow into discord from such tiny things—wrong adjectives, or a chance inflection of the voice. Frances had a right to her views of life as much as I had. At least, I reflected comfortably, we had separated upon an agreement this time, recognised mutually, though not actually stated.

And this point of meeting was, oddly enough, our way of regarding some one who was dead. For we had both disliked the husband with a great dislike, and during his three years' married life had only been to the house once—for a week-end visit; arriving late on Saturday, we had left after an early breakfast on Monday morning. Ascribing my sister's dislike to a natural jealousy at losing her old friend, I said merely that he displeased me. Yet we both knew that the real emotion lay much deeper. Frances, loyal, honourable creature, had kept silence; and beyond saying that house and grounds—he altered one and laid out the other—distressed her as an expression of his personality somehow ("distressed" was the word she used), no further explanation had passed her lips.

Our dislike of his personality was easily accounted for—up to a point, since both of us shared the artist's point of view that a creed, cut to measure and carefully dried, was an ugly thing, and that a dogma to which believers must subscribe or perish everlastingly was a barbarism resting upon cruelty. But while my own dislike was purely due to an abstract worship of Beauty, my sister's had another twist in it, for with her "new" tendencies, she believed that all religions were an aspect of truth and that no one, even the lowest wretch, could escape "heaven" in the long run.

Samuel Franklyn, the rich banker, was a man universally respected and admired, and the marriage, though Mabel was fifteen years his junior, won general applause; his bride was an heiress in her own right—breweries—and the story of her conversion at a revivalist meeting where Samuel Franklyn had spoken fervidly of heaven, and terrifyingly of sin, hell and damnation, even contained a touch of genuine romance. She was a brand snatched from the burning; his detailed eloquence had frightened her into heaven; salvation came in the nick of time; his words had plucked her from the edge of that lake of fire and brimstone where their worm dieth not and the fire is not quenched. She regarded him as a hero, sighed her relief upon his saintly shoulder, and accepted the peace he offered her with a grateful resignation.

For her husband was a "religious man" who successfully combined great riches with the glamour of winning souls. He was a portly figure, though tall, with masterful, big hands, the fingers rather thick and red; and his dignity, that just escaped being pompous, held in it something that was implacable. A convinced assurance, almost remorseless, gleamed in his eyes when he preached especially, and his threats of hell fire must have scared souls stronger than the timid, receptive Mabel whom he married. He clad himself in long frock-coats that buttoned unevenly, big square boots, and trousers that invariably bagged at the knee and were a little short; he wore low collars, spats occasionally, and a tall black hat that was not of silk. His voice was alternately hard and unctuous; and he regarded theatres, ballrooms and race-courses as the vestibule of that brimstone lake of whose geography he was as positive as of his great banking offices in the City. A philanthropist up to the hilt, however, no one ever doubted his complete sincerity; his convictions were ingrained, his faith borne out by his life—as witness his name upon so many admirable Societies, as treasurer, patron, or heading the donation list. He bulked large in the world of doing good, a broad and stately stone in the rampart against evil. And his heart was genuinely kind and soft for others—who believed as he did.

Yet in spite of this true sympathy with suffering and his desire to help, he was narrow as a telegraph wire and unbending as a church pillar; he was intensely selfish; intolerant as an officer of the Inquisition, his bourgeois soul constructed a revolting scheme of heaven that was reproduced in miniature in all he did and planned. Faith was the *sine qua non* of salvation, and by "faith" he meant belief in his own particular view of things—"which faith, except every one do keep whole and undefiled, without doubt he shall perish everlastingly." All the world but his own small, exclusive sect must be damned eternally—a pity, but alas, inevitable. *He* was right.

Yet he prayed without ceasing, and gave heavily to the poor—the only thing he could not give being big ideas to his provincial and suburban deity. Pettier than an insect, and more obstinate than a mule, he had also the superior, sleek humility of a "chosen one." He was churchwarden, too. He read the Lessons in a "place of worship," either chilly or overheated, where neither organ, vestments, nor lighted candles were permitted, but where the odour of hairwash on the boys' heads in the back rows pervaded the entire building.

This portrait of the banker, who accumulated riches both on earth and in heaven, may possibly be overdrawn, however, because Frances and I were "artistic temperaments" that viewed the type with a dislike and distrust amounting to contempt. The majority considered Samuel Franklyn a worthy man and a good citizen. The majority, doubtless, held the saner view. A few years more, and he certainly would have been made a baronet. He relieved much suffering in the world, as assuredly as he caused many souls the agonies of torturing fear by his emphasis upon damnation. Had there been one point of beauty in him, we might have been more lenient; only we found it not, and, I admit, took little pains to search. I shall never forget the look of dour forgiveness with which he heard our excuses for missing Morning Prayers that Sunday morning of our single visit to The Towers. My sister learned that a change was made soon afterwards, prayers being "conducted" after breakfast instead of before.

The Towers stood solemnly upon a Sussex hill amid park-like modern grounds, but the house cannot better be described—it would be so wearisome for one thing—than by saying that it was a cross between an overgrown, pretentious Norwood villa and one of those saturnine Institutes for cripples the train passes as it slinks ashamed through South London into Surrey. It was "wealthily" furnished and at first sight imposing, but on closer acquaintance revealed a meagre personality, barren and austere. One looked for Rules and Regulations on the walls, all signed By Order. The place was a prison that shut out "the world." There was, of course, no billiard-room, no smoking-room, no room for play of any kind, and the great hall at the back, once a chapel which might have been used for dancing, theatricals, or other innocent amusements, was consecrated in his day to meetings of various kinds, chiefly brigades, temperance or missionary societies. There was a harmonium at one end—on the level floor—a raised dais or platform at the other and a gallery above for the servants, gardeners and coachmen. It was heated with hot-water pipes, and hung with Doré's pictures, though these latter were soon removed and stored out of sight in the attics as being too unspiritual. In polished, shiny wood, it was a representation in miniature of that poky exclusive Heaven he took about with him, externalising it in all he did and planned, even in the grounds about the house.

Changes in The Towers, Frances told me, had been made during Mabel's year of widowhood abroad—an organ put into the big hall, the library made liveable and recatalogued—when it was permissible to suppose she had found her soul again and returned to her normal, healthy views of life, which included enjoyment and play, literature, music and the arts, without, however, a touch of that trivial thoughtlessness usually termed worldliness. Mrs. Franklyn, as I remembered her, was a quiet little woman, shallow, perhaps, and easily influenced, but sincere as a dog and thorough in her faithful friendships. Her tastes at heart were catholic, and that heart was simple and unimaginative. That she took up with the various movements of the day was sign merely that she was searching in her limited way for a belief that should bring her peace. She was, in fact, a very ordinary woman, her calibre a little less than that of Frances. I knew they used to discuss all kinds of theories together, but as these discussions never resulted in action, I had come to regard her as harmless. Still, I was not sorry when she married, and I did not welcome now a renewal of the former intimacy. The philanthropist had given her no children, or she would have made a good and sensible mother. No doubt she would marry again.

"Mabel mentions that she's been alone at The Towers since the end of August," Frances told me at tea-time; "and I'm sure she feels out of it and lonely. It would be a kindness to go. Besides, I always liked her."

I agreed. I had recovered from my attack of selfishness. I expressed my pleasure.

"You've written to accept," I said, half statement and half question.

Frances nodded. "I thank for you," she added quietly, "explaining that you were not free at the moment, but that later, if not inconvenient, you might come down for a bit and join me."

I stared. Frances sometimes had this independent way of deciding things. I was convicted, and punished into the bargain.

Of course there followed argument and explanation, as between brother and sister who were affectionate, but the recording of our talk could be of little interest. It was arranged thus, Frances and I both satisfied. Two days later she departed for The Towers, leaving me alone in the flat with everything planned for my comfort and good behaviour—she was rather a tyrant in her quiet way—and her last words as I saw her off from Charing Cross rang in my head for a long time after she was gone:

"I'll write and let you know, Bill. Eat properly, mind, and let me know if anything goes wrong."

She waved her small gloved hand, nodded her head till the feather brushed the window, and was gone.

II

After the note announcing her safe arrival a week of silence passed, and then a letter came; there were various suggestions for my welfare, and the rest was the usual rambling information and description Frances loved, generously italicised.

". . . and we are quite alone," she went on in her enormous handwriting that seemed such a waste of space and labour, "though some others are coming presently, I believe. You could work here to your heart's content. Mabel *quite* understands, and says she would love to have you when you feel free to come.

She has changed a bit—back to her old natural self: she never mentions *him*. The place has changed too in certain ways: it has more cheerfulness, I think. *She* has put it in, this cheerfulness, spaded it in, if you know what I mean; but it lies about uneasily and is not natural—quite. The organ is a beauty. She must be very rich now, but she's as gentle and sweet as ever. Do you know, Bill, I think he must have *frightened* her into marrying him. I get the impression she was afraid of him." This last sentence was inked out, but I read it through the scratching; the letters being too big to hide. "He had an inflexible will beneath all that oily kindness which passed for spiritual. He was a real personality, I mean. I'm sure he'd have sent you and me cheerfully to the stake in another century—*for our own good*. Isn't it odd she never speaks of him, even to me?" This, again, was stroked through, though without the intention to obliterate—merely because it was repetition, probably. "The only reminder of him in the house now is a big copy of the presentation portrait that stands on the stairs of the Multitechnic Institute at Peckham—you know—that life-size one with his fat hand sprinkled with rings resting on a thick Bible and the other slipped between the buttons of a tight frock-coat. It hangs in the dining-room and rather dominates our meals. I wish Mabel would take it down. I think she'd like to, if she *dared*. There's not a single photograph of him anywhere, even in her own room. Mrs. Marsh is here—you remember her, *his* housekeeper, the wife of the man who got penal servitude for killing a baby or something,—*you* said she robbed him and justified her stealing because the story of the unjust steward was in the Bible! How we laughed over that! *She's* just the same, too, gliding about all over the house and turning up when least expected."

Other reminiscences filled the next two sides of the letter, and ran, without a trace of punctuation, into instructions about a Salamander stove for heating my work-room in the flat; these were followed by things I was to tell the cook, and by requests for several articles she had forgotten and would like sent after her, two of them blouses, with descriptions so lengthy and contradictory that I sighed as I read them—"unless you come down soon, in which case perhaps you wouldn't mind bringing them; not the mauve one I wear in the evening sometimes, but the pale blue one with lace round the collar and the crinkly front. They're in the cupboard—or the drawer, I'm not sure which—of my bedroom. *Ask Annie* if you're in doubt. Thanks most *awfully*. Send a telegram, remember, and we'll meet you in the motor *any time*. I don't quite know if I shall stay the whole month—*alone*. It all depends. . . ." And she closed the letter, the italicised words increasing recklessly towards the end, with a repetition that Mabel would love to have me "for myself," as also to have a "man in the house," and that I only had to telegraph the day and the train. . . . This letter, coming by the second post, interrupted me in a moment of absorbing work, and, having read it through to make sure there was nothing requiring instant attention, I threw it aside and went on with my notes and reading. Within five minutes, however, it was back at me again. That restless thing called "between the lines" fluttered about my mind. My interest in the Balkan States—political article that had been "ordered"—faded. Somewhere, somehow I felt disquieted, disturbed. At first I persisted in my work, forcing myself to concentrate, but soon found that a layer of new impressions floated between the article and my attention. It was like a shadow, though a shadow that dissolved upon inspection. Once or twice I glanced up, expecting to find some one in the room, that the door had opened unobserved and Annie, was waiting for instructions. I heard the 'buses thundering across the bridge. I was aware of Oakley Street. Montenegro and the blue Adriatic melted into the October haze along that depressing Embankment that aped a river bank, and sentences from the letter flashed before my eyes and stung me. Picking it up and reading it through more carefully, I rang the bell and told Annie to find the blouses and pack them for the post, showing her finally the written description, and resenting the superior smile with which she at once interrupted, "*I* know them, sir," and disappeared.

But it was not the blouses: it was that exasperating thing "between the lines" that put an end to my work with its elusive teasing nuisance. The first sharp impression is alone of value in such a case, for once analysis begins the imagination constructs all kinds of false interpretation. The more I thought, the more I grew fuddled. The letter, it seemed to me, wanted to say another thing; instead the eight sheets *conveyed* it merely. It came to the edge of disclosure, then halted. There was something on the writer's mind, and I felt uneasy. Studying the sentences brought, however, no revelation, but increased confusion only; for while the uneasiness remained, the first clear hint had vanished. In the end I closed my books and went out to look up another matter at the British Museum Library. Perhaps I should discover it that way—by turning the mind in a totally new direction. I lunched at the Express Dairy in Oxford Street close by, and telephoned to Annie that I would be home to tea at five.

And at tea, tired physically and mentally after breathing the exhausted air of the Rotunda for five hours, my mind suddenly delivered up its original impression, vivid and clear-cut; no proof accompanied the revelation; it was mere presentiment, but convincing. Frances was disturbed in her mind, her orderly, sensible, housekeeping mind; she was uneasy, even perhaps afraid; something in the house distressed her, and she had need of me. Unless I went down, her time of rest and change, her quite necessary holiday, in fact, would be spoilt. She was too unselfish to say this, but it ran everywhere between the lines. I saw it clearly now. Mrs. Franklyn, moreover—and that meant Frances, too—would like a "man in the house." It was a disagreeable phrase, a sugges-tive way of hinting something she dared not state definitely. The two women in that great, lonely barrack of a house were afraid.

My sense of duty, affection, unselfishness, whatever the composite emo-tion may be termed, was stirred; also my vanity. I acted quickly, lest reflection should warp clear, decent judgment. "Annie," I said, when she answered the bell, "you need not send those blouses by the post. I'll take them down to-morrow when I go. I shall be away a week or two, possibly longer." And, hav-ing looked up a train, I hastened out to telegraph before I could change my fickle mind.

But no desire came that night to change my mind. I was doing the right, the necessary thing. I was even in something of a hurry to get down to The Towers as soon as possible. I chose an early afternoon train.

III

A telegram had told me to come to a town ten miles from the house, so I was saved the crawling train to the local station, and travelled down by an express. As soon as we left London the fog cleared off, and an autumn sun, though without heat in it, painted the landscape with golden browns and yellows. My spirits rose as I lay back in the luxurious motor and sped between the woods and hedges. Oddly enough, my anxiety of overnight had disappeared. It was due, no doubt, to that exaggeration of detail which reflection in loneliness brings. Frances and I had not been separated for over a year, and her letters from The Towers told so little. It had seemed unnatural to be deprived of those intimate particulars of mood and feeling I was accustomed to. We had such confidence in one another, and our affection was so deep. Though she was but five years younger than myself, I regarded her as a child. My attitude was fatherly. In return, she certainly mothered me with a solicitude that never cloyed. I felt no desire to marry while she was still alive. She painted in water-colours with a reasonable success, and kept house for me; I wrote, reviewed books and lectured on æsthetics; we were a humdrum couple of quasi-artists, well satisfied with life, and all I feared for her was that she might become a suffragette or be taken captive by one of these wild theories that caught her imagination sometimes, and that Mabel, for one, had fostered. As for myself, no doubt she deemed me a trifle solid or stolid—I forget which word she pre-ferred—but on the whole there was just sufficient difference of opinion to make intercourse suggestive without monotony, and certainly without quarrel-ling. Drawing in deep draughts of the stinging autumn air, I felt happy and exhilarated. It was like going for a holiday, with comfort at the end of the journey instead of bargaining for centimes.

But my heart sank noticeably the moment the house came into view. The long drive, lined with hostile monkey trees and formal Wellingtonias that were solemn and sedate, was mere extension of the miniature approach to a thousand semi-detached suburban "residences"; and the appearance of The Towers, as we turned the corner with a rush, suggested a commonplace climax to a story that had begun interestingly, almost thrillingly. A villa had escaped from the shadow of the Crystal Palace, thumped its way down by night, grown suddenly monstrous in a shower of rich rain, and settled itself insolently to stay. Ivy climbed about the opulent red-brick walls, but climbed neatly and with disfiguring effect, sham as on a prison or—the simile made me smile—an orphan asylum. There was no hint of the comely roughness of untidy ivy on a ruin. Clipped, trained and precise it was, as on a brand-new protestant church. I swear there was not a bird's nest nor a single earwig in it anywhere. About the porch it was particularly thick, smothering a seventeenth-century lamp with a contrast that was quite horrible. Extensive glass-houses spread away on the further side of the house; the numerous towers to which the building owed its name seemed made to hold school bells; and the window-sills thick with potted flowers, made me think of the desolate suburbs of Brighton or Bexhill. In a commanding position upon the crest of a hill, it overlooked miles of undulating, wooded country southwards to the Downs, but behind it, to the north, thick banks of ilex, holly, and privet protected it from the cleaner and more stimulating winds. Hence, though highly placed, it was shut in. Three years had passed since I last set eyes upon it, but the unsightly memory I had retained was justified by the reality. The place was deplorable.

It is my habit to express my opinions audibly sometimes, when impressions are strong enough to warrant it; but now I only sighed "Oh, dear," as I extricated my legs from many rugs and went into the house. A tall parlourmaid, with the bearing of a grenadier, received me, and standing behind her was Mrs. Marsh, the housekeeper, whom I remembered because her untidy back hair had suggested to me that it had been burnt. I went at once to my room, my hostess already dressing for dinner, but Frances came in to see me just as I was struggling with my black tie that had got tangled like a bootlace. She fastened it for me in a neat, effective bow, and while I held my chin up, for the operation, staring blankly at the ceiling, the impression came—I wondered, was it her touch that caused it?—that something in her trembled. Shrinking perhaps is the truer word. Nothing in her face or manner betrayed it, nor in her pleasant, easy talk while she tidied my things and scolded my slovenly packing, as her habit was, questioning me about the servants at the flat. The blouses, though right, were crumpled, and my scolding was deserved. There was no impatience even. Yet somehow or other the suggestion of a shrinking reserve and holding back reached my mind. She had been lonely, of course, but it was more than that; she was glad that I had come, yet for some reason unstated she could have wished that I had stayed away. We discussed the news that had accumulated during our brief separation, and in doing so the impression, at best exceedingly slight, was forgotten. My chamber was large and beautifully furnished; the hall and dining-room of our flat would have gone into it with a good remainder; yet it was not a place I could settle down in for work. It conveyed the idea of impermanence, making me feel transient as in a hotel bedroom. This, of course, was the fact. But some rooms convey a settled, lasting hospitality even in a hotel; this one did not; and as I was accustomed to work in the room I slept in, at least when visiting, a slight frown must have crept between my eyes.

"Mabel has fitted a work-room for you just out of the library," said the clairvoyant Frances. "No one will disturb you there, and you'll have fifteen thousand books all catalogued within easy reach. There's a private staircase, too. You can breakfast in your room and slip down in your dressing-gown if you want to." She laughed. My spirits took a turn upwards as absurdly as they had gone down.

"And how are *you?*" I asked, giving her a belated kiss. "It's jolly to be together again. I did feel rather lost without you, I'll admit."

"That's natural," she laughed. "I'm so glad!"

She looked well and had country colour in her cheeks. She informed me that she was eating and sleeping well, going out for little walks with Mabel, painting bits of scenery again, and enjoying a complete change and rest; and yet, for all her brave description, the words somehow did not quite ring true. Those last words in particular did not ring true. There lay in her manner, just out of sight, I felt, this suggestion of the exact reverse—of unrest, shrinking, almost of anxiety. Certain small strings in her seemed overtight. "Keyed-up" was the slang expression that crossed my mind. I looked rather searchingly into her face as she was telling me this.

"Only—the evenings," she added, noticing my query, yet rather avoiding my eyes, "the evenings are—well, rather heavy sometimes, and I find it difficult to keep awake."

"The strong air after London makes you drowsy," I suggested, "and you like to get early to bed."

Frances turned and looked at me for a moment steadily. "On the contrary, Bill, I dislike going to bed—here. And Mabel goes so early." She said it lightly enough, fingering the disorder upon my dressing-table in such a stupid way that I saw her mind was working in another direction altogether. She looked up suddenly with a kind of nervousness from the brush and scissors.

"Billy," she said abruptly, lowering her voice, "isn't it odd, but I *hate* sleeping alone here? I can't make it out quite; I've never felt such a thing before in my life. Do you—think it's all nonsense?" And she laughed, with her lips but not with her eyes; there was a note of defiance in her I failed to understand.

"Nothing a nature like yours feels strongly is nonsense, Frances," I replied soothingly.

But I, too, answered with my lips only, for another part of my mind was working elsewhere, and among uncomfortable things. A touch of bewilderment passed over me. I was not certain how best to continue. If I laughed she would tell me no more, yet if I took her too seriously the strings would tighten further. Instinctively, then, this flashed rapidly across me: that something of what she felt, I had also felt, though interpreting it differently. Vague it was, as the coming of rain or storm that announce themselves hours in advance with their hint of faint, unsettling excitement in the air. I had been but a short hour in the house,—big, comfortable, luxurious house,—but had experienced this sense of being unsettled, unfixed, fluctuating—a kind of impermanence that transient lodgers in hotels must feel, but that a guest in a friend's home ought not to feel, be the visit short or long. To Frances, an impressionable woman, the feeling had come in the terms of alarm. She disliked sleeping alone, while yet she longed to sleep. The precise idea in my mind evaded capture, merely brushing through me, three-quarters out of sight; I realised only that we both felt the same thing, and that neither of us could get at it clearly. Degrees of unrest we felt, but the actual thing did not disclose itself. It did not happen.

I felt strangely at sea for a moment. Frances would interpret hesitation as endorsement, and encouragement might be the last thing that could help her.

"Sleeping in a strange house," I answered at length, "is often difficult at first, and one feels lonely. After fifteen months in our tiny flat one feels lost and uncared for in a big house. It's an uncomfortable feeling—I know it well. And this *is* a barrack, isn't it? The masses of furniture only make it worse. One feels in storage somewhere underground—the furniture doesn't furnish. One must never yield to fancies, though—"

Frances looked away towards the windows; she seemed disappointed a little.

"After our thickly-populated Chelsea," I went on quickly, "it seems isolated here."

But she did not turn back, and clearly I was saying the wrong thing. A wave of pity rushed suddenly over me. Was she really frightened, perhaps? She was imaginative, I knew, but never moody; common sense was strong in her, though she had her times of hypersensitiveness. I caught the echo of some unreasoning, big alarm in her. She stood there, gazing across my balcony towards the sea of wooded country that spread dim and vague in the obscurity of the dusk. The deepening shadows entered the room, I fancied, from the grounds below. Following her abstracted gaze a moment, I experienced a curious sharp desire to leave, to escape. Out yonder was wind and space and freedom. This enormous building was oppressive, silent, still. Great catacombs occurred to me, things beneath the ground, imprisonment and capture. I believe I even shuddered a little.

I touched her shoulder. She turned round slowly, and we looked with a certain deliberation into each other's eyes.

"Fanny," I asked, more gravely than I intended, "you are not frightened, are you? Nothing has happened, has it?"

She replied with emphasis. "Of course not! How could it—I mean, why should I?" She stammered, as though the wrong sentence flustered her a second. "It's simply—that I have this ter—this dislike of sleeping alone."

Naturally, my first thought was how easy it would be to cut our visit short. But I did not say this. Had it been a true solution, Frances would have said it for me long ago.

"Wouldn't Mabel double-up with you?" I said instead, "or give you an adjoining room, so that you could leave the door between you open? There's space enough, Heaven knows."

And then, as the gong sounded in the hall below for dinner, she said, as with an effort, this thing:

"Mabel did ask me—on the third night—after I had told her. But I declined."

"You'd rather be alone than with her?" I asked, with a certain relief.

Her reply was so gravely given, a child would have known there was more behind it: "Not that; but that she did not really want it."

I had a moment's intuition and acted on it impulsively. "She feels it too, perhaps, but wishes to face it by herself—and get over it?"

My sister bowed her head, and the gesture made me realise of a sudden how grave and solemn our talk had grown, as though some portentous thing were under discussion. It had come of itself—indefinite as a gradual change of temperature. Yet neither of us knew its nature, for apparently neither of us could state it plainly. Nothing happened, even in our words.

"That *was* my impression," she said, "—that if she yields to it she encourages it. And a habit forms so easily. Just think," she added, with a faint smile that was the first sign of lightness she had yet betrayed, "what a nuisance it would be—everywhere—if everybody was afraid of being alone—like that."

I snatched readily at the chance. We laughed a little, though it was a quiet kind of laughter that seemed wrong. I took her arm and led her towards the door.

"Disastrous, in fact," I agreed.

She raised her voice to its normal pitch again, as I had done. "No doubt it will pass," she said, "now that you have come. Of course, it's chiefly my imagination." Her tone was lighter, though nothing could convince me that the matter itself was light—just then. "And in any case," tightening her grip on my arm as we passed into the bright enormous corridor and caught sight of Mrs. Franklyn waiting in the cheerless hall below, "I'm *very* glad you're here, Bill, and Mabel, I know, is too."

"If it doesn't pass," I just had time to whisper with a feeble attempt at jollity, "I'll come at night and snore outside your door. After that you'll be so glad to get rid of me that you won't mind being alone."

"That's a bargain," said Frances.

I shook my hostess by the hand, made a banal remark about the long interval since last we met, and walked behind them into the great dining-room, dimly lit by candles, wondering in my heart how long my sister and I should stay, and why in the world we had ever left our cosy little flat to enter this desolation of riches and false luxury at all. The unsightly picture of the late Samuel Franklyn, Esq., stared down upon me from the further end of the room above the mighty mantelpiece. He looked, I thought, like some pompous Heavenly Butler who denied to all the world, and to us in particular, the right of entry without presentation cards signed by his hand as proof that we belonged to his own exclusive set. The majority, to his deep grief, and in spite of all his prayers on their behalf, must burn and "perish everlastingly."

IV

With the instinct of the healthy bachelor I always try to make myself a nest in the place I live in, be it for long or short. Whether visiting, in lodging-house, or in hotel, the first essential is this nest—one's own things built into the walls as a bird builds in its feathers. It may look desolate and uncomfortable enough to others, because the central detail is neither bed nor wardrobe, sofa nor arm-chair, but a good solid writing-table that does not wriggle, and that has wide elbow-room. And The Towers is vividly described for me by the single fact that I could not "nest" there. I took several days to discover this, but the first impression of impermanence was truer than I knew. The feathers of the mind refused here to lie one way. They ruffled, pointed and grew wild.

Luxurious furniture does not mean comfort; I might as well have tried to settle down in the sofa and arm-chair department of a big shop. My bedroom was easily managed; it was the private work-room, prepared especially for my reception, that made me feel alien and outcast. Externally, it was all one could desire: an ante-chamber to the great library, with not one, but two generous oak tables, to say nothing of smaller ones against the walls with capacious drawers. There were reading-desks, mechanical devices for holding books, perfect light, quiet as in a church, and no approach but across the huge adjoining room. Yet it did not invite.

"I hope you'll be able to work here," said my little hostess the next morning, as she took me in—her only visit to it while I stayed in the house—and showed me the ten-volume Catalogue. "It's absolutely quiet and no one will disturb you."

"If you can't, Bill, you're not much good," laughed Frances, who was on her arm. "Even I could write in a study like this!"

I glanced with pleasure at the ample tables, the sheets of thick blotting-paper, the rulers, sealing-wax, paper-knives, and all the other immaculate paraphernalia. "It's perfect," I answered, with a secret thrill, yet feeling a little foolish. This was for Gibbon or Carlyle, rather than for my pot-boiling insignificancies. "If I can't write masterpieces here, it's certainly not *your* fault," and I turned with gratitude to Mrs. Franklyn. She was looking straight at me, and there was a question in her small pale eyes I did not understand. Was she noting the effect upon me, I wondered?

"You'll write here—perhaps a story about the house," she said; "Thompson will bring you anything you want; you only have to ring." She pointed to the electric bell on the central table, the wire running neatly down the leg. "No one has ever worked here before, and the library has been hardly used since it was put in. So there's no previous atmosphere to affect your imagination—er—adversely."

We laughed. "Bill isn't that sort," said my sister; while I wished they would go out and leave me to arrange my little nest and set to work.

I thought, of course, it was the huge listening library that made me feel so inconsiderable—the fifteen thousand silent, staring books, the solemn aisles, the deep, eloquent shelves. But when the women had gone and I was alone, the beginning of the truth crept over me, and I felt that first hint of disconsolateness which later became an imperative No. The mind shut down, images ceased to rise and flow. I read, made copious notes, but I wrote no single line at The Towers. Nothing completed itself there. Nothing happened.

The morning sunshine poured into the library through ten long narrow windows; birds were singing; the autumn air, rich with a faint aroma of November melancholy that stung the imagination pleasantly, filled my ante-chamber. I looked out upon the undulating wooded landscape, hemmed in by the sweep of distant Downs, and I tasted a whiff of the sea. Rooks cawed as they floated above the elms, and there were lazy cows in the nearer meadows. A dozen times I tried to make my nest and settle down to work, and a dozen times, like a turning fastidious dog upon a hearth-rug, I rearranged my chair and books and papers. The temptation of the Catalogue and shelves, of course, was accountable for much, yet not, I felt, for all. That was a manageable seduction. My work, moreover, was not of the creative kind that requires absolute absorption; it was the mere readable presentation of data I had accumulated. My note-books were charged with facts ready to tabulate—facts, too, that interested me keenly. A mere effort of the will was necessary, and concentration of no difficult kind. Yet, somehow, it seemed beyond me: something for ever pushed the facts into disorder . . . and in the end I sat in the sunshine, dipping into a dozen books selected from the shelves outside, vexed with myself and only half-enjoying it. I felt restless. I wanted to be elsewhere.

And even while I read, attention wandered. Frances, Mabel, her late husband, the house and grounds, each in turn and sometimes all together, rose uninvited into the stream of thought, hindering any consecutive flow of work. In disconnected fashion came these pictures that interrupted concentration, yet presenting themselves as broken fragments of a bigger thing my mind already groped for unconsciously. They fluttered round this hidden thing of which they were aspects, fugitive interpretations, no one of them bringing complete revelation. There was no adjective, such as pleasant or unpleasant, that I could attach to what I felt, beyond that the result was unsettling. Vague as the atmosphere of a dream, it yet persisted, and I could not dissipate it. Isolated words or phrases in the lines I read sent questions scouring across my mind, sure sign that the deeper part of me was restless and ill at ease.

Rather trivial questions, too—half-foolish interrogations, as of a puzzled or curious child: Why was my sister afraid to sleep alone, and why did her friend feel a similar repugnance, yet seek to conquer it? Why was the solid luxury of the house without comfort, its shelter without the sense of permanence? Why had Mrs. Franklyn asked *us* to come, artists, unbelieving vagabonds, types at the furthest possible remove from the saved sheep of her husband's household? Had a reaction set in against the hysteria of her conversion? I had seen no signs of religious fervour in her; her atmosphere was that of an ordinary, high-minded woman, yet a woman of the world. Lifeless, though, a little, perhaps, now that I came to think about it: she had made no definite impression upon me of any kind. And my thoughts ran vaguely after this fragile clue.

Closing my book, I let them run. For, with this chance reflection came the discovery that I could not *see* her clearly—could not feel her soul, her personality. Her face, her small pale eyes, her dress and body and walk, all these stood before me like a photograph; but her Self evaded me. She seemed not there, lifeless, empty, a shadow—nothing. The picture was disagreeable, and I put it by. Instantly she melted out, as though light thought had conjured up a phantom that had no real existence. And at that very moment, singularly enough, my eye caught sight of her moving past the window, going silently along the gravel path. I watched her, a sudden new sensation gripping me. "There goes a prisoner," my thought instantly ran, "one who wishes to escape, but cannot."

What brought the outlandish notion, heaven only knows. The house was of her own choice, she was twice an heiress, and the world lay open at her feet. Yet she stayed—unhappy, frightened, caught. All this flashed over me, and made a sharp impression even before I had time to dismiss it as absurd. But a moment later explanation offered itself, though it seemed as far-fetched as the original impression. My mind, being logical, was obliged to provide something, apparently. For Mrs. Franklyn, while dressed to go out, with thick walking-boots, a pointed stick, and a motor-cap tied on with a veil as for the windy lanes, was obviously content to go no further than the little garden paths. The costume was a sham and a pretence. It was this, and her lithe, quick movements that suggested a caged creature—a creature tamed by fear and cruelty that cloaked themselves in kindness—pacing up and down, unable to realise why it got no further, but always met the same bars in exactly the same place. The mind in her was barred.

I watched her go along the paths and down the steps from one terrace to another, until the laurels hid her altogether; and into this mere imagining of a moment came a hint of something slightly disagreeable, for which my mind, search as it would, found no explanation at all. I remembered then certain other little things. They dropped into the picture of their own accord. In a mind not deliberately hunting for clues, pieces of a puzzle sometimes come together in this way, bringing revelation, so that for a second there flashed across me, vanishing instantly again before I could consider it, a large, distressing thought that I can only describe vaguely as a Shadow. Dark and ugly, oppressive certainly it might be described, with something torn and dreadful about the edges that suggested pain and strife and terror. The interior of a prison with two rows of occupied condemned cells, seen years ago in New York, sprang to memory after it—the connection between the two impossible to surmise even. But the "certain other little things" mentioned above were these: that Mrs. Franklyn, in last night's dinner talk, had always referred to "this house," but never called it "home"; and had emphasised unnecessarily, for a well-bred woman, our "great kindness" in coming down to stay so long with her. Another time, in answer to my futile compliment about the "stately rooms," she said quietly, "It is an enormous house for so small a party; but I stay here very little, and only till I get it straight again." The three of us were going up the great staircase to bed as this was said, and, not knowing quite her meaning, I dropped the subject. It edged delicate ground, I felt. Frances added no word of her own. It now occurred to me abruptly that "stay" was the word made use of, when "live" would have been more natural. How insignificant to recall! Yet why did they suggest themselves just at this moment? . . . And, on going to Frances's room to make sure she was not nervous or lonely, I realised abruptly, that Mrs. Franklyn, of course, had talked with *her* in a confidential sense that I, as a mere visiting brother, could not share. Frances had told me nothing. I might easily have wormed it out of her, had I not felt that for us to discuss further our hostess and her house merely because we were under the roof together, was not quite nice or loyal.

"I'll call you, Bill, if I'm scared," she had laughed as we parted, my room being just across the big corridor from her own. I had fallen asleep, thinking what in the world was meant by "getting it straight again."

And now in my ante-chamber to the library, on the second morning, sitting among piles of foolscap and sheets of spotless blotting-paper, all useless to me, these slight hints came back and helped to frame the big, vague Shadow I have mentioned. Up to the neck in this Shadow, almost drowned, yet just treading water, stood the figure of my hostess in her walking costume. Frances and I seemed swimming to her aid. The Shadow was large enough to include both house and grounds, but further than that I could not see. . . . Dismissing it, I fell to reading my purloined book again. Before I turned another page, however, another startling detail leaped out at me: the figure of Mrs. Franklyn in the Shadow was not living. It floated helplessly, like a doll or puppet that has no life in it. It was both pathetic and dreadful.

Any one who sits in reverie thus, of course, may see similar ridiculous pictures when the will no longer guides construction. The incongruities of dreams are thus explained. I merely record the picture as it came. That it remained by me for several days, just as vivid dreams do, is neither here nor there. I did not allow myself to dwell upon it. The curious thing, perhaps, is that from this moment I date my inclination, though not yet my desire, to leave. I purposely say "to leave." I cannot quite remember when the word changed to that aggressive, frantic thing which is escape.

V

We were left delightfully to ourselves in this pretentious country mansion with the soul of a villa. Frances took up her painting again, and, the weather being propitious, spent hours out of doors, sketching flowers, trees and nooks of woodland, garden, even the house itself where bits of it peered suggestively across the orchards. Mrs. Franklyn seemed always busy about something or other, and never interfered with us except to propose motoring, tea in another part of the lawn, and so forth. She flitted everywhere, preoccupied, yet apparently doing nothing. The house engulfed her rather. No visitors called. For one thing, she was not supposed to be back from abroad yet; and for another, I think, the neighbourhood—her husband's neighbourhood—was puzzled by her sudden cessation from good works. Brigades and temperance societies did not ask to hold their meetings in the big hall, and the vicar arranged the school-treats in another's field without explanation. The full-length portrait in the dining-room, and the presence of the housekeeper with the "burnt" back-hair, indeed, were the only reminders of the man who once had lived here. Mrs. Marsh retained her place in silence, well-paid sinecure as it doubtless was, yet with no hint of that suppressed disapproval one might have expected from her. Indeed, there was nothing positive to disapprove, since nothing "worldly" entered grounds or building. In her master's lifetime she had been another "brand snatched from the burning," and it had then been her custom to give vociferous "testimony" at the revival meetings where he adorned the platform and led in streams of prayer. I saw her sometimes on the stairs, hovering, wandering, half-watching and half-listening, and the idea came to me once that this woman somehow formed a link with the departed influence of her bigoted employer. She, alone among us, *belonged* to the house, and looked at home there. When I saw her talking—oh, with such correct and respectful mien—to Mrs. Franklyn, I had the feeling that for all her unaggressive attitude, she yet exerted some influence that sought to make her mistress stay in the building for ever—live there. She would prevent her escape, prevent her "getting it straight again," thwart somehow her will to freedom, if she could. The idea in me was of the most fleeting kind. But another time, when I came down late at night to get a book from the library ante-chamber, and found her sitting in the hall—alone—the impression left upon me was the reverse of fleeting. I can never forget the vivid, disagreeable effect it produced upon me. What was she doing there at half-past eleven at night, all alone in the darkness? She was sitting upright, stiff, in a big chair below the clock. It gave me a turn. It was so incongruous and odd. She rose quietly as I turned the corner of the stairs, and asked me respectfully, her eyes cast down as usual, whether I had finished with the library, so that she might lock up. There was no more to it than that; but the picture stayed with me—unpleasantly.

These various impressions came to me at odd moments, of course, and not in a single sequence as I now relate them. I was hard at work before three days were past, not writing, as explained, but reading, making notes, and gathering material from the library for future use. It was in chance moments that these curious flashes came, catching me unawares with a touch of surprise that sometimes made me start. For they proved that my under-mind was still conscious of the Shadow, and that far away out of sight lay the cause of it that left me with a vague unrest, unsettled, seeking to "nest" in a place that did not want me. Only when this deeper part knows harmony, perhaps, can good brain work result, and my inability to write was thus explained. Certainly, I was always seeking for something here I could not find—an explanation that continually evaded me. Nothing but these trivial hints offered themselves. Lumped together, however, they had the effect of defining the Shadow a little. I became more and more aware of its very real existence. And, if I have made little mention of Frances and my hostess in this connection, it is because they contributed at first little or nothing towards the discovery of what this story tries to tell. Our life was wholly external, normal, quiet, and uneventful; conversation banal—Mrs. Franklyn's conversation in particular. They said nothing that suggested revelation. Both were in this Shadow, and both knew that they were in it, but neither betrayed by word or act a hint of interpretation. They talked privately, no doubt, but of that I can report no details.

And so it was that, after ten days of a very commonplace visit, I found myself looking straight into the face of a Strangeness that defied capture at close quarters. "There's something here that never happens," were the words that rose in my mind, "and that's why none of us can speak of it." And as I looked out of the window and watched the vulgar blackbirds, with toes turned in, boring out their worms, I realised sharply that even they, as indeed everything large and small in the house and grounds, shared this strangeness, and was twisted out of normal appearance because of it. Life, as expressed in the entire place, was crumpled, dwarfed, emasculated. God's meanings here were crippled, His love of joy was stunted. Nothing in the garden danced or sang. There was hate in it. "The Shadow," my thought hurried on to completion, "is a manifestation of hate; and hate is the Devil." And then I sat back frightened in my chair, for I knew that I had partly found the truth.

Leaving my books, I went out into the open. The sky was overcast, yet the day by no means gloomy, for a soft, diffused light oozed through the clouds and turned all things warm and almost summery. But I saw the grounds now in their nakedness because I understood. Hate means strife, and the two together weave the robe that terror wears. Having no so-called religious beliefs myself, nor belonging to any set of dogmas called a creed, I could stand outside these feelings and observe. Yet they soaked into me sufficiently for me to grasp sympathetically what others, with more cabined souls (I flattered myself) might feel. That picture in the dining-room stalked everywhere, hid behind every tree, peered down upon me from the peaked ugliness of the bourgeois towers, and left the impress of its powerful hand upon every bed of flowers. "You must not do this, you must not do that," went past me through the air. "You must not leave these narrow paths," said the rigid iron railings of black. "You shall not walk here," was written on the lawns. "Keep to the steps," "Don't pick the flowers; make no noise of laughter, singing, dancing," was placarded all over the rose-garden, and "Trespassers will be—not prosecuted but—*destroyed*" hung from the crest of monkey-tree and holly. Guarding the ends of each artificial terrace stood gaunt, implacable policemen, warders, gaolers. "Come with us," they chanted, "or be damned eternally."

I remember feeling quite pleased with myself that I had discovered this obvious explanation of the prison-feeling the place breathed out. That the posthumous influence of heavy old Samuel Franklyn might be an inadequate solution did not occur to me. By "getting the place straight again," his widow, of course, meant forgetting the glamour of fear and foreboding his depressing creed had temporarily forced upon her; and Frances, delicately-minded being, did not speak of it because it was the influence of the man her friend had loved. I felt lighter; a load was lifted from me. "To trace the unfamiliar to the familiar," came back a sentence I had read somewhere, "is to understand." It was a real relief. I could talk with Frances now, even with my hostess, no danger of treading clumsily. For the key was in my hands. I might even help to dissipate the Shadow, "to get it straight again." It seemed, perhaps, our long invitation was explained!

I went into the house laughing—at myself a little. "Perhaps after all the artist's outlook, with no hard and fast dogmas, is as narrow as the others! How small humanity is! And why is there no possible and true combination of *all* outlooks?"

The feeling of "unsettling" was very strong in me just then, in spite of my big discovery which was to clear everything up. And at that moment I ran into Frances on the stairs, with a portfolio of sketches under her arm.

It came across me then abruptly that, although she had worked a great deal since we came, she had shown me nothing. It struck me suddenly as odd, unnatural. The way she tried to pass me now confirmed my new-born suspicion that—well, that her results were hardly what they ought to be.

"Stand and deliver!" I laughed, stepping in front of her. "I've seen nothing you've done since you've been here, and as a rule you show me all your things. I believe they are atrocious and degrading!" Then my laughter froze.

She made a sly gesture to slip past me, and I almost decided to let her go, for the expression that flashed across her face shocked me. She looked uncomfortable and ashamed; the colour came and went a moment in her cheeks, making me think of a child detected in some secret naughtiness. It was almost fear.

"It's because they're not finished then?" I said, dropping the tone of banter, "or because they're too good for me to understand?" For my criticism of painting, she told me, was crude and ignorant sometimes. "But you'll let me see them later, won't you?"

Frances, however, did not take the way of escape I offered. She changed her mind. She drew the portfolio from beneath her arm instead. "You can see them if you *really* want to, Bill," she said quietly, and her tone reminded me of a nurse who says to a boy just grown out of childhood, "you are old enough now to look upon horror and ugliness—only I don't advise it."

"I do want to," I said, and made to go downstairs with her. But, instead, she said in the same low voice as before, "Come up to my room, we shall be undisturbed there." So I guessed that she had been on her way to show the paintings to our hostess, but did not care for us all three to see them together. My mind worked furiously.

"Mabel asked me to do them," she explained, in a tone of submissive horror, once the door was shut, "in fact, she begged it of me. You know how persistent she is in her quiet way. I—er—had to."

She flushed and opened the portfolio on the little table by the window, standing behind me as I turned the sketches over—sketches of the grounds and trees and garden. In the first moment of inspection, however, I did not take in clearly why my sister's sense of modesty had been offended. For my attention flashed a second elsewhere. Another bit of the puzzle had dropped into place, defining still further the nature of what I called "the Shadow." Mrs. Franklyn, I now remembered, had suggested to me in the library that I might perhaps write something about the place, and I had taken it for one of her banal sentences and paid no further attention. I realised now that it was said in earnest. She wanted our interpretations, as expressed in our respective "talents," painting and writing. Her invitation *was* explained. She left us to ourselves on purpose.

"I should like to tear them up," Frances was whispering behind me with a shudder, "only I promised—" She hesitated a moment.

"Promised not to?" I asked, with a queer feeling of distress, my eyes glued to the papers.

"Promised always to show them to her first," she finished so low I barely caught it.

I have no intuitive, immediate grasp of the value of paintings; results come to me slowly, and though every one believes his own judgment to be good, I dare not claim that mine is worth more than that of any other layman. Frances had too often convicted me of gross ignorance and error. I can only say that I examined these sketches with a feeling of amazement that contained revulsion, if not actually horror and disgust. They were outrageous. I felt hot for my sister, and it was a relief to know she had moved across the room on some pretence or other, and did not examine them with me. Her talent, of course, is mediocre, yet she has her moments of inspiration—moments, that is to say, when a view of Beauty not normally her own flames divinely through her. And these interpretations struck me forcibly as being thus "inspired,"—not her own. They were uncommonly well done; they were also atrocious. The meaning in them, however, was never more than hinted. There the unholy skill and power came in; they suggested so abominably, leaving most to the imagination. To find such significance in a bourgeois villa garden, and to interpret it with such delicate yet legible certainty, was a kind of symbolism that was sinister, even diabolical. The delicacy was her own, but the point of view was another's. And the word that rose in my mind was not the gross description of "impure," but the more fundamental qualification—"un-pure."

In silence I turned the sketches over one by one, as a boy hurries through the pages of an evil book lest he be caught.

"What does Mabel do with them?" I asked presently, in a low tone, as I neared the end. "Does she keep them?"

"She makes notes about them in a book and then destroys them," was the reply from the end of the room. I heard a sigh of relief. "I'm glad you've seen them, Bill. I wanted you to—but was afraid to show them. You understand?"

"I understand," was my reply, though it was not a question intended to be answered. All I understood really was that Mabel's mind was as sweet and pure as my sister's, and that she had some good reason for what she did. She destroyed the sketches, but first made notes! It was an interpretation of the place she sought. Brother-like, I felt resentment, though, that Frances should waste her time and talent, when she might be doing work that she could sell. Naturally, I felt other things as well. . . .

"Mabel pays me five guineas for each one," I heard. "Absolutely insists."

I stared at her stupidly a moment, bereft of speech or wit.

"I must either accept, or go away," she went on calmly, but a little white. "I've tried everything. There was a scene the third day I was here—when I showed her my first result. I wanted to write to you, but hesitated—"

"It's unintentional, then, on your part—forgive my asking it, Frances, dear?" I blundered, hardly knowing what to think or say. "Between the lines" of her letter came back to me. "I mean, you make the sketches in your ordinary way and—the result comes out of itself, so to speak?"

She nodded, throwing her hands out like a Frenchman. "We needn't keep the money for ourselves, Bill. We can give it away, but—I must either accept or leave," and she repeated the shrugging gesture. She sat down on the chair facing me, staring helplessly at the carpet.

"You say there was a scene?" I went on presently. "She insisted?"

"She begged me to continue," my sister replied very quietly. "She thinks—that is, she has an idea or theory that there's something about the place—something she can't get at quite." Frances stammered badly. She knew I did not encourage her wild theories.

"Something she feels, yes," I helped her, more than curious.

"Oh, you know what I mean, Bill," she said desperately. "That the place is saturated with some influence that she is herself too positive or too stupid to interpret. She's trying to make herself negative and receptive, as she calls it, but can't, of course, succeed. Haven't you noticed how dull and impersonal and insipid she seems, as though she had no personality? She thinks impressions will come to her that way. But they don't—"

"Naturally."

"So she's trying me—us—what she calls the sensitive and impressionable artistic temperament. She says that until she is sure exactly what this influence is, she can't fight it, turn it out, 'get the house straight,' as she phrases it."

Remembering my own singular impressions, I felt more lenient than I might otherwise have done. I tried to keep impatience out of my voice.

"And this influence, what—whose is it?"

We used the pronoun that followed in the same breath, for I answered my own question at the same moment as she did:

"His." Our heads nodded involuntarily towards the floor, the dining-room being directly underneath.

And my heart sank, my curiosity died away on the instant, I felt bored. A commonplace haunted house was the last thing in the world to amuse or interest me. The mere thought exasperated, with its suggestions of imagination, overwrought nerves, hysteria, and the rest. Mingled with my other feelings was certainly disappointment. To see a figure or feel a "presence," and report from day to day strange incidents to each other would be a form of weariness I could never tolerate.

"But really, Frances," I said firmly, after a moment's pause, "it's too far-fetched, this explanation. A curse, you know, belongs to the ghost stories of early Victorian days." And only my positive conviction that there *was* something after all worth discovering, and that it most certainly was *not* this, prevented my suggesting that we terminate our visit forthwith, or as soon as we decently could. "This is not a haunted house, whatever it is," I concluded somewhat vehemently, bringing my hand down upon her odious portfolio.

My sister's reply revived my curiosity sharply.

"I was waiting for you to say that. Mabel says exactly the same. *He* is in it—but it's something more than that alone, something far bigger and more complicated." Her sentence seemed to indicate the sketches, and though I caught the inference I did not take it up, having no desire to discuss them with her just then, indeed, if ever.

I merely stared at her and listened. Questions, I felt sure, would be of little use. It was better she should say her thought in her own way.

"He is one influence, the most recent," she went on slowly, and always very calmly, "but there are others—deeper layers, as it were—underneath. If his were the only one, something would happen. But nothing ever does happen. The others hinder and prevent—as though each were struggling to predominate."

I had felt it already myself. The idea was rather horrible. I shivered.

"That's what is so ugly about it—that nothing ever happens," she said. "There is this endless anticipation—always on the dry edge of a result that never materializes. It is torture. Mabel is at her wits' ends, you see. And when she begged me—what I felt about my sketches—I mean—" She stammered badly as before.

I stopped her. I had judged too hastily. That queer symbolism in her paintings, pagan and yet not innocent, was, I understood, the result of mixture. I did not pretend to understand, but at least I could be patient. I consequently held my peace. We did talk on a little longer, but it was more general talk that avoided successfully our hostess, the paintings, wild theories, and *him*—until at length the emotion Frances had hitherto so successfully kept under burst vehemently forth again. It had hidden between her calm sentences, as it had hidden between the lines of her letter. It swept her now from head to foot, packed tight in the thing she then said.

"Then, Bill, if it is not an ordinary haunted house," she asked, *"what is it?"*

The words were commonplace enough. The emotion was in the tone of her voice that trembled; in the gesture she made, leaning forward and clasping both hands upon her knees, and in the slight blanching of her cheeks as her brave eyes asked the question and searched my own with anxiety that bordered upon panic. In that moment she put herself under my protection. I winced.

"And why," she added, lowering her voice to a still and furtive whisper, "does nothing ever happen? If only,"—this with great emphasis—"something *would* happen—break this awful tension—bring relief. It's the waiting I cannot stand." And she shivered all over as she said it, a touch of wildness in her eyes.

I would have given much to have made a true and satisfactory answer. My mind searched frantically for a moment, but in vain. There lay no sufficient answer in me. I felt what she felt, though with differences. No conclusive explanation lay within reach. Nothing happened. Eager as I was to shoot the entire business into the rubbish heap where ignorance and superstition discharge their poisonous weeds, I could not honestly accomplish this. To treat Frances as a child, and merely "explain away" would be to strain her confidence in my protection, so affectionately claimed. It would further be dishonest to myself—weak, besides—to deny that I had also felt the strain and tension even as she did. While my mind continued searching, I returned her stare in silence; and Frances then, with more honesty and insight than my own, gave suddenly the answer herself—an answer whose truth and adequacy, so far as they went, I could not readily gainsay:

"I think, Bill, because it is too big to happen here—to happen anywhere, indeed, all at once—and too awful!"

To have tossed the sentence aside as nonsense, argued it away, proved that it was really meaningless, would have been easy—at any other time or in any other place; and, had the past week brought me none of the vivid impressions it had brought me, this is doubtless what I should have done. My narrowness again was proved. We understand in others only what we have in ourselves. But her explanation, in a measure, I knew was true. It hinted at the strife and struggle that my notion of a Shadow had seemed to cover thinly.

"Perhaps," I murmured lamely, waiting in vain for her to say more. "But you said just now that you felt the thing was 'in layers,' as it were. Do you mean each one—each influence—fighting for the upper hand?"

I used her phraseology to conceal my own poverty. Terminology, after all, was nothing, provided we could reach the idea itself.

Her eyes said yes. She had her clear conception, arrived at independently, as was her way. And, unlike her sex, she kept it clear, unsmothered by too many words.

"One set of influences gets at me, another gets at you. It's according to our temperaments, I think." She glanced significantly at the vile portfolio. "Sometimes they are mixed—and therefore false. There has always been in me, more than in you, the pagan thing, perhaps, though never, thank God, like *that*."

The frank confession of course invited my own, as it was meant to do. Yet it was difficult to find the words.

"What I have felt in this place, Frances, I honestly can hardly tell you, because—er—my impressions have not arranged themselves in any definite form I can describe. The strife, the agony of vainly-sought escape, and the unrest—a sort of prison atmosphere—this I have felt at different times and with varying degrees of strength. But I find, as yet, no final label to attach. I couldn't say pagan, Christian, or anything like that, I mean, as you do. As with the blind and deaf, you may have an intensification of certain senses denied to me, or even another sense altogether in embryo—"

"Perhaps," she stopped me, anxious to keep to the point, "you feel it as Mabel does. She feels the whole thing *complete*."

"That also is possible," I said very slowly. I was thinking behind my words. Her odd remark that it was "big and awful" came back upon me as true. A vast sensation of distress and discomfort swept me suddenly. Pity was in it, and a fierce contempt, a savage, bitter anger as well. Fury against some sham authority was part of it.

"Frances," I said, caught unawares, and dropping all pretence, "what in the world can it be?" I looked hard at her. For some minutes neither of us spoke.

"Have *you* felt no desire to interpret it?" she asked presently.

"Mabel did suggest my writing something about the house," was my reply, "but I've felt nothing imperative. That sort of writing is not my line, you know. My own feeling," I added, noticing that she waited for more, "is the impulse to explain, discover, get it out of me somehow, and so get rid of it. Not by writing, though—as yet." And again I repeated my former question: "What in the world do you think it is?" My voice had become involuntarily hushed. There was awe in it.

Her answer, given with slow emphasis, brought back all my reserve: the phraseology provoked me rather:—

"Whatever it is, Bill, it is not of God."

I got up to go downstairs. I believe I shrugged my shoulders. "Would you like to leave, Frances? Shall we go back to town?" I suggested this at the door, and hearing no immediate reply, I turned back to look. Frances was sitting with her head bowed over and buried in her hands. The attitude horribly suggested tears. No woman, I realised, can keep back the pressure of strong emotion as long as Frances had done, without ending in a fluid collapse. I waited a moment uneasily, longing to comfort, yet afraid to act—and in this way discovered the existence of the appalling emotion in myself, hitherto but half guessed. At all costs a scene must be prevented: it would involve such exaggeration and over-statement. Brutally, such is the weakness of the ordinary man, I turned the handle to go out, but my sister then raised her head. The sunlight caught her face, framed untidily in its auburn hair, and I saw her wonderful expression with a start. Pity, tenderness and sympathy shone in it like a flame. It was undeniable. There shone through all her features the imperishable love and yearning to sacrifice self for others which I have seen in only one type of human being. It was the great mother look.

"We must stay by Mabel and help her get it straight," she whispered, making the decision for us both.

I murmured agreement. Abashed and half ashamed, I stole softly from the room and went out into the grounds. And the first thing clearly realised when alone was this: that the long scene between us was without definite result. The exchange of confidence was really nothing but hints and vague suggestion. We had decided to stay, but it was a negative decision not to leave rather than a positive action. All our words and questions, our guesses, inferences, explanations, our most subtle allusions and insinuations, even the odious paintings themselves, were without definite result. Nothing had happened.

VI

And instinctively, once alone, I made for the places where she had painted her extraordinary pictures; I tried to see what she had seen. Perhaps, now that she had opened my mind to another view, I should be sensitive to some similar interpretation and possibly by way of literary expression. If I were to write about the place, I asked myself, how should I treat it? I deliberately invited an interpretation in the way that came easiest to me—writing.

But in this case there came no such revelation. Looking closely at the trees and flowers, the bits of lawn and terrace, the rose-garden and corner of the house where the flaming creeper hung so thickly, I discovered nothing of the odious, unpure thing her colour and grouping had unconsciously revealed. At first, that is, I discovered nothing. The reality stood there, commonplace and ugly, side by side with her distorted version of it that lay in my mind. It seemed incredible. I tried to force it, but in vain. My imagination, ploughed less deeply than hers, or to another pattern, grew different seed. Where I saw the gross soul of an overgrown suburban garden, inspired by the spirit of a vulgar, rich revivalist who loved to preach damnation, she saw this rush of pagan liberty and joy, this strange licence of primitive flesh which, tainted by the other, produced the adulterated, vile result.

Certain things, however, gradually then became apparent, forcing themselves upon me, willy nilly. They came slowly, but overwhelmingly. Not that facts had changed, or natural details altered in the grounds—this was impossible—but that I noticed for the first time various aspects I had not noticed before—trivial enough, yet for me, just then, significant. Some I remembered from previous days; others I saw now as I wandered to and fro, uneasy, uncomfortable,—almost, it seemed, watched by some one who took note of my impressions. The details were so foolish, the total result so formidable. I was half aware that others tried hard to make me see. It was deliberate. My sister's phrase, "one layer got at me, another gets at you," flashed, undesired, upon me.

For I saw, as with the eyes of a child, what I can only call a goblin garden—house, grounds, trees, and flowers belonged to a goblin world that children enter through the pages of their fairy tales. And what made me first aware of it was the whisper of the wind behind me, so that I turned with a sudden start, feeling that something had moved closer. An old ash tree, ugly and ungainly, had been artificially trained to form an arbour at one end of the terrace that was a tennis lawn, and the leaves of it now went rustling together, swishing as they rose and fell. I looked at the ash tree, and felt as though I had passed that moment between doors into this goblin garden that crouched behind the real one. Below, at a deeper layer perhaps, lay hidden the one my sister had entered.

To deal with my own, however, I call it goblin, because an odd aspect of the quaint in it yet never quite achieved the picturesque. Grotesque, probably, is the truer word, for everywhere I noticed, and for the first time, this slight alteration of the natural due either to the exaggeration of some detail, or to its suppression, generally, I think, to the latter. Life everywhere appeared to me as blocked from the full delivery of its sweet and lovely message. Some counter influence stopped it—suppression; or sent it awry—exaggeration. The house itself, mere expression, of course, of a narrow, limited mind, was sheer ugliness; it required no further explanation. With the grounds and garden, so far as shape and general plan were concerned, this was also true; but that trees and flowers and other natural details should share the same deficiency perplexed my logical soul, and even dismayed it. I stood and stared, then moved about, and stood and stared again. Everywhere was this mockery of a sinister, unfinished aspect. I sought in vain to recover my normal point of view. My mind had found this goblin garden and wandered to and fro in it, unable to escape.

The change was in myself, of course, and so trivial were the details which illustrated it, that they sound absurd, thus mentioned one by one. For me, they proved it, is all I can affirm. The goblin touch lay plainly everywhere: in the forms of the trees, planted at neat intervals along the lawns; in this twisted ash that rustled just behind me; in the shadow of the gloomy Wellingtonias, whose sweeping skirts obscured the grass; but especially, I noticed, in the tops and crests of them. For here, the delicate, graceful curves of last year's growth seemed to shrink back into themselves. None of them pointed upwards. Their life had failed and turned aside just when it should have become triumphant. The character of a tree reveals itself chiefly at the extremities, and it was precisely here that they all drooped and achieved this hint of goblin distortion—in the growth, that is, of the last few years. What ought to have been fairy, joyful, natural, was instead uncomely to the verge of the grotesque. Spontaneous expression was arrested. My mind perceived a goblin garden, and was caught in it. The place grimaced at me.

With the flowers it was similar, though far more difficult to detect in detail for description. I saw the smaller vegetable growth as impish, half-malicious. Even the terraces sloped ill, as though their ends had sagged since they had been so lavishly constructed; their varying angles gave a queerly bewildering aspect to their sequence that was unpleasant to the eye. One might wander among their deceptive lengths and get lost—lost among open terraces!—with the house quite close at hand. Unhomely seemed the entire garden, unable to give repose, restlessness in it everywhere, almost strife, and discord certainly.

Moreover, the garden grew into the house, the house into the garden, and in both was this idea of resistance to the natural—the spirit that says No to joy. All over it I was aware of the effort to achieve another end, the struggle to burst forth and escape into free, spontaneous expression that should be happy and natural, yet the effort for ever frustrated by the weight of this dark shadow that rendered it abortive. Life crawled aside into a channel that was a cul-de-sac, then turned horribly upon itself. Instead of blossom and fruit, there were weeds. This approach of life I was conscious of—then dismal failure. There was no fulfilment. Nothing happened.

And so, through this singular mood, I came a little nearer to understand the unpure thing that had stammered out into expression through my sister's talent. For the unpure is merely negative; it has no existence; it is but the cramped expression of what is true, stammering its way brokenly over false boundaries that seek to limit and confine. Great, full expression of anything is pure, whereas here was only the incomplete, unfinished, and therefore ugly. There was strife and pain and desire to escape. I found myself shrinking from house and grounds as one shrinks from the touch of the mentally arrested, those in whom life has turned awry. There was almost mutilation in it.

Past items, too, now flocked to confirm this feeling that I walked, liberty captured and half-maimed, in a monstrous garden. I remembered days of rain that refreshed the countryside, but left these grounds, cracked with the summer heat, unsatisfied and thirsty; and how the big winds, that cleaned the woods and fields elsewhere, crawled here with difficulty through the dense foliage that protected The Towers from the North and West and East. They were ineffective, sluggish currents. There was no real wind. Nothing happened. I began to realise—far more clearly than in my sister's fanciful explanation about "layers"—that here were many contrary influences at work, mutually destructive of one another. House and grounds were not haunted merely; they were the arena of past thinking and feeling, perhaps of terrible, impure beliefs, each striving to suppress the others, yet no one of them achieving supremacy because no one of them was strong enough, no one of them was true. Each, moreover, tried to win me over, though only one was able to reach my mind at all. For some obscure reason—possibly because my temperament had a natural bias towards the grotesque—it was the goblin layer. With me, it was the line of least resistance. . . .

In my own thoughts this "goblin garden" revealed, of course, merely my personal interpretation. I felt now objectively what long ago my mind had felt subjectively. My work, essential sign of spontaneous life with me, had stopped dead; production had become impossible. I stood now considerably closer to the cause of this sterility. The Cause, rather, turned bolder, had stepped insolently nearer. Nothing happened anywhere; house, garden, mind alike were barren, abortive, torn by the strife of frustrate impulse, ugly, hateful, sinful. Yet behind it all was still the desire of life—desire to escape—accomplish. Hope—an intolerable hope—I became startlingly aware—crowned torture.

And, realising this, though in some part of me where Reason lost her hold, there rose upon me then another and a darker thing that caught me by the throat and made me shrink with a sense of revulsion that touched actual loathing. I knew instantly whence it came, this wave of abhorrence and disgust, for even while I saw red and felt revolt rise in me, it seemed that I grew partially aware of the layer next below the goblin. I perceived the existence of this deeper stratum. One opened the way for the other, as it were. There were so many, yet all inter-related; to admit one was to clear the way for all. If I lingered I should be caught—horribly. They struggled with such violence for supremacy among themselves, however, that this latest uprising was instantly smothered and crushed back, though not before a glimpse had been revealed to me, and the redness in my thoughts transferred itself to colour my surroundings thickly and appallingly—with blood. This lurid aspect drenched the garden, smeared the terraces, lent to the very soil a tinge as of sacrificial rites, that choked the breath in me, while it seemed to fix me to the earth my feet so longed to leave. It was so revolting that at the same time I felt a dreadful curiosity as of fascination—I wished to stay. Between these contrary impulses I think I actually reeled a moment, transfixed by a fascination of the Awful. Through the lighter goblin veil I felt myself sinking down, down, down into this turgid layer that was so much more violent and so much more ancient. The upper layer, indeed, seemed fairy by comparison with this terror born of the lust for blood, thick with the anguish of human sacrificial victims.

Upper! Then I was already sinking; my feet were caught; I was actually in it! What atavistic strain, hidden deep within me, had been touched into vile response, giving this flash of intuitive comprehension, I cannot say. The coatings laid on by civilisation are probably thin enough in all of us. I made a supreme effort. The sun and wind came back. I could almost swear I opened my eyes. Something very atrocious surged back into the depths, carrying with it a thought of tangled woods, of big stones standing in a circle, motionless white figures, the one form bound with ropes, and the ghastly gleam of the knife. Like smoke upon a battlefield, it rolled away. . . .

I was standing on the gravel path below the second terrace when the familiar goblin garden danced back again, doubly grotesque now, doubly mocking, yet, by way of contrast, almost welcome. My glimpse into the depths was momentary, it seems, and had passed utterly away. The common world rushed back with a sense of glad relief, yet ominous now for ever, I felt, for the knowledge of what its past had built upon. In street, in theatre, in the festivities of friends, in music-room or playing-field, even indeed in church—how could the memory of what I had seen and felt not leave its hideous trace? The very structure of my Thought, it seemed to me, was stained. What has been thought by others can never be obliterated until . . .

With a start my reverie broke and fled, scattered by a violent sound that I recognised for the first time in my life as wholly desirable. The returning motor meant that my hostess was back. Yet, so urgent had been my temporary obsession, that my first presentation of her was—well, not as I knew her now. Floating along with a face of anguished torture I saw Mabel, a mere effigy captured by others' thinking, pass down into those depths of fire and blood that only just had closed beneath my feet. She dipped away. She vanished, her fading eyes turned to the last towards some saviour who had failed her. And that strange intolerable hope was in her face.

The mystery of the place was pretty thick about me just then. It was the fall of dusk, and the ghost of slanting sunshine was as unreal as though badly painted. The garden stood at attention all about me. I cannot explain it, but I can tell it, I think, exactly as it happened, for it remains vivid in me for ever—that, for the first time, something *almost happened,* myself apparently the combining link through which it pressed towards delivery:

I had already turned towards the house. In my mind were pictures—not actual thoughts—of the motor, tea on the verandah, my sister, Mabel—when there came behind me this tumultuous, awful rush—as I left the garden. The ugliness, the pain, the striving to escape, the whole negative and suppressed agony that *was* the Place, focussed that second into a concentrated effort to produce a result. It was a blinding tempest of long frustrate desire that heaved at me, surging appallingly behind me like an anguished mob. I was in the act of crossing the frontier into my normal self again, when it came, catching fearfully at my skirts. I might use an entire dictionary of descriptive adjectives yet come no nearer to it than this—the conception of a huge assemblage determined to escape with me, or to snatch me back among themselves. My legs trembled for an instant, and I caught my breath—then turned and ran as fast as possible up the ugly terraces.

At the same instant, as though the clanging of an iron gate cut short the unfinished phrase, I *thought* the beginning of an awful thing:

"The Damned . . ."

Like this it rushed after me from that goblin garden that had sought to keep me:

"The Damned!"

For there was sound in it. I know full well it was subjective, not actually heard at all; yet somehow sound was in it—a great volume, roaring and booming thunderously, far away, and below me. The sentence dipped back into the depths that gave it birth, unfinished. Its completion was prevented. As usual, nothing happened. But it drove behind me like a hurricane as I ran towards the house, and the sound of it I can only liken to those terrible undertones you may hear standing beside Niagara. They lie behind the mere crash of the falling flood, within it somehow, not audible to all—felt rather than definitely heard.

It seemed to echo back from the surface of those sagging terraces as I flew across their sloping ends, for it was somehow underneath them. It was in the rustle of the wind that stirred the skirts of the drooping Wellingtonias. The beds of formal flowers passed it on to the creepers, red as blood, that crept over the unsightly building. Into the structure of the vulgar and forbidding house it sank away; The Towers took it home. The uncomely doors and windows seemed almost like mouths that had uttered the words themselves, and on the upper floors at that very moment I saw two maids in the act of closing them again.

And on the verandah, as I arrived breathless, and shaken in my soul, Frances and Mabel, standing by the tea-table, looked up to greet me. In the faces of both were clearly legible the signs of shock. They watched me coming, yet so full of their own distress that they hardly noticed the state in which I came. In the face of my hostess, however, I read another and a bigger thing than in the face of Frances. Mabel *knew*. She had experienced what I had experienced. She had heard that awful sentence I had heard, but heard it not for the first time; heard it, moreover, I verily believe, complete and to its dreadful end.

"Bill, did you hear that curious noise just now?" Frances asked it sharply before I could say a word. Her manner was confused; she looked straight at me; and there was a tremor in her voice she could not hide.

"There's wind about," I said, "wind in the trees and sweeping round the walls. It's risen rather suddenly." My voice faltered rather.

"No. It wasn't wind," she insisted, with a significance meant for me alone, but badly hidden. "It was more like distant thunder, we thought. How you ran too!" she added. "What a pace you came across the terraces!"

I knew instantly from the way she said it that they both had already heard the sound before and were anxious to know if I had heard it, and how. My interpretation was what they sought.

"It was a curiously deep sound, I admit. It may have been big guns at sea," I suggested, "forts or cruisers practising. The coast isn't so very far, and with the wind in the right direction—"

The expression on Mabel's face stopped me dead.

"Like huge doors closing," she said softly in her colourless voice, "enormous metal doors shutting against a mass of people clamouring to get out." The gravity, the note of hopelessness in her tones, was shocking.

Frances had gone into the house the instant Mabel began to speak. "I'm cold," she had said; "I think I'll get a shawl." Mabel and I were alone. I believe it was the first time we had been really alone since I arrived. She looked up from the teacups, fixing her pallid eyes on mine. She had made a question of the sentence.

"You hear it like that?" I asked innocently. I purposely used the present tense.

She changed her stare from one eye to the other; it was absolutely expressionless. My sister's step sounded on the floor of the room behind us.

"If only—" Mabel began, then stopped, and my own feelings leaping out instinctively completed the sentence I felt was in her mind:

"—something would happen."

She instantly corrected me. I had caught her thought, yet somehow phrased it wrongly.

"We could escape!" She lowered her tone a little, saying it hurriedly. The "we" amazed and horrified me; but something in her voice and manner struck me utterly dumb. There was ice and terror in it. It was a dying woman speaking—a lost and hopeless soul.

In that atrocious moment I hardly noticed what was said exactly, but I remember that my sister returned with a grey shawl about her shoulders, and that Mabel said, in her ordinary voice again, "It is chilly, yes; let's have tea inside," and that two maids, one of them the grenadier, speedily carried the loaded trays into the morning-room and put a match to the logs in the great open fireplace. It was, after all, foolish to risk the sharp evening air, for dusk was falling steadily, and even the sunshine of the day just fading could not turn autumn into summer. I was the last to come in. Just as I left the verandah a large black bird swooped down in front of me past the pillars; it dropped from overhead, swerved abruptly to one side as it caught sight of me, and flapped heavily towards the shrubberies on the left of the terraces, where it disappeared into the gloom. It flew very low, very close. And it startled me, I think because in some way it seemed like my Shadow materialised—as though the dark horror that was rising everywhere from house and garden, then settling back so thickly yet so imperceptibly upon us all, were incarnated in that whirring creature that passed between the daylight and the coming night.

I stood a moment, wondering if it would appear again, before I followed the others indoors, and as I was in the act of closing the windows after me, I caught a glimpse of a figure on the lawn. It was some distance away, on the other side of the shrubberies, in fact where the bird had vanished. But, in spite of the twilight that half magnified, half obscured it, the identity was unmistakable. I knew the housekeeper's stiff walk too well to be deceived. "Mrs. Marsh taking the air," I said to myself. I felt the necessity of saying it, and I wondered why she was doing so at this particular hour. If I had other thoughts they were so vague, and so quickly and utterly suppressed, that I cannot recall them sufficiently to relate them here.

And, once indoors, it was to be expected that there would come explanation, discussion, conversation, at any rate, regarding the singular noise and its cause, some uttered evidence of the mood that had been strong enough to drive us all inside. Yet there was none. Each of us purposely, and with various skill, ignored it. We talked little, and when we did it was of anything in the world but that. Personally, I experienced a touch of that same bewilderment which had come over me during my first talk with Frances on the evening of my arrival, for I recall now the acute tension, and the hope, yet dread, that one or other of us must sooner or later introduce the subject. It did not happen, however; no reference was made to it even remotely. It was the presence of Mabel, I felt positive, that prohibited. As soon might we have discussed Death in the bedroom of a dying woman.

The only scrap of conversation I remember, where all was ordinary and commonplace, was when Mabel spoke casually to the grenadier asking why Mrs. Marsh had omitted to do something or other—what it was I forget—and that the maid replied respectfully that "Mrs. Marsh was very sorry, but her 'and still pained her." I enquired, though so casually that I scarcely know what prompted the words, whether she had injured herself severely, and the reply, "She upset a lamp and burnt herself," was said in a tone that made me feel my curiosity was indiscreet, "but she always has an excuse for not doing things she ought to do." The little bit of conversation remained with me, and I remember particularly the quick way Frances interrupted and turned the talk upon the delinquencies of servants in general, telling incidents of her own at our flat with a volubility that perhaps seemed forced, and that certainly did not encourage general talk as it may have been intended to do. We lapsed into silence immediately she finished.

But for all our care and all our calculated silence, each knew that something had, in these last moments, come very close; it had brushed us in passing; it had retired; and I am inclined to think now that the large dark thing I saw, riding the dusk, probably bird of prey, was in some sense a symbol of it in my mind—that actually there had been no bird at all, I mean, but that my mood of apprehension and dismay had formed the vivid picture in my thoughts. It had swept past us, it had retreated, but it was now, at this moment, in hiding very close. And it was watching us.

Perhaps, too, it was mere coincidence that I encountered Mrs. Marsh, *his* housekeeper, several times that evening in the short interval between tea and dinner, and that on each occasion the sight of this gaunt, half-saturnine woman fed my prejudice against her. Once, on my way to the telephone, I ran into her just where the passage is somewhat jammed by a square table carrying the Chinese gong, a grandfather's clock and a box of croquet mallets. We both gave way, then both advanced, then again gave way—simultaneously. It seemed impossible to pass. We stepped with decision to the same side, finally colliding in the middle, while saying those futile little things, half apology, half excuse, that are inevitable at such times. In the end she stood upright against the wall for me to pass, taking her place against the very door I wished to open. It was ludicrous.

"Excuse me—I was just going in—to telephone," I explained. And she sidled off, murmuring apologies, but opening the door for me while she did so. Our hands met a moment on the handle. There was a second's awkwardness—it was so stupid. I remembered her injury, and by way of something to say, I enquired after it. She thanked me; it was entirely healed now, but it might have been much worse; and there was something about the "mercy of the Lord" that I didn't quite catch. While telephoning, however—a London call, and my attention focussed on it—I realised sharply that this was the first time I had spoken with her; also, that I had—touched her.

It happened to be a Sunday, and the lines were clear. I got my connection quickly, and the incident was forgotten while my thoughts went up to London. On my way upstairs, then, the woman came back into my mind, so that I recalled other things about her—how she seemed all over the house, in unlikely places often; how I had caught her sitting in the hall alone that night; how she was for ever coming and going with her lugubrious visage and that untidy hair at the back that had made me laugh three years ago with the idea that it looked singed or burnt; and how the impression on my first arrival at The Towers was that this woman somehow kept alive, though its evidence was outwardly suppressed, the influence of her late employer and of his sombre teachings. Somewhere with her was associated the idea of punishment, vindictiveness, revenge. I remembered again suddenly my odd notion that she sought to keep her present mistress here, a prisoner in this bleak and comfortless house, and that really, in spite of her obsequious silence, she was intensely opposed to the change of thought that had reclaimed Mabel to a happier view of life.

All this in a passing second flashed in review before me, and I discovered, or at any rate reconstructed, the real Mrs. Marsh. She was decidedly in the Shadow. More, she stood in the forefront of it, stealthily leading an assault, as it were, against The Towers and its occupants, as though, consciously or unconsciously, she laboured incessantly to this hateful end.

I can only judge that some state of nervousness in me permitted the series of insignificant thoughts to assume this dramatic shape, and that what had gone before prepared the way and led her up at the head of so formidable a procession. I relate it exactly as it came to me. My nerves were doubtless somewhat on edge by now. Otherwise I should hardly have been a prey to the exaggeration at all. I seemed open to so many strange impressions.

Nothing else, perhaps, can explain my ridiculous, conversation with her, when, for the third time that evening, I came suddenly upon the woman halfway down the stairs, standing by an open window as if in the act of listening. She was dressed in black, a black shawl over her square shoulders and black gloves on her big, broad hands. Two black objects, prayer-books apparently, she clasped, and on her head she wore a bonnet with shaking beads of jet. At first I did not know her, as I came running down upon her from the landing; it was only when she stood aside to let me pass that I saw her profile against the tapestry and recognised Mrs. Marsh. And to catch her on the front stairs, dressed like this, struck me as incongruous—impertinent. I paused in my dangerous descent. Through the opened window came the sound of bells— church bells—a sound more depressing to me than superstition, and as nauseating. Though the action was ill-judged, I obeyed the sudden prompting— was it a secret desire to attack, perhaps?—and spoke to her.

"Been to church, I suppose, Mrs. Marsh?" I said. "Or just going, perhaps?"

Her face, as she looked up a second to reply, was like an iron doll that moved its lips and turned its eyes, but made no other imitation of life at all.

"Some of us still goes, sir," she said unctuously.

It was respectful enough, yet the implied judgment of the rest of the world made me almost angry. A deferential insolence lay behind the affected meekness.

"For those who believe no doubt it *is* helpful," I smiled. "True religion brings peace and happiness, I'm sure—joy, Mrs. Marsh, JOY!" I found keen satisfaction in the emphasis.

She looked at me like a knife. I cannot describe the implacable thing that shone in her fixed, stern eyes, nor the shadow of felt darkness that stole across her face. She glittered. I felt hate in her. I knew—she knew too—who was in the thoughts of us both at that moment.

She replied softly, never forgetting her place for an instant:

"There is joy, sir—in 'eaven—over one sinner that repenteth, and in church there goes up prayer to Gawd for those 'oo—well, for the others, sir, 'oo—"

She cut short her sentence thus. The gloom about her as she said it was like the gloom about a hearse, a tomb, a darkness of great hopeless dungeons. My tongue ran on of itself with a kind of bitter satisfaction:

"We must believe there are *no* others, Mrs. Marsh. Salvation, you know, would be such a failure if there were. No merciful, all-foreseeing God could ever have devised such a fearful plan—"

Her voice, interrupting me, seemed to rise out of the bowels of the earth:

"They rejected the salvation when it was hoffered to them, sir, on earth."

"But you wouldn't have them tortured for ever because of one mistake in ignorance," I said, fixing her with my eye. "Come now, would you, Mrs. Marsh? No God worth worshipping could permit such cruelty. Think a moment what it means."

She stared at me, a curious expression in her stupid eyes. It seemed to me as though the "woman" in her revolted, while yet she dared not suffer her grim belief to trip. That is, she would willingly have had it otherwise but for a terror that prevented.

"We may pray for them, sir, and we do—we *may* 'ope." She dropped her eyes to the carpet.

"Good, good!" I put in cheerfully, sorry now that I had spoken at all. "That's more hopeful, at any rate, isn't it?"

She murmured something about Abraham's bosom, and the "time of salvation not being for ever," as I tried to pass her. Then a half gesture that she made stopped me. There was something more she wished to say—to ask. She looked up furtively. In her eyes I saw the "woman" peering out through fear.

"Per'aps, sir," she faltered, as though lightning must strike her dead, "per'aps, would you think, a drop of cold water, given in His name, might moisten—?"

But I stopped her, for the foolish talk had lasted long enough.

"Of course," I exclaimed, "of course. For God is love, remember, and love means charity, tolerance, sympathy, and sparing others pain," and I hurried past her, determined to end the outrageous conversation for which yet I knew myself entirely to blame. Behind me, she stood stock-still for several minutes, half bewildered, half alarmed, as I suspected. I caught the fragment of another sentence, one word of it, rather—"punishment"—but the rest escaped me. Her arrogance and condescending tolerance exasperated me, while I was at the same time secretly pleased that I might have touched some string of remorse or sympathy in her after all. Her belief was iron; she dared not let it go; yet somewhere underneath there lurked the germ of a wholesome revulsion. She would help "them"—if she dared. Her question proved it.

Half-ashamed of myself, I turned and crossed the hall quickly lest I should be tempted to say more, and in me was a disagreeable sensation as though I had just left the Incurable Ward of some great hospital. A reaction caught me as of nausea. Ugh! I wanted such people cleansed by fire. They seemed to me as centres of contamination whose vicious thoughts flowed out to stain God's glorious world. I saw myself, Frances, Mabel too especially, on the rack, while that odious figure of cruelty and darkness stood over us and ordered the awful handles turned in order that we might be "saved"—forced, that is, to think and believe exactly as *she* thought and believed.

I found relief for my somewhat childish indignation by letting myself loose upon the organ then. The flood of Bach and Beethoven brought back the sense of proportion. It proved, however, at the same time that there *had* been this growth of distortion in me, and that it had been provided apparently by my closer contact—for the first time—with that funereal personality, the woman who, like her master, believed that all holding views of God that differed from her own, must be damned eternally. It gave me, moreover, some faint clue perhaps, though a clue I was unequal to following up, to the nature of the strife and terror and frustrate influence in the house. That housekeeper had to do with it. She kept it alive. Her thought was like a spell she waved above her mistress's head.

VII

That night I was wakened by a hurried tapping at my door, and before I could answer, Frances stood beside my bed. She had switched on the light as she came in. Her hair fell straggling over her dressing-gown. Her face was deathly pale, its expression so distraught it was almost haggard. The eyes were very wide. She looked almost like another woman.

She was whispering at a great pace: "Bill, Bill, wake up, quick!"

"I *am* awake. What is it?" I whispered too. I was startled.

"Listen!" was all she said. Her eyes stared into vacancy.

There was not a sound in the great house. The wind had dropped, and all was still. Only the tapping seemed to continue endlessly in my brain. The clock on the mantelpiece pointed to half-past two.

"I heard nothing, Frances. What is it?" I rubbed my eyes; I had been very deeply asleep.

"Listen!" she repeated very softly, holding up one finger and turning her eyes towards the door she had left ajar. Her usual calmness had deserted her. She was in the grip of some distressing terror.

For a full minute we held our breath and listened. Then her eyes rolled round again and met my own, and her skin went even whiter than before.

"It woke me," she said beneath her breath, and moving a step nearer to my bed. "It was the Noise." Even her whisper trembled.

"The Noise!" The word repeated itself dully of its own accord. I would rather it had been anything in the world but that—earthquake, foreign cannon, collapse of the house above our heads! "The noise, Frances! Are you *sure?*" I was playing really for a little time.

"It was like thunder. At first I thought it *was* thunder. But a minute later it came again—from underground. It's appalling." She muttered the words, her voice not properly under control.

There was a pause of perhaps a minute, and then we both spoke at once. We said foolish, obvious things that neither of us believed in for a second. The roof had fallen in, there were burglars downstairs, the safes had been blown open. It was to comfort each other as children do that we said these things; also it was to gain further time.

"There's some one in the house, of course," I heard my voice say finally, as I sprang out of bed and hurried into dressing-gown and slippers. "Don't be alarmed. I'll go down and see," and from the drawer I took a pistol it was my habit to carry everywhere with me. I loaded it carefully while Frances stood stock-still beside the bed and watched. I moved towards the open door.

"You stay here, Frances," I whispered, the beating of my heart making the words uneven, "while I go down and make a search. Lock yourself in, girl. Nothing can happen to you. It was downstairs, you said?"

"Underneath," she answered faintly, pointing through the floor.

She moved suddenly between me and the door.

"Listen! Hark!" she said, the eyes in her face quite fixed; "it's coming again," and she turned her head to catch the slightest sound. I stood there watching her, and while I watched her, shook. But nothing stirred. From the halls below rose only the whirr and quiet ticking of the numerous clocks. The blind by the open window behind us flapped out a little into the room as the draught caught it.

"I'll come with you, Bill—to the next floor," she broke the silence. "Then I'll stay with Mabel—till you come up again." The blind sank down with a long sigh as she said it.

The question jumped to my lips before I could repress it:

"Mabel is awake. She heard it too?"

I hardly know why horror caught me at her answer. All was so vague and terrible as we stood there playing the great game of this sinister house where nothing ever happened.

"We met in the passage. She was on her way to me."

What shook in me, shook inwardly. Frances, I mean, did not see it. I had the feeling just then that the Noise was upon us, that any second it would boom and roar about our ears. But the deep silence held. I only heard my sister's little whisper coming across the room in answer to my question:

"Then what is Mabel doing now?"

And her reply proved that she was yielding at last beneath the dreadful tension, for she spoke at once, unable longer to keep up the pretence. With a kind of relief, as it were, she said it out, looking helplessly at me like a child:

"She is weeping and gna—"

My expression must have stopped her. I believe I clapped both hands upon her mouth, though when I realised things clearly again, I found they were covering my own ears instead. It was a moment of unutterable horror. The revulsion I felt was actually physical. It would have given me pleasure to fire off all the five chambers of my pistol into the air above my head; the sound—a definite, wholesome sound that explained itself—would have been a positive relief. Other feelings, though, were in me too, all over me, rushing to and fro. It was vain to seek their disentanglement; it was impossible. I confess that I experienced, among them, a touch of paralysing fear—though for a moment only; it passed as sharply as it came, leaving me with a violent flush of blood to the face such as bursts of anger bring, followed abruptly by an icy perspiration over the entire body. Yet I may honestly avow that it was not ordinary personal fear I felt, nor any common dread of physical injury. It was, rather, a vast, impersonal shrinking—a sympathetic shrinking—from the agony and terror that countless others, somewhere, somehow, felt for themselves. The first sensation of a prison overwhelmed me in that instant, of bitter strife and frenzied suffering, and the fiery torture of the yearning to escape that was yet hopelessly uttered. . . . It was of incredible power. It was real. The vain, intolerable hope swept over me.

I mastered myself, though hardly knowing how, and took my sister's hand. It was as cold as ice, as I led her firmly to the door and out into the passage. Apparently she noticed nothing of my so near collapse, for I caught her whisper as we went. "You *are* brave, Bill; splendidly brave."

The upper corridors of the great sleeping house were brightly lit; on her way to me she had turned on every electric switch her hand could reach; and as we passed the final flight of stairs to the floor below, I heard a door shut softly and knew that Mabel had been listening—waiting for us. I led my sister up to it. She knocked, and the door was opened cautiously an inch or so. The room was pitch black. I caught no glimpse of Mabel standing there. Frances turned to me with a hurried whisper, "Billy, you *will* be careful, won't you?" and went in. I just had time to answer that I would not be long, and Frances to reply, "You'll find us here—" when the door closed and cut her sentence short before its end.

But it was not alone the closing door that took the final words. Frances—by the way she disappeared I knew it—had made a swift and violent movement into the darkness that was as though she sprang. She leaped upon that other woman who stood back among the shadows, for, simultaneously with the clipping of the sentence, another sound was also stopped—stifled, smothered, choked back lest I should also hear it. Yet not in time. I heard it—a hard and horrible sound that explained both the leap and the abrupt cessation of the whispered words.

I stood irresolute a moment. It was as though all the bones had been withdrawn from my body, so that I must sink and fall. That sound plucked them out, and plucked out my self-possession with them. I am not sure that it was a sound I had ever heard before, though children, I half remembered, made it sometimes in blind rages when they knew not what they did. In a grown-up person certainly I had never known it. I associated it with animals rather—horribly. In the history of the world, no doubt, it has been common enough, alas, but fortunately to-day there can be but few who know it, or would recognise it even when heard. The bones shot back into my body the same instant, but red-hot and burning; the brief instant of irresolution passed; I was torn between the desire to break down the door and enter, and to run—run for my life from a thing I dared not face.

Out of the horrid tumult, then, I adopted neither course. Without reflection, certainly without analysis of what was best to do for my sister, myself or Mabel, I took up my action where it had been interrupted. I turned from the awful door and moved slowly towards the head of the stairs. But that dreadful little sound came with me. I believe my own teeth chattered. It seemed all over the house—in the empty halls that opened into the long passages towards the music-room, and even in the grounds outside the building. From the lawns and barren garden, from the ugly terraces themselves, it rose into the night, and behind it came a curious driving sound, incomplete, unfinished, as of wailing for deliverance, the wailing of desperate souls in anguish, the dull and dry beseeching of hopeless spirits in prison.

That I could have taken the little sound from the bedroom where I actually heard it, and spread it thus over the entire house and grounds, is evidence, perhaps, of the state my nerves were in. The wailing assuredly was in my mind alone. But the longer I hesitated, the more difficult became my task, and, gathering up my dressing-gown, lest I should trip in the darkness, I passed slowly down the staircase into the hall below. I carried neither candle nor matches; every switch in room and corridor was known to me. The covering of darkness was indeed rather comforting than otherwise, for if it prevented seeing, it also prevented being seen. The heavy pistol, knocking against my thigh as I moved, made me feel I was carrying a child's toy, foolishly. I experienced in every nerve that primitive vast dread which is the Thrill of darkness. Merely the child in me was comforted by that pistol.

The night was not entirely black; the iron bars across the glass front door were visible, and, equally, I discerned the big, stiff wooden chairs in the hall, the gaping fireplace, the upright pillars supporting the staircase, the round table in the centre with its books and flower-vases, and the basket that held visitors' cards. There, too, was the stick and umbrella-stand and the shelf with railway guides, directory, and telegraph forms. Clocks ticked everywhere with sounds like quiet footfalls. Light fell here and there in patches from the floor above. I stood a moment in the hall, letting my eyes grow more accustomed to the gloom, while deciding on a plan of search. I made out the ivy trailing outside over one of the big windows . . . and then the tall clock by the front door made a grating noise deep down inside its body—it was the Presentation clock, large and hideous, given by the congregation of his church—and, dreading the booming strike it seemed to threaten, I made a quick decision. If others beside myself were about in the night, the sound of that striking might cover their approach.

So I tiptoed to the right, where the passage led towards the dining-room. In the other direction were the morning- and drawing-room, both little used, and various other rooms beyond that had been *his*, generally now kept locked. I thought of my sister, waiting upstairs with that frightened woman for my return. I went quickly, yet stealthily.

And, to my surprise, the door of the dining-room was open. It had been opened. I paused on the threshold, staring about me. I think I fully expected to see a figure blocked in the shadows against the heavy sideboard, or looming on the other side beneath his portrait. But the room was empty; I *felt* it empty.

Through the wide bow-windows that gave on to the verandah came an uncertain glimmer that even shone reflected in the polished surface of the dinner-table, and again I perceived the stiff outline of chairs, waiting tenantless all round it, two larger ones with high carved backs at either end. The monkey-trees on the upper terrace, too, were visible outside against the sky, and the solemn crests of the Wellingtonias on the terraces below. The enormous clock on the mantelpiece ticked very slowly, as though its machinery were running down, and I made out the pale round patch that was its face. Resisting my first inclination to turn the lights up—my hand had gone so far as to finger the friendly knob—I crossed the room so carefully that no single board creaked, nor a single chair, as I rested a hand upon its back, moved on the parquet flooring. I turned neither to the right nor left, nor did I once look back.

I went towards the long corridor, filled with priceless *objets d'art,* that led through various ante-chambers into the spacious music-room, and only at the mouth of this corridor did I next halt a moment in uncertainty. For this long corridor, lit faintly by high windows on the left from the verandah, was very narrow, owing to the mass of shelves and fancy tables it contained. It was not that I feared to knock over precious things as I went, but that, because of its ungenerous width, there would be no room to pass another person—if I met one. And the certainty had suddenly come upon me that somewhere in this corridor another person at this actual moment stood. Here, somehow, amid all this dead atmosphere of furniture, and impersonal emptiness, lay the hint of a living human presence; and with such conviction did it come upon me, that my hand instinctively gripped the pistol in my pocket before I could even think. Either some one had passed along this corridor just before me, or some one lay waiting at its further end—withdrawn or flattened into one of the little recesses, to let me pass. It was the person who had opened the door. And the blood ran from my heart as I realised it.

It was not courage that sent me on, but rather a strong impulse from behind that made it impossible to retreat: the feeling that a throng pressed at my back, drawing nearer and nearer; that I was already half surrounded, swept, dragged, coaxed into a vast prison-house where there was wailing and gnashing of teeth, where their worm dieth not and their fire is not quenched. I can neither explain nor justify the storm of irrational emotion that swept me as I stood in that moment, staring down the length of the silent corridor towards the music-room at the far end, I can only repeat that no personal bravery sent me down it, but that the negative emotion of fear was swamped in this vast sea of pity and commiseration for others that surged upon me.

My senses, at least, were no whit confused; if anything, my brain registered impressions with keener accuracy than usual. I noticed, for instance, that the two swinging doors of baize that cut the corridor into definite lengths, making little rooms of the spaces between them, were both wide open—in the dim light no mean achievement. Also that the fronds of a palm plant, some ten feet in front of me, still stirred gently from the air of some one who had recently gone past them. The long green leaves waved to and fro like hands. Then I went stealthily forward down the narrow space, proud even that I had this command of myself, and so carefully that my feet made no sound upon the Japanese matting on the floor.

It was a journey that seemed timeless. I have no idea how fast or slow I went, but I remember that I deliberately examined articles on each side of me, peering with particular closeness into the recesses of wall and window. I passed the first baize doors, and the passage beyond them widened out to hold shelves of books; there were sofas and small reading-tables against the wall. It narrowed again presently, as I entered the second stretch. The windows here were higher and smaller, and marble statuettes of classical subjects lined the walls, watching me like figures of the dead. Their white and shining faces saw me, yet made no sign. I passed next between the second baize doors. They, too, had been fastened back with hooks against the wall. Thus all doors were open—had been recently opened.

And so, at length, I found myself in the final widening of the corridor which formed an antechamber to the music-room itself. It had been used formerly to hold the overflow of meetings. No door separated it from the great hall beyond, but heavy curtains hung usually to close it off, and these curtains were invariably drawn. They now stood wide. And here—I can merely state the impression that came upon me—I knew myself at last surrounded. The throng that pressed behind me, also surged in front: facing me in the big room, and waiting for my entry, stood a multitude; on either side of me, in the very air above my head, the vast assemblage paused upon my coming. The pause, however, was momentary, for instantly the deep, tumultuous movement was resumed that yet was silent as a cavern underground. I felt the agony that was in it, the passionate striving, the awful struggle to escape. The semi-darkness held beseeching faces that fought to press themselves upon my vision, yearning yet hopeless eyes, lips scorched and dry, mouths that opened to implore but found no craved delivery in actual words, and a fury of misery and hate that made the life in me stop dead, frozen by the horror of vain pity. That intolerable, vain Hope was everywhere.

And the multitude, it came to me, was not a single multitude, but many; for, as soon as one huge division pressed too close upon the edge of escape, it was dragged back by another and prevented. The wild host was divided against itself. Here dwelt the Shadow I had "imagined" weeks ago, and in it struggled armies of lost souls as in the depths of some bottomless pit whence there is no escape. The layers mingled, fighting against themselves in endless torture. It was in this great Shadow I had clairvoyantly seen Mabel, but about its fearful mouth, I now was certain, hovered another figure of darkness, a figure who sought to keep it in existence, since to her thought were due those lampless depths of woe without escape. . . . Towards me the multitudes now surged.

It was a sound and a movement that brought me back into myself. The great clock at the further end of the room just then struck the hour of three. That was the sound. And the movement—? I was aware that a figure was passing across the distant centre of the floor. Instantly I dropped back into the arena of my little human terror. My hand again clutched stupidly at the pistol butt. I drew back into the folds of the heavy curtain. And the figure advanced.

I remember every detail. At first it seemed to me enormous—this advancing shadow—far beyond human scale; but as it came nearer, I measured it, though not consciously, by the organ pipes that gleamed in faint colours, just above its gradual soft approach. It passed them, already half-way across the great room. I saw then that its stature was that of ordinary men. The prolonged booming of the clock died away. I heard the footfall, shuffling upon the polished boards. I heard another sound—a voice, low and monotonous, droning as in prayer. The figure was speaking. It was a woman. And she carried in both hands before her a small object that faintly shimmered—a glass of water. And then I recognised her.

There was still an instant's time before she reached me, and I made use of it. I shrank back, flattening myself against the wall. Her voice ceased a moment, as she turned and carefully drew the curtains together behind her, closing them with one hand. Oblivious of my presence, though she actually touched my dressing-gown with the hand that pulled the cords, she resumed her dreadful, solemn march, disappearing at length down the long vista of the corridor like a shadow. But as she passed me, her voice began again, so that I heard each word distinctly as she uttered it, her head aloft, her figure upright, as though she moved at the head of a procession:

"A drop of cold water, given in His name, shall moisten their burning tongues."

It was repeated monotonously over and over again, droning down into the distance as she went, until at length both voice and figure faded into the shadows at the further end.

For a time, I have no means of measuring precisely, I stood in that dark corner, pressing my back against the wall, and would have drawn the curtains down to hide me had I dared to stretch an arm out. The dread that presently the woman would return passed gradually away. I realised, that the air had emptied, the crowd her presence had stirred into activity had retreated; I was alone in the gloomy under-spaces of the odious building. . . . Then I remembered suddenly again the terrified women waiting for me on that upper landing; and realised that my skin was wet and freezing cold after a profuse perspiration. I prepared to retrace my steps. I remember the effort it cost me to leave the support of the wall and covering darkness of my corner, and step out into the grey light of the corridor. At first I sidled, then, finding this mode of walking impossible, turned my face boldly and walked quickly, regardless that my dressing-gown set the precious objects shaking as I passed. A wind that sighed mournfully against the high, small windows seemed to have got inside the corridor as well; it felt so cold; and every moment I dreaded to see the outline of the woman's figure as she waited in recess or angle against the wall for me to pass.

Was there another thing I dreaded even more? I cannot say. I only know that the first baize doors had swung-to behind me, and the second ones were close at hand, when the great dim thunder caught me, pouring up with prodigious volume so that it seemed to roll out from another world. It shook the very bowels of the building. I was closer to it than that other time, when it had followed me from the goblin garden. There was strength and hardness in it, as of metal reverberation. Some touch of numbness, almost of paralysis, must surely have been upon me that I felt no actual terror, for I remember even turning and standing still to hear it better.

"That is the Noise," my thought ran stupidly, and I think I whispered it aloud; *"the Doors are closing."*

The wind outside against the windows was audible, so it cannot have been really loud, yet to me it was the biggest, deepest sound I have ever heard, but so far away, with such awful remoteness in it, that I had to doubt my own ears at the same time. It seemed underground—the rumbling of earthquake gates that shut remorselessly within the rocky Earth—stupendous, ultimate thunder. *They* were shut off from help again. The doors had closed.

I felt a storm of pity, an agony of bitter, futile hate sweep through me. My memory of the figure changed then. The Woman with the glass of cooling water had stepped down from Heaven; but the Man—or was it Men?—who smeared this terrible layer of belief and Thought upon the world! . . .

I crossed the dining-room—it was fancy, of course, that held my eyes from glancing at the portrait for fear I should see it smiling approval—and so finally reached the hall, where the light from the floor above seemed now quite bright in comparison. All the doors I closed carefully behind me; but first I had to open them. The woman had closed every one. Up the stairs, then, I actually ran, two steps at a time. My sister was standing outside Mabel's door. By her face I knew that she had also heard. There was no need to ask. I quickly made my mind up.

"There's nothing," I said, and detailed briefly my tour of search. "All is quiet and undisturbed downstairs." May God forgive me!

She beckoned to me, closing the door softly behind her. My heart beat violently a moment, then stood still.

"Mabel," she said aloud.

It was like the sentence of a judge, that one short word.

I tried to push past her and go in, but she stopped me with her arm. She was wholly mistress of herself, I saw.

"Hush!" she said in a lower voice. "I've got her round again with brandy. She's sleeping quietly now. We won't disturb her."

She drew me further out into the landing, and as she did so, the clock in the hall below struck half-past three. I had stood, then, thirty minutes in the corridor below. "You've been such a long time," she said simply. "I feared for you," and she took my hand in her own that was cold and clammy.

VIII

And then, while that dreadful house stood listening about us in the early hours of this chill morning upon the edge of winter, she told me, with laconic brevity, things about Mabel that I heard as from a distance. There was nothing so unusual or tremendous in the short recital, nothing indeed I might not have already guessed for myself. It was the time and scene, the inference, too, that made it so afflicting: the idea that Mabel believed herself so utterly and hopelessly lost—beyond recovery *damned*.

That she had loved him with so passionate a devotion that she had given her soul into his keeping, this certainly I had not divined—probably because I had never thought about it one way or the other. He had "converted" her, I knew, but that she had subscribed whole-heartedly to that most cruel and ugly of his dogmas—this was new to me, and came with a certain shock as I heard it. In love, of course, the weaker nature is receptive to all manner of suggestion. This man had "suggested" his pet brimstone lake so vividly that she had listened and believed. He had frightened her into heaven; and his heaven, a definite locality in the skies, had its foretaste here on earth in miniature— The Towers, house and garden. Into his dolorous scheme of a handful saved and millions damned, his enclosure, as it were, of sheep and goats, he had swept her before she was aware of it. Her mind no longer was her own. And it was Mrs. Marsh who kept the thought-stream open, though tempered, as she deemed, with that touch of craven, superstitious mercy.

But what I found it difficult to understand, and still more difficult to accept, was that, during her year abroad, she had been so haunted with a secret dread of that hideous after-death that she had finally revolted and tried to recover that clearer state of mind she had enjoyed before the religious bully had stunned her—yet had tried in vain. She had returned to The Towers to find her soul again, only to realise that it was lost eternally. The cleaner state of mind lay then beyond recovery. In the reaction that followed the removal of his terrible "suggestion," she felt the crumbling of all that he had taught her, but searched in vain for the peace and beauty his teachings had destroyed. Nothing came to replace these. She was empty, desolate, hopeless; craving her former joy and carelessness, she found only hate and diabolical calculation. This man, whom she had loved to the point of losing her soul for him, had bequeathed to her one black and fiery thing—the terror of the damned. His thinking wrapped her in this iron garment that held her fast.

All this Frances told me, far more briefly than I have here repeated it. In her eyes and gestures and laconic sentences lay the conviction of great beating issues and of menacing drama my own description fails to recapture. It was all so incongruous and remote from the world I lived in that more than once a smile, though a smile of pity, fluttered to my lips; but a glimpse of my face in the mirror showed rather the leer of a grimace. There was no real laughter anywhere that night. The entire adventure seemed so incredible, here, in this twentieth century—but yet delusion, that feeble word, did not occur once in the comments my mind suggested though did not utter. I remembered that forbidding Shadow too; my sister's water-colours; the vanished personality of our hostess; the inexplicable, thundering Noise, and the figure of Mrs. Marsh in her midnight ritual that was so childish yet so horrible. I shivered in spite of my own "emancipated" cast of mind.

"There *is* no Mabel," were the words with which my sister sent another shower of ice down my spine. "He has killed her in his lake of fire and brimstone."

I stared at her blankly, as in a nightmare where nothing true or possible ever happened.

"He killed her in his lake of fire and brimstone," she repeated more faintly.

A desperate effort was in me to say the strong, sensible thing which should destroy the oppressive horror that grew so stiflingly about us both, but again the mirror drew the attempted smile into the merest grin, betraying the distortion that was everywhere in the place.

"You mean," I stammered beneath my breath, "that her faith has gone, but that the terror has remained?" I asked it, dully groping. I moved out of the line of the reflection in the glass.

She bowed her head as though beneath a weight; her skin was the pallor of grey ashes.

"You mean," I said louder, "that she has lost her—mind?"

"She is terror incarnate," was the whispered answer. "Mabel has lost her soul. Her soul is—there!" She pointed horribly below. "She is seeking it . . .?"

The word "soul" stung me into something of my normal self again.

"But her terror, poor thing, is not—cannot be—transferable to *us!*" I exclaimed more vehemently. "It certainly is not convertible into feelings, sights and—even sounds!"

She interrupted me quickly, almost impatiently, speaking with that conviction by which she conquered me so easily that night.

"It is her terror that has revived 'the Others.' It has brought her into touch with them. They are loose and driving after her. Her efforts at resistance have given them also hope—that escape, after all, *is* possible. Day and night they strive."

"Escape! Others!" The anger first rising in me dropped of its own accord at the moment of birth. It shrank into a shuddering beyond my control. In that moment, I think, I would have believed in the possibility of anything and everything she might tell me. To argue or contradict seemed equally futile.

"His strong belief, as also the beliefs of others who have preceded him," she replied, so sure of herself that I actually turned to look over my shoulder, "have left their shadow like a thick deposit over the house and grounds. To them, poor souls imprisoned by thought, it was hopeless as granite walls—until her resistance, her effort to dissipate it—let in light. Now, in their thousands, they are flocking to this little light, seeking escape. Her own escape, don't you see, may release them all!"

It took my breath away. Had his predecessors, former occupants of this house, also preached damnation of all the world but their own exclusive sect? Was this the explanation of her obscure talk of "layers," each striving against the other for domination? And if men are spirits, and these spirits survive, could strong Thought thus determine their condition even afterwards?

So many questions flooded into me that I selected no one of them, but stared in uncomfortable silence, bewildered, out of my depth, and acutely, painfully distressed. There was so odd a mixture of possible truth and incredible, unacceptable explanation in it all; so much confirmed, yet so much left darker than before. What she said did, indeed, offer a quasi-interpretation of my own series of abominable sensations—strife, agony, pity, hate, escape—but so far-fetched that only the deep conviction in her voice and attitude made it tolerable for a second even. I found myself in a curious state of mind. I could neither think clearly nor say a word to refute her amazing statements, whispered there beside me in the shivering hours of the early morning with only a wall between ourselves and—Mabel. Close behind her words I remember this singular thing, however—that an atmosphere as of the Inquisition seemed to rise and stir about the room, beating awful wings of black above my head.

Abruptly, then, a moment's common-sense returned to me. I faced her.

"And the Noise?" I said aloud, more firmly, "the roar of the closing doors? We have *all* heard that! Is that subjective too?"

Frances looked sideways about her in a queer fashion that made my flesh creep again. I spoke brusquely, almost angrily. I repeated the question, and waited with anxiety for her reply.

"What noise?" she asked, with the frank expression of an innocent child. "What closing doors?"

But her face turned from grey to white, and I saw that drops of perspiration glistened on her forehead. She caught at the back of a chair to steady herself, then glanced about her again with that sidelong look that made my blood run cold. I understood suddenly then. She did not take in what I said. I knew now. She was listening—for something else.

And the discovery revived in me a far stronger emotion than any mere desire for immediate explanation. Not only did I not insist upon an answer, but I was actually terrified lest she *would* answer. More, I felt in me a terror lest I should be moved to describe my own experiences below-stairs, thus increasing their reality and so the reality of all. She might even explain them too!

Still listening intently, she raised her head and looked me in the eyes. Her lips opened to speak. The words came to me from a great distance, it seemed, and her voice had a sound like a stone that drops into a deep well, its fate though hidden, known.

"We are in it with her, too, Bill. We are in it with her. Our interpretations vary—because we are—in parts of it only. Mabel is in it—*all*."

The desire for violence came over me. If only she would say a definite thing in plain King's English! If only I could find it in me to give utterance to what shouted so loud within me! If only—the same old cry—something would happen! For all this elliptic talk that dazed my mind left obscurity everywhere. Her atrocious meaning, none the less, flashed through me, though vanishing before it wholly divulged itself.

It brought a certain reaction with it. I found my tongue. Whether I actually believed what I said is more than I can swear to; that it seemed to me wise at the moment is all I remember. My mind was in a state of obscure perception less than that of normal consciousness.

"Yes, Frances, I believe that what you say is the truth, and that we are in it with her"—I meant to say it with loud, hostile emphasis, but instead I whispered it lest she should hear the trembling of my voice—"and for that reason, my dear sister, we leave to-morrow, you and I—to-day, rather, since it is long past midnight—we leave this house of the damned. We go back to London."

Frances looked up, her face distraught almost beyond recognition. But it was not my words that caused the tumult in her heart. It was a sound—the sound she had been listening for—so faint I barely caught it myself, and had she not pointed I could never have known the direction whence it came. Small and terrible it rose again in the stillness of the night, the sound of gnashing teeth. And behind it came another—the tread of stealthy footsteps. Both were just outside the door.

The room swung round me for a second. My first instinct to prevent my sister going out—she had dashed past me frantically to the door—gave place to another when I saw the expression in her eyes. I followed her lead instead; it was surer than my own. The pistol in my pocket swung uselessly against my thigh. I was flustered beyond belief and ashamed that I was so.

"Keep close to me, Frances," I said huskily, as the door swung wide and a shaft of light fell upon a figure moving rapidly. Mabel was going down the corridor. Beyond her, in the shadows on the staircase, a second figure stood beckoning, scarcely visible.

"Before they get her! Quick!" was screamed into my ears, and our arms were about her in the same moment. It was a horrible scene. Not that Mabel struggled in the least, but that she collapsed as we caught her and fell with her dead weight, as of a corpse, limp, against us. And her teeth began again. They continued, even beneath the hand that Frances clapped upon her lips. . . .

We carried her back into her own bedroom, where she lay down peacefully enough. It was so soon over. . . . The rapidity of the whole thing robbed it of reality almost. It had the swiftness of something remembered rather than of something witnessed. She slept again so quickly that it was almost as if we had caught her sleep-walking. I cannot say. I asked no questions at the time; I have asked none since; and my help was needed as little as the protection of my pistol. Frances was strangely competent and collected. . . . I lingered for some time uselessly by the door, till at length, looking up with a sigh, she made a sign for me to go.

"I shall wait in your room next door," I whispered, "till you come." But, though going out, I waited in the corridor instead, so as to hear the faintest call for help. In that dark corridor upstairs I waited, but not long. It may have been fifteen minutes when Frances reappeared, locking the door softly behind her. Leaning over the banisters, I saw her.

"I'll go in again about six o'clock," she whispered, "as soon as it gets light. She is sound asleep now. Please don't wait. If anything happens I'll call—you might leave your door ajar, perhaps." And she came up, looking like a ghost.

But I saw her first safely into bed, and the rest of the night I spent in an armchair close to my opened door, listening for the slightest sound. Soon after five o'clock I heard Frances fumbling with the key, and, peering over the railing again, I waited till she reappeared and went back into her own room. She closed her door. Evidently she was satisfied that all was well.

Then, and then only, did I go to bed myself, but not to sleep. I could not get the scene out of my mind, especially that odious detail of it which I hoped and believed my sister had not seen—the still, dark figure of the housekeeper waiting on the stairs below—waiting, of course, for Mabel.

IX

It seems I became a mere spectator after that; my sister's lead was so assured for one thing, and for another, the responsibility of leaving Mabel alone— Frances laid it bodily upon my shoulders—was a little more than I cared about. Moreover, when we all three met later in the day, things went on so exactly as before, so absolutely without friction or distress, that to present a sudden, obvious excuse for cutting our visit short seemed ill judged. And on the lowest grounds it would have been desertion. At any rate, it was beyond my powers, and Frances was quite firm that *she* must stay. We therefore did stay. Things that happen in the night always seem exaggerated and distorted when the sun shines brightly next morning; no one can reconstruct the terror of a nightmare afterwards, nor comprehend why it seemed so overwhelming at the time.

I slept till ten o'clock, and when I rang for breakfast, a note from my sister lay upon the tray, its message of counsel couched in a calm and comforting strain. Mabel, she assured me, was herself again and remembered nothing of what had happened; there was no need of any violent measures; I was to treat her exactly as if I knew nothing. "And, if you don't mind, Bill, let us leave the matter unmentioned between ourselves as well. Discussion exaggerates; such things are best not talked about. I'm sorry I disturbed you so unnecessarily; I was stupidly excited. Please forget all the things I said at the moment." She had written "nonsense" first instead of "things," then scratched it out. She wished to convey that hysteria had been abroad in the night, and I readily gulped the explanation down, though it could not satisfy me in the smallest degree.

There was another week of our visit still, and we stayed it out to the end without disaster. My desire to leave at times became that frantic thing, desire to escape; but I controlled it, kept silent, watched and wondered. Nothing happened. As before, and everywhere, there was no sequence of development, no connection between cause and effect; and climax, none whatever. The thing swayed up and down, backwards and forwards like a great loose curtain in the wind, and I could only vaguely surmise what caused the draught or why there was a curtain at all. A novelist might mould the queer material into coherent sequence that would be interesting but could not be true. It remains, therefore, not a story but a history. Nothing happened.

Perhaps my intense dislike of the fall of darkness was due wholly to my stirred imagination, and perhaps my anger when I learned that Frances now occupied a bed in our hostess's room was unreasonable. Nerves were unquestionably on edge. I was for ever on the look-out for some event that should make escape imperative, but yet that never presented itself. I slept lightly, left my door ajar to catch the slightest sound, even made stealthy tours of the house below-stairs while everybody dreamed in their beds. But I discovered nothing; the doors were always locked; I neither saw the housekeeper again in unreasonable times and places, nor heard a footstep in the passages and halls. The Noise was never once repeated. That horrible, ultimate thunder, my intensest dread of all, lay withdrawn into the abyss whence it had twice arisen. And though in my thoughts it was sternly denied existence, the great black reason for the fact afflicted me unbelievably. Since Mabel's fruitless effort to escape, the Doors kept closed remorselessly. She had failed; *they* gave up hope. For this was the explanation that haunted the region of my mind where feelings stir and hint before they clothe themselves in actual language. Only I firmly kept it there; it never knew expression.

But, if my ears were open, my eyes were opened too, and it were idle to pretend that I did not notice a hundred details that were capable of sinister interpretation had I been weak enough to yield. Some protective barrier had fallen into ruins round me, so that Terror stalked behind the general collapse, feeling for me through all the gaping fissures. Much of this, I admit, must have been merely the elaboration of those sensations I had first vaguely felt, before subsequent events and my talks with Frances had dramatised them into living thoughts. I therefore leave them unmentioned in this history, just as my mind left them unmentioned in that interminable final week.

Our life went on precisely as before—Mabel unreal and outwardly so still; Frances, secretive, anxious, tactful to the point of slyness, and keen to save to the point of self-forgetfulness. There were the same stupid meals, the same wearisome long evenings, the stifling ugliness of house and grounds, the

Shadow settling in so thickly that it seemed almost a visible, tangible thing. I came to feel the only friendly things in all this hostile, cruel place were the robins that hopped boldly over the monstrous terraces and even up to the windows of the unsightly house itself. The robins alone knew joy; they danced, believing no evil thing was possible in all God's radiant world. They believed in everybody; *their* god's plan of life had no room in it for hell, damnation and lakes of brimstone. I came to love the little birds. Had Samuel Franklyn known them, he might have preached a different sermon, bequeathing love in place of terror! . . .

Most of my time I spent writing; but it was a pretence at best, and rather a dangerous one besides. For it stirred the mind to production, with the result that other things came pouring in as well. With reading it was the same. In the end I found an aggressive, deliberate resistance to be the only way of feasible defence. To walk far afield was out of the question, for it meant leaving my sister too long alone, so that my exercise was confined to nearer home. My saunters in the grounds, however, never surprised the goblin garden again. It was close at hand, but I seemed unable to get wholly into it. Too many things assailed my mind for any one to hold exclusive possession, perhaps.

Indeed, all the interpretations, all the "layers," to use my sister's phrase, slipped in by turns and lodged there for a time. They came day and night, and though my reason denied them entrance they held their own as by a kind of squatters' right. They stirred moods already in me, that is, and did not introduce entirely new ones; for every mind conceals ancestral deposits that have been cultivated in turn along the whole line of its descent. Any day a chance shower may cause this one or that to blossom. Thus it came to me, at any rate. After darkness the Inquisition paced the empty corridors and set up ghastly apparatus in the dismal halls; and once, in the library, there swept over me that easy and delicious conviction that by confessing my wickedness I could resume it later, since Confession is expression, and expression brings relief and leaves one ready to accumulate again. And in such mood I felt bitter and unforgiving towards all others who thought differently. Another time it was a Pagan thing that assaulted me—so trivial yet oh, so significant at the time—when I dreamed that a herd of centaurs rolled up with a great stamping of hoofs round the house to destroy it, and then woke to hear the horses tramping across the field below the lawns; they neighed ominously and their noisy panting was audible as if it were just outside my windows.

But the tree episode, I think, was the most curious of all—except, perhaps, the incident with the children which I shall mention in a moment—for its closeness to reality was so unforgettable. Outside the east window of my room stood a giant Wellingtonia on the lawn, its head rising level with

the upper sash. It grew some twenty feet away, planted on the highest terrace, and I often saw it when closing my curtains for the night, noticing
how it drew its heavy skirts about it, and how the light from other windows
threw glimmering streaks and patches that turned it into the semblance of a
towering, solemn image. It stood there then so strikingly, somehow like a
great old-world idol, that it claimed attention. Its appearance was curiously
formidable. Its branches rustled without visibly moving and it had a certain
portentous, forbidding air, so grand and dark and monstrous in the night
that I was always glad when my curtains shut it out. Yet, once in bed, I had
never thought about it one way or the other, and by day had certainly never
sought it out.

One night, then, as I went to bed and closed this window against a cutting easterly wind, I saw—that there were two of these trees. A brother Wellingtonia rose mysteriously beside it, equally huge, equally towering, equally
monstrous. The menacing pair of them faced me there upon the lawn. But in
this new arrival lay a strange suggestion that frightened me before I could argue it away. Exact counterpart of its giant companion, it revealed also that
gross, odious quality that all my sister's paintings held. I got the odd impression that the rest of these trees, stretching away dimly in a troop over the further lawns, were similar, and that, led by this enormous pair, they had all
moved boldly closer to my windows. At the same moment a blind was drawn
down over an upper room; the second tree disappeared into the surrounding
darkness. It was, of course, this chance light that had brought it into the field
of vision, but when the black shutter dropped over it, hiding it from view, the
manner of its vanishing produced the queer effect that it had slipped into its
companion—almost that it had been an emanation of the one I so disliked,
and not really a tree at all! In this way the garden turned vehicle for expressing
what lay behind it all! . . .

The behaviour of the doors, the little, ordinary doors, seemed scarcely
worth mention at all, their queer way of opening and shutting of their own
accord; for this was accountable in a hundred natural ways, and to tell the
truth, I never caught one in the act of moving. Indeed, only after frequent
repetitions, did the detail force itself upon me, when, having noticed one, I
noticed all. It produced, however, the unpleasant impression of a continual
coming and going in the house, as though, screened cleverly and purposely
from actual sight, some one in the building held constant invisible intercourse
with others.

Upon detailed descriptions of these uncertain incidents I do not venture,
individually so trivial, but taken all together so impressive and so insolent. But
the episode of the children, mentioned above, was different. And I give it be-

cause it showed how vividly the intuitive child-mind received the impression—one impression, at any rate—of what was in the air. It may be told in a very few words. I believe they were the coachman's children, and that the man had been in Mr. Franklyn's service; but of neither point am I quite positive. I heard screaming in the rose-garden that runs along the stable walls—it was one afternoon not far from the tea-hour—and on hurrying up I found a little girl of nine or ten fastened with ropes to a rustic seat, and two other children—boys, one about twelve and one much younger—gathering sticks beneath the climbing rose-trees. The girl was white and frightened, but the others were laughing and talking among themselves so busily while they picked that they did not notice my abrupt arrival. Some game, I understood, was in progress, but a game that had become too serious for the happiness of the prisoner, for there was a fear in the girl's eyes that was a very genuine fear indeed. I unfastened her at once; the ropes were so loosely and clumsily knotted that they had not hurt her skin; it was not that which made her pale. She collapsed a moment upon the bench, then picked up her tiny skirts and dived away at full speed into the safety of the stable-yard. There was no response to my brief comforting, but she ran as though for her life, and I divined that some horrid boys' cruelty had been afoot. It was probably mere thoughtlessness, as cruelty with children usually is, but something in me decided to discover exactly what it was.

And the boys, not one whit alarmed at my intervention, merely laughed shyly when I explained that their prisoner had escaped, and told me frankly what their "gime" had been. There was no vestige of shame in them, nor any idea, of course, that they aped a monstrous reality. That it was mere pretence was neither here nor there. To them, though make-believe, it was a make-believe of something that was right and natural and in no sense cruel. Grown-ups did it too. It was necessary for her good.

"We were going to burn her up, sir," the older one informed me, answering my "Why?" with the explanation, "Because she wouldn't believe what we wanted 'er to believe."

And, game though it was, the feeling of reality about the little episode was so arresting, so terrific in some way, that only with difficulty did I confine my admonitions on this occasion to mere words. The boys slunk off, frightened in their turn, yet not, I felt, convinced that they had erred in principle. It was their inheritance. They had breathed it in with the atmosphere of their bringing-up. They would renew the salutary torture when they could—till she "believed" as they did.

I went back into the house, afflicted with a passion of mingled pity and distress impossible to describe, yet on my short way across the garden was attacked by other moods in turn, each more real and bitter than its predecessor. I received the whole series, as it were, at once. I felt like a diver rising to the surface through layers of water at different temperatures, though here the natural order was reversed, and the cooler strata were uppermost, the heated ones below. Thus, I was caught by the goblin touch of the willows that fringed the field; by the sensuous curving of the twisted ash that formed a gateway to the little grove of sapling oaks where fauns and satyrs lurked to play in the moonlight before Pagan altars; and by the cloaking darkness, next, of the copse of stunted pines, close gathered each to each, where hooded figures stalked behind an awful cross. The episode with the children seemed to have opened me like a knife. The whole Place rushed at me.

I suspect this synthesis of many moods produced in me that climax of loathing and disgust which made me feel the limit of bearable emotion had been reached, so that I made straight to find Frances in order to convince her that at any rate *I* must leave. For, although this was our last day in the house, and we had arranged to go next day, the dread was in me that she would still find some persuasive reason for staying on. And an unexpected incident then made my dread unnecessary. The front door was open and a cab stood in the drive; a tall, elderly man was gravely talking in the hall with the parlourmaid we called the Grenadier. He held a piece of paper in his hand. "I have called to see the house," I heard him say, as I ran up the stairs to Frances, who was peering like an inquisitive child over the banisters. . . .

"Yes," she told me, with a sigh, I know not whether of resignation or relief, "the house *is* to be let or sold. Mabel has decided. Some Society or other, I believe—"

I was overjoyed: this made our leaving right and possible. "You never told me, Frances!"

"Mabel only heard of it a few days ago. She told me herself this morning. It is a chance, she says. Alone she cannot get it 'straight.'"

"Defeat?" I asked, watching her closely.

"She thinks she has found a way out. It's not a family, you see, it's a Society, a sort of Community—they go in for thought—"

"A Community!" I gasped. "You mean religious?"

She shook her head. "Not exactly," she said, smiling, "but some kind of association of men and women who want a headquarters in the country—a place where they can write and meditate—*think*—mature their plans and all the rest—I don't know exactly what."

"Utopian dreamers?" I asked, yet feeling an immense relief come over me as I heard. But I asked in ignorance, not cynically. Frances would know. She knew all this kind of thing.

"No, not that exactly," she smiled. "Their teachings are grand and simple—old as the world too, really—the basis of every religion before men's mind perverted them with their manufactured creeds—"

Footsteps on the stairs, and the sound of voices, interrupted our odd impromptu conversation, as the Grenadier came up, followed by the tall, grave gentleman who was being shown over the house. My sister drew me along the corridor towards her room, where she went in and closed the door behind me, yet not before I had stolen a good look at the caller—long enough, at least, for his face and general appearance to have made a definite impression on me. For something strong and peaceful emanated from his presence; he moved with such quiet dignity; the glance of his eyes was so steady and reassuring, that my mind labelled him instantly as a type of man one would turn to in an emergency and not be disappointed. I had seen him but for a passing moment, but I had seen him twice, and the way he walked down the passage, looking competently about him, conveyed the same impression as when I saw him standing at the door—fearless, tolerant, wise. "A sincere and kindly character," I judged instantly, "a man whom some big kind of love has trained in sweetness towards the world; no hate in him anywhere." A great deal, no doubt, to read in so brief a glance! Yet his voice confirmed my intuition, a deep and very gentle voice, great firmness in it too.

"Have I become suddenly sensitive to people's atmospheres in this extraordinary fashion?" I asked myself, smiling, as I stood in the room and heard the door close behind me. "Have I developed some clairvoyant faculty here?" At any other time I should have mocked.

And I sat down and faced my sister, feeling strangely comforted and at peace for the first time since I had stepped beneath The Towers' roof a month ago. Frances, I then saw, was smiling a little as she watched me.

"You know him?" I asked.

"You felt it too?" was her question in reply. "No," she added, "I don't know him—beyond the fact that he is a leader in the Movement and has devoted years and money to its objects. Mabel felt the same thing in him that you have felt—and jumped at it."

"But you've seen him before?" I urged, for the certainty was in me that he was no stranger to her.

She shook her head. "He called one day early this week, when you were out. Mabel saw him. I believe"—she hesitated a moment, as though expecting me to stop her with my usual impatience of such subjects—"I believe he has explained everything to her—the beliefs he embodies, she declares, are her salvation—might be, rather, if she could adopt them."

"Conversion again?" For I remembered her riches, and how gladly a Society would gobble them.

"The layers I told you about," she continued calmly, shrugging her shoulders slightly—"the deposits that are left behind by strong thinking and *real*
belief—but especially by ugly, hateful belief, because, you see—unfortunately
there's more vital passion in that sort—"

"Frances, I don't understand a bit," I said out loud, but said it a little
humbly, for the impression the man had left was still strong upon me and I
was grateful for the steady sense of peace and comfort he had somehow in
troduced. The horrors had been so dreadful. My nerves, doubtless, were more
than a little overstrained. Absurd as it must sound, I classed him in my mind
with the robins, the happy, confiding robins, who believed in everybody and
thought no evil! I laughed a moment at my ridiculous idea, and my sister, encouraged by this sign of patience in me, continued more fluently:

"Of course you don't understand, Bill. Why should you? You've never
thought about such things. Needing no creed yourself, you think all creeds are
rubbish."

"I'm open to conviction—I'm tolerant," I interrupted.

"You're as narrow as Sam Franklyn, and as crammed with prejudice," she
answered, knowing that she had me at her mercy.

"Then, pray, what may be his, or his Society's beliefs?" I asked, feeling no
desire to argue, "and how are they going to prove your Mabel's salvation? Can
they bring beauty into all this aggressive hate and ugliness?"

"Certain hope and peace," she said, "that peace which is understanding,
and that understanding which explains *all* creeds and therefore tolerates
them."

"Toleration! The one word a religious man loathes above all others! His
pet word is damnation—"

"Tolerates them," she repeated patiently, unperturbed by my explosion,
"because it includes them all."

"Fine, if true," I admitted, "very fine. But how, pray, does it include them
all?"

"Because the key-word, the motto, of their Society is, 'There is no religion higher than Truth,' and it has no single dogma of any kind. Above all,"
she went on, "because it claims that no individual can be 'lost.' It teaches universal salvation. To damn outsiders is uncivilised, childish, impure. Some take
longer than others—it's according to the way they think and live—but all find
peace, through development, in the end. What the creeds call a hopeless soul,
it regards as a soul having further to go. There is no damnation—"

"Well, well," I exclaimed, feeling that she rode her hobby-horse too wildly, too roughly over me, "but what is the bearing of all this upon this dreadful place, and upon Mabel? I'll admit that there is this atmosphere—this—er—inexplicable horror in the house and grounds, and that if not of damnation exactly, it is certainly damnable. I'm not too prejudiced to deny *that*, for I've felt it myself."

To my relief she was brief. She made her statement, leaving me to take it or reject it as I would.

"The thought and belief its former occupants—have left behind. For there has been coincidence here, a coincidence that must be rare. The site on which this modern house now stands was Roman, before that early Britain, with burial mounds, before that again, Druid—the Druid stones still lie in that copse below the field, the Tumuli among the ilexes behind the drive. The older building Sam Franklyn altered and practically pulled down was a monastery; he changed the chapel into a meeting hall, which is now the music room; but, before he came here, the house was occupied by Manetti, a violent Catholic without tolerance or vision; and in the interval between these two, Julius Weinbaum had it, Hebrew of most rigid orthodox type imaginable—so they all have left their—"

"Even so," I repeated, yet interested to hear the rest, "what of it?"

"Simply this," said Frances with conviction, "that each in turn has left his layer of concentrated thinking and belief behind him; because each believed intensely, absolutely, beyond the least weakening of any doubt—the kind of strong belief and thinking that is rare anywhere to-day, the kind that wills, impregnates objects, saturates the atmosphere, haunts, in a word. And each, believing he was utterly and finally right, damned with equally positive conviction the rest of the world. One and all preached that implicitly if not explicitly. It's the root of every creed. Last of the bigoted, grim series came Samuel Franklyn."

I listened in amazement that increased as she went on. Up to this point her explanation was so admirable. It was, indeed, a pretty study in psychology if it were true.

"Then why does nothing ever happen?" I enquired mildly. "A place so thickly haunted ought to produce a crop of no ordinary results!"

"There lies the proof," she went on, in a lowered voice, "the proof of the horror and the ugly reality. The thought and belief of each occupant in turn kept all the others under. They gave no sign of life at the time. But the results of thinking never die. They crop out again the moment there's an opening. And, with the return of Mabel in her negative state, believing nothing positive herself, the place for the first time found itself free to reproduce its buried stores. Damnation, hell-fire, and the rest—the most permanent and vital thought of all those creeds, since it was applied to the majority of the world—broke loose again, for there was no restraint to hold it back. Each sought to obtain its former supremacy. None conquered. There results a pandemonium of hate and fear, of striving to escape, of agonised, bitter warring to find safety, peace—salvation. The place is saturated by that appalling stream of thinking—the terror of the damned. It concentrated upon Mabel, whose negative attitude furnished the channel of deliverance. You and I, according to our sympathy with her, were similarly involved. Nothing happened, because no one layer could ever gain the supremacy."

I was so interested—I dare not say amused—that I stared in silence while she paused a moment, afraid that she would draw rein and end the fairy tale too soon.

"The beliefs of this man, of his Society rather, vigorously thought and therefore vigorously given out here, will put the whole place straight. It will act as a solvent. These vitriolic layers actively denied, will fuse and disappear in the stream of gentle, tolerant sympathy which is love. For each member, worthy of the name, loves the world, and all creeds go into the melting pot; Mabel, too, if she joins them out of real conviction, will find salvation—"

"Thinking, I know, is of the first importance," I objected, "but don't you, perhaps, exaggerate the power of feeling and emotion which in religion are *au fond* always hysterical?"

"What is the world," she told me, "but thinking and feeling? An individual's world is entirely what that individual thinks and believes—interpretation. There is no other. And unless he really thinks and really believes, he has no permanent world at all. I grant that few people think, and still fewer believe, and that most take ready-made suits and make them do. Only the strong make their own things; the lesser fry, Mabel among them, are merely swept up into what has been manufactured for them. They get along somehow. You and I have made for ourselves, Mabel has not. She is a nonentity, and when her belief is taken from her, she goes with it."

It was not in me just then to criticise the evasion, or pick out the sophistry from the truth. I merely waited for her to continue.

"None of us have Truth, my dear Frances," I ventured presently, seeing that she kept silent.

"Precisely," she answered, "but most of us have beliefs. And what one believes and thinks affects the world at large. Consider the legacy of hatred and cruelty involved in the doctrines men have built into their creeds where the *sine quâ non* of salvation is absolute acceptance of one particular set of views or else perishing everlastingly—for only by repudiating history can they disavow it—"

"You're not quite accurate," I put in. "Not all the creeds teach damnation, do they? Franklyn did, of course; but the others are a bit modernised now surely?"

"Trying to get out of it," she admitted, "perhaps they are, but damnation of unbelievers—of most of the world, that is—is their rather favourite idea if you talk with them."

"I never have."

She smiled. "But I have," she said significantly, "so, if you consider what the various occupants of this house have so strongly held and thought and believed, you need not be surprised that the influence they have left behind them should be a dark and dreadful legacy. For thought, you know, does leave—"

The opening of the door, to my great relief, interrupted her, as the Grenadier led in the visitor to see the room. He bowed to both of us with a brief word of apology, looked round him, and withdrew, and with his departure the conversation between us came naturally to an end. I followed him out. Neither of us in any case, I think, cared to argue further.

And, so far as I am aware, the curious history of The Towers ends here, too. There was no climax in the story sense. Nothing ever really happened. We left next morning for London. I only know that the Society in question took the house and have since occupied it to their entire satisfaction, and that Mabel, who became a member shortly afterwards, now stays there frequently when in need of repose from the arduous and unselfish labours she took upon herself under its ægis. She dined with us only the other night, here in our tiny Chelsea flat, and a jollier, saner, more interesting and happy guest I could hardly wish for. She was vital—in the best sense; the lay-figure had come to life. I found it difficult to believe she was the same woman whose fearful effigy had floated down those dreary corridors and almost disappeared in the depths of that atrocious Shadow.

What her beliefs were now I was wise enough to leave unquestioned, and Frances, to my great relief, kept the conversation well away from such inappropriate topics. It was clear, however, that the woman had in herself some secret source of joy, that she was now an aggressive, positive force, sure of herself, and apparently afraid of nothing in heaven or hell. She radiated something very like hope and courage about her, and talked as though the world were a glorious place and everybody in it kind and beautiful. Her optimism was certainly infectious.

The Towers were mentioned only in passing. The name of Marsh came up—not *the* Marsh, it so happened, but a name in some book that was being discussed—and I was unable to restrain myself. Curiosity was too strong. I threw out a casual enquiry Mabel could leave unanswered if she wished. But there was no desire to avoid it. Her reply was frank and smiling.

"Would you believe it? She married," Mabel told me, though obviously surprised that I remembered the housekeeper at all; "and is happy as the day is long. She's found her right niche in life. A sergeant—"

"The army!" I ejaculated.

"Salvation Army," she explained merrily.

Frances exchanged a glance with me. I laughed too, for the information took me by surprise. I cannot say why exactly, but I expected at least to hear that the woman had met some dreadful end, not impossibly by burning.

"And The Towers, now called the Rest House," Mabel chattered on, "seems to me the most peaceful and delightful spot in England—"

"Really," I said politely.

"When I lived there in the old days—while you were there, perhaps, though I won't be sure," Mabel went on, "the story got abroad that it was haunted. Wasn't it odd? A less likely place for a ghost I've never seen. Why, it had no atmosphere at all." She said this to Frances, glancing up at me with a smile that apparently had no hidden meaning. "Did *you* notice anything queer about it when you were there?"

This was plainly addressed to me.

"I found it—er—difficult to settle down to anything," I said, after an instant's hesitation. I couldn't work there—"

"But I thought you wrote that wonderful book on the Deaf and Blind while you stayed with me," she asked innocently.

I stammered a little. "Oh, no, not then. I only made a few notes—er—at The Towers. My mind, oddly enough, refused to produce at all down there. But—why do you ask? Did anything—was anything *supposed* to happen there?"

She looked searchingly into my eyes a moment before she answered.

"Not that I know of," she said simply.

A Descent into Egypt

He was an accomplished, versatile man whom some called brilliant. Behind his talents lay a wealth of material that right selection could have lifted into genuine distinction. He did too many things, however, to excel in one, for a restless curiosity kept him ever on the move. George Isley was an able man. His short career in diplomacy proved it; yet, when he abandoned this for travel and exploration, no one thought it a pity. He would do big things in any line. He was merely finding himself.

Among the rolling stones of humanity a few acquire moss of considerable value. They are not necessarily shiftless; they travel light; the comfortable pockets in the game of life that attract the majority are too small to retain them; they are in and out again in a moment. The world says, "What a pity! They stick to nothing!" but the fact is that, like questing wild birds, they seek the nest they need. It is a question of values. They judge swiftly, change their line of flight, are gone, not even hearing the comment that they might have "retired with a pension."

And to this homeless, questing type George Isley certainly belonged. He was by no means shiftless. He merely sought with insatiable yearning that soft particular nest where he could settle down in permanently. And to an accompaniment of sighs and regrets from his friends he found it; he found it, however, not in the present, but by retiring from the world "without a pension," unclothed with honours and distinctions. He withdrew from the present and slipped softly back into a mighty Past where he belonged. Why; how; obeying what strange instincts—this remains unknown, deep secret of an inner life that found no resting-place in modern things. Such instincts are not disclosable in twentieth-century language, nor are the details of such a journey properly describable at all. Except by the few—poets, prophets, psychiatrists and the like—such experiences are dismissed with the neat museum label—"queer."

So, equally, must the recorder of this experience share the honour of that little label—he who by chance witnessed certain external and visible signs of this inner and spiritual journey. There remains, nevertheless, the amazing reality of the experience; and to the recorder alone was some clue of interpretation possible, perhaps, because in himself also lay the lure, though less imperative, of a similar journey. At any rate the interpretation may be offered to the handful who realize that trains and motors are not the only means of travel left to our progressive race.

In his younger days I knew George Isley intimately. I know him now. But the George Isley I knew of old, the arresting personality with whom I travelled, climbed, explored, is no longer with us. He is not here. He disappeared—gradually—into the past. There is no George Isley. And that such an individuality could vanish, while still his outer semblance walks the familiar streets, normal apparently, and not yet fifty in the number of his years, seems a tale, though difficult, well worth the telling. For I witnessed the slow submergence. It was very gradual. I cannot pretend to understand the entire significance of it. There was something questionable and sinister in the business that offered hints of astonishing possibilities. Were there a corps of spiritual police, the matter might be partially cleared up, but since none of the churches have yet organised anything effective of this sort, one can only fall back upon variants of the blessed "Mesopotamia," and whisper of derangement, and the like. Such labels, of course, explain as little as most other *clichés* in life. That well-groomed, soldierly figure strolling down Piccadilly, watching the Races, dining out—there is no derangement there. The face is not melancholy, the eye not wild; the gestures are quiet and the speech controlled. Yet the eye is empty, the face expressionless. Vacancy reigns there, provocative and significant. If not unduly noticeable, it is because the majority in life neither expect, nor offer, more.

At closer quarters you may think questioning things, or you may think—nothing; probably the latter. You may wonder why something continually expected does not make its appearance; and you may watch for the evidence of "personality" the general presentment of the man has led you to expect. Disappointed, therefore, you may certainly be; but I defy you to discover the smallest hint of mental disorder, and of derangement or nervous affliction, absolutely nothing. Before long, perhaps, you may feel you are talking with a dummy, some well-trained automaton, a nonentity devoid of spontaneous life; and afterwards you may find that memory fades rapidly away, as though no impression of any kind has really been made at all. All this, yes; but nothing pathological. A few may be stimulated by this startling discrepancy between promise and performance, but most, accustomed to accept face values, would say, "a pleasant fellow, but nothing in him much . . ." and an hour later forgot him altogether.

For the truth is as you, perhaps, divined. You have been sitting beside no one, you have been talking to, looking at, listening to—no one. The intercourse has conveyed nothing that can waken human response in you, good, bad or indifferent. There is no George Isley. And the discovery, if you make it, will not even cause you to creep with the uncanniness of the experience, because the exterior is so wholly pleasing. George Isley to-day is a picture with no meaning in it that charms merely by the harmonious colouring of an inoffensive subject. He moves undiscovered in the little world of society to which he was born, secure in the groove first habit has made comfortably automatic for him. No one guesses; none, that is, but the few who knew him intimately in early life. And his wandering existence has scattered these; they have forgotten what he was. So perfect, indeed, is he in the manners of the commonplace fashionable man, that no woman in his "set" is aware that he differs from the type she is accustomed to. He turns a compliment with the accepted language of her text-book, motors, golfs and gambles in the regulation manner of his particular world. He is an admirable, perfect automaton. He is nothing. He is a human shell.

II

The name of George Isley had been before the public for some years when, after a considerable interval, we met again in a hotel in Egypt, I for my health, he for I knew not what—at first. But I soon discovered: archæology and excavation had taken hold of him, though he had gone so quietly about it that no one seemed to have heard. I was not sure that he was glad to see me, for he had first withdrawn, annoyed, it seemed, at being discovered, but later, as though after consideration, had made tentative advances. He welcomed me with a curious gesture of the entire body that seemed to shake himself free from something that had made him forget my identity. There was pathos somewhere in his attitude, almost as though he asked for sympathy. "I've been out here, off and on, for the last three years," he told me, after describing something of what he had been doing. "I find it the most repaying hobby in the world. It leads to a reconstruction—an imaginative reconstruction, of course, I mean—of an enormous thing the world had entirely lost. A very gorgeous, stimulating hobby, believe me, and a very entic—" he quickly changed the word—"exacting one indeed."

I remember looking him up and down with astonishment. There was a change in him, a lack; a note was missing in his enthusiasm, a colour in the voice, a quality in his manner. The ingredients were not mixed quite as of old. I did not bother him with questions, but I noted thus at the very first a subtle alteration. Another facet of the man presented itself. Something that had been independent and aggressive was replaced by a certain emptiness that invited sympathy. Even in his physical appearance the change was manifested—this odd suggestion of lessening. I looked again more closely. Lessening *was* the word. He had somehow dwindled. It was startling, vaguely unpleasant too.

The entire subject, as usual, was at his fingertips; he knew all the important men; and had spent money freely on his hobby. I laughed, reminding him of his

remark that Egypt had no attractions for him, owing to the organised adver-
tisement of its somewhat theatrical charms. Admitting his error with a gesture,
he brushed the objection easily aside. His manner, and a certain glow that rose
about his atmosphere as he answered, increased my first astonishment. His
voice was significant and suggestive. "Come out with me," he said in a low tone,
"and see how little the tourists matter, how inappreciable the excavation is compared to what remains to be done, how gigantic"—he emphasised the word impressively—"the scope for discovery remains." He made a movement with his
head and shoulders that conveyed a sense of the prodigious, for he was of massive build, his cast of features stern, and his eyes, set deep into the face, shone
past me with a sombre gleam in them I did not quite account for. It was the
voice, however, that brought the mystery in. It vibrated somewhere below the
actual sound of it. "Egypt," he continued—and so gravely that at first I made
the mistake of thinking he chose the curious words on purpose to produce a
theatrical effect—"that has enriched her blood with the pageant of so many civi-
lisations, that has devoured Persians, Greeks and Romans, Saracens and Mame-
lukes, a dozen conquests and invasions besides,—what can mere tourists or
explorers matter to her? The excavators scratch their skin and dig up mummies;
and as for tourists!"—he laughed contemptuously—"flies that settle for a moment on her covered face, to vanish at the first signs of heat! Egypt is not even
aware of them. The real Egypt lies underground in darkness. Tourists must have
light, to be seen as well as to see. And the diggers—!"

He paused, smiling with something between pity and contempt I did not
quite appreciate, for, personally, I felt a great respect for the tireless excavators.
And then he added, with a touch of feeling in his tone as though he had a griev-
ance against them, and had not also "dug" himself, "Men who uncover the
dead, restore the temples, and reconstruct a skeleton, thinking they have read its
beating heart. . . ." He shrugged his great shoulders, and the rest of the sentence
may have been but the protest of a man in defence of his own hobby, but that
there seemed an undue earnestness and gravity about it that made me wonder
more than ever. He went on to speak of the strangeness of the land as a mere
ribbon of vegetation along the ancient river, the rest all ruins, desert, sun-
drenched wilderness of death, yet so breakingly alive with wonder, power and a
certain disquieting sense of deathlessness. There seemed, for him, a revelation of
unusual spiritual kind in this land where the Past survived so potently. He spoke
almost as though it obliterated the Present.

Indeed, the hint of something solemn behind his words made it difficult
for me to keep up the conversation, and the pause that presently came I filled
in with some word of questioning surprise, which yet, I think, was chiefly in
concurrence. I was aware of some big belief in him, some enveloping emotion

that escaped my grasp. Yet, though I did not understand, his great mood swept me. . . . His voice lowered, then, as he went on to mention temples, tombs and deities, details of his own discoveries and of their effect upon him, but to this I listened with half an ear, because in the unusual language he had first made use of I detected this other thing that stirred my curiosity more— stirred it uncomfortably.

"Then the spell," I asked, remembering the effect of Egypt upon myself two years before, "has worked upon you as upon most others, only with greater power?"

He looked hard at me a moment, signs of trouble showing themselves faintly in his rugged, interesting face. I think he wanted to say more than he could bring himself to confess. He hesitated.

"I'm only glad," he replied after a pause, "it didn't get hold of me earlier in life. It would have absorbed me. I should have lost all other interests. Now,"—that curious look of helplessness, of asking sympathy, flitted like a shadow through his eyes—"now that I'm on the decline . . . it matters less."

On the decline! I cannot imagine by what blundering I missed this chance he never offered again; somehow or other the singular phrase passed un-noticed at the moment, and only came upon me with its full significance later when it was too awkward to refer to it. He tested my readiness to help, to sympathise, to share his inner life. I missed the clue. For, at the moment, a more practical consideration interested me in his language. Being of those who regretted that he had not excelled by devoting his powers to a single ob-ject, I shrugged my shoulders. He caught my meaning instantly. Oh, he was glad to talk. He felt the possibility of my sympathy underneath, I think.

"No, no, you take me wrongly there," he said with gravity. "What I mean—and I ought to know if any one does!—is that while most countries give, others take away. Egypt changes you. No one can live here and remain exactly what he was before."

This puzzled me. It startled, too, again. His manner was so earnest.. "And Egypt, you mean, is one of the countries that takes away?" I asked. The strange idea unsettled my thoughts a little.

"First takes away from you," he replied, "but in the end takes *you* away. Some lands enrich you," he went on, seeing that I listened, "while others im-poverish. From India, Greece, Italy, all ancient lands, you return with memo-ries you can use. From Egypt you return with—nothing. Its splendour stupefies; it's useless. There is a change in your inmost being, an emptiness, an unaccountable yearning, but you find nothing that can fill the lack you're con-scious of. Nothing comes to replace what has gone. You have been drained."

I stared; but I nodded a general acquiescence. Of a sensitive, artistic temperament this was certainly true, though by no means the superficial and generally accepted verdict. The majority imagine that Egypt has filled them to the brim. I took his deeper reading of the facts. I was aware of an odd fascination in his idea.

"Modern Egypt," he continued, "is, after all, but a trick of civilisation," and there was a kind of breathlessness in his measured tone, "but ancient Egypt lies waiting, hiding, underneath. Though dead, she is amazingly alive. And you feel her touching you. She takes from you. She enriches herself. You return from Egypt—less than you were before."

What came over my mind is hard to say. Some touch of visionary imagination burned its flaming path across my mind. I thought of some old Grecian hero speaking of his delicious battle with the gods—battle in which he knew he must be worsted, but yet in which he delighted because at death his spirit would join their glorious company beyond this world. I was aware, that is to say, of resignation as well as resistance in him. He already felt the effortless peace which follows upon long, unequal battling, as of a man who has fought the rapids with a strain beyond his strength, then sinks back and goes with the awful mass of water smoothly and indifferently—over the quiet fall.

Yet, it was not so much his words which clothed picturesquely an undeniable truth, as the force of conviction that drove behind them, shrouding my mind with mystery and darkness. His eyes, so steadily holding mine, were lit, I admit, yet they were calm and sane as those of a doctor discussing the symptoms of that daily battle to which we all finally succumb. This analogy occurred to me.

"There *is*"—I stammered a little, faltering in my speech—"an incalculable element in the country . . . somewhere, I confess. You put it—rather strongly, though, don't you?"

He answered quietly, moving his eyes from my face towards the window that framed the serene and exquisite sky towards the Nile.

"The real, invisible Egypt," he murmured, "I do find rather—strong. I find it difficult to deal with. You see," and he turned towards me, smiling like a tired child, "I think the truth is that Egypt deals with me."

"It draws—" I began, then started as he interrupted me at once.

"Into the Past." He uttered the little word in a way beyond me to describe. There came a flood of glory with it, a sense of peace and beauty, of battles over and of rest attained. No saint could have brimmed "Heaven" with as much passionately enticing meaning. He went willingly, prolonging the struggle merely to enjoy the greater relief and joy of the consummation.

For again he spoke as though a struggle were in progress in his being. I got the impression that he somewhere wanted help. I understood the pathetic quality I had vaguely discerned already. His character naturally was so strong and independent. It now seemed weaker, as though certain fibres had been drawn out. And I understood then that the spell of Egypt, so lightly chattered about in its sensational aspect, so rarely known in its naked power, the nameless, creeping influence that begins deep below the surface and thence sends delicate tendrils outwards, was in his blood. I, in my untaught ignorance, had felt it too; it is undeniable; one is aware of unaccountable, queer things in Egypt; even the utterly prosaic feel them. Dead Egypt is marvellously alive. . .

.

I glanced past him out of the big windows where the desert glimmered in its featureless expanse of yellow leagues, two monstrous pyramids signalling from across the Nile, and for a moment—inexplicably, it seemed to me afterwards—I lost sight of my companion's stalwart figure that was yet so close before my eyes. He had risen from his chair; he was standing near me; yet my sight missed him altogether. Something, dim as a shadow, faint as a breath of air, rose up and bore my thoughts away, obliterating vision too. I forgot for a moment who I was; identity slipped from me. Thought, sight, feeling, all sank away into the emptiness of those sun-baked sands, sank, as it were, into nothingness, caught away from the Present, enticed, absorbed. . . . And when I looked back again to answer him, or rather to ask what his curious words could mean—he was no longer there. More than surprised—for there was something of shock in the disappearance—I turned to search. I had not seen him go. He had stolen from my side so softly, slipped away silently, mysteriously, and—so easily. I remember that a faint shiver ran down my back as I realised that I was alone.

Was it that, momentarily, I had caught a reflex of his state of mind? Had my sympathy induced in myself an echo of what he experienced in full—a going backwards, a loss of present vigour, the enticing, subtle draw of those immeasurable sands that hide the living dead from the interruptions of the careless living . . .?

I sat down to reflect and, incidentally, to watch the magnificence of the sunset; and the thing he had said returned upon me with insistent power, ringing like distant bells within my mind. His talk of the tombs and temples passed, but this remained. It stimulated oddly. His talk, I remembered, had always excited curiosity in this way. Some countries give, while others take away. What did he mean precisely? What had Egypt taken away from him? And I realised more definitely that something in him *was* missing, something he possessed in former years that was now no longer there. He had grown shadowy already in my thoughts. The mind searched keenly, but in vain . . . and after some time I left my chair and moved over to another window, aware that a vague discomfort stirred within me that involved uneasiness—for him. I felt pity. But behind the pity was an eager, absorbing curiosity as well. He seemed receding curiously into misty distance, and the strong desire leaped in me to overtake, to travel with him into some vanished splendour that he had re-discovered. The feeling was a most remarkable one, for it included yearning—the yearning for some nameless, forgotten loveliness the world has lost. It was in me too.

At the approach of twilight the mind loves to harbour shadows. The room, empty of guests, was dark behind me; darkness, too, was creeping across the desert like a veil, deepening the serenity of its grim, unfeatured face. It turned pale with distance; the whole great sheet of it went rustling into night. The first stars peeped and twinkled, hanging loosely in the air as though they could be plucked like golden berries; and the sun was already below the Lybian horizon, where gold and crimson faded through violet into blue. I stood watching this mysterious Egyptian dusk, while an eerie glamour seemed to bring the incredible within uneasy reach of the half-faltering senses. . . . And suddenly the truth dropped into me. Over George Isley, over his mind and energies, over his thoughts and over his emotions too, a kind of darkness was also slowly creeping. Something in him had dimmed, yet not with age; it had gone out. Some inner night, stealing over the Present, obliterated it. And yet he looked towards the dawn. Like the Egyptian monuments his eyes turned—eastwards.

And so it came to me that what he had lost was personal ambition. He was glad, he said, that these Egyptian studies had not caught him earlier in life; the language he made use of was peculiar: "Now I am on the decline it matters less." A slight foundation, no doubt, to build conviction on, and yet I felt sure that I was partly right. He was fascinated, but fascinated against his will. The Present in him battled against the Past. Still fighting, he had yet lost hope. The desire *not* to change was now no longer in him. . . .

I turned away from the window so as not to see that grey, encroaching desert, for the discovery produced a certain agitation in me. Egypt seemed suddenly a living entity of enormous power. She stirred about me. She was stirring now. This flat and motionless land pretending it had no movement, was actually busy with a million gestures that came creeping round the heart. She was reducing him. Already from the complex texture of his personality she had drawn one vital thread that in its relation to the general woof was of central importance—ambition. The mind chose the simile; but in my heart where thought fluttered in singular distress, another suggested itself as truer.

"Thread" changed to "artery." I turned quickly and went up to my room where I could be alone. The idea was somewhere ghastly.

III

Yet, while dressing for dinner, the idea exfoliated as only a living thing exfoliates. I saw in George Isley this great question mark that had not been there formerly. All have, of course, some question mark, and carry it about, though with most it rarely becomes visible until the end. With him it was plainly visible in his atmosphere at the hey-day of his life. He wore it like a fine curved scimitar above his head. So full of life, he yet seemed willingly dead. For, though imagination sought every possible explanation, I got no further than the somewhat negative result—that a certain energy, wholly unconnected with mere physical health, had been withdrawn. It was more than ambition, I think, for it included intention, desire, self-confidence as well. It was life itself. He was no longer in the Present. He was no longer *here*.

"Some countries give while others take away. . . . I find Egypt difficult to deal with. I find it . . ." and then that simple, uncomplex adjective—"strong." In memory and experience the entire globe was mapped for him; it remained for Egypt, then, to teach him this marvellous new thing. But not Egypt of to-day; it was vanished Egypt that had robbed him of his strength. He had described it as underground, hidden, waiting. . . . I was again aware of a faint shuddering—as though something crept secretly from my inmost heart to share the experience with him, and as though my sympathy involved a willing consent that this should be so. With sympathy there must always be a shedding of the personal self; each time I felt this sympathy, it seemed that something left me. I thought in circles, arriving at no definite point where I could rest and say "that's it; I understand." The giving attitude of a country was easily comprehensible; but this idea of robbery, of deprivation baffled me. An obscure alarm took hold of me—for myself as well as for him.

At dinner, where he invited me to his table, the impression passed off a good deal, however, and I convicted myself of a woman's exaggeration; yet, as we talked of many a day's adventure together in other lands, it struck me that we oddly left the present out. We ignored to-day. His thoughts, as it were, went most easily backwards. And each adventure led, as by its own natural weight and impetus, towards one thing—the enormous glory of a vanished age. Ancient Egypt was "home" in this mysterious game life played with death. The specific gravity of his being, to say nothing for the moment of my own, had shifted lower, further off, backwards and below, or as he put it—underground. The sinking sensation I experienced was of a literal kind. . . .

And so I found myself wondering what had led him to this particular hotel. I had come out with an affected organ the specialist promised me would heal in the marvellous air of Helouan, but it was queer that my companion also should have chosen it. Its clientèle was mostly invalid, German and Russian invalid at that. The Management set its face against the lighter, gayer side of life that hotels in Egypt usually encourage eagerly. It was a true rest-house, a place of repose and leisure, a place where one could remain undiscovered and unknown. No English patronised it. One might easily—the idea came unbidden, suddenly—hide in it.

"Then you're doing nothing just now," I asked, "in the way of digging? No big expeditions or excavating at the moment?"

"I'm recuperating," he answered carelessly. "I've had two years up at the Valley of the Kings, and overdid it rather. But I'm by way of working at a little thing near here across the Nile." And he pointed in the direction of Sakkhâra, where the huge Memphian cemetery stretches underground from the Dachûr Pyramids to the Gizeh monsters, four miles lower down. "There's a matter of a hundred years in that alone!"

"You must have accumulated a mass of interesting material. I suppose later you'll make use of it—a book or—"

His expression stopped me—that strange look in the eyes that had stirred my first uneasiness. It was as if something struggled up a moment, looked bleakly out upon the present, then sank away again.

"More," he answered listlessly, "than I can ever use. It's much more likely to use me." He said it hurriedly, looking over his shoulder as though some one might be listening, then smiled significantly, bringing his eyes back upon my own again. I told him that he was far too modest. "If all the excavators thought like that," I added, "we ignorant ones should suffer." I laughed, but the laughter was only on my lips.

He shook his head indifferently. "They do their best; they do wonders," he replied, making an indescribable gesture as though he withdrew willingly from the topic altogether, yet could not quite achieve it. "I know their books; I know the writers too—of various nationalities." He paused a moment, and his eyes turned grave. "I cannot understand quite—how they do it," he added half below his breath.

"The labour, you mean? The strain of the climate, and so forth?" I said this purposely, for I knew quite well he meant another thing. The way he looked into my face, however, disturbed me so that I believe I visibly started. Something very deep in me sat up alertly listening, almost on guard.

"I mean," he replied, "that they must have uncommon powers of resistance."

There! He had used the very word that had been hiding in me! "It puzzles me," he went on, "for, with one exception, they are not unusual men. In the way of gifts—oh, yes. It's in the way of resistance and protection that I mean. Self-protection," he added with emphasis.

It was the way he said resistance and self-protection that sent a touch of cold through me: I learned later that he himself had made surprising discoveries in these two years, penetrating closer to the secret life of ancient sacerdotal Egypt than any of his predecessors or co-labourers—then, inexplicably, had ceased. But this was told to me afterwards and by others. At the moment I was only conscious of this odd embarrassment. I did not understand, yet felt that he touched upon something intimately personal to himself. He paused, expecting me to speak.

"Egypt, perhaps, merely pours through them," I ventured. "They give out mechanically, hardly realising how much they give. They report facts devoid of interpretation. Whereas with you it's the actual spirit of the past that is discovered and laid bare. You live it. You feel old Egypt and disclose her. That divining faculty was always yours—uncannily, I used to think."

The flash of his sombre eyes betrayed that my aim was singularly good. It seemed a third had silently joined our little table in the corner. Something intruded, evoked by the power of what our conversation skirted but ever left unmentioned. It was huge and shadowy; it was also watchful. Egypt came gliding, floating up beside us. I saw her reflected in his face and gaze. The desert slipped in through walls and ceiling, rising from beneath our feet, settling about us, listening, peering, waiting. The strange obsession was sudden and complete. The gigantic scale of her swam in among the very pillars, arches, and windows of that modern dining-room. I felt against my skin the touch of chilly air that sunlight never reaches, stealing from beneath the granite monoliths. Behind it came the stifling breath of the heated tombs, of the Serapeum, of the chambers and corridors in the pyramids. There was a rustling as of myriad footsteps far away, and as of sand the busy winds go shifting through the ages. And in startling contrast to this impression of prodigious size, Isley himself wore suddenly an air of strangely dwindling. For a second he shrank visibly before my very eyes. He was receding. His outline seemed to retreat and lessen, as though he stood to the waist in what appeared like flowing mist, only his head and shoulders still above the ground. Far, far away I saw him.

It was a vivid inner picture that I somehow transferred objectively. It was a dramatised sensation, of course. His former phrase "now that I am declining" flashed back upon me with sharp discomfort. Again, perhaps, his state of mind was reflected into me by some emotional telepathy. I waited, conscious of an almost sensible oppression that would not lift. It seemed an age before he spoke, and when he did there was the tremor of feeling in his voice he sought nevertheless to repress. I kept my eyes on the table for some reason. But I listened intently.

"It's you that have the divining faculty, not I," he said, an odd note of distance even in his tone, yet a resonance as though it rose up between reverberating walls. "There *is*, I believe, something here that resents too close inquiry, or rather that resists discovery—almost—takes offence."

I looked up quickly, then looked down again. It was such a startling thing to hear on the lips of a modern Englishman. He spoke lightly, but the expression of his face belied the careless tone. There was no mockery in those earnest eyes, and in the hushed voice was a little creeping sound that gave me once again the touch of goose-flesh. The only word I can find is subterranean: all that was mental in him had sunk, so that he seemed speaking underground, head and shoulders alone visible. The effect was almost ghastly.

"Such extraordinary obstacles are put in one's way," he went on, "when the prying gets too close to the—reality; physical, external obstacles, I mean. Either that, or—the mind loses its assimilative faculties. One or other happens—" his voice died down into a whisper—"and discovery ceases of its own accord."

The same minute, then, he suddenly raised himself like a man emerging from a tomb; he leaned across the table; he made an effort of some violent internal kind, on the verge, I fully believe, of a pregnant personal statement. There was confession in his attitude; I think he was about to speak of his work at Thebes and the reason for its abrupt cessation. For I had the feeling of one about to hear a weighty secret, the responsibility unwelcome. This uncomfortable emotion rose in me, as I raised my eyes to his somewhat unwillingly, only to find that I was wholly at fault. It was not me he was looking at. He was staring past me in the direction of the wide, unshuttered windows. The expression of yearning was visible in his eyes again. Something had stopped his utterance.

And instinctively I turned and saw what he saw. So far as external details were concerned, at least, I saw it.

Across the glare and glitter of the uncompromising modern dining-room, past crowded tables, and over the heads of Germans feeding unpicturesquely, I saw—the moon. Her reddish disc, hanging unreal and enormous, lifted the spread sheet of desert till it floated off the surface of the world. The great window faced the east, where the Arabian desert breaks into a ruin of gorges, cliffs, and flat-topped ridges; it looked unfriendly, ominous, with danger in it; unlike the serener sand-dunes of the Lybian desert, there lay both menace and seduction behind its flood of shadows. And the moonlight emphasised this aspect: its ghostly desolation, its cruelty, its bleak hostility, turning it murderous. For no river sweetens this Arabian desert; instead of sandy softness, it has fangs of limestone rock, sharp and aggressive. Across it, just visible in the moonlight as a thread of paler grey, the old camel-trail to Suez beckoned faintly. And it was this that he was looking at so intently.

It was, I know, a theatrical stage-like glimpse, yet in it a seductiveness most potent. "Come out," it seemed to whisper, "and taste my awful beauty. Come out and lose yourself, and die. Come out and follow my moonlit trail into the Past . . . where there is peace and immobility and silence. My kingdom is unchanging underground. Come down, come softly, come through sandy corridors below this tinsel of your modern world. Come back, come down into my golden past. . . ."

A poignant desire stole through my heart on moonlit feet; I was personally conscious of a keen yearning to slip away in unresisting obedience. For it was uncommonly impressive, this sudden, haunting glimpse of the world outside. The hairy foreigners, uncouthly garbed, all busily eating in full electric light, provided a sensational contrast of emphatically distressing kind. A touch of what is called unearthly hovered about that distance through the window. There was weirdness in it. Egypt looked in upon us. Egypt watched and listened, beckoning through the moonlit windows of the heart to come and find her. Mind and imagination might flounder as they pleased, but something of this kind happened undeniably, whether expression in language fails to hold the truth or not. And George Isley, aware of being seen, looked straight into the awful visage—fascinated.

Over the bronze of his skin there stole a shade of grey. My own feeling of enticement grew—the desire to go out into the moonlight, to leave my kind and wander blindly through the desert, to see the gorges in their shining silver, and taste the keenness of the cool, sharp air. Further than this with me it did not go, but that my companion felt the bigger, deeper draw behind this surface glamour, I have no reasonable doubt. For a moment, indeed, I thought he meant to leave the table; he had half risen in his chair; it seemed he struggled and resisted—and then his big frame subsided again; he sat back; he looked, in the attitude his body took, less impressive, smaller, actually shrunken into the proportions of some minuter scale. It was as though something in that second had been drawn out of him, decreasing even his physical appearance. The voice, when he spoke presently with a touch of resignation, held a lifeless quality as though deprived of virile timbre.

"It's always there," he whispered, half collapsing back into his chair, "it's always watching, waiting, listening. Almost like a monster of the fables, isn't it? It makes no movement of its own, you see. It's far too strong for that. It just hangs there, half in the air and half upon the earth—a gigantic web. Its prey flies into it. That's Egypt all over. D'you feel like that too, or does it seem to you just imaginative rubbish? To me it seems that she just waits her time; she gets you quicker that way; in the end you're bound to go."

"There's power certainly," I said after a moment's pause to collect my wits, my distress increased by the morbidness of his simile. "For some minds there may be a kind of terror too—for weak temperaments that are all imagination." My thoughts were scattered, and I could not readily find good words. "There is startling grandeur in a sight like that, for instance," and I pointed to the window. "You feel drawn—as if you simply *had* to go." My mind still buzzed with his curious words, "In the end you're bound to go." It betrayed his heart and soul. "I suppose a fly does feel drawn," I added, "or a moth to the destroying flame. Or is it just unconscious on their part?"

He jerked his big head significantly. "Well, well," he answered, "but the fly isn't necessarily weak, or the moth misguided. Over-adventurous, perhaps, yet both obedient to the laws of their respective beings. They get warnings too—only, when the moth wants to know too much, the fire stops it. Both flame and spider enrich themselves by understanding the natures of their prey; and fly and moth return again and again until this is accomplished."

Yet George Isley was as sane as the head waiter who, noticing our interest in the window, came up just then and enquired whether we felt a draught and would prefer it closed. Isley, I realised, was struggling to express a passionate state of soul for which, owing to its rarity, no adequate expression lies at hand. There is a language of the mind, but there is none as yet of the spirit. I felt ill at ease. All this was so foreign to the wholesome, strenuous personality of the man as I remembered it.

"But, my dear fellow," I stammered, "aren't you giving poor old Egypt a bad name she hardly deserves? I feel only the amazing strength and beauty of it; awe, if you like, but none of this resentment you so mysteriously hint at."

"You understand, for all that," he answered quietly; and again he seemed on the verge of some significant confession that might ease his soul. My uncomfortable emotion grew. Certainly he was at high pressure somewhere. "And, if necessary, you could help. Your sympathy, I mean, *is* a help already." He said it half to himself and in a suddenly lowered tone again.

"A help!" I gasped. "My sympathy! Of course, if—"

"A witness," he murmured, not looking at me, "some one who understands, yet does not think me mad."

There was such appeal in his voice that I felt ready and eager to do anything to help him. Our eyes met, and my own tried to express this willingness in me; but what I said I hardly know, for a cloud of confusion was on my mind, and my speech went fumbling like a schoolboy's. I was more than disconcerted. Through this bewilderment, then, I just caught the tail-end of another sentence in which the words "relief it is to have . . . some one to hold to . . . when the disappearance comes . . ." sounded like voices heard in dream. But I missed the complete phrase and shrank from. asking him to repeat it.

Some sympathetic answer struggled to my lips, though what it was I know not. The thing I murmured, however, seemed apparently well chosen. He leaned across and laid his big hand a moment on my own with eloquent pressure. It was cold as ice. A look of gratitude passed over his sunburned features. He sighed. And we left the table then and passed into the inner smoking-rooms for coffee—a room whose windows gave upon columned terraces that allowed no view of the encircling desert. He led the conversation into channels less personal and, thank heaven, less intensely emotional and mysterious. What we talked about I now forget; it was interesting but in another key altogether. His old charm and power worked; the respect I had always felt for his character and gifts returned in force, but it was the pity I now experienced that remained chiefly in my mind. For this change in him became more and more noticeable. He was less impressive, less convincing, less suggestive. His talk, though so knowledgeable, lacked that spiritual quality that drives home. He was uncannily less *real.* And I went up to bed, uneasy and disturbed. "It is not age," I said to myself, "and assuredly it is not death he fears, although he spoke of disappearance. It is mental—in the deepest sense. It is what religious people would call soul. Something is happening to his soul."

IV

And this word "soul" remained with me to the end. Egypt was taking his soul away into the Past. What was of value in him went willingly; the rest, some lesser aspect of his mind and character, resisted, holding to the present. A struggle, therefore, was involved. But this was being gradually obliterated too.

How I arrived gaily at this monstrous conclusion seems to me now a mystery; but the truth is that from a conversation one brings away a general idea that is larger than the words actually heard and spoken. I have reported, naturally, but a fragment of what passed between us in language, and of what was suggested—by gesture, expression, silence—merely perhaps a hint. I can only assert that this troubling verdict remained a conviction in my mind. It came upstairs with me; it watched and listened by my side. That mysterious Third evoked in our conversation was bigger than either of us separately; it might be called the spirit of ancient Egypt, or it might be called with equal generalisation, the Past. This Third, at any rate, stood by me, whispering this astounding thing. I went out on to my little balcony to smoke a pipe and enjoy the comforting presence of the stars before turning in. It came out with me. It was everywhere. I heard the barking of dogs, the monotonous beating of a distant drum towards Bedraschien, the sing-song voices of the natives in their booths and down the dim-lit streets. I was aware of this invisible Third behind all these familiar sounds. The enormous night-sky, drowned in stars, conveyed it too. It was in the breath of chilly wind that whispered round the walls, and it brooded everywhere above the sleepless desert. I was alone as little as though George Isley stood beside me in person—and at that moment a moving figure caught my eye below. My window was on the sixth storey, but there was no mistaking the tall and soldierly bearing of the man who was strolling past the hotel. George Isley was going slowly out into the desert.

There was actually nothing unusual in the sight. It was only ten o'clock; but for doctor's orders I might have been doing the same myself. Yet, as I leaned over the dizzy ledge and watched him, a chill struck through me, and a feeling nothing could justify, nor pages of writing describe, rose up and mastered me. His words at dinner came back with curious force. Egypt lay round him, motionless, a vast grey web. His feet were caught in it. It quivered. The silvery meshes in the moonlight announced the fact from Memphis up to Thebes, across the Nile, from underground Sakkhâra to the Valley of the Kings. A tremor ran over the entire desert, and again, as in the dining-room, the leagues of sand went rustling. It seemed to me that I caught him in the act of disappearing.

I realised in that moment the haunting power of this mysterious still atmosphere which is Egypt, and some magical emanation of its mighty past broke over me suddenly like a wave. Perhaps in that moment I felt what he himself felt; the withdrawing suction of the huge spent wave swept something out of me into the past with it. An indescribable yearning drew something living from my heart, something that longed with a kind of burning, searching sweetness for a glory of spiritual passion that was gone. The pain and happiness of it were more poignant than may be told, and my present personality—some vital portion of it, at any rate—wilted before the power of its enticement.

I stood there, motionless as stone, and stared. Erect and steady, knowing resistance vain, eager to go yet striving to remain, and half with an air of floating off the ground, he went towards the pale grey thread which was the track to Suez and the far Red Sea. There came upon me this strange, deep sense of pity, pathos, sympathy that was beyond all explanation, and mysterious as a pain in dreams. For a sense of his awful loneliness stole into me, a loneliness nothing on this earth could possibly relieve. Robbed of the Present, he sought this chimera of his Soul, an unreal Past. Not even the calm majesty of this exquisite Egyptian night could soothe the dream away; the peace and silence were marvellous, the sweet perfume of the desert air intoxicating; but all these intensified it only.

And though at a loss to explain my own emotion, its poignancy was so real that a sigh escaped me and I felt that tears lay not too far away. I watched him, yet felt I had no right to watch. Softly I drew back from the window with the sensation of eavesdropping upon his privacy; but before I did so I had seen his outline melt away into the dim world of sand that began at the very walls of the hotel. He wore a cloak of green that reached down almost to his heels, and its colour blended with the silvery surface of the desert's dark sea-tint. This sheen first draped and then concealed him. It covered him with a fold of its mysterious garment that, without seam or binding, veiled Egypt for a thousand leagues. The desert took him. Egypt caught him in her web. He was gone.

Sleep for me just then seemed out of the question. The change in *him* made me feel less sure of myself. To see him thus invertebrate shocked me. I was aware that I had nerves.

For a long time I sat smoking by the window, my body weary, but my imagination irritatingly stimulated. The big sign-lights of the hotel went out; window after window closed below me; the electric standards in the streets were already extinguished; and Helouan looked like a child's white blocks scattered in ruin upon the nursery carpet. It seemed so wee upon the vast expanse. It lay in a twinkling pattern, like a cluster of glow-worms dropped into a negligible crease of the tremendous desert. It peeped up at the stars, a little frightened.

The night was very still. There hung an enormous brooding beauty everywhere, a hint of the sinister in it that only the brilliance of the blazing stars relieved. Nothing really slept. Grouped here and there at intervals about this dun-coloured world stood the everlasting watchers in solemn, tireless guardianship—the soaring pyramids, the Sphinx, the grim Colossi, the empty temples, the long-deserted tombs. The mind was aware of them, stationed like sentries through the night. "This is Egypt; you are actually in Egypt," whispered the silence. "Eight thousand years of history lie fluttering outside your window. *She* lies there underground, sleepless, mighty, deathless, not to be trifled with. Beware! Or she will change you too!"

My imagination offered this hint: Egypt *is* difficult to realise. It remains outside the mind, a fabulous, half-legendary idea. So many enormous elements together refuse to be assimilated; the heart pauses, asking for time and breath; the senses reel a little, and in the end a mental torpor akin to stupefaction creeps upon the brain. With a sigh the struggle is abandoned and the mind surrenders to Egypt on her own terms. Alone the diggers and archæologists, confined to definite facts, offer successful resistance. My friend's use of the words "resistance" and "protection" became clearer to me. While logic halted, intuition fluttered round this clue to the solution of the influences at work. George Isley realised Egypt more than most—but as she had been.

And I recalled its first effect upon myself, and how my mind had been unable to cope with the memory of it afterwards. There had come to its summons a colossal medley, a gigantic, coloured blur that merely bewildered. Only lesser points lodged comfortably in the heart. I saw a chaotic vision: sands drenched in dazzling light, vast granite aisles, stupendous figures that stared unblinking at the sun, a shining river and a shadowy desert, both endless as the sky, mountainous pyramids and gigantic monoliths, armies of heads, of paws, of faces—all set to a scale of size that was prodigious. The items stunned; the composite effect was too unwieldy to be grasped. Something that blazed with splendour rolled before the eyes, too close to be seen distinctly—at the same time very distant—unrealised.

Then, with the passing of the weeks, it slowly stirred to life. It had attacked unseen; its grip was quite tremendous; yet it could neither be told, nor painted, nor described. It flamed up unexpectedly—in the foggy London streets, at the Club, in the theatre. A sound recalled the street-cries of the Arabs, a breath of scented air brought back the heated sand beyond the palm groves. Up rose the huge Egyptian glamour, transforming common things; it had lain buried all this time in deep recesses of the heart that are inaccessible to ordinary daily life. And there hid in it something of uneasiness that was inexplicable; awe, a hint of cold eternity, a touch of something unchanging and terrific, something sublime made lovely yet unearthly with shadowy time and distance. The melancholy of the Nile and the grandeur of a hundred battered temples dropped some unutterable beauty upon the heart. Up swept the desert air, the luminous pale shadows, the naked desolation that yet brims with sharp vitality. An Arab on his donkey tripped in colour across the mind, melting off into tiny perspective, strangely vivid. A string of camels stood in silhouette against the crimson sky. Great winds, great blazing spaces, great solemn nights, great days of golden splendour rose from the pavement or the theatre-stall, and London, dim-lit England, the whole of modern life, indeed, seemed suddenly reduced to a paltry insignificance that produced an aching longing for the pageantry of those millions of vanished souls. Egypt rolled through the heart for a moment—and was gone.

I remembered that some such fantastic experience had been mine. Put it as one may, the fact remains that for certain temperaments Egypt can rob the Present of some thread of interest that was formerly there. The memory became for me an integral part of personality; something in me yearned for its curious and awful beauty. He who has drunk of the Nile shall return to drink of it again. . . . And if for myself this was possible, what might not happen to a character of George Isley's type? Some glimmer of comprehension came to me. The ancient, buried, hidden Egypt had cast her net about his soul. Grown shadowy in the present, his life was being transferred into some golden, reconstructed Past, where it was real. Some countries give, while others take away. And George Isley was worth robbing. . . .

Disturbed by these singular reflections, I moved away from the open window, closing it. But the closing did not exclude the presence of the Third. The biting night air followed me in. I drew the mosquito curtains round the bed, but the light I left still burning; and, lying there, I jotted down upon a scrap of paper this curious impression as best I could, only to find that it escaped easily between the words. Such visionary and spiritual perceptions are too elusive to be trapped in language. Reading it over after an interval of years, it is difficult to recall with what intense meaning, what uncanny emotion, I wrote those faded lines in pencil. Their rhetoric seems cheap, their content much exaggerated; yet at the time truth burned in every syllable. Egypt, which since time began has suffered robbery with violence at the hands of all the world, now takes her vengeance, choosing her individual prey. Her time has come. Behind a modern mask she lies in wait, intensely active, sure of her hidden power. Prostitute of dead empires, she lies now at peace beneath the same old stars, her loveliness unimpaired, bejewelled with the beaten gold of ages, her breasts uncovered, and her grand limbs flashing in the sun. Her shoulders of alabaster are lifted above the sand-drifts; she surveys the little figures of to-day. She takes her choice. . . .

That night I did not dream, but neither did the whole of me lie down in sleep. During the long dark hours I was aware of that picture endlessly repeating itself, the picture of George Isley stealing out into the moonlight desert. The night so swiftly dropped her hood about him; so mysteriously he merged into the unchanging thing which cloaks the past. It lifted. Some huge shadowy hand, gloved softly yet of granite, stretched over the leagues to take him. He disappeared.

They say the desert is motionless and has no gestures! That night I saw it moving, hurrying. It went tearing after him. You understand my meaning? No! Well, when excited it produces this strange impression, and the terrible moment is—when you surrender helplessly—you desire it shall swallow you. You let it come. George Isley spoke of a web. It is, at any rate, some central power that conceals itself behind the surface glamour folk call the spell of Egypt. Its home is not apparent. It dwells with ancient Egypt—underground.

Behind the stillness of hot windless days, behind the peace of calm, gigantic nights, it lurks unrealised, monstrous and irresistible. My mind grasped it as little as the fact that our solar system with all its retinue of satellites and planets rushes annually many million miles towards a star in Hercules, while yet that constellation appears no closer than it did six thousand years ago. But the clue dropped into me. George Isley, with his entire retinue of thought and life and feeling, was being similarly drawn. And I, a minor satellite, had become aware of the horrifying pull. It was magnificent. . . . And I fell asleep on the crest of this enormous wave.

V

The next few days passed idly; weeks passed too, I think; hidden away in this cosmopolitan hotel we lived apart, unnoticed. There was the feeling that time went what pace it pleased, now fast, now slow, now standing still. The similarity of the brilliant days, set between wondrous dawns and sunsets, left the impression that it was really one long, endless day without divisions. The mind's machinery of measurement suffered dislocation. Time went backwards; dates were forgotten; the month, the time of year, the century itself went down into undifferentiated life.

The Present certainly slipped away curiously. Newspapers and politics became unimportant, news uninteresting, English life so remote as to be unreal, European affairs shadowy. The stream of life ran in another direction altogether—backwards. The names and faces of friends appeared through mist. People arrived as though dropped from the skies. They suddenly were there; one saw them in the dining-room, as though they had just slipped in from an outer world that once was real—somewhere. Of course, a steamer sailed four times a week, and the journey took five days, but these things were merely known, not realised. The fact that here it was summer, whereas over there winter reigned, helped to make the distance not quite thinkable. We looked at the desert and made plans. "We will do this, we will do that; we must go there, we'll visit such and such a place . . ." yet nothing happened. It always was to-morrow or yesterday, and we shared the discovery of Alice that there was no real "to-day." For our thinking made everything happen. That was enough. It *had* happened. It was the reality of dreams. Egypt was a dream-world that made the heart live backwards.

It came about, thus, that for the next few weeks I watched a fading life, myself alert and sympathetic, yet unable somehow to intrude and help. Noticing various little things by which George Isley betrayed the progress of the unequal struggle, I found my assistance negatived by the fact that I was in similar case myself. What he experienced in large and finally, I, too, experienced in little and for the moment. For I seemed also caught upon the fringe of the invisible web. My feelings were entangled sufficiently for me to understand. . . . And the decline of his being was terrible to watch. His character went with it; I saw his talents fade, his personality dwindle, his very soul dissolve before the insidious and invading influence. He hardly struggled. I thought of those abominable insects that paralyse the motor systems of their victims and then devour them at their leisure—alive. The incredible adventure was literally true, but, being spiritual, may not be told in the terms of a detective story. This version must remain an individual rendering—an aspect of *one* possible version. All who know the real Egypt, that Egypt which has nothing to do with dams and Nationalists and the external welfare of the falaheen, will understand. The pilfering of her ancient dead she suffers still; she, in revenge, preys at her leisure on the living.

The occasions when he betrayed himself were ordinary enough; it was the glimpse they afforded of what was in progress beneath his calm exterior that made them interesting. Once, I remember, we had lunched together at Mena, and, after visiting certain excavations beyond the Gizeh pyramids, we made our way homewards by way of the Sphinx. It was dusk, and the main army of tourists had retired, though some few dozen sight-seers still moved about to the cries of donkey-boys and baksheesh. The vast head and shoulders suddenly emerged, riding undrowned above the sea of sand. Dark and monstrous in the fading light, it loomed, as ever, a being of non-human lineage; no amount of familiarity could depreciate its grandeur, its impressive setting, the lost expression of the countenance that is too huge to focus as a face. A thousand visits leaves its power undiminished. It has intruded upon our earth from some uncommon world. George Isley and myself both turned aside to acknowledge the presence of this alien, uncomfortable thing. We did not linger, but we slackened pace. It was the obvious, inevitable thing to do. He pointed then, with a suddenness that made me start. He indicated the tourists standing round.

"See," he said, in a lowered tone, "day and night you'll always find a crowd obedient to that thing. But notice their behaviour. People don't do that before any other ruin in the world I've ever seen." He referred to the attempts of individuals to creep away alone and stare into the stupendous visage by themselves. At different points in the deep sandy basin were men and women, standing solitary, lying, crouching, apart from the main company where the dragomen mouthed their exposition with impertinent glibness.

"The desire to be alone," he went on, half to himself, as we paused a moment, "the sense of worship which insists on privacy."

It *was* significant, for no amount of advertising could dwarf the impressiveness of the inscrutable visage into whose eyes of stone the silent humans gazed. Not even the red-coat, standing inside one gigantic ear, could intro-duce the commonplace. But my companion's words let another thing into the spectacle, a less exalted thing, dropping a hint of horror about that sandy cup: It became easy, for a moment, to imagine these tourists worshipping—against their will; to picture the monster noticing that they were there; that it might slowly turn its awful head; that the sand might visibly trickle from a stirring paw; that, in a word, they might be taken—changed.

"Come," he whispered in a dropping tone, interrupting my fancies as though he half-divined them, "it is getting late, and to be alone with the thing is intolerable to me just now. But you notice, don't you," he added, as he took my arm to hurry me away, "how little the tourists matter? Instead of injuring the effect, they increase it. It uses *them*."

And again a slight sensation of chill, communicated possibly by his nerv-ous touch, or possibly by his earnest way of saying these curious words, passed through me. Some part of me remained behind in that hollow trough of sand, prostrate before an immensity that symbolised the past. A curious, wild yearning caught me momentarily, an intense desire to understand exactly why that terror stood there, its actual meaning long ago to the hearts that set it waiting for the sun, what definite rôle it played, what souls it stirred and why, in that system of towering belief and faith whose indestructible emblem it still remained. The past stood grouped so solemnly about its menacing pre-sentment. I was distinctly aware of this spiritual suction backwards that my companion yielded to so gladly, yet against his normal, modern self. For it made the past appear magnificently desirable, and loosened all the rivets of the present. It bodied forth three main ingredients of this deep Egyptian spell—size, mystery, and immobility.

Yet, to my relief, the cheaper aspect of this Egyptian glamour left him cold. He remained unmoved by the commonplace mysterious; he told no mummy stories, nor ever hinted at the supernatural quality that leaps to the mind of the majority. There was no play in him. The influence was grave and vital. And, although I knew he held strong views with regard to the impiety of disturbing the dead, he never in my hearing attached any possible revengeful character to the energy of an outraged past. The current tales of this descrip-tion he ignored; they were for superstitious minds or children; the deities that claimed his soul were of a grander order altogether. He lived, if it may be so expressed, already in a world his heart had reconstructed or remembered; it drew him in another direction altogether; with the modern, sensational view of life his spirit held no traffic any longer; he was living backwards. I saw his figure receding mournfully, yet never sentimentally, into the spacious, golden atmosphere of recaptured days. The enormous soul of buried Egypt drew him

down. The dwindling of his physical appearance was, of course, a mental interpretation of my own; but another, stranger interpretation of a spiritual kind
moved parallel with it—marvellous and horrible. For, as he diminished outwardly and in his modern, present aspect, he grew within—gigantic. The size
of Egypt entered into him. Huge proportions now began to accompany any
presentment of his personality to my inner vision. He towered. These two
qualities of the land already obsessed him—magnitude and immobility.

And that awe which modern life ignores contemptuously woke in my
heart. I almost feared his presence at certain times. For one aspect of the
Egyptian spell is explained by sheer size and bulk. Disdainful of mere speed
to-day, the heart is still uncomfortable with magnitude; and in Egypt there is
size that may easily appal, for every detail shunts it laboriously upon the mind.
It elbows out the present. The desert's vastness is not made comprehensible
by mileage, and the sources of the Nile are so distant that they exist less on
the map than in the imagination. The effort to realise suffers paralysis; they
might equally be in the moon or Saturn. The undecorated magnificence of the
desert remains unknown, just as the proportions of pyramid and temple, of
pylons and Colossi approach the edge of the mind yet never enter in. All
stand outside, clothed in this prodigious measurement of the past. And the
old beliefs not only share this titanic effect upon the consciousness, but carry
it stages further. The entire scale haunts with uncomfortable immensity, so
that the majority run back with relief to the measurable details of a more
manageable scale. Express trains, flying machines, Atlantic liners—these produce no unpleasant stretching of the faculties compared to the influence of
the Karnak pylons, the pyramids, or the interior of the Serapeum.

Close behind this magnitude, moreover, steps the monstrous. It is revealed
not in sand and stone alone, in queer effects of light and shadow, of glittering
sunsets and of magical dusks, but in the very aspect of the bird and animal life.
The heavy-headed buffaloes betray it equally with the vultures, the myriad kites,
the grotesqueness of the mouthing camels. The rude, enormous scenery has it
everywhere. There is nothing lyrical in this land of passionate mirages. Uncouth
immensity notes the little human flittings. The days roll by in a tide of golden
splendour; one goes helplessly with the flood; but it is an irresistible flood that
sweeps backwards and below. The silent-footed natives in their coloured robes
move before a curtain, and behind that curtain dwells the soul of ancient
Egypt—the Reality, as George Isley called it—watching, with sleepless eyes of
grey infinity. Then, sometimes the curtain stirs and lifts an edge; an invisible
hand creeps forth; the soul is touched. And some one disappears.

VI

The process of disintegration must have been at work a long time before I appeared upon the scene; the changes went forward with such rapidity.

It was his third year in Egypt, two of which had been spent without interruption in company with an Egyptologist named Moleson, in the neighbourhood of Thebes. I soon discovered that this region was for him the centre of attraction, or as he put it, of the web. Not Luxor, of course, nor the images of reconstructed Karnak; but that stretch of grim, forbidding mountains where royalty, earthly and spiritual, sought eternal peace for the physical remains. There amid surroundings of superb desolation, great priests and mighty kings had thought themselves secure from sacrilegious touch. In caverns underground they kept their faithful tryst with centuries, guarded by the silence of magnificent gloom. There they waited, communing with passing ages in their sleep, till Ra, their glad divinity, should summon them to the fulfilment of their ancient dream. And there, in the Valley of the Tombs of the Kings, their dream was shattered, their lovely prophecies derided, and their glory dimmed by the impious desecration of the curious.

That George Isley and his companion had spent their time, not merely digging and deciphering like their practical confrères, but engaged in some strange experiments of recovery and reconstruction, was matter for open comment among the fraternity. That incredible things had happened there was the big story of two Egyptian seasons at least. I heard this later only— tales of utterly incredible kind, that the desolate vale of rock was seen repeopled on moonlit nights, that the smoke of unaccustomed fires rose to cap the flat-topped peaks, that the pageantry of some forgotten worship had been seen to issue from the openings of these hills, and that sounds of chanting, sonorous and marvellously sweet, had been heard to echo from those bleak, repellent precipices. The tales apparently were grossly exaggerated; wandering Bedouins brought them in; the guides and dragomen repeated them with mysterious additions; till they filtered down through the native servants in the hotels and reached the tourists with highly picturesque embroidery. They reached the authorities too. The only accurate fact I gathered at the time, however, was that they had abruptly ceased. George Isley and Moleson, moreover, had parted company. And Moleson, I heard, was the originator of the business. He was, at this time, unknown to me; his arresting book on "A Modern Reconstruction of Sun-worship in Ancient Egypt" being my only link with his unusual mind. Apparently he regarded the sun as the deity of the scientific religion of the future which would replace the various anthropomorphic gods of childish creeds. He discussed the possibility of the zodiacal signs being some kind of Celestial Intelligences.

Belief blazed on every page. Men's life is heat, derived solely from the sun, and men were, therefore, part of the sun in the sense that a Christian is part of his personal deity. And absorption was the end. His description of "sun-worship ceremonials" conveyed an amazing reality and beauty. This singular book, however, was all I knew of him until he came to visit us in Helouan, though I easily discerned that his influence somehow was the original cause of the change in my companion.

At Thebes, then, was the active centre of the influence that drew my friend away from modern things. It was there, I easily guessed, that "obstacles" had been placed in the way of these men's too close enquiry. In that haunted and oppressive valley, where profane and reverent come to actual grips, where modern curiosity is most busily organised, and even tourists are aware of a masked hostility that dogs the prying of the least imaginative mind—there, in the neighbourhood of the hundred-gated city, had Egypt set the headquarters of her irreconcilable enmity. And it was there, amid the ruins of her loveliest past, that George Isley had spent his years of magical reconstruction and met the influence that now dominated his entire life.

And though no definite avowal of the struggle betrayed itself in speech between us, I remember fragments of conversation, even at this stage, that proved his willing surrender of the present. We spoke of fear once, though with the indirectness of connection I have mentioned. I urged that the mind, once it is forewarned, can remain master of itself and prevent a thing from happening.

"But that does not make the thing unreal," he objected.

"The mind can deny it," I said. "It then becomes unreal."

He shook his head. "One does not deny an unreality. Denial is a childish act of self-protection against something you expect to happen." He caught my eye a moment. "You deny what you are afraid of," he said. "Fear invites." And he smiled uneasily. "You know it must get you in the end." And, both of us being aware secretly to what our talk referred, it seemed bold-blooded and improper; for actually we discussed the psychology of his disappearance. Yet, while I disliked it, there was a fascination about the subject that compelled attraction. . . . "Once fear gets in," he added presently, "confidence is undermined, the structure of life is threatened, and you—go gladly. The foundation of everything is belief. A man is what he believes about himself; and in Egypt you can believe things that elsewhere you would not even think about. It attacks the essentials." He sighed, yet with a curious pleasure; and a smile of resignation and relief passed over his rugged features and was gone again. The luxury of abandonment lay already in him.

"But even belief," I protested, "must be founded on some experience or other." It seemed ghastly to speak of his spiritual malady behind the mask of indirect allusion. My excuse was that he so obviously talked willingly.

He agreed instantly. "Experience of one kind or another," he said darkly, "there always is. Talk with the men who live out here; ask any one who thinks, or who has the imagination which divines. You'll get only one reply, phrase it how they may. Even the tourists and the little commonplace officials feel it. And it's not the climate, it's not nerves, it's not any definite tendency that they can name or lay their finger on. Nor is it mere orientalising of the mind. It's something that first takes you from your common life, and that later takes common life from you. You willingly resign an unremunerative Present. There are no half-measures either—once the gates are open."

There was so much undeniable truth in this that I found no corrective by way of strong rejoinder. All my attempts, indeed, were futile in this way. He meant to go; my words could not stop him. He wanted a witness,—he dreaded the loneliness of going—but he brooked no interference. The contradictory position involved a perplexing state of heart and mind in both of us. The atmosphere of this majestic land, to-day so trifling, yesterday so immense, most certainly induced a lifting of the spiritual horizon that revealed amazing possibilities.

VII

It was in the windless days of a perfect December that Moleson, the Egyptologist, found us out and paid a flying visit to Helouan. His duties took him up and down the land, but his time seemed largely at his own disposal. He lingered on. His coming introduced a new element I was not quite able to estimate; though, speaking generally, the effect of his presence upon my companion was to emphasise the latter's alteration. It underlined the change, and drew attention to it. The new arrival, I gathered, was not altogether welcome. "I should never have expected to find you *here*," laughed Moleson when they met, and whether he referred to Helouan or to the hotel was not quite clear. I got the impression he meant both; I remembered my fancy that it was a good hotel to hide in. George Isley had betrayed a slight involuntary start when the visiting card was brought to him at tea-time. I think he had wished to escape from his former co-worker. Moleson had found him out. "I heard you had a friend with you and were contemplating further exper—work," he added. He changed the word "experiment" quickly to the other.

"The former, as you see, is true, but not the latter," replied my companion dryly, and in his manner was a touch of opposition that might have been hostility. Their intimacy, I saw, was close and of old standing. In all they said and did and looked, there was an undercurrent of other meaning that just escaped me. They were up to something—they *had* been up to something; but Isley would have withdrawn if he could!

Moleson was an ambitious and energetic personality, absorbed in his profession, alive to the poetical as well as to the practical value of archæology, and he made at first a wholly delightful impression upon me. An instinctive flair for his subject had early in life brought him success and a measure of fame as well. His knowledge was accurate and scholarly, his mind saturated in the lore of a vanished civilisation. Behind an exterior that was quietly careless, I divined a passionate and complex nature, and I watched him with interest as the man for whom the olden sun-worship of unscientific days held some beauty of reality and truth. Much in his strange book that had bewildered me now seemed intelligible when I saw the author. I cannot explain this more closely. Something about him somehow made it possible. Though modern to the finger-tips and thoroughly equipped with all the tendencies of the day, there seemed to hide in him another self that held aloof with a dignified detachment from the interests in which his "educated" mind was centred. He read living secrets beneath museum labels, I might put it. He stepped out of the days of the Pharaohs if ever man did, and I realised early in our acquaintance that this was the man who had exceptional powers of "resistance and self-protection," and was, in his particular branch of work, "unusual." In manner he was light and gay, his sense of humour strong, with a way of treating everything as though laughter was the sanest attitude towards life. There is, however, the laughter that hides—other things. Moleson, as I gathered from many clues of talk and manner and silence, was a deep and singular being. His experiences in Egypt, if any, he had survived admirably. There were at least two Molesons. I felt him more than double—multiple.

In appearance tall, thin and fleshless, with a dried-up skin and features withered as a mummy's, he said laughingly that Nature had picked him physically for his "job"; and, indeed, one could see him worming his way down narrow tunnels into the sandy tombs, and writhing along sunless passages of suffocating heat without too much personal inconvenience. Something sinuous, almost fluid in his mind expressed itself in his body too. He might go in any direction without causing surprise. He might go backwards or forwards. He might go in two directions at once.

And my first impression of the man deepened before many days were past. There was irresponsibility in him, insincerity somewhere, almost want of heart. His morality was certainly not to-day's, and the mind in him was slippery. I think the modern world, to which he was unattached, confused and irritated him. A sense of insecurity came with him. His interest in George Isley was the interest in a psychological "specimen." I remembered how in his book he described the selection of individuals for certain functions of that marvellous worship, and the odd idea flashed through me—well, that Isley exactly suited some purpose of his re-creating energies. The man was keenly observant from top to toe, but not with his sight alone; he seemed to be aware of motives and emotions before he noticed the acts or gestures that these caused. I felt that he took me in as well. Certainly he eyed me up and down by means of this inner observation that seemed automatic with him.

Moleson was not staying in our hotel; he had chosen one where social life was more abundant; but he came up frequently to lunch and dine, and sometimes spent the evening in Isley's rooms, amusing us with his skill upon the piano, singing Arab songs, and chanting phrases from the ancient Egyptian rituals to rhythms of his own invention. The old Egyptian music, both in harmony and melody, was far more developed than I had realised, the use of sound having been of radical importance in their ceremonies. The chanting in particular he did with extraordinary effect, though whether its success lay in his sonorous voice, his peculiar increasing of the vowel sounds, or to anything deeper, I cannot pretend to say. The result at any rate was of a unique description. It brought buried Egypt to the surface; the gigantic Presence entered sensibly into the room. It came, huge and gorgeous, rolling upon the mind the instant he began, and something in it was both terrible and oppressive. The repose of eternity lay in the sound. Invariably, after a few moments of that transforming music, I saw the Valley of the Kings, the deserted temples, titanic faces of stone, great effigies coifed with zodiacal signs, but above all—the twin Colossi.

I mentioned this latter detail.

"Curious *you* should feel that too—curious you should say it, I mean," Moleson replied, not looking at me, yet with an air as if I had said something he expected. "To me the Memnon figures express Egypt better than all the other monuments put together. Like the desert, they are featureless. They sum her up, as it were, yet leave the message unuttered. For, you see, they cannot." He laughed a little in his throat. "They have neither eyes nor lips nor nose; their features are gone."

"Yet they tell the secret—to those who care to listen," put in Isley in a scarcely noticeable voice. "Just because they have no words. They still sing at dawn," he added in a louder, almost a challenging tone. It startled me.

Moleson turned round at him, opened his lips to speak, hesitated, stopped. He said nothing for a moment. I cannot describe what it was in the lightning glance they exchanged that put me on the alert for something other than was obvious. My nerves quivered suddenly, and a breath of colder air stole in among us. Moleson swung round to me again. "I almost think," he said, laughing when I complimented him upon the music, "that I must have been a priest of Aton-Ra in an earlier existence, for all this comes to my fin-ger-tips as if it were instinctive knowledge. Plotinus, remember, lived a few miles away at Alexandria with his great idea that knowledge is recollection," he said, with a kind of cynical amusement. "In those days, at any rate," he added more significantly, "worship was real and ceremonials actually ex-pressed great ideas and teaching. There was power in them." Two of the Mo-lesons spoke in that contradictory utterance.

I saw that Isley was fidgeting where he sat, betraying by certain gestures that uneasiness was in him. He hid his face a moment in his hands; he sighed; he made a movement—as though to prevent something coming. But Moleson resisted his attempt to change the conversation, though the key shifted a little of its own accord. There were numerous occasions like this when I was aware that both men skirted something that had happened, something that Moleson wished to resume, but that Isley seemed anxious to postpone.

I found myself studying Moleson's personality, yet never getting beyond a certain point. Shrewd, subtle, with an acute rather than a large intelligence, he was cynical as well as insincere, and yet I cannot describe by what means I ar-rived at two other conclusions as well about him; first, that this insincerity and want of heart had not been so always; and secondly, that he sought social di-version with deliberate and un-ordinary purpose. I could well believe that the first was Egypt's mark upon him, and the second an effort at resistance and self-protection.

"If it wasn't for the gaiety," he remarked once in a flippant way that thinly hid significance, "a man out here would go under in a year. Social life gets rather reckless—exaggerated—people do things they would never dream of doing at home. Perhaps you've noticed it," he added, looking suddenly at me; "Cairo and the rest—they plunge at it as though driven—a sort of excess about it somewhere." I nodded agreement. The way he said it was unpleasant rather. "It's an antidote," he said, a sub-acid flavour in his tone. "I used to loathe society myself. But now I find gaiety—a certain irresponsible excite-ment—of importance. Egypt gets on the nerves after a bit. The moral fibre fails. The will grows weak." And he glanced covertly at Isley as with a desire to point his meaning. "It's the clash between the ugly present and the majestic past, perhaps." He smiled.

Isley shrugged his shoulders, making no reply; and the other went on to tell stories of friends and acquaintances whom Egypt had adversely affected: Barton, the Oxford man, school teacher, who had insisted on living in a tent until the Government relieved him of his job. He took to his tent, roamed the desert, drawn irresistibly, practical considerations of the present of no avail.

This yearning took him, though he could never define the exact attraction. In the end his mental balance was disturbed. "But now he's all right again; I saw him in London only this year; he can't say what he felt or why he did it. Only—he's different." Of John Lattin, too, he spoke, whom agoraphobia caught so terribly in Upper Egypt; of Malahide, upon whom some fascination of the Nile induced suicidal mania and attempts at drowning; of Jim Moleson, a cousin (who had camped at Thebes with himself and Isley), whom megalomania of a most singular type attacked suddenly in a sandy waste—all radically cured as soon as they left Egypt, yet, one and all, changed and made otherwise in their very souls.

He talked in a loose, disjointed way, and though much he said was fantastic, as if meant to challenge opposition, there was impressiveness about it somewhere, due, I think, to a kind of cumulative emotion he produced.

"The monuments do not impress merely by their bulk, but by their majestic symmetry," I remember him saying. "Look at the choice of form alone—the pyramids, for instance. No other shape was possible: dome, square, spires, all would have been hideously inadequate. The wedge-shaped mass, immense foundations and pointed apex were the *mot juste* in outline. Do you think people without greatness in themselves chose that form? There was no unbalance in the minds that conceived the harmonious and magnificent structures of the temples. There was stately grandeur in their consciousness that could only be born of truth and knowledge. The power in their images is a direct expression of eternal and essential things they knew."

We listened in silence. He was off upon his hobby. But behind the careless tone and laughing questions, there was this lurking passionateness that made me feel uncomfortable. He was edging up, I felt, towards some climax that meant life and death to himself and Isley. I could not fathom it. My sympathy let me in a little, yet not enough to understand completely. Isley, I saw, was also uneasy, though for reasons that equally evaded me.

"One can almost believe," he continued, "that something still hangs about in the atmosphere from those olden times." He half-closed his eyes, but I caught the gleam in them. "It affects the mind through the imagination. With some it changes the point of view. It takes the soul back with it to former, quite different conditions, that must have been almost another kind of consciousness."

He paused an instant and looked up at us. "The *intensity* of belief in those days," he resumed, since neither of us accepted the challenge, "was amazing—something quite unknown anywhere in the world to-day. It was so sure, so positive; no mere speculative theories, I mean;—as though something in the climate, the exact position beneath the stars, the 'attitude' of this particular stretch of earth in relation to the sun—thinned the veil between humanity—and other things. Their hierarchies of gods, you know, were not mere idols; animals, birds, monsters, and what-not, all typified spiritual forces and powers that influenced their daily life. But the strong thing is—they *knew*. People who were scientific as they were did not swallow foolish superstitions. They made colours that could last six thousand years, even in the open air; and without instruments they measured accurately—an enormously difficult and involved calculation—the precession of the equinoxes. You've been to Denderah?"—he suddenly glanced again at me. "No! Well, the minds that realised the zodiacal signs could hardly believe, you know, that Hathor was a cow!"

Isley coughed. He was about to interrupt, but before he could find words, Moleson was off again, some new quality in his tone and manner that was almost aggressive. The hints he offered seemed more than hints. There was a strange conviction in his heart. I think he was skirting a bigger thing that he and his companion knew, yet that his real object was to see in how far I was open to attack—how far my sympathy might be with them. I became aware that he and George Isley shared this bigger thing. It was based, I felt, on some certain knowledge that experiment had brought them.

"Think of the grand teaching of Aknahton, that young Pharaoh who regenerated the entire land and brought it to its immense prosperity. He taught the worship of the sun, but not of the visible sun. The deity had neither form nor shape. The great disk of glory was but the manifestation, each beneficent ray ending in a hand that blessed the world. It was a god of everlasting energy, love and power, yet men could know it at first hand in their daily lives, worshipping it at dawn and sunset with passionate devotion. No anthropomorphic idol masqueraded in *that!*"

An extraordinary glow was about him as he said it. The same minute he lowered his voice, shifting the key perceptibly. He kept looking up at me through half-closed eyelids.

"And another thing they wonderfully knew," he almost whispered, "was that, with the precession of their deity across the equinoctial changes, there came new powers down into the world of men. Each cycle—each zodiacal sign—brought its special powers which they quickly typified in the monstrous effigies we label to-day in our dull museums. Each sign took some two thousand years to traverse. Each sign, moreover, involved a change in human consciousness. There was this relation between the heavens and the human heart. All that they knew. While the sun crawled through the sign of Taurus, it was the Bull they worshipped; with Aries, it was the ram that coifed their granite symbols. Then came, as you remember, with Pisces the great New Arrival, when already they sank from their grand zenith, and the Fish was taken as the emblem of the changing powers which the Christ embodied. For the human soul, they held, echoed the changes in the immense journey of the original deity, who is its source, across the Zodiac, and the truth of 'As above, so Below,' remains the key to all manifested life. And to-day the sun, just entering Aquarius, new powers are close upon the world. The old—that which has been for two thousand years—again is crumbling, passing, dying. New powers and a new consciousness are knocking at our doors. It is a time of change. It is also"—he leaned forward so that his eyes came close before me—"the time to make the change. The soul can choose its own conditions. It can—"

A sudden crash smothered the rest of the sentence. A chair had fallen with a clatter upon the wooden floor where the carpet left it bare. Whether Isley in rising had stumbled against it, or whether he had purposely knocked it over, I could not say. I only knew that he had abruptly risen and as abruptly sat down again. A curious feeling came to me that the sign was somehow pre-arranged. It was so sudden. His voice, too, was forced, I thought.

"Yes, but we can do without all that, Moleson," he interrupted, with acute abruptness. "Suppose we have a tune instead."

VIII

It was after dinner in his private room, and he had sat very silent in his corner until this sudden outburst. Moleson got up quietly without a word and moved over to the piano. I saw—or was it imagination merely?—a new expression slide upon his withered face. He meant mischief somewhere.

From that instant—from the moment he rose and walked over the thick carpet—he fascinated me. The atmosphere his talk and stories had brought remained. His lean fingers ran over the keys, and at first he played fragments from popular musical comedies that were pleasant enough, but made no demand upon the attention. I heard them without listening. I was thinking of another thing—his walk. For the way he moved across those few feet of carpet had power in it. He looked different; he seemed another man; he was changed. I saw him curiously—as I sometimes now saw Isley too—bigger. In some manner that was both enchanting and oppressive, his presence from that moment drew my imagination as by an air of authority it held.

I left my seat in the far corner and dropped into a chair beside the window, nearer to the piano. Isley, I then noticed, had also turned to watch him. But it was George Isley not quite as he was now. I felt rather than saw the change. Both men had subtly altered. They seemed extended, their outlines shadowy.

Isley, alert and anxious, glanced up at the player, his mind of earlier years—for the expression of his face was plain—following the light music, yet with difficulty that involved effort, almost struggle. "Play that again, will you?" I heard him say from time to time. He was trying to take hold of it, to climb back to a condition where that music had linked him to the present, to seize a mental structure that was gone, to grip hold tightly of it—only to find that it was too far forgotten and too fragile. It would not bear him. I am sure of it, and I can swear I divined his mood. He fought to realise himself as he had been, but in vain. In his dim corner opposite I watched him closely. The big black Blüthner blocked itself between us. Above it swayed the outline, lean and half shadowy, of Moleson as he played. A faint whisper floated through the room. "You are in Egypt." Nowhere else could this queer feeling of presentiment, of anticipation, have gained a footing so easily. I was aware of intense emotion in all three of us. The least reminder of To-day seemed ugly. I longed for some ancient forgotten splendour that was lost.

The scene fixed my attention very steadily, for I was aware of something deliberate and calculated on Moleson's part. The thing was well considered in his mind, intention only half concealed. It was Egypt he interpreted by sound, expressing what in him was true, then observing its effect, as he led us cleverly towards—the past. Beginning with the present, he played persuasively, with penetration, with insistent meaning, too. He had that touch which conjured up real atmosphere, and, at first, that atmosphere termed modern. He rendered vividly the note of London, passing from the jingles of musical comedy, nervous rag-times and sensuous Tango dances, into the higher strains of concert rooms and "cultured" circles. Yet not too abruptly. Most dexterously he shifted the level, and with it our emotion. I recognised, as in a parody, various ultra-modern thrills: the tumult of Strauss, the pagan sweetness of primitive Debussy, the weirdness and ecstasy of metaphysical Scriabin. The composite note of To-day in both extremes, he brought into this private sitting-room of the desert hotel, while George Isley, listening keenly, fidgeted in his chair.

"'Après-midi d'un Faune,'" said Moleson dreamily, answering the question as to what he played. "Debussy's, you know. And the thing before it was from 'Til Eulenspiegel'—Strauss, of course."

He drawled, swaying slowly with the rhythm, and leaving pauses between the words. His attention was not wholly on his listener, and in the voice was a quality that increased my uneasy apprehension. I felt distress for Isley somewhere. Something, it seemed, was coming; Moleson brought it. Unconsciously in his walk, it now appeared consciously in his music; and it came from what was underground in him. A charm, a subtle change, stole oddly over the room. It stole over my heart as well. Some power of estimating left me, as though my mind were slipping backwards and losing familiar, common standards.

"The true modern note in it, isn't there?" he drawled; "cleverness, I think—intellectual—surface ingenuity—no depth or permanence—just the sensational brilliance of To-day." He turned and stared at me fixedly an instant. "Nothing *everlasting*," he added impressively. "It tells everything it knows—because it's small enough—"

And the room turned pettier as he said it; another, bigger shadow draped its little walls. Through the open windows came a stealthy gesture of eternity. The atmosphere stretched visibly. Moleson was playing a marvellous fragment from Scriabin's "Prometheus." It sounded thin and shallow. This modern music, all of it, was out of place and trivial. It was almost ridiculous. The scale of our emotion changed insensibly into a deeper thing that has no name in dictionaries, being of another age. And I glanced at the windows where stone columns framed dim sections of great Egypt listening outside. There was no moon; only deep draughts of stars blazed, hanging in the sky. I thought with awe of the mysterious knowledge that vanished people had of these stars, and of the Sun's huge journey through the Zodiac. . . .

And, with astonishing suddenness as of dream, there rose a pictured image against that starlit sky. Lifted into the air, between heaven and earth, I saw float swiftly past a panorama of the stately temples, led by Denderah, Edfu, Abou Simbel. It paused, it hovered, it disappeared. Leaving incalculable solemnity behind it in the air, it vanished, and to see so vast a thing move at that easy yet unhasting speed unhinged some sense of measurement in me. It was, of course, I assured myself, mere memory objectified owing to something that the music summoned, yet the apprehension rose in me that the whole of Egypt presently would stream past in similar fashion—Egypt as she was in the zenith of her unrecoverable past. Behind the tinkling of the modern piano passed the rustling of a multitude, the tramping of countless feet on sand. . . . It was singularly vivid. It arrested in me something that normally went flowing. . . . And when I turned my head towards the room to call attention to my strange experience, the eyes of Moleson, I saw, were laid upon my own. He stared at me. The light in them transfixed me, and I understood that the illusion was due in some manner to his evocation. Isley rose at the same moment from his chair. The thing I had vaguely been expecting had shifted closer. And the same moment the musician abruptly changed his key.

"You may like this better," he murmured, half to himself, but in tones he somehow made echoing. "It's more suited to the place." There was a resonance in the voice as though it emerged from hollows underground. "The other seems almost sacrilegious—here." And his voice drawled off in the rhythm of slower modulations that he played. It had grown muffled. There was an impression, too, that he did not strike the piano, but that the music issued from himself.

"Place! What place?" asked Isley quickly. His head turned sharply as he spoke. His tone, in its remoteness, made me tremble.

The musician laughed to himself. "I meant that this hotel seems really an impertinence," he murmured, leaning down upon the notes he played upon so softly and so well; "and that it's but the thinnest kind of pretence—when you come to think of it. We are in the desert really. The Colossi are outside, and all the emptied temples. Or ought to be," he added, raising his tone abruptly with a glance at me.

He straightened up and stared out into the starry sky past George Isley's shoulders.

"That," he exclaimed, with betraying vehemence, "is where we are and what we play to!" His voice suddenly increased; there was a roar in it. "That," he repeated, "is the thing that takes our hearts away." The volume of intonation was astonishing.

For the way he uttered the monosyllable suddenly revealed the man beneath the outer sheath of cynicism and laughter, explained his heartlessness, his secret stream of life. He, too, was soul and body in the past. "That" revealed more than pages of descriptive phrases. His heart lived in the temple aisles, his mind unearthed forgotten knowledge; his soul had clothed itself anew in the seductive glory of antiquity: he dwelt with a quickening magic of existence in the reconstructed splendour of what most term only ruins. He and George Isley together had revivified a power that enticed them backwards; but whereas the latter struggled still, the former had already made his permanent home there. The faculty in me that saw the vision of streaming temples saw also this—remorselessly definite. Moleson himself sat naked at that piano. I saw him clearly then. He no longer masqueraded behind his sneers and laughter. He, too, had long ago surrendered, lost himself, gone out, and from the place his soul now dwelt in he watched George Isley sinking down to join him. He lived in ancient, subterranean Egypt. This great hotel stood precariously on the merest upper crust of desert. A thousand tombs, a hundred temples lay outside, within reach almost of our very voices. Moleson was merged with "that."

This intuition flashed upon me like the picture in the sky; and both were true.

And, meanwhile, this other thing he played had a surge of power in it impossible to describe. It was sombre, huge and solemn. It conveyed the power that his walk conveyed. There was distance in it, but a distance not of space alone. A remoteness of time breathed through it with that strange sadness and melancholy yearning that enormous interval brings. It marched, but very far away; it held refrains that assumed the rhythms of a multitude the centuries muted; it sang, but the singing was underground in passages that fine sand muffled. Lost, wandering winds sighed through it, booming. The contrast, after the modern, cheaper music, was dislocating. Yet the change had been quite naturally effected.

"It would sound empty and monotonous elsewhere—in London, for instance," I heard Moleson drawling, as he swayed to and fro, "but here it is big and splendid—true. You hear what I mean," he added gravely. "You understand?"

"What is it?" asked Isley thickly, before I could say a word. "I forget exactly. It has tears in it—more than I can bear." The end of his sentence died away in his throat.

Moleson did not look at him as he answered. He looked at me.

"You surely ought to know," he replied, the voice rising and falling as though the rhythm forced it. "You have heard it all before—that chant from the ritual we—"

Isley sprang up and stopped him. I did not hear the sentence complete. An extraordinary thought blazed into me that the voices of both men were not quite their own. I fancied—wild, impossible as it sounds—that I heard the twin Colossi singing to each other in the dawn. Stupendous ideas sprang past me, leaping. It seemed as though eternal symbols of the cosmos, discovered and worshipped in this ancient land, leaped into awful life. My consciousness became enveloping. I had the distressing feeling that ages slipped out of place and took me with them; they dominated me; they rushed me off my feet like water. I was drawn backwards. I, too, was changing—being changed.

"I remember," said Isley softly, a reverence of worship in his voice. But there was anguish in it too, and pity; he let the present go completely from him; the last strands severed with a wrench of pain. I imagined I heard his soul pass weeping far away—below.

"I'll sing it," murmured Moleson, "for the voice is necessary. The sound and rhythm are utterly divine!"

IX

And forthwith his voice began a series of long-drawn cadences that seemed somehow the root-sounds of every tongue that ever was. A spell came over me I could touch and feel. A web encompassed me; my arms and feet became entangled; a veil of fine threads wove across my eyes. The enthralling power of the rhythm produced some magical movement in the soul. I was aware of life everywhere about me, far and near, in the dwellings of the dead, as also in the corridors of the iron hills. Thebes stood erect, and Memphis teemed upon the river banks. For the modern world fell, swaying, at this sound that restored the past, and in this past both men before me lived and had their being. The storm of present life passed o'er their heads, while they dwelt underground, obliterated, gone. Upon the wave of sound they went down into their recovered kingdom.

I shivered, moved vigorously, half rose up, then instantly sank back again, resigned and helpless. For I entered by their side, it seemed, the conditions of their strange captivity. My thoughts, my feelings, my point of view were transplanted to another centre. Consciousness shifted in me. I saw things from another's point of view—antiquity's.

The present forgotten but the past supreme, I lost Reality. Our room became a pin-point picture seen in a drop of water, while this subterranean world, replacing it, turned immense. My heart took on the gigantic, leisured stride of what had been. Proportions grew; size captured me; and magnitude, turned monstrous, swept mere measurement away. Some hand of golden sunshine picked me up and set me in the quivering web beside those other two. I heard the rustle of the settling threads; I heard the shuffling of the feet in sand; I heard the whispers in the dwellings of the dead. Behind the monotony of this sacerdotal music I heard them in their dim carved chambers. The ancient galleries were awake. The Life of unremembered ages stirred in multitudes about me.

The reality of so incredible an experience evaporates through the stream of language. I can only affirm this singular proof—that the deepest, most satisfying knowledge the Present could offer seemed insignificant beside some stalwart majesty of the Past that utterly usurped it. This modern room, holding a piano and two figures of To-day, appeared as a paltry miniature pinned against a vast transparent curtain, whose foreground was thick with symbols of temple, sphinx, and pyramid, but whose background of stupendous hanging grey slid off towards a splendour where the cities of the Dead shook off their sand and thronged space to its ultimate horizons. . . . The stars, the entire universe, vibrating and alive, became involved in it. Long periods of time slipped past me. I seemed living ages ago. . . . I was living backwards. . . .

The size and eternity of Egypt took me easily. There was an overwhelming grandeur in it that elbowed out all present standards. The whole place towered and stood up. The desert reared, the very horizons lifted; majestic figures of granite rose above the hotel, great faces hovered and drove past; huge arms reached up to pluck the stars and set them in the ceilings of the labyrinthine tombs. The colossal meaning of the ancient land emerged through all its ruined details . . . reconstructed—burningly alive. . . .

It became at length unbearable. I longed for the droning sounds to cease, for the rhythm to lessen its prodigious sweep. My heart cried out for the gold of the sunlight on the desert, for the sweet air by the river's banks, for the violet lights upon the hills at dawn. And I resisted, I made an effort to return.

"Your chant is horrible. For God's sake, let's have an Arab song—or the music of To-day!"

The effort was intense, the result was—nothing. I swear I used these words. I heard the actual sound of my voice, if no one else did, for I remember that it was pitiful in the way great space devoured it, making of its appreciable volume the merest whisper as of some bird or insect cry. But the figure that I took for Moleson instead of answer or acknowledgment, merely grew and grew as things grow in a fairy tale. I hardly know; I certainly cannot say. That dwindling part of me which offered comments on the entire occurrence noted this extraordinary effect as though it happened naturally—that Moleson himself was marvellously increasing.

The entire spell became operative all at once. I experienced both the delight of complete abandonment and the terror of letting go what *had* seemed real. I understood Moleson's sham laughter, and the subtle resignation of George Isley. And an amazing thought flashed birdlike across my changing consciousness—that this resurrection into the Past, this rebirth of the spirit which they sought, involved taking upon themselves the guise of these ancient symbols each in turn. As the embryo assumes each evolutionary stage below it before the human semblance is attained, so the souls of those two adventurers took upon themselves the various emblems of that intense belief. The devout worshipper takes on the qualities of his deity. They wore the entire series of the old-world gods so potently that I perceived them, and even objectified them by my senses. The present was their pre-natal stage; to enter the past they were being born again.

But it was not Moleson's semblance alone that took on this awful change. Both faces, scaled to the measure of Egypt's outstanding quality of size, became in this little modern room distressingly immense. Distorting mirrors can suggest no simile, for the symmetry of proportion was not injured. I lost their human physiognomies. I saw their thoughts, their feelings, their augmented, altered hearts, the thing that Egypt put there while she stole their love from modern life. There grew an awful stateliness upon them that was huge, mysterious, and motionless as stone.

For Moleson's narrow face at first turned hawklike in the semblance of the sinister deity, Horus, only stretched to tower above the toy-scaled piano; it was keen and sly and monstrous after prey, while a swiftness of the sunrise leaped from both the brilliant eyes. George Isley, equally immense of outline, was in general presentment more magnificent, a breadth of the Sphinx about his spreading shoulders, and in his countenance an inscrutable power of calm temple images. These were the first signs of obsession; but others followed. In rapid series, like lantern-slides upon a screen, the ancient symbols flashed one after another across these two extended human faces and were gone. Disentanglement became impossible. The successive signatures seemed almost superimposed as in a composite photograph, each appearing and vanished before recognition was even possible, while I interpreted the inner alchemy by means of outer tokens familiar to my senses. Egypt, possessing them, expressed herself thus marvellously in their physical aspect, using the symbols of her intense, regenerative power. . . .

The changes merged with such swiftness into one another that I did not seize the half of them—till, finally, the procession culminated in a single one that remained fixed awfully upon them both. The entire series merged. I was aware of this single masterful image which summed up all the others in sublime repose. The gigantic thing rose up in this incredible statue form. The spirit of Egypt synthesised in this monstrous symbol, obliterated them both. I saw the seated figures of the grim Colossi, dipped in sand, night over them, waiting for the dawn. . . .

X

I made a violent effort, then, at self-assertion—an effort to focus my mind upon the present. And, searching for Moleson and George Isley, its nearest details, I was aware that I could not find them. The familiar figures of my two companions were not discoverable.

I saw it as plainly as I also saw that ludicrous, wee piano—for a moment. But the moment remained; the Eternity of Egypt stayed. For that lonely and terrific pair had stooped their shoulders and bowed their awful heads. They were in the room. They imaged forth the power of the everlasting Past through the little structures of two human worshippers. Room, walls, and ceiling fled away. Sand and the open sky replaced them.

The two of them rose side by side before my bursting eyes. I knew not where to look. Like some child who confronts its giants upon the nursery floor, I turned to stone, unable to think or move. I stared. Sight wrenched itself to find the men familiar to it, but found instead this symbolising vision. I could not see them properly. Their faces were spread with hugeness, their features lost in some uncommon magnitude, their shoulders, necks, and arms grown vast upon the air. As with the desert, there was physiognomy yet no personal expression, the human thing all drowned within the mass of battered stone. I discovered neither cheeks nor mouth nor jaw, but ruined eyes and lips of broken granite. Huge, motionless, mysterious, Egypt informed them and took them to herself. And between us, curiously presented in some false perspective, I saw the little symbol of To-day—the Blüthner piano. It was appalling. I knew a second of majestic horror. I blenched. Hot and cold gushed through me. Strength left me, power of speech and movement, too, as in a moment of complete paralysis.

The spell, moreover, was not within the room alone; it was outside and everywhere. The Past stood massed about the very walls of the hotel. Distance, as well as time, stepped nearer. That chanting summoned the gigantic items in all their ancient splendour. The shadowy concourse grouped itself upon the sand about us, and I was aware that the great army shifted noiselessly into place; that pyramids soared and towered; that deities of stone stood by; that temples ranged themselves in reconstructed beauty, grave as the night of time whence they emerged; and that the outline of the Sphinx, motionless but aggressive, piled its dim bulk upon the atmosphere. Immensity answered to immensity. . . . There were vast intervals of time and there were reaches of enormous distance, yet all happened in a moment, and all happened within a little space. It was now and here. Eternity whispered in every second as in every grain of sand. Yet, while aware of so many stupendous details all at once, I was really aware of one thing only—that the spirit of ancient Egypt faced me in these two terrific figures, and that my consciousness, stretched painfully yet gloriously, included all, as She also unquestionably included them—and me.

For it seemed I shared the likeness of my two companions. Some lesser symbol, though of similar kind, obsessed me too. I tried to move, but my feet were set in stone; my arms lay fixed; my body was embedded in the rock. Sand beat sharply upon my outer surface, urged upwards in little flurries by a chilly wind. There was nothing felt: I *heard* the rattle of the scattering grains against my hardened body. . . .

And we waited for the dawn; for the resurrection of that unchanging deity who was the source and inspiration of all our glorious life. . . . The air grew keen and fresh. In the distance a line of sky turned from pink to violet and gold; a delicate rose next flushed the desert; a few pale stars hung fainting overhead; and the wind that brought the sunrise was already stirring. The whole land paused upon the coming of its mighty God. . . .

Into the pause there rose a curious sound for which we had been waiting. For it came familiarly, as though expected. I could have sworn at first that it was George Isley who sang, answering his companion. There beat behind its great volume the same note and rhythm, only so prodigiously increased that, while Moleson's chant had waked it, it now was independent and apart. The resonant vibrations of what he sang had reached down into the places where it slept. *They* uttered synchronously. Egypt spoke. There was in it the deep muttering as of a thousand drums, as though the desert uttered in prodigious syllables. I listened while my heart of stone stood still. There were two voices in the sky. *They* spoke tremendously with each other in the dawn:

"So easily we still remain possessors of the land. . . . While the centuries roar past us and are gone."

Soft with power the syllables rolled forth, yet with a booming depth as though caverns underground produced them.

"Our silence is disturbed. Pass on with the multitude towards the East. . . . Still in the dawn we sing the old-world wisdom. . . . They shall hear our speech, yet shall not hear it with their ears of flesh. At dawn our words go forth, searching the distances of sand and time across the sunlight. . . . At dusk they return, as upon eagles' wings, entering again our lips of stone. . . . Each century one syllable, yet no sentence yet complete. While our lips are broken with the utterance. . . ."

It seemed that hours and months and years went past me while I listened in my sandy bed. The fragments died far away, then sounded very close again. It was as though mountain peaks sang to one another above clouds. Wind caught the muffled roar away. Wind brought it back. . . . Then, in a hollow pause that lasted years, conveying marvellously the passage of long periods, I heard the utterance more clearly. The leisured roll of the great voice swept through me like a flood:

"We wait and watch and listen in our loneliness. We do not close our eyes. The moon and stars sail past us, and our river finds the sea. We bring Eternity upon your broken lives. . . . We see you build your little lines of steel across our territory behind the thin white smoke. We hear the whistle of your messengers of iron through the air. . . . The nations rise and pass. The empires flutter westwards and are gone. . . . The sun grows older and the stars turn pale. . . . Winds shift the line of the horizons, and our River moves its bed. But we, everlasting and unchangeable, remain. Of water, sand and fire is our essential being, yet built within the universal air. . . . There is no pause in life, there is no break in death. The changes bring no end. The sun returns. . . . There is eternal resurrection. But our kingdom is underground in shadow, unrealised of your little day. . . . Come, come! The temples still are crowded, and our Desert blesses you. Our River takes your feet. Our sand shall purify, and the fire of our God shall burn you sweetly into wisdom. . . . Come, then, and worship, for the time draws near. It is the dawn. . . ."

The voices died down into depths that the sand of ages muffled, while the flaming dawn of the East rushed up the sky. Sunrise, the great symbol of life's endless resurrection, was at hand. About me, in immense but shadowy array, stood the whole of ancient Egypt, hanging breathlessly upon the moment of adoration. No longer stern and terrible in the splendour of their long neglect, the effigies rose erect with passionate glory, a forest of stately stone. Their granite lips were parted and their ancient eyes were wide. All faced the east. And the sun drew nearer to the rim of the attentive Desert.

XI

Emotion there seemed none, in the sense that *I* knew feeling. I knew, if anything, the ultimate secrets of two primitive sensations—joy and awe. . . . The dawn grew swiftly brighter. There was gold, as though the sands of Nubia spilt their brilliance on each shining detail; there was glory, as though the retreating tide of stars spilt their light foam upon the world; and there was passion, as though the beliefs of all the edges floated back with abandonment into the—Sun. Ruined Egypt merged into a single temple of elemental vastness whose floor was the empty desert, but whose walls rose to the stars.

Abruptly, then, chanting and rhythm ceased; they dipped below. Sand muffled them. And the Sun looked down upon its ancient world. . . .

A radiant warmth poured through me. I found that I could move my limbs again. A sense of triumphant life ran through my stony frame. For one passing second I heard the shower of gritty particles upon my surface like sand blown upwards by a gust of wind, but this time I could *feel* the sting of it upon my skin. It passed. The drenching heat bathed me from head to foot, while stony insensibility gave place with returning consciousness to flesh and blood. The sun had risen. . . . I was alive, but I was—changed.

It seemed I opened my eyes. An immense relief was in me. I turned; I drew a deep, refreshing breath; I stretched one leg upon a thick, green carpet. Something had left me; another thing had returned. I sat up, conscious of welcome release, of freedom, of escape.

There was some violent, disorganising break. I found myself; I found Moleson; I found George Isley, too. He had got shifted in that room without my being aware of it. Isley had risen. He came upon me like a blow. I saw him move his arms. Fire flashed from below his hands; and I realised then that he was turning on the electric lights. They emerged from different points along the walls, in the alcove, beneath the ceiling, by the writing-table; and one had just that minute blazed into my eyes from a bracket close above me. I was back again in the Present among modern things.

But, while most of the details presented themselves gradually to my recovered senses, Isley returned with this curious effect of speed and distance—like a blow upon the mind. From great height and from prodigious size—he dropped. I seemed to find him rushing at me. Moleson was simply "there"; there was no speed or sudden change in him as with the other. Motionless at the piano, his long thin hands lay down upon the keys yet did not strike them. But Isley came back like lightning into the little room, signs of the monstrous obsession still about his altering features. There was battle and worship mingled in his deep-set eyes. His mouth, though set, was smiling. With a shudder I positively saw the vastness slipping from his face as shadows from a stretch of broken cliff. There was this awful mingling of proportions. The colossal power that had resumed his being drew slowly inwards. There was collapse in him. And upon the sun-burned cheek of his rugged face I saw a tear.

Poignant revulsion caught me then for a moment. The present showed itself in rags. The reduction of scale was painful. I yearned for the splendour that was gone, yet still seemed so hauntingly almost within reach. The cheapness of the hotel room, the glaring ugliness of its tinsel decoration, the baseness of ideals where utility instead of beauty, gain instead of worship, governed life—this, with the dwindled aspect of my companions to the insignificance of marionettes, brought a hungry pain that was at first intolerable. In the glare of light I noticed the small round face of the portable clock upon the mantelpiece, showing half-past eleven. Moleson had been two hours at the piano. And this measuring faculty of my mind completed the disillusionment. I was, indeed, back among present things. The mechanical spirit of To-day imprisoned me again.

For a considerable interval we neither moved nor spoke; the sudden change left the emotions in confusion; we had leaped from a height, from the top of the pyramid, from a star—and the crash of landing scattered thought. I stole a glance at Isley, wondering vaguely why he was there at all; the look of resignation had replaced the power in his face; the tear was brushed away. There was no struggle in him now, no sign of resistance; there was abandonment only; he seemed insignificant. The real George Isley was elsewhere: he himself had not returned.

By jerks, as it were, and by awkward stages, then, we all three came back to common things again. I found that we were talking ordinarily, asking each other questions, answering, lighting cigarettes, and all the rest. Moleson played some commonplace chords upon the piano, while he leaned back listlessly in his chair, putting in sentences now and again and chatting idly to whichever of us would listen. And Isley came slowly across the room towards me, holding out cigarettes. His dark brown face had shadows on it. He looked exhausted, worn, like some soldier broken in the wars.

"You liked it?" I heard his thin voice asking. There was no interest, no expression; it was not the real Isley who spoke; it was the little part of him that had come back. He smiled like a marvellous automaton.

Mechanically I took the cigarette he offered me, thinking confusedly what answer I could make.

"It's irresistible," I murmured; "I understand that it's easier to go."

"Sweeter as well," he whispered with a sigh, "and very wonderful!"

XII

The hand that lit my cigarette, I saw, was trembling. A desire to do something violent woke in me suddenly—to move energetically, to push or drive something away.

"What was it?" I asked abruptly, in a louder, half-challenging voice, intended for the man at the piano. "Such a performance—upon others—without first asking their permission—seems to me unpermissible—it's—"

And it was Moleson who replied. He ignored the end of my sentence as though he had not heard it. He strolled over to our side, taking a cigarette and pressing it carefully into shape between his long thin fingers.

"You may well ask," he answered quietly; "but it's not so easy to tell. We discovered it"—he nodded towards Isley—"two years ago in the 'Valley.' It lay beside a Priest, a very important personage, apparently, and was part of the Ritual he used in the worship of the sun. In the Museum now—you can see it any day at the Boulak—it is simply labelled 'Hymn to Ra.' The period was Aknahton's."

"The words, yes," put in Isley, who was listening closely.

"The words?" repeated Moleson in a curious tone. "There *are* no words. It's all really a manipulation of the vowel sounds. And the rhythm, or chanting, or whatever you like to call it, I—I invented myself. The Egyptians did not write their music, you see." He suddenly searched my face a moment with questioning eyes. "Any words you heard," he said, "or thought you heard, were merely your own interpretation."

I stared at him, making no rejoinder.

"They made use of what they called a 'root-language' in their rituals," he went on, "and it consisted entirely of vowel sounds. There were no consonants. For vowel sounds, you see, run on for ever without end or beginning, whereas consonants interrupt their flow and break it up and limit it. A consonant has no sound of its own at all. Real language is continuous."

We stood a moment, smoking in silence. I understood then that this thing Moleson had done was based on definite knowledge. He had rendered some fragment of an ancient Ritual he and Isley had unearthed together, and while he knew its effect upon the latter, he chanced it on myself. Not otherwise, I feel, could it have influenced me in the extraordinary way it did. In the faith and poetry of a nation lies its soul-life, and the gigantic faith of Egypt blazed behind the rhythm of that long, monotonous chant. There was blood and heart and nerves in it. Millions had heard it sung; millions had wept and prayed and yearned; it was ensouled by the passion of that marvellous civilisation that loved the godhead of the Sun, and that now hid, waiting but still alive, below the ground. The majestic faith of ancient Egypt poured up with it—that tremendous, burning elaboration of the after-life and of Eternity that was the pivot of those spacious days. For centuries vast multitudes, led by their royal priests, had uttered this very form and ritual—believed it, lived it, felt it. The rising of the sun remained its climax. Its spiritual power still clung to the great ruined symbols. The faith of a buried civilisation had burned back into the present and into our hearts as well.

And a curious respect for the man who was able to produce this effect upon two modern minds crept over me, and mingled with the repulsion that I felt. I looked furtively at his withered, dried-up features. He wore some vague and shadowy impress still of what had just been in him. There was a stony appearance in his shrunken cheeks. He looked smaller. I saw him lessened. I thought of him as he had been so short a time before, imprisoned in his great stone captors that had obsessed him. . . .

"There's tremendous power in it,—an awful power," I stammered, more to break the oppressive pause than for any desire in me to speak with him. "It brings back Egypt in some extraordinary way—ancient Egypt, I mean—brings it close—into the heart." My words ran on of their own accord almost. I spoke with a hush, unwittingly. There was awe in me. Isley had moved away towards the window, leaving me face to face with this strange incarnation of another age.

"It must," he replied, deep light still glowing in his eyes, "for the soul of the old days is in it. No one, I think, can hear it and remain the same. It expresses, you see, the essential passion and beauty of that gorgeous worship, that splendid faith, that reasonable and intelligent worship of the sun, the only scientific belief the world has ever known. Its popular form, of course, was largely superstitious, but the sacerdotal form—the form used by the priests, that is—who understood the relationship between colour, sound and symbol, was—"

He broke off suddenly, as though he had been speaking to himself. We sat down. George Isley leaned out of the window with his back to us, watching the desert in the moonless night.

"You have tried its effect before upon—others?" I asked point-blank.

"Upon myself," he answered shortly.

"Upon others?" I insisted.

He hesitated an instant.

"Upon one other—yes," he admitted.

"Intentionally?" And something quivered in me as I asked it.

He shrugged his shoulders slightly. "I'm merely a speculative archæolo-gist," he smiled, "and—and an imaginative Egyptologist. My bounden duty is to reconstruct the past so that it lives for others."

An impulse rose in me to take him by the throat.

"You know perfectly well, of course, the magical effect it's sure—likely, at least—to have?"

He stared steadily at me through the cigarette smoke. To this day I can-not think exactly what it was in this man that made me shudder.

"I'm sure of nothing," he replied smoothly, "but I consider it quite le-gitimate to try. Magical—the word you used—has no meaning for me. If such a thing exists, it is merely scientific—undiscovered or forgotten knowledge." An insolent, aggressive light shone in his eyes as he spoke; his manner was almost truculent. "You refer, I take it, to—our friend—rather than to your-self?"

And with difficulty I met his singular stare. From his whole person some-thing still emanated that was forbidding, yet overmasteringly persuasive. It brought back the notion of that invisible Web, that dim gauze curtain, that motionless Influence lying waiting at the centre for its prey, those monstrous and mysterious Items standing, alert, and watchful, through the centuries. "You mean," he added lower, "his altered attitude to life—his going?"

To hear him use the words, the very phrase, struck me with sudden chill. Before I could answer, however, and certainly before I could master the touch of horror that rushed over me, I heard him continuing in a whisper. It seemed again that he spoke to himself as much as he spoke to me.

"The soul, I suppose, has the right to choose its own conditions and sur-roundings. To pass elsewhere involves translation, not extinction." He smoked a moment in silence, then said another curious thing, looking up into my face with an expression of intense earnestness. Something genuine in him again replaced the pose of cynicism. "The soul is eternal and can take its place anywhere, regardless of mere duration. What is there in the vulgar and super-ficial Present that should hold it so exclusively; and where can it find to-day the belief, the faith, the beauty that are the very essence of its life—where in the rush and scatter of this tawdry age can it make its home? Shall it flutter for ever in a valley of dry bones, when a living Past lies ready and waiting with loveliness, strength, and glory?" He moved closer; he touched my arm; I felt his breath upon my face. "Come with us," he whispered awfully; "come back with us! Withdraw your life from the rubbish of this futile ugliness! Come back and worship with us in the spirit of the Past. Take up the old, old splen-dour, the glory, the immense conceptions, the wondrous certainty, the ineffable knowledge of essentials. It all lies about you still; it's calling, ever calling; it's very close; it draws you day and night—calling, calling, calling. . . ."

His voice died off curiously into distance on the word; I can hear it to this day, and the soft, droning quality in the intense yet fading tone: "Calling, calling, calling." But his eyes turned wicked. I felt the sinister power of the man. I was aware of madness in his thought and mind. The Past he sought to glorify I saw black, as with the forbidding Egyptian darkness of a plague. It was not beauty but Death that I heard calling, calling, calling.

"It's real," he went on, hardly aware that I shrank, "and not a dream. These ruined symbols still remain in touch with that which was. They are potent to-day as they were six thousand years ago. The amazing life of those days brims behind them. They are not mere masses of oppressive stone; they express in visible form great powers that still are—*knowable.*" He lowered his head, peered up into my face, and whispered. Something secret passed into his eyes.

"I saw you change," came the words below his breath, "as you saw the change in us. But only worship can produce that change. The soul assumes the qualities of the deity it worships. The powers of its deity possess it and transform it into its own likeness. You also felt it. *You* also were possessed. I saw the stone-faced deity upon your own."

I seemed to shake myself as a dog shakes water from its body. I stood up. I remember that I stretched my hands out as though to push him from me and expel some creeping influence from my mind. I remember another thing as well. But for the reality of the sequel, and but for the matter-of-fact result still facing me to-day in the disappearance of George Isley—the loss to the present time of all George Isley *was*—I might have found subject for laughter in what I saw. Comedy was in it certainly. Yet it was both ghastly and terrific. Deep horror crept below the aspect of the ludicrous, for the apparent mimicry cloaked truth. It was appalling because it was real.

In the large mirror that reflected the room behind me I saw myself and Moleson; I saw Isley too in the background by the open window. And the attitude of all three was the attitude of hieroglyphics come to life. My arms indeed were stretched, but not stretched, as I had thought, in mere self-defence. They were stretched—unnaturally. The forearms made those strange obtuse angles that the old carved granite wears, the palms of the hands held upwards, the heads thrown back, the legs advanced, the bodies stiffened into postures that expressed forgotten, ancient minds. The physical conformation of all three was monstrous; and yet reverence and truth dictated even the uncouthness of the gestures. Something in all three of us inspired the forms our bodies had assumed. Our attitudes expressed buried yearnings, emotions, tendencies— whatever they may be termed—that the spirit of the Past evoked.

I saw the reflected picture but for a moment. I dropped my arms, aware of foolishness in my way of standing. Moleson moved forward with his long, significant stride, and at the same instant Isley came up quickly and joined us from his place by the open window. We looked into each other's faces without a word. There was this little pause that lasted perhaps ten seconds. But in that pause I felt the entire world slide past me. I heard the centuries rush by at headlong speed. The present dipped away. Existence was no longer in a line that stretched two ways; it was a circle in which ourselves, together with Past and Future, stood motionless at the centre, all details equally accessible at once. The three of us were falling, falling backwards. . . .

"Come!" said the voice of Moleson solemnly, but with the sweetness as of a child anticipating joy, "Come! Let us go together, for the boat of Ra has crossed the Underworld. The darkness has been conquered. Let us go out together and find the dawn. Listen! It is calling, calling, calling. . . ."

XIII

I was aware of rushing, but it was the soul in me that rushed. It experienced dizzy, unutterable alterations. Thousands of emotions, intense and varied, poured through me at lightning speed, each satisfyingly known, yet gone before its name appeared. The life of many centuries tore headlong back with me, and, as in drowning, this epitome of existence shot in a few seconds the steep slopes the Past had so laboriously built up. The changes flashed and passed. I wept and prayed and worshipped; I loved and suffered; I battled, lost and won. Down the gigantic scale of ages that telescoped thus into a few brief moments, the soul in me went sliding backwards towards a motionless, reposeful Past.

I remember foolish details that interrupted the immense descent—I put on coat and hat; I remember some one's words, strangely sounding as when some bird wakes up and sings at midnight—"We'll take the little door; the front one's locked by now"; and I have a vague recollection of the outline of the great hotel, with its colonnades and terraces, fading behind me through the air. But these details merely flickered and disappeared, as though I fell earthwards from a star and passed feathers or blown leaves upon the way. There was no friction as my soul dropped backwards into time; the flight was easy and silent as a dream. I felt myself sucked down into gulfs whose emptiness offered no resistance . . . until at last the appalling speed decreased of its own accord, and the dizzy flight became a kind of gentle floating. It changed imperceptibly into a gliding motion, as though the angle altered. My feet, quite naturally, were on the ground, moving through something soft that clung to them and rustled while it clung.

I looked up and saw the bright armies of the stars. In front of me I recognised the flat-topped, shadowy ridges; on both sides lay the open expanses of familiar wilderness; and beside me, one on either hand, moved two figures who were my companions. We were in the desert, but it was the desert of thousands of years ago. My companions, moreover, though familiar to some part of me, seemed strangers or half known. Their names I strove in vain to capture; Mosely, Ilson, sounded in my head, mingled together falsely. And when I stole a glance at them, I saw dark lines of mannikins unfilled with substance, and was aware of the grotesque gestures of living hieroglyphics. It seemed for an instant that their arms were bound behind their backs impossibly, and that their heads turned sharply across their lineal shoulders.

But for a moment only; for at a second glance I saw them solid and compact; their names came back to me; our arms were linked together as we walked. We had already covered a great distance, for my limbs were aching and my breath was short. The air was cold, the silence absolute. It seemed, in this faint light, that the desert flowed beneath our feet, rather than that we advanced by taking steps. Cliffs with hooded tops moved past us, boulders glided, mounds of sand slid by. And then I heard a voice upon my left that was surely Moleson speaking:

"Towards Enet our feet are set," he half sang, half murmured, "towards Enet-te-ntōrē. There, in the House of Birth, we shall dedicate our hearts and lives anew."

And the language, no less than the musical intonation of his voice, enraptured me. For I understood he spoke of Denderah, in whose majestic temple recent hands had painted with deathless colours the symbols of our cosmic relationships with the zodiacal signs. And Denderah was our great seat of worship of the goddess Hathor, the Egyptian Aphrodite, bringer of love and joy. The falcon-headed Horus was her husband, from whom, in his home at Edfu, we imbibed swift kinds of power. And—it was the time of the New Year, the great feast when the forces of the living earth turn upwards into happy growth.

We were on foot across the desert towards Denderah, and this sand we trod was the sand of thousands of years ago.

The paralysis of time and distance involved some amazing lightness of the spirit that, I suppose, touched ecstasy. There was intoxication in the soul. I was not divided from the stars, nor separate from this desert that rushed with us. The unhampered wind blew freshly from my nerves and skin, and the Nile, glimmering faintly on our right, lay with its lapping waves in both my hands. I knew the life of Egypt, for it was in me, over me, round me. I was a part of it. We went happily, like birds to meet the sunrise. There were no pits of measured time and interval that could detain us. We flowed, yet were at rest; we were endlessly alive; present and future alike were inconceivable; we were in the Kingdom of the Past.

The Pyramids were just a-building, and the army of Obelisks looked about them, proud of their first balance; Thebes swung her hundred gates upon the world. New, shining Memphis glittered with myriad reflections into waters that the tears of Isis sweetened, and the cliffs of Abou Simbel were still innocent of their gigantic progeny. Alone, the Sphinx, linking timelessness with time, brooded unguessed and underived upon an alien world. We marched within antiquity towards Denderah. . . .

How long we marched, how fast, how far we went, I can remember as little as the marvellous speech that passed across me while my two companions spoke together. I only remember that suddenly a wave of pain disturbed my wondrous happiness and caused my calm, which had seemed beyond all reach of break, to fall away. I heard their voices abruptly with a kind of terror. A sensation of fear, of loss, of nightmare bewilderment came over me like cold wind. What *they* lived naturally, true to their inmost hearts, *I* lived merely by means of a temperamental sympathy. And the stage had come at which my powers failed. Exhaustion overtook me. I wilted. The strain—the abnormal backwards stretch of consciousness that was put upon me by another—gave way and broke. I heard their voices faint and horrible. My joy was extinguished. A glare of horror fell upon the desert and the stars seemed evil. An anguishing desire for the safe and wholesome Present usurped all this mad yearning to obtain the Past. My feet fell out of step. The rushing of the desert paused. I unlinked my arms. We stopped all three.

The actual spot is to this day well known to me. I found it afterwards, I even photographed it. It lies actually not far from Helouan—a few miles at most beyond the Solitary Palm, where slopes of undulating sand mark the opening of a strange, enticing valley called the Wadi Gerraui. And it is enticing because it beckons and leads on. Here, amid torn gorges of a limestone wilderness, there is suddenly soft yellow sand that flows and draws the feet onward. It slips away with one too easily; always the next ridge and basin must be seen, each time a little further. It has the quality of decoying. The cliffs say, No; but this streaming sand invites. In its flowing curves of gold there is enchantment.

And it was here upon its very lips we stopped, the rhythm of our steps broken, our hearts no longer one. My temporary rapture vanished. I was aware of fear. For the Present rushed upon me with attack in it, and I felt that my mind was arrested close upon the edge of madness. Something cleared and lifted in my brain.

The soul, indeed, could "choose its dwelling-place"; but to live elsewhere completely was the choice of madness, and to live divorced from all the sweet wholesome business of To-day involved an exile that was worse than madness. It was death. My heart burned for George Isley. I remembered the tear upon his cheek. The agony of his struggle I shared suddenly with him. Yet with him was the reality, with me a sympathetic reflection merely. *He* was already too far gone to fight. . . .

I shall never forget the desolation of that strange scene beneath the morning stars. The desert lay down and watched us. We stood upon the brink of a little broken ridge, looking into the valley of golden sand. This sand gleamed soft and wonderful in the starlight some twenty feet below. The descent was easy—but I would not move. I refused to advance another step. I saw my companions in the mysterious half-light beside me peering over the edge, Moleson in front a little.

And I turned to him, sure of the part I meant to play, yet conscious painfully of my helplessness. My personality seemed a straw in mid-stream that spun in a futile effort to arrest the flood that bore it. There was vivid human conflict in the moment's silence. It was an eddy that paused in the great body of the tide. And then I spoke. Oh, I was ashamed of the insignificance of my voice and the weakness of my little personality.

"Moleson, we go no further with you. We have already come too far. We now turn back."

Behind my words were a paltry thirty years. His answer drove sixty centuries against me. For his voice was like the wind that passed whispering down the stream of yellow sand below us. He smiled.

"Our feet are set towards Enet-te-ntōrē. There is no turning back. Listen! It is calling, calling, calling!"

"We will go home," I cried, in a tone I vainly strove to make imperative.

"Our home is there," he sang, pointing with one long thin arm towards the brightening east, "for the Temple calls us and the River takes our feet. We shall be in the House of Birth to meet the sunrise—"

"You lie," I cried again, "you speak the lies of madness, and this Past you seek is the House of Death. It is the kingdom of the underworld."

The words tore wildly, impotently out of me. I seized George Isley's arm.

"Come back with me," I pleaded vehemently, my heart aching with a nameless pain for him. "We'll retrace our steps. Come home with me! Come back! Listen! The Present calls you sweetly!"

His arm slipped horribly out of my grasp that had seemed to hold it so tightly. Moleson, already below us in the yellow sand, looked small with distance. He was gliding rapidly further with uncanny swiftness. The diminution of his form was ghastly. It was like a doll's. And his voice rose up, faint as with the distance of great gulfs of space.

"Calling . . . calling. . . . You hear it for ever calling. . . ."

It died away with the wind along that sandy valley, and the Past swept in a flood across the brightening sky. I swayed as though a storm was at my back. I reeled. Almost I went too—over the crumbling edge into the sand.

"Come back with me! Come home!" I cried more faintly. "The Present alone is real. There is work, ambition, duty. There is beauty, too—the beauty of good living! And there is love! There is—a woman . . . calling, calling . . .!"

That other voice took up the word below me. I heard the faint refrain sing down the sandy walls. The wild, sweet pang in it was marvellous.

"Our feet are set for Enet-te-ntōrē. It is calling, calling . . .!"

My voice fell into nothingness. George Isley was below me now, his outline tiny against the sheet of yellow sand. And the sand was moving. The desert rushed again. The human figures receded swiftly into the Past they had reconstructed with the creative yearning of their souls.

I stood alone upon the edge of crumbling limestone, helplessly watching them. It was amazing what I witnessed, while the shafts of crimson dawn rose up the sky. The enormous desert turned alive to the horizon with gold and blue and silver. The purple shadows melted into grey. The flat-topped ridges shone. Huge messengers of light flashed everywhere at once. The radiance of sunrise dazzled my outer sight.

But if my eyes were blinded, my inner sight was focussed the more clearly upon what followed. I witnessed the disappearance of George Isley. There was a dreadful magic in the picture. The pair of them, small and distant below me in that little sandy hollow, stood out sharply defined as in a miniature. I saw their outlines neat and terrible like some ghastly inset against the enormous scenery. Though so close to me in actual space, they were centuries away in time. And a dim, vast shadow was about them that was not mere shadow of the ridges. It encompassed them; it moved, crawling over the sand, obliterating them. Within it, like insects lost in amber, they became visibly imprisoned, dwindled in size, borne deep away, absorbed.

And then I recognised the outline. Once more, but this time recumbent and spread flat upon the desert's face, I knew the monstrous shapes of the twin obsessing symbols. The spirit of ancient Egypt lay over all the land, tremendous in the dawn. The sunrise summoned her. She lay prostrate before the deity. The shadows of the towering Colossi lay prostrate too. The little humans, with their worshipping and conquered hearts, lay deep within them.

George Isley I saw clearest. The distinctness, the reality were appalling. He was naked, robbed, undressed. I saw him a skeleton, picked clean to the very bones as by an acid. His life lay hid in the being of that mighty Past. Egypt had absorbed him. He was gone. . . .

I closed my eyes, but I could not keep them closed. They opened of their own accord. The three of us were nearing the great hotel that rose yellow, with shuttered windows, in the early sunshine. A wind blew briskly from the north across the Mokattam Hills. There were soft cannon-ball clouds dotted about the sky, and across the Nile, where the mist lay in a line of white, I saw the tops of the Pyramids gleaming like mountain peaks of gold. A string of camels, laden with white stone, went past us. I heard the crying of the natives in the streets of Helouan, and as we went up the steps the donkeys arrived and camped in the sandy road beside their *bersim* till the tourists claimed them.

"Good morning," cried Abdullah, the man who owned them. "You all go Sakkhârah to-day, or Memphis? Beat'ful day to-day, and vair good donkeys!"

Moleson went up to his room without a word, and Isley did the same. I thought he staggered a moment as he turned the passage corner from my sight. His face wore a look of vacancy that some call peace. There was radiance in it. It made me shudder. Aching in mind and body, and no word spoken, I followed their example. I went upstairs to bed, and slept a dreamless sleep till after sunset. . . .

XIV

And I woke with a lost, unhappy feeling that a withdrawing tide had left me on the shore, alone and desolate. My first instinct was for my friend, George Isley. And I noticed a square, white envelope with my name upon it in his writing.

Before I opened it I knew quite well what words would be inside:

"We are going up to Thebes," the note informed me simply. "We leave by the night train. If you care to—" But the last four words were scratched out again, though not so thickly that I could not read them. Then came the address of the Egyptologist's house and the signature, very firmly traced, "Yours ever, GEORGE ISLEY." I glanced at my watch and saw that it was after seven o'clock. The night train left at half-past six. They had already started. . . .

The pain of feeling forsaken, left behind, was deep and bitter, for myself; but what I felt for him, old friend and comrade, was even more intense, since it was hopeless. Fear and conventional emotion had stopped me at the very gates of an amazing possibility—some state of consciousness that, *realizing* the Past, might doff the Present, and by slipping out of Time, experience Eternity. That was the seduction I had escaped by the uninspired resistance of my pettier soul. Yet he, my friend, yielding in order to conquer, had obtained an awful prize—ah, I understood the picture's other side as well, with an unutterable poignancy of pity—the prize of immobility which is sheer stagnation, the imagined bliss which is a false escape, the dream of finding beauty away from present things. From that dream the awakening must be rude indeed. Clutching at vanished stars, he had clutched the oldest illusion in the world. To me it seemed the negation of life that had betrayed him. The pity of it burned me like a flame.

But I did not "care to follow" him and his companion. I waited at Helouan for his return, filling the empty days with yet emptier explanations. I felt as a man who sees what he loves sinking down into clear, deep water, still within visible reach, yet gone beyond recovery. Moleson had taken him back to Thebes; and Egypt, monstrous effigy of the Past, had caught her prey.

The rest, moreover, is easily told. Moleson I never saw again. To this day I have never seen him, though his subsequent books are known to me, with the banal fact that he is numbered with those energetic and deluded enthusiasts who start a new religion, obtain notoriety, a few hysterical followers and—oblivion.

George Isley, however, returned to Helouan after a fortnight's absence. I saw him, knew him, talked and had my meals with him. We even did slight expeditions together. He was gentle and delightful as a woman who has loved a wonderful ideal and attained to it—in memory. All roughness was gone out of him; he was smooth and polished as a crystal surface that reflects whatever is near enough to ask a picture. Yet his appearance shocked me inexpressibly: there was nothing in him—*nothing*. It was the representation of George Isley that came back from Thebes; the outer simulacra; the shell that walks the London streets to-day. I met no vestige of the man I used to know. George Isley had disappeared.

With this marvellous automaton I lived another month. The horror of him kept me company in the hotel where he moved among the cosmopolitan humanity as a ghost that visits the sunlight yet has its home elsewhere.

This empty image of George Isley lived with me in our Helouan hotel until the winds of early March informed his physical frame that discomfort was in the air, and that he might as well move elsewhere, elsewhere happening to be northwards.

And he left just as he stayed—automatically. His brain obeyed the conventional stimuli to which his nerves, and consequently his muscles, were accustomed. It sounds so foolish. But he took his ticket automatically; he gave the natural and adequate reasons automatically; he chose his ship and landing-place in the same way that ordinary people chose these things; he said good-bye like any other man who leaves casual acquaintances and "hopes" to meet them again; he lived, that is to say, entirely in his brain. His heart, his emotions, his temperament and personality, that nameless sum-total for which the great sympathetic nervous system is accountable—all this, his soul, had gone elsewhere. This once vigorous, gifted being had become a normal, comfortable man that everybody could understand—a commonplace nonentity. He was precisely what the majority expected him to be—ordinary; a good fellow; a man of the world; he was "delightful." He merely reflected daily life without partaking of it. To the majority it was hardly noticeable; "very pleasant" was a general verdict. His ambition, his restlessness, his zeal had gone; that tireless zest whose driving power is yearning had taken flight, leaving behind it physical energy without spiritual desire. His soul had found its nest and flown to it. He lived in the chimera of the Past, serene, indifferent, detached. I saw him immense, a shadowy, majestic figure, standing—ah, not moving!—in a repose that was satisfying because it *could* not change. The size, the mystery, the immobility that caged him in seemed to me—terrible. For I dared not intrude upon his awful privacy, and intimacy between us there was none. Of his experiences at Thebes I asked no single question—it was somehow not possible or legitimate; he, equally, vouchsafed no word of explanation—it was uncommunicable to a dweller in the Present. Between us was this barrier we both respected. He peered at modern life, incurious, listless, apathetic, through a dim, gauze curtain. He was behind it.

People round us were going to Sakkhâra and the Pyramids, to see the Sphinx by moonlight, to dream at Edfu and at Denderah. Others described their journeys to Assouan, Khartoum and Abou Simbel, and gave details of their encampments in the desert. Wind, wind, wind! The winds of Egypt blew and sang and sighed. From the White Nile came the travellers, and from the Blue Nile, from the Fayum, and from nameless excavations without end. They talked and wrote their books. They had the magpie knowledge of the present. The Egyptologists, big and little, read the writing on the wall and put the hieroglyphs and papyri into modern language. Alone George Isley *knew* the secret. He lived it.

And the high passionate calm, the lofty beauty, the glamour and enchantment that are the spell of this thrice-haunted land, were in *my* soul as well—sufficiently for me to interpret his condition. I could not leave, yet having left I could not stay away. I yearned for the Egypt that he knew. No word I uttered; speech could not approach it. We wandered by the Nile together, and through the groves of palms that once were Memphis. The sandy wastes beyond the Pyramids knew our footsteps; the Mokattam Ridges, purple at evening and golden in the dawn, held our passing shadows as we silently went by. At no single dawn or sunset was he to be found indoors, and it became my habit to accompany him—the joy of worship in his soul was marvellous. The great, still skies of Egypt watched us, the hanging stars, the gigantic dome of blue; we felt together that burning southern wind; the golden sweetness of the sun lay in our blood as we saw the great boats take the northern breeze upstream. Immensity was everywhere and this golden magic of the sun. . . .

But it was in the Desert especially, where only sun and wind observe the faint signalling of Time, where space is nothing because it is not divided, and where no detail reminds the heart that the world is called To-Day—it was in the desert this curtain hung most visibly between us, he on that side, I on this. It was transparent. He was with a multitude no man can number. Towering to the moon, yet spreading backwards towards his burning source of life, drawn out by the sun and by the crystal air into some vast interior magnitude, the spirit of George Isley hung beside me, close yet far away, in the haze of olden days.

And, sometimes, he moved. I was aware of gestures. His head was raised to listen. One arm swung shadowy across the sea of broken ridges. From leagues away a line of sand rose slowly. There was a rustling. Another—an enormous—arm emerged to meet his own, and two stupendous figures drew together. Poised above Time, yet throned upon the centuries, They knew eternity. So easily they remained possessors of the land. Facing the east, they waited for the dawn. And their marvellously forgotten singing poured across the world. . . .

Wayfarers

I missed the train at Evain, and, after infinite trouble, discovered a motor that would take me, ice-axe and all, to Geneva. By hurrying, the connection might be just possible. I telegraphed to Haddon to meet me at the station, and lay back comfortably, dreaming of the precipices of Haute Savoie. We made good time; the roads were excellent, traffic of the slightest, when—crash! There was an instant's excruciating pain, the sun went out like a snuffed candle, and I fell into something as soft as a bed of flowers and as yielding to my weight as warm water. . . .

It was *very* warm. There was a perfume of flowers. My eyes opened, focussed vividly upon a detailed picture for a moment, then closed again. There was no context—at least, none that I could recall—for the scene, though familiar as home, brought nothing that I definitely remembered. Broken away from any sequence, unattached to any past, unaware even of my own identity, I simply saw this picture as a camera snaps it off from the world, a scene apart, with meaning only for those who knew the context:

The warm, soft thing I lay in was a bed—big, deep, comfortable; and the perfume came from flowers that stood beside it on a little table. It was in a stately, ancient chamber, with lofty ceiling and immense open fireplace of stone; old-fashioned pictures—familiar portraits and engravings I knew intimately—hung upon the walls; the floor was bare, with dignified, carved furniture of oak and mahogany, huge chairs and massive cupboards. And there were latticed windows set within deep embrasures of grey stone, where clambering roses patterned the sunshine that cast their moving shadows on the polished boards. With the perfume of the flowers there mingled, too, that delicate, elusive odour of age—of wood, of musty tapestries in spacious halls and corridors, and of chambers long unopened to the sun and air.

By the door that stood ajar far away at the end of the room—very far away it seemed—an old lady, wearing a little cap of silk embroidery, was whispering to a man of stern, uncompromising figure, who, as he listened, bent down to her with a grave and even solemn face. A wide stone corridor was just visible through the crack of the open door behind her.

The picture flashed, and vanished. The numerous details I took in because they were well known to me already. That I could not supply the context was merely a trick of the mind, the kind of trick that dreams play. Darkness swamped vision again. I sank back into the warm, soft, comfortable bed of delicious oblivion. There was not the slightest desire to know; sleep and soft forgetfulness were all I craved.

But a little later—or was it a very great deal later?—when I opened my eyes again, there was a thin trail of memory. I remembered my name and age. I remembered vaguely, as though from some unpleasant dream, that I was on the way to meet a climbing friend in the Alps of Haute Savoie, and that there was need to hurry and be very active. Something had gone wrong, it seemed. There had been a stupid, violent disaster, pain in it somewhere, an accident. Where were my belongings? Where, for instance, was my precious ice-axe—tried old instrument on which my life and safety depended? A rush of jumbled questions poured across my mind. The effort to sort them hurt atrociously. . . .

A figure stood beside my bed. It was the same old lady I had seen a moment ago—or was it a month ago, even last year perhaps? And this time she was alone. Yet, though familiar to me as my own right hand, I could not for the life of me attract her name. Searching for it brought the pain again. Instead, I asked an easier question; it seemed the most important somehow, though a feeling of shame came with it, as though I knew I was talking nonsense:

"My ice-axe—is it safe? It should have stood any ordinary strain. It's ash. . . ." My voice failed absurdly, caught away by a whisper half-way down my throat. What was I talking about? There was vile confusion somewhere.

She smiled tenderly, sweetly, as she placed her small, cool hand upon my forehead. Her touch calmed me as it always did, and the pain retreated a little.

"All your things are safe," she answered, in a voice so soft beneath the distant ceiling it was like a bird's note singing in the sky. "And *you* are also safe. There is no danger now. The bullet has been taken out and all is going well. Only you must be patient, and lie very still, and rest." And then she added the morsel of delicious comfort she knew quite well I waited for: "Marion is near you all day long, and most of the night besides. She rarely leaves you. She is in and out all day."

I stared, thirsting for more. Memory put certain pieces in their place again. I heard them click together as they joined. But they only tried to join. There were several pieces missing. They must have been lost in the disaster. The pattern was too ridiculous.

"I ought to tel—telegraph—" I began, seizing at a fragment that poked its end up, then plunged out of sight again before I could read more of it. The pieces fell apart; they would not hold together without these missing fragments. Anger flamed up in me.

"They're badly made," I said, with a petulance I was secretly ashamed of; "you have chosen the wrong pieces! I'm not a child—to be treated—" A shock of heat tore through me, led by a point of iron, with blasting pain.

"Sleep, my poor dear Félix, sleep," she murmured soothingly, while her tiny hand stroked my forehead, just in time to prevent that pointed, hot thing entering my heart. "Sleep again now, and a little later you shall tell me their names, and I will send on horseback quickly—"

"Telegraph—" I tried to say, but the word went lost before I could pronounce it. It was a nonsense word, caught up from dreams. Thought fluttered and went out.

"I will send," she whispered, "in the quickest possible way. You shall explain to Marion. Sleep first a little longer; promise me to lie quite still and sleep. When you wake again, she will come to you at once."

She sat down gently on the edge of the enormous, bed, so that I saw her outline against the window where the roses clambered to come in. She bent over me—or was it a rose that bent in the wind across the stone embrasure? I saw her clear blue eyes—or was it two raindrops upon a withered roseleaf that mirrored the summer sky?

"Thank you," my voice murmured with intense relief, as everything sank away and the old-world garden seemed to enter by the latticed windows. For there was a power in her way that made obedience sweet, and her little hand, besides, cushioned the attack of that cruel iron point so that I hardly felt its entrance. Before the fierce heat could reach me, darkness again put out the world. . . .

Then, after a prodigious interval, my eyes once more opened to the stately, old-world chamber that I knew so well; and this time I found myself alone. In my brain was a stinging, splitting sensation, as though Memory shook her pieces together with angry violence, pieces, moreover, made of clashing metal. A degrading nausea almost vanquished me. Against my feet was a heated metal body, too heavy for me to move, and bandages were tight round my neck and the back of my head. Dimly, it came back to me that hands had been about me hours ago, soft, ministering hands that I loved. Their perfume lingered still. Faces and names fled in swift procession past me, yet without my making any attempt to bid them stay. I asked myself no questions. Effort of any sort was utterly beyond me. I lay and watched and waited, helpless and strangely weak.

One or two things alone were clear. They came, too, without the effort to think them:

There had been a disaster; they had carried me into the nearest house; and—the mountain heights, so keenly longed for, were suddenly denied me. I was being cared for by kind people somewhere far from the world's high routes. They were familiar people, yet for the moment I had lost the name. But it was the bitterness of losing my holiday climbing that chiefly savaged me, so that strong desire returned upon itself unfulfilled. And, knowing the danger of frustrated yearnings, and the curious states of mind they may engender, my trembling brain registered a decision automatically:

"Keep careful watch upon yourself," it whispered.

For I saw the peaks that towered above the world, and felt the wind rise from the hidden valleys. The perfume of lonely ridges came to me, and I saw the snow against the blue-black sky. Yet I could not reach them. I lay, instead, broken and useless upon my back, in a soft, deep, comfortable bed. And I loathed the thought. A dull and evil fury rose within me. Where was Haddon? He would get me out of it if any one could. And where was my dear, old trusted ice-axe? Above all, who were these gentle, old-world people who cared for me? . . . And, with this last thought, came some fairy touch of sweetness so delicious that I was conscious of sudden resignation—more, even of delight and joy.

This joy and anger ran races for possession of my mind, and I knew not which to follow: both seemed real, and both seemed true. The cruel confusion was an added torture. Two sets of places and people seemed to mingle.

"Keep a careful watch upon yourself," repeated the automatic caution.

Then, with returning, blissful darkness, came another thing—a tiny point of wonder, where light entered in. I thought of a woman. . . . It was a vehement, commanding thought; and though at first it was very close and real—as much of To-day as Haddon and my precious ice-axe—the next second it was leagues away in another world somewhere. Yet, before the confusion twisted it all askew, I knew her; I remembered clearly even where she lived; that I knew her husband, too—had stayed with them in—in Scotland—yes, in Scotland. Yet no word in this life had ever crossed my lips, for she was not free to come. Neither of us, with eyes or lips or gesture, had ever betrayed a hint to the other of our deeply hidden secret. And, although for me she was *the* woman, my great yearning—long, long ago it was, in early youth—had been sternly put aside and buried with all the vigour nature gave me. Her husband was my friend as well.

Only, now, the shock had somehow strained the prison bars, and the yearning escaped for a moment full-edged, and vehement with passion long denied. The inhibition was destroyed. The knowledge swept deliciously upon me that we had the right to be together, because we always *were* together. I had the right to ask for her.

My mind was certainly a mere field of confused, ungoverned images. No thinking was possible, for it hurt too vilely. But this one memory stood out with violence. I distinctly remember that I called to her to come, and that she had the right to come because my need was so peremptory. To the one most loved of all this life had brought me, yet to whom I had never spoken because she was in another's keeping, I called for help, and called, I verily believe, aloud:

"Please come!" Then, close upon its heels, the automatic warning again: "Keep close watch upon yourself . . .!"

It was as though one great yearning had loosed the other that was even greater, and had set it free.

Disappearing consciousness then followed the cry for an incalculable distance. Down into subterraneans within myself that were positively frightening it plunged away. But the cry was real; the yearning appeal held authority in it as of command. Love gave the right, supplied the power as well. For it seemed to me a tiny answer came, but from so far away that it was scarcely audible. And names were nowhere in it, either in answer or appeal.

"I am always here. I have never, never left you!"

The unconsciousness that followed was not complete, apparently. There was a memory of effort in it, of struggle, and, as it were, of searching. Some one was trying to get at me. I tossed in a troubled sea upon a piece of wreckage that another swimmer also fought to reach. Huge waves of transparent green now brought this figure nearer, now concealed it, but it came steadily on, holding out a rope. My exhaustion was too great for me to respond, yet this swimmer swept up nearer, brought by enormous rollers that threatened to engulf us both. The rope was for my safety, too. I saw hands outstretched. In the deep water I saw the outline of the body, and once I even saw the face. But for a second, merely. The wave that bore it crashed with a horrible roar that smothered us both and swept me from my piece of wreckage. In the violent flood of water the rope whipped against my feeble hands. I grasped it. A sense of divine security at once came over me—an intolerable sweetness of utter bliss and comfort, then blackness and suffocation as of the grave. The white-hot point of iron struck me. It beat audibly against my heart. I heard the knocking. The pain brought me up to the surface, and the knocking of my dreams was in reality a knocking on the door. Some one was gently tapping.

Such was the confusion of images in my pain-wracked mind, that I expected to see the old lady enter, bringing ropes and ice-axes, and followed by Haddon, my mountaineering friend; for I thought that I had fallen down a deep crevasse and had waited hours for help in the cold, blue darkness of the ice. I was too weak to answer, and the knocking for that matter was not repeated. I did not even hear the opening of the door, so softly did she move into the room. I only knew that before I actually saw her, this wave of intolerable sweetness drenched me once again with bliss and peace and comfort, my pain retreated, and I closed my eyes, knowing I should feel that cool and soothing hand upon my forehead.

The same minute I did feel it. There was a perfume of old gardens in the air. I opened my eyes to look the gratitude I could not utter, and saw, close against me—not the old lady, but the young and lovely face my worship had long made familiar. With lips that smiled their yearning and eyes of brown that held tears of sympathy, she sat down beside me on the bed. The warmth and fragrance of her atmosphere enveloped me. I sank away into a garden where spring melts magically into summer. Her arms were round my neck. Her face dropped down, so that I felt her hair upon my cheek and eyes. And then, whispering my name twice over, she kissed me on the lips.

"Marion," I murmured.

"Hush! Mother sends you this," she answered softly. "You are to take it all; she made it with her own hands. But *I* bring it to you. You must be quite obedient, please."

She tried to rise, but I held her against my breast.

"Kiss me again and I'll promise obedience always," I strove to say. But my voice refused so long a sentence, and anyhow her lips were on my own before I could have finished it. Slowly, very carefully, she disentangled herself, and my arms sank back upon the coverlet. I sighed in happiness. A moment longer she stood beside my bed, gazing down with love and deep anxiety into my face.

"And when all is eaten, all, mind, *all,*" she smiled, "you are to sleep until the doctor comes this afternoon. You are much better. Soon you shall get up. Only, remember," shaking her finger with a sweet pretence of looking stern, "I shall exact complete obedience. You must yield your will utterly to mine. You are in my heart, and my heart must be kept very warm and happy."

Her eyes were tender as her mother's, and I loved the authority and strength that were so real in her. I remembered how it was this strength that had sealed the contract her beauty first drew up for me to sign. She bent down once more to arrange my pillows.

"What happened to—to the motor?" I asked hesitatingly, for my thoughts *would* not regulate themselves. The mind presented such incongruous fragments.

"The—what?" she asked, evidently puzzled. The word seemed strange to her. "What is that?" she repeated, anxiety in her eyes.

I made an effort to tell her, but I could not. Explanation was suddenly impossible. The whole idea dived away out of sight. It utterly evaded me. I had again invented a word that was without meaning. I was talking nonsense.

In its place my dream came up. I tried to tell her how I had dreamed of climbing dangerous heights with a stranger, and had spoken another language with him than my own—English, was it?—at any rate, not my native French.

"Darling," she whispered close into my ear, "the bad dreams will not come back. You are safe here, quite safe." She put her little hand like a flower on my forehead and drew it softly down the cheek. "Your wound is already healing. They took the bullet out four days ago. I have got it," she added with a touch of shy embarrassment, and kissed me tenderly upon my eyes.

"How long have you been away from me?" I asked, feeling exhaustion coming back.

"Never once for more than ten minutes," was the reply. "I watched with you all night. Only this morning, while mother took my place, I slept a little. But, hush!" she said, with dear authority again; "you are not to talk so much. You must eat what I have brought, then sleep again. You must rest and sleep. Good-bye, good-bye, my love. I shall come back in an hour, and I shall always be within reach of your dear voice."

Her tall, slim figure, dressed in the grey I loved, crossed silently to the door. She gave me one more look—there was all the tenderness of passionate love in it—and then was gone.

I followed instructions meekly, and when a delicious sleep stole over me soon afterwards, I had forgotten utterly the ugly dream that I was climbing dangerous heights with another man, forgotten as well everything else, except that it seemed so many days since my love had come to me, and that my bullet wound would after all be healed in time for our wedding on the day so long, so eagerly waited for.

And when, several hours later, her mother came in with the doctor—his face less grave and solemn this time—the news that I might get up next day and lie a little in the garden, did more to heal me than a thousand bandages or twice that quantity of medical instructions.

I watched them as they stood a moment by the open door. They went out very slowly together, speaking in whispers. But the only thing I caught was the mother's voice, talking brokenly of the great wars. Napoleon, the doctor was saying in a low, hushed tone, was in full retreat from Moscow, though the news had only just come through. They passed into the corridor then, and there was a sound of weeping as the old lady murmured something about her son and the cruelty of Heaven. "Both will be taken from me," she was sobbing softly, while he stooped to comfort her; "one in marriage, and the other in death." They closed the door then, and I heard no more.

I

Convalescence seemed to follow very quickly then, for I was utterly obedient as I had promised, and never spoke of what could excite me to my own detriment—the wars and my own unfortunate part in them. We talked instead of our love, our already too-long engagement, and of the sweet dream of happiness that life held waiting for us in the future. And, indeed, I was sufficiently weary of the world to prefer repose to much activity, for my body was almost incessantly in pain, and this old garden where we lay between high walls of stone, aloof from the busy world and very peaceful, was far more to my taste just then than wars and fighting.

The orchards were in blossom, and the winds of spring showered their rain of petals upon the long, new grass. We lay, half in sunshine, half in shade, beneath the poplars that lined the avenue towards the lake, and behind us rose the ancient grey-stone towers where the jackdaws nested in the ivy and the pigeons cooed and fluttered from the woods beyond.

There was loveliness everywhere, but there was sadness too, for though we both knew that the wars had taken her brother whence there is no return, and that only her aged, failing mother's life stood between ourselves and the stately property, there hid a sadness yet deeper than either of these thoughts in both our hearts. And it was, I think, the sadness that comes with spring. For spring, with her lavish, short-lived promises of eternal beauty is ever a symbol of passing human happiness, incomplete and always unfulfilled. Promises made on earth are playthings, after all, for children. Even while we make them so solemnly, we seem to know they are not meant to hold. They are made, as spring is made, with a glory of soft, radiant blossoms that pass away before there is time to realise them. And yet they come again with the return of spring, as unashamed and glorious as if Time had utterly forgotten.

And this sadness was in her too. I mean it was part of her and she was part of it. Not that our love could change to pass or die, but that its sweet, so long-desired accomplishment must hold sway, and, like the spring, must melt and vanish before it had been fully known. I did not speak of it. I well understood that the depression of a broken body can influence the spirit with its poisonous melancholy, but it must have betrayed itself in my words and gestures, even in my manner too. At any rate, she was aware of it. I think, if truth be told, she felt it too. It seemed so painfully inevitable.

My recovery, meanwhile, was rapid, and from spending an hour or two in the garden, I soon came to spend the entire day. For the spring came on with a rush, and the warmth increased deliciously. While the cuckoos called to one another in the great beech-woods behind the château, we sat and talked and sometimes had our simple meals or coffee there together, and I particularly recall the occasion when solid food was first permitted me and she gave me a delicate young *bondelle,* fresh caught that very morning in the lake. There were leaves of sweet, crisp lettuce with it, and she picked the bones out for me with her own white hands.

The day was radiant, with a sky of cloudless blue, soft airs stirred the poplar crests; the little waves fell on the pebbly beach not fifty metres away, and the orchard floor was carpeted with flowers that seemed to have caught from heaven's stars the patterns of their yellow blossoms. The bees droned peacefully among the fruit trees; the air was full of musical deep hummings. My former vigour stirred delightfully in my blood, and I knew no pain, beyond occasional dull twinges in the head that came with a rush of temporary darkness over my mind. The scar was healed, however, and the hair had grown over it again. This temporary darkness alarmed her more than it alarmed me. There were grave complications, apparently, that I did not know of.

But the deep-lying sadness in me seemed independent of the glorious weather, due to causes so intangible, so far off, that I never could dispel them by arguing them away. For I could not discover what they actually were. There was a vague, distressing sense of restlessness that I ought to have been elsewhere and otherwise, that we were together for a few days only, and that these few days I had snatched unlawfully from stern, imperative duties. These duties were immediate, but neglected. In a sense, I had no right to this spring-tide of bliss her presence brought me. I was playing truant somehow, somewhere. It was *not* my absence from the regiment; that I know. It was infinitely deeper, set to some enormous scale that vaguely frightened me, while it deepened the sweetness of the stolen joy.

Like a child, I sought to pin the sunny hours against the sky and make them stay. They passed with such a mocking swiftness, snatched momentarily from some big oblivion. The twilights swallowed our days together before they had been properly tasted, and on looking back, each afternoon of happiness seemed to have been a mere moment in a flying dream. And I must have somehow betrayed the aching mood, for Marion turned of a sudden and gazed into my face with yearning and anxiety in the sweet brown eyes.

"What is it, dearest?" I asked, "and why do your eyes bring questions?"

"You sighed," she answered, smiling a little sadly; "and sighed so deeply. You are in pain again. The darkness, perhaps, is over you?" And her hand stole out to meet my own. "You are in pain?"

"Not physical pain," I said, "and not *the* darkness either. I see *you* clearly," and would have told her more, as I carried her soft fingers to my lips, had I not divined from the expression in her eyes that she read my heart and knew all my strange, mysterious forebodings in herself.

"I know," she whispered before I could find speech, "for I feel it too. It is the shadow of separation that oppresses you—yet of no common, measurable separation you can understand. Is it not that?"

Leaning over then, I took her close into my arms, since words in that moment were mere foolishness. I held her so that she could not get away; but even while I did so it was like trying to hold the spring, or fasten the flying hour with a fierce desire. All slipped from me, and my arms caught at the sunshine and the wind.

"We have both felt it all these weeks," she said bravely, as soon as I had released her, "and we both have struggled to conceal it. But now"—she hesitated for a second, and with so exquisite a tenderness that I would have caught her to me again but for my anxiety to hear her further words—"now that you are well, we may speak plainly to each other, and so lessen our pain by sharing it." And then she added, still more softly: "You feel there is 'something' that shall take you from me—yet what it is you cannot discover nor divine. Tell me, Félix—all your thought, that I in turn may tell you mine."

Her voice floated about me in the sunny air. I stared at her, striving to focus the dear face more clearly for my sight. A shower of apple blossoms fell about us, and her words seemed floating past me like those passing petals of white. They drifted away. I followed them with difficulty and confusion. With the wind, I fancied, a veil of indefinable change slipped across her face and eyes.

"Yet nothing that could alter feeling," I answered; for she had expressed my own thought completely. "Nor anything that either of us can control. Only—perhaps, that everything must fade and pass away, just as this glory of the spring must fade and pass away—"

"Yet leaving its sweetness in us," she caught me up passionately, "and to come again, my beloved, to come again in every subsequent life, each time with an added sweetness in it, too!" Her little face showed suddenly the courage of a lion in its eyes. Her heart was ever braver than my own, a vigorous, fighting soul. She spoke of lives, I prattled of days and hours merely.

A touch of shame stole over me. But that delicate, swift change in her spread, too. With a thrill of ominous warning I noticed how it rose and grew about her. From within, outwards, it seemed to pass—like a shadow of great blue distance. Shadow was somewhere in it, so that she dimmed a little before my very eyes. The dreadful yearning searched and shook me, for I could not understand it, try as I would. She seemed going from me—drifting like her words and like the apple blossoms.

"But when we shall no longer be here to know it," I made answer quickly, yet as calmly as I could, "and when we shall have passed to some other place—to other conditions—where we shall not recognise the joy and wonder. When barriers of mist shall have rolled between us—our love and passion so made-over that we shall not know each other"—the words rushed out feverishly, half beyond control—"and perhaps shall not even dare to speak to each other of our deep desire—"

I broke off abruptly, conscious that I was speaking out of some unfamiliar place where I floundered, helpless among strange conditions. I was saying things I hardly understood myself. Her bigger, deeper mood spoke through me, perhaps.

Her darling face came back again; she moved close within reach once more.

"Hush, hush!" she whispered, terror and love both battling in her eyes. "It is the truth, perhaps, but you must not say such things. To speak them brings them closer. A chain is about our hearts, a chain of fashioning lives without number, but do not seek to draw upon it with anxiety or fear. To do so can only cause the pain of wrong entanglement, and interrupt the natural running of the iron links." And she placed her hand swiftly upon my mouth, as though divining that the bleak attack of anguish was again upon me with its throbbing rush of darkness.

But for once I was disobedient and resisted. The physical pain, I realised vividly, was linked closely with this spiritual torture. One caused the other somehow. The disordered brain received, though brokenly, some hints of darker and unusual knowledge. It had stammered forth in me, but through her it flowed easily and clear. I saw the change move more swiftly then across her face. Some ancient look passed into both her eyes.

And it was inevitable; I must speak out, regardless of mere bodily well-being.

"We shall have to face them some day," I cried, although the effort hurt abominably, "then why not now?" And I drew her hand down and kissed it passionately over and over again. "We are not children, to hide our faces among shadows and pretend we are invisible. At least we have the Present—the Moment that is here and now. We stand side by side in the heart of this deep spring day. This sunshine and these flowers, this wind across the lake, this sky of blue and this singing of the birds—all, all are ours *now*. Let us use the moment that Time gives, and so strengthen the chain you speak of that shall bring us again together times without number. We shall then, perhaps, remember. Oh, my heart, think what that would mean—to remember!"

Exhaustion caught me, and I sank back among my cushions. But Marion rose up suddenly and stood beside me. And as she did so, another Sky dropped softly down upon us both, and I smelt again the incense of old, old gardens that brought long-forgotten perfumes, incredibly sweet, but with it an ache of far-off, passionate remembrance that was pain. This great ache of distance swept over me like a wave.

I know not what grand change then was wrought upon her beauty, so that I saw her defiant and erect, commanding Fate because she understood it. She towered over me, but it was her soul that towered. The rush of internal darkness in me blotted out all else. The familiar, present sky grew dim, the sunshine faded, the lake and flowers and poplars dipped away. Conditions a thousand times more vivid took their place. She stood out, dear and shining in the glory of an undressed soul, brave and confident with an eternal love that separation strengthened but could never, never change. The deep sadness, I abruptly realised, was very little removed from joy—because, somehow, it was the condition of joy. I could not explain it more than that.

And her voice, when she spoke, was firm with a note of steel in it; intense, yet devoid of the wasting anger that passion brings. She was determined beyond Death itself, upon a foundation sure and lasting as the stars. The heart in her was calm, because she *knew*. She was magnificent.

"We are together—always," she said, her voice rich with the knowledge of some unfathomable experience, "for separation is temporary merely, forging new links in the ancient chain of lives that binds our hearts eternally together." She looked like one who has conquered the adversity Time brings, by accepting it. "You speak of the Present as though our souls were already fitted now to bid it stay, needing no further fashioning. Looking only to the Future, you forget our ample Past that has made us what we are. Yet our Past is here and now, beside us at this very moment. Into the hollow cups of weeks and months, of years and centuries, Time pours its flood beneath our eyes. Time is our schoolroom. . . . Are you so soon afraid? Does not separation achieve that which companionship never could accomplish? And how shall we dare eternity together if we cannot be strong in separation first?"

I listened while a flood of memories broke up through film upon film and layer upon layer that had long covered them.

"This Present that we seem to hold between our hands," she went on in that earnest, distant voice, "*is* our moment of sweet remembrance that you speak of, of renewal, perhaps, too, of reconciliation—a fleeting instant when we may kiss again and say good-bye, but with strengthened hope and courage revived. But we may not stay together finally—we *cannot*—until long discipline and pain shall have perfected sympathy and schooled our love by searching, difficult tests, that it may last for ever."

I stretched my arms out dumbly to take her in. Her face shone down upon me, bathed in an older, fiercer sunlight. The change in her seemed in an instant then complete. Some big, soft wind blew both of us ten thousand miles away. The centuries gathered us back together.

"Look, rather, to the Past," she whispered grandly, "where first we knew the sweet opening of our love. Remember, if you can, how the pain and separation have made it so worth while to continue. And be braver thence."

She turned her eyes more fully upon my own, so that their light persuaded me utterly away with her. An immense new happiness broke over me. I listened, and with the stirrings of an ampler courage. It seemed I followed her down an interminable vista of remembrance till I was happy with her among the flowers and fields of our earliest pre-existence.

Her voice came to me with the singing of birds and the hum of summer insects.

"Have you so soon forgotten," she sighed, "when we knew together the perfume of the hanging Babylonian Gardens, or when the Hesperides were so soft to us in the dawn of the world? And do you not remember," with a little rise of passion in her voice, "the sweet plantations of Chaldea, and how we tasted the odour of many a drooping flower in the gardens of Alcinous and Adonis, when the bees of olden time picked out the honey for our eating? It is the fragrance of those first hours we knew together that still lies in our hearts to-day, sweetening our love to this apparent suddenness. Hence comes the full, deep happiness we gather so easily To-day. . . . The breast of every ancient forest is torn with storms and lightning . . . that's why it is so soft and full of little gardens. You have forgotten too easily the glades of Lebanon, where we whispered our earliest secrets while the big winds drove their chariots down those earlier skies . . ."

There rose an indescribable tempest of remembrance in my heart as I strove to bring the pictures into focus; but words failed me, and the hand I eagerly stretched out to touch her own, met only sunshine and the rain of apple blossoms.

"The myrrh and frankincense," she continued, in a sighing voice that seemed to come with the wind from invisible caverns in the sky, "the grapes and pomegranates—have they all passed from you, with the train of apes and peacocks, the tigers and the ibis, and the hordes of dark-faced slaves? And this little sun that plays so lightly here upon our woods of beech and pine— does it bring back nothing of the old-time scorching when the olive slopes, the figs and ripening cornfields heard our vows and watched our love mature?

. . . Our spread encampment in the Desert—do not these sands upon our little beach revive its lonely majesty for you, and have you forgotten the gleaming towers of Semiramis . . . or, in Sardis, those strange lilies that first tempted our souls to their divine disclosure . . .?"

Conscious of a violent struggle between pain and joy, both too deep for me to understand, I rose to seize her in my arms. But the effort dimmed the flying pictures. The wind that bore her voice down the stupendous vista fled back into the caverns whence it came. And the pain caught me in a vice of agony so searching that I could not move a muscle. My tongue lay dry against my lips. I could not frame a word of any sentence. . . .

Her voice presently came back to me, but fainter, like a whisper from the stars. The light dimmed everywhere; I saw no more the vivid, shining scenery she had summoned. A mournful dusk instead crept down upon the world she had momentarily revived.

". . . we may not stay together," I heard her little whisper, "until long discipline shall have perfected sympathy, and schooled our love to last. For this love of ours *is* for ever, and the pain that tries it is the furnace that fashions precious stones. . . ."

Again I stretched my arms out. Her face shone a moment longer in that forgotten fiercer sunlight, then faded very swiftly. The change, like a veil, passed over it. From the place of prodigious distance where she had been, she swept down towards me with such dizzy speed. As she was To-day I saw her again, more and more.

"Pain and separation, then, are welcome," I tried to stammer, "and we will desire them"—but my thought got no further into expression than the first two words. Aching blotted out coherent utterance.

She bent down very close against my face. Her fragrance was about my lips. But her voice ran off like a faint thrill of music, far, far away. I caught the final words, dying away as wind dies in high branches of a wood. And they reached me this time through the droning of bees and of waves that murmured close at hand upon the shore.

". . . for our love is of the soul, and our souls are moulded in Eternity. It is not yet, it is not now, our perfect consummation. Nor shall our next time of meeting know it. We shall not even speak. . . . For I shall not be free. . . ." was what I heard. She paused.

"You mean we shall not know each other?" I cried, in an anguish of spirit that mastered the lesser physical pain.

I barely caught her answer:

"My discipline then will be in another's keeping—yet only that I may come back to you . . . more perfect . . . in the end. . . ."

The bees and waves then cushioned her whisper with their humming. The trail of a deeper silence led them far away. The rush of temporary darkness passed and lifted. I opened my eyes. My love sat close beside me in the shadow of the poplars. One hand held both my own, while with the other she arranged my pillows and stroked my aching head. The world dropped back into a tiny scale once more.

"You have had the pain again," Marion murmured anxiously, "but it is better now. It is passing." She kissed my cheek. "You must come in. . . ."

But I would not let her go. I held her to me with all the strength that was in me. "I had it, but it's gone again. An awful darkness came with it," I whispered in the little ear that was so close against my mouth. "I've been dreaming," I told her, as memory dipped away, "dreaming of you and me—together somewhere—in old gardens, or forests—where the sun was—"

But she would not let me finish. I think, in any case, I could not have said more, for thought evaded me, and any language of coherent description was in the same instant beyond my power. Exhaustion came upon me, that vile, compelling nausea with it.

"The sun here is too strong for you, dear love," I heard her saying, "and you must rest more. We have been doing too much these last few days. You must have more repose." She rose to help me move indoors.

"I have been unconscious, then?" I asked, in the feeble whisper that was all I could manage.

"For a little while. You slept, while I watched over you."

"But I was away from you! Oh, how could you let me sleep, when our time together is so short?"

She soothed me instantly in the way she knew we both loved so. I clung to her until she released herself again.

"Not away from me," she smiled, "for I was with you in your dreaming."

"Of course, of course you were"; but already I knew not exactly why I said it, nor caught the deep meaning that struggled up into my words from such unfathomable distance.

"Come," she added, with her sweet authority again, "we must go in now. Give me your arm, and I will send out for the cushions. Lean on me. I am going to put you back to bed."

"But I shall sleep again," I said petulantly, "and we shall be separated."

"We shall dream together," she replied, as she helped me slowly and painfully towards the old grey walls of the Château.

II

Half an hour later I slept deeply, peacefully, upon my bed in the big stately chamber where the roses watched beside the latticed windows.

And to say I dreamed again is not correct, for it can only be expressed by saying that I saw and knew. The figures round the bed were actual, and in life. Nothing could be more real than the whisper of the doctor's voice—that solemn, grave-faced man who was so tall—as he said, sternly yet brokenly, to some one: "You must say good-bye; and you had better say it *now*." Nor could anything be more definite and sure, more charged with the actuality of living, than the figure of Marion, as she stooped over me to obey the terrible command. For I saw her face float down towards me like a star, and a shower of pale spring blossoms rained upon me with her hair. The perfume of old, old gardens rose about me as she slipped to her knees beside the bed and kissed my lips—so softly it was like the breath of wind from lake and orchard, and so lingeringly it was as though the blossoms lay upon my mouth and grew into flowers that she planted there.

"Good-bye, my love; be brave. It is only separation."

"It is death," I tried to say, but could only feebly stir my lips against her own.

I drew her breath of flowers into my mouth . . . and there came then the darkness which is final.

The voices grew louder. I heard a man struggling with an unfamiliar language. Turning restlessly, I opened my eyes—upon a little, stuffy room, with white walls whereon no pictures hung. It was very hot. A woman was standing beside the bed, and the bed was very short. I stretched, and my feet kicked against the boarding at the end.

"Yes, he *is* awake," the woman said in French. "Will you come in? The doctor said you might see him when he woke. I think he'll know you." She spoke in French. I just knew enough to understand.

And of course I knew him. It was Haddon. I heard him thanking her for all her kindness, as he blundered in. His French, if anything, was worse than my own. I felt inclined to laugh. I did laugh.

"By Jove! old man, this is bad luck, isn't it? You've had a narrow shave. This good lady telegraphed—"

"Have you got my ice-axe? Is it all right?" I asked. I remembered clearly the motor accident, everything.

"The ice-axe is right enough," he laughed, looking cheerfully at the woman, "but what about yourself? Feel bad still? Any pain, I mean?"

"Oh, I feel all right," I answered, searching for the pain of broken bones, but finding none. "What happened? I was stunned, I suppose?"

"Bit stunned, yes," said Haddon. "You got a nasty knock on the head, it seems. The point of the axe ran into you, or something."

"Was that all?"

He nodded. "But I'm afraid it's knocked our climbing on the head. Shocking bad luck, isn't it?"

"I telegraphed last night," the kind woman was explaining.

"But I couldn't get here till this morning," Haddon said. "The telegram didn't find me till midnight, you see." And he turned to thank the woman in his voluble, dreadful French. She kept a little pension on the shores of the lake. It was the nearest house, and they had carried me in there and got the doctor to me all within the hour. It proved slight enough, apart from the shock. It was not even concussion. I had merely been stunned. Sleep had cured me, as it seemed.

"Jolly little place," said Haddon, as he moved me that afternoon to Geneva, whence, after a few days' rest, we went on into the Alps of Haute Savoie, "and lucky the old body was so kind and quick. Odd, wasn't it?" He glanced at me.

Something in his voice betrayed he hid another thought. I saw nothing "odd" in it at all, only very tiresome. "What's its name?" I asked, taking a shot at a venture.

He hesitated a second. Haddon, the climber, was not skilled in the delicacies of tact.

"Don't know its present name," he answered, looking away from me across the lake, "but it stands on the site of an old château—destroyed a hundred years ago—the Château de Bellerive."

And then I understood my old friend's absurd confusion. For Bellerive chanced also to be the name of a married woman I knew in Scotland—at least, it was her maiden name, and she was of French extraction.